Praise for *Wish You Were Here*

'[O'Nan's] finest and deepest novel to date.'   *New York Times Book Review*

'Succeeds beautifully . . . showcases some of the finest character studies a contemporary reader could ask for.'   *Boston Globe*

'Offers a stark and brilliantly mesmerising glimpse into the lives of the Maxwells, the most aggressively average American family this side of *The Corrections*.'   *Los Angeles Times*

'Stewart O'Nan loves us and forgives us and watches us when we aren't looking. And he has given us this big, fine, openhearted book in which the inner and outer lives of a family come together, with depth and art.'

Amy Bloom

'An unflinching portrait of an American family that's remarkable for its precision, intelligence and heart. You will not soon forget these people.'

Richard Russo

ALSO BY STEWART O'NAN

FICTION
City of Secrets
West of Sunset
The Odds
Emily, Alone
Songs for the Missing
Last Night at the Lobster
The Good Wife
The Night Country
Everyday People
A Prayer for the Dying
A World Away
The Speed Queen
The Names of the Dead
Snow Angels
In the Walled City

NONFICTION
Faithful (with Stephen King)
The Circus Fire
The Vietnam Reader (editor)
On Writers and Writing by John Gardner (editor)

SCREENPLAY
Poe

WISH YOU WERE HERE

STEWART O'NAN

ALLEN&UNWIN

First published in the United States in 2002 by Grove/Atlantic, Inc.
First published in Great Britain in 2017 by Allen & Unwin

Allen & Unwin
c/o Atlantic Books
Ormond House
26–27 Boswell Street
London WC1N 3JZ

Phone: 020 7269 1610
Fax: 020 7430 0916
Email: UK@allenandunwin.com
Web: www.allenandunwin.com/uk

A CIP catalogue record of this book is available from the British Library.

Paperback ISBN 978 1 76029 388 8
E-book ISBN 978 1 95253 522 2

Designed by Laura Hammond Hough

Printed in Italy by Grafica Veneta S.p.A.

10 9 8 7 6 5 4 3 2 1

for Dewey and Diamond,

our two Rufuses

It's not like anything

they compare it to—

    the summer moon.

Bashō

Last night I dreamt I went to Manderley again.

Daphne du Maurier

Wish
You
Were
Here

Saturday

They took Arlene's car because it had air-conditioning and Emily wasn't sure the Olds would make it. That and Arlene's was bigger, a wagon, better for bringing things back.

Emily knew she wouldn't be able to resist. She'd never learned to take even the smallest loss gracefully—a glass cracked in the dishwasher, a sweater shrunk by the dryer. She'd stuff the Taurus full of junk she didn't have room for at home. All of it would end up down in the basement, moldering next to the extra fridge still filled to clinking with Henry's Iron Citys. She didn't drink beer, and she couldn't bring herself to twist them open one by one and tip them foaming down the sink, so they stayed there, the crimped edges of the bottle caps going rusty, giving her vegetables a steely tinge. She would save what she could, she knew, though Henry himself would have shaken his head at the mess.

It would be the last time she made the trip up, the last time she saw the cottage. The closing would be handled by her attorney—Henry's, really. She'd only spoken with him once in person, last fall, numbly going over the estate. Everything else was done by phone, or Federal Express, an expense she considered extravagant and feared she was paying for, but Henry had used Barney Pontzer for thirty years, and she trusted Henry's judgment, in this case more than her own.

The cottage was three hours from the house, depending on 79. Saturdays could be bad. She wanted to leave around nine so they'd be there by lunchtime, but Arlene was late and then gave her a hard time about Rufus, ceremoniously laying a faded Steelers towel over the backseat. Emily assured her that he hadn't been fed this morning, but Arlene kept tucking the towel into the crack. They'd had the exact same argument over Christmas, visiting Kenneth. It was so pointless. The car stunk of her Luckies and always would.

"He's fine," Emily insisted.

"Better safe."

"He's good about it now."

"I was thinking more for the hair."

"Oh please," Emily said, trying to laugh, "a towel's not going to do anything. I'll vacuum it when we get there."

"*Some*one will have to."

"*I* will."

These everlasting battles, Emily thought. Couldn't Arlene see this trip was different? Henry attributed his sister's obtuseness to her school-teacher's practicality, but Emily thought it was more ingrained than will-ful. Arlene seemed constantly on guard, afraid of somehow being cheated. It made sense: Henry had been the baby, their parents' favorite, an engi-neer like his father. Her entire life Arlene had had to fight for the least bit of attention.

But they were all gone, Emily wanted to say. She could stop now.

Rufus had hip trouble, and she had to help him in. Arlene said nothing while she rearranged the towel. Truthfully, Rufus still got carsick, though no longer to the point of upchucking. Over the years he'd learned to keep his head down so the endless carousel of trees and fields no longer dizzied him, but he still hitched and hiccupped as if he was going to let loose. Instead he drooled, long gelatinous strings depending from his jowls, catching in his coat like spiderwebs. And all right, he *was* shedding heavily. It had been a beastly summer. The baseboards in the bedroom were drifted with dark clumps of fur that scattered at the approach of the vacuum, but that was natural for a springer spaniel.

Could she or Arlene say they'd aged more gracefully? Rufus was fourteen and had spent his every summer at the cottage. He deserved a last romp with the grandchildren, a last swim off the dock, a last snooze on the cool slab of the screenporch. She would Hoover Arlene's seats if it came to that.

The house was locked, the windows closed, the machine on. She'd stopped the mail and cleaned out the hydrator. The Olds was purposely low, in case anyone broke into the garage with an idea of stealing it. Marcia next door had a key and the number up at Chautauqua. If she'd forgot-ten anything, she couldn't think of it.

"And they're off," Emily said, turning her wrist over to check Henry's Hamilton.

Arlene drove slowly, cozied up to the wheel, peering over her hands like the pilot of a ship in fog. It was already hot and the air-conditioning was heavenly. Shadows of trees fell sharply across the empty sidewalks. In yards browned with drought, sprinklers whisked and tilted. It felt good to be moving, leaving the still city, as if they were escaping a great palace while everyone slept.

Traffic was surprisingly light on the Boulevard of the Allies, the Monongahela brown and sluggish below, a coal train crawling along the far shore. The mile-long mills were gone, nothing but graded fields protected by chain-link fences. Downtown, the glittering new buildings rose behind them as they crossed the green Allegheny, the fountain at the Point spraying perfect white arcs, a barge pushing upriver beneath them, all of it like a postcard. In a week she would be back and it would seem hateful to her, she knew—or just discouraging, a reminder of what she'd given up and how little there was left.

Time, that was the difficulty now (it always was, only now she had no one to help her through it, someone besides herself to concentrate on). Mornings in her garden, afternoons at the Edgewood Club pool, nights reading while the radio played Brahms. She'd found her own quiet way of getting through the days, biding her time, trying not to badger Kenneth or Margaret to visit with the children. And it was right that she should still feel Henry, it was not so long that she shouldn't miss him. Winter had been a trial, with the dark coming down early, but there were always those hardy perennials—British mysteries from the library, the new PBS special, lunch with Louise Pickering. She had her health, her teeth, her memory. She refused to become one of those old ladies who did nothing but moon aloud about the old days, speaking of their dead husbands as if they were just drinking in the next room. She'd never considered it a possibility before Henry got sick. Now she feared it had already happened, that transformation, as if—like Henry—she'd discovered the disease only well after it had ravaged her.

Far below, to their left, the Ohio started, the Allegheny and the Mon blending, the surface swirled like a stirred can of paint, lapping furrows covering the heavy undertow. She imagined following the water, driving all night through the little river towns with their brick taverns and row houses and rusting pickup trucks, the railroad tracing the oxbows and eddies downstream, pushing on for Cairo, St. Louis, New Orleans. She'd lived in Pittsburgh more than forty years; now, suddenly, there was nothing keeping her here.

"The new stadium's almost done," Arlene nodded at the far shore, and it was true, they were even working weekends, the scaffolds around the facade dotted with hard hats, an orange crane draped with a huge Steelers banner.

"They're playing someone today," Emily said. "It's barely August."

"Buffalo."

"Oh great, we're headed straight into enemy territory."

"Maybe I'll finally buy that T-shirt," Arlene said.

It was an old joke. The Bills trained at Fredonia, so the grocery stores were filled with Bills merchandise, the seasonal aisle a party of hats and glasses and beer cozies, lamps and license plates and chip-n-dip trays. Fans showed up in Winnebagos painted the team colors, and some of their neighbors at Chautauqua flew blue-and-red flags.

Strange how things changed. When she was a teenager growing up in Kersey, in the wooded hills of central Pennsylvania, her friends all saw Buffalo and Pittsburgh as their deliverance, the only way out of their small town. Of the two, Pittsburgh was the more glamorous, a notion that now struck her as sad in its innocence. She'd been such a hick; Henry never tired of reminding her. The two cities had seemed magical back then, home to radio stations she struggled to bring in on her father's console. Both were famous for hard work. Now they seemed like relics, lost and emptied, the heavy industry fled or extinct. She and Henry had honeymooned, like everyone else, at Niagara Falls. They'd had their picture taken in slickers on the *Maid of the Mist*. She remembered kissing him, how the water ran down their faces like a shower.

She hadn't been to Buffalo in years, would probably never go again.

"Were there any bills in Buffalo?" Emily asked.

"Were there any pirates in Pittsburgh?"

"Besides Andy Carnegie and Mr. Frick."

"How's Rufus doing?"

"He's fine," Emily said, before turning to check. Rufus lay with his head resting on his crossed paws, looking up at her guiltily. At each corner his rubbery lips held a gluey drop of slobber. "He's a good boy."

"Rufus the Doofus." It was the children's nickname, but coming from Arlene it didn't sound loving.

"Be nice."

"I am being. As long as he's on the towel."

"He is."

Arlene lighted up a Lucky, and Emily flicked down her window. The air rushed in with the sound of a blowtorch. It did nothing to clear the smoke, if anything pushed more in her direction.

"Shoot," Arlene said, and smacked the wheel.

"What?"

"I forgot to bring film. I wanted to take pictures of the house."

For old times' sake, Emily thought. "You can get some there."

"I know, but . . . I bought some special. I know right where it is, it's sitting on the kitchen table."

"You can borrow some from me, I've got extra."

Emily hadn't thought of taking pictures of the cottage, just of Kenneth and Margaret and the children. When Mrs. Klinginsmith, the realtor, had asked for a recent photo, Emily couldn't find one. Mrs. Klinginsmith said it was okay, she'd take one, and produced on the spot a digital camera from her massive bag. Emily and Henry had taken hundreds of shots of the house, but always in the background. They had hours of videos—Sam and Ella playing croquet, Sarah and Justin shooing a younger Rufus away from the doomed geraniums.

She'd watched some this winter, trying to catch a glimpse of Henry, but he was behind the camera, at best a shadow on the screenporch, tipped back in his chair. The only good one she found was of him playing wiffle ball with Sam and Ella. Kenneth must have taken it from behind home plate, because there was Lisa on first and Henry wearing his Pirates cap sideways, pitching behind his back and through his legs, doing a goofy windmilling windup only to deliver a soft lob that Ella smacked past him. And then the scene changed to Ella's seventh birthday, and Emily could tell Henry was shooting because Lisa was bringing in the lit cake and Emily herself was standing beside Sam's chair, singing, her hair a mess from swimming, and she stopped the tape and rewound it.

"Here comes the old radio ball," Henry joked. "You can hear it but you can't see it."

She'd only watched the scene a few times, the last standing right by the set as if she could get closer to him that way.

They'd relied on the video when the grandchildren were little, made an event of sitting around the Zenith watching themselves, but since last fall she couldn't remember using it once. For Christmas she was at Kenneth and Lisa's, Easter at Margaret's (Jeff had showed up perfunctorily for the egg hunt but had other dinner plans). Today, like then, it had never crossed her mind to bring the camera, and now she was sorry.

She looked out at the grassy embankment rising beside the highway, pink with mountain laurel despite the drought, a rock wash laid neatly down one manicured flank. The trees were bright, the darkness beneath absolute. She wondered how far back they ran, and what lived in them, but without any real interest, just something to look at, to stop her from chewing on things she could do nothing about.

It wasn't just riding in the car that sent her off like this. Watching TV or reading, she found her mind wrapping itself around the irreducible new facts of her life, like Rufus winding his chain around the sycamore out back. Like him, she only managed to tear off more bark, leave even more raw scars. To soothe them, she remembered, and the remembering became a full world, a dream she could walk through. It felt real, and then it went away and she was left with the kitchen, the garbage can nearly full, the fly that wandered the downstairs, knocking into screens, making her chase it with a magazine.

Arlene had gotten them behind a silver tank truck. A stream of cars passed them on the left while Arlene darted her head at her mirrors and over her shoulder. A space opened in the chain. At the last second Arlene said, "I can't make it," and backed off. She waited until everyone had overtaken them, then signaled primly and swung around the truck, their reflection dimpling as they passed. A green sign on the side said CORROSIVE. Another diamond beside it showed a test tube dripping liquid on a disembodied hand spiced with cartoon shock marks.

"Lovely."

"What's lovely?" Arlene asked, concentrating on her lane.

Emily explained.

"What do you think it is?"

"Some sort of industrial acid, I imagine."

It was an answer Henry would have given, noncommittal but promising. Emily had no idea what might be in the truck and didn't care. Some chemical. The driver would deliver it to some factory, and they would make something people would buy and put in their homes and use until whatever it was broke or was relegated to the attic or a tag sale, then eventually thrown away, left to rust in some dump or to rot under tons of garbage at a landfill while more trucks rolled past day and night.

A dead deer slid by on their right. It was a spotted fawn, its neck bent back unnaturally, black blood coating the nose, staining the pavement. Arlene obviously saw it but said nothing—to spare her feelings, Emily supposed.

She wanted to respond, to remind Arlene that she was a country girl from a family of dedicated hunters, intimate with back roads littered spring and fall with fat, soggy possums and capsized raccoons. And really, she'd gotten used to death. There were as many dead things as living in the world. More. Everywhere you looked there was a cemetery, a dried leaf, a husk of a fly. And yet the world rolled on, green and busy as ever.

The thing that secretly moved her to tears now was not death but parting. Watching TV, she would be reduced to sniffling and wiping her eyes by soldiers waving from trains, mothers putting children onto school buses, confetti snowing over the decks of cruise ships. It didn't have to be some sweeping movie she was caught up in. A long-distance commercial could do it. And the quality didn't matter—it could be the most obvious, manipulative, sepia-toned slow motion, it still hit her like a brick. It was funny, because in real life she had no trouble saying good-bye, simply did it and walked away (a trait she credited to her mother's stringent Lutheranism). She and Henry had had a year to tell each other good-bye, and she thought she was happy with the job they'd done. There was nothing lingering, nothing left to say between them. Then why did these clichéd scenes tear at her?

"I brought paper plates," Arlene said.

"So did I. How about napkins?"

They would need to stop at the Golden Dawn after they got there.

"We should make a list," Emily said, and dug in her purse. "Paper towels, film . . . what else?"

Pie from a roadside stand. Blackberry was in season for another week. They could wait till tomorrow for corn, and get two of those rotisserie chickens from the Lighthouse. Did they have to call and reserve those? Probably, on the weekend. Peaches. Tomatoes. They would have to make a separate trip to the cheese place and pick up a block of the extra-sharp cheddar the children liked.

Miles in the car, the air-conditioning growing too cold. Forest, crows, police. She had made this drive so many times, yet parts of it still surprised her. She'd forgotten the barn they pointed out to the children when they were little, the faded advertisement dull but legible: CHEW MAIL POUCH TREAT YOURSELF TO THE BEST. A rest area was barricaded, a customized van with back windows faceted like diamonds inexplicably sitting in the middle of the empty lot. Clouds repeated in the sky to the horizon, a fleet steaming out of harbor. The woods gave way to dairy land, slouching red barns and fields overgrown with burdock and Queen Anne's lace. Outside Mercer they ran into a thundershower, the rain so heavy that Arlene braked and Emily braced for a collision. A mile later it was sunny, a rainbow rising from the hills.

"Make a wish," Emily said, then cleared a space in her mind and thought, slowly, as if speaking to God, I wish: that they will all understand.

They left 79 and headed east along Lake Erie, Arlene tentatively joining the four lanes of I-90. In back, Rufus gulped for air, huffed and swallowed hard, and to placate Arlene, Emily twisted in her seat and sweet-talked him.

"You're all right," she said, but Rufus didn't look convinced. He lifted his head, woozy and confused.

"No!" Emily said. "Down!"

He did, his muzzle jumping with a hiccup.

"Should I pull over?" Arlene asked.

"He's fine. It's not far."

"It's another hour."

"Forty minutes," Emily said. "Just drive. He's not going to throw up on your precious seats, and if he does I'll clean it up."

"I was just trying to help," Arlene said.

"I'm sorry. I know you don't like him."

"I like him, I just don't want him throwing up in my car."

"Well, that's just what dogs do, I can't do anything about that."

Emily sighed at the pettiness of the argument and the needling fact that she was in the wrong. "Listen, I appreciate you driving, and I'm sorry he's not the best passenger. I don't mean to be rude, I just want us to get there."

"I don't mind him, really," Arlene said, as if she'd already accepted her apology.

The sign welcoming them to New York was pocked with yellow paintball splotches, the one panel with the new governor's name a darker green. Crossing the border, Kenneth and Margaret used to lift their feet off the floor and hold their hands in the air, something they'd learned on the bus to church camp. She thought of doing it now but knew Arlene would be baffled.

She could almost hear Henry tell her to simmer down, could almost see the sideways look he'd give her that meant please take it easy on Arlene—or, more often, on Margaret, whose whole personality seemed designed to drive Emily to violence. She still could not get over the way Margaret had treated Jeff. Neither could Jeff, apparently, because he'd left her. That it had likely been the one trait they shared that finally drove him away seemed fitting to Emily. For Margaret, it was all the proof she needed that once again her mother had ruined her life. They'd been officially separated less than a year, but from Margaret's scattered calls and what Kenneth let slip, divorce seemed more probable than reconciliation.

Wouldn't her own mother feel justified now, always telling her to calm down and hold her tongue? "Why can't you be nice?" her mother once said, gripping her forearm hard, and what answer could Emily give her? She saw the same helpless anger in her daughter and was just as powerless to save her. And who would save Emily when everything piled up?

Henry had, his placid heart the perfect balm for hers. Now that he was gone, she feared she would turn sour, take it out on those around her. Sometimes it seemed that was exactly what was happening. It was hard to tell. It was like menopause all over again, the crazy swings—or like being pregnant. Half the time she had no idea why she felt the way she did, except the overall excuse that Henry was dead.

"Here," Arlene said of a sign coming up. "Nineteen miles."

Route 17 was so new through here the bridges were still under construction. Orange-and-white-striped pylons funneled the two lanes into a chute between concrete barriers. Arlene brought her face closer over the wheel, and Emily sat up straight, as if lending her attention. No one was working, but a state trooper had tucked his cruiser in behind a dusty water truck.

Arlene was going slow enough that it didn't matter, but from reflex Emily stiffened as if caught, a jagged spasm shooting through her. Henry had been a fast driver, a great believer in the Olds V-8.

"Tricky tricky," Emily said.

"And it's a work zone, so the fines are doubled."

"Even if no one's working. What a racket."

A sign for Panama came, and then, off in a disused field, a billboard for Panama Rocks, where they'd taken Kenneth and Margaret as children. Margaret had been pudgy then, and refused to even try Fat Man's Misery, standing outside while the rest of them squeezed through, the lichened walls cold against their bellies. She'd always stood apart from them somehow, and Emily had failed to bring her in.

Rufus had settled back into his tuck, a thread of slobber dried over his nose. "We're almost there," Emily promised.

They got off at the exit for the Institute, tracking a balding blacktop past lopsided Greek Revivals with washing machines on the porches and horses grazing in with cows. The road dissolved in spots, cinders clinking beneath them, wildflowers in the ditches. It reminded her of Kersey, the roller-coaster shortcuts through the state forest full of dips and switchbacks. The old homesteads were the same, the gingerbread Gothics on hilltops safe inside windbreaks of oaks and willows, mailboxes jutting from whitewashed milk cans, ponds with stubby docks for the kids to swim off, ducks sunning on an overturned rowboat. She could live here, give up the house in the city and watch the mist settle in the trees at dusk, the cows come lowing home.

Another billboard loomed over a slight rise: RUNNING ON EMPTY? FILL UP WITH JESUS.

Well, that would be nice, she thought.

"Corn's high," Arlene noted.

"They're north enough to get the lake effect."

"I hope it doesn't rain like last year."

Emily had not been up last summer because of Henry, but she'd heard the horror stories—the children playing video games all day and fighting. She could see Arlene abandoning the house, throwing on a poncho and going for her walk by the fishery, cupping her Luckies against the drops.

"It won't," Emily said. "And if it does, we'll find something to do. There's always cards."

"Justin was big into chess, I remember."

"And Ella's pretty good about the TV. It's Sam who gets weird."

"Maybe if we set a time limit. Who's going to get there first?"

"Kenneth."

"Maybe if you talk with Lisa."

"I can try," Emily said.

"The two of you make up yet?"

"We're civil. Let me put it that way."

"Oh my," Arlene said, slowing to take in a massive Victorian painted garish shades of mustard and raspberry. PLUMBUSH BED AND BREAK-FAST, proclaimed a fussy placard hung pub-style out front. The wraparound porch commanded a view of a makeshift hay wagon across the road, and farther down the sloping field, the browned shell of a pickup.

"Plum bushed," Arlene said. "I get it."

"I'm sure the neighbors are amused," Emily said.

Closer to the lake, they saw more new houses, all modular, trailered in from the same factory. One had a satellite dish beside it the size of a small plane, another a Bills flag in its bay window.

"You wonder if they keep that up all year," Arlene said.

Finally they came to the intersection of 394, just above the Institute. Andriaccio's was still there, its parking lot jammed with the lunch-time rush. The sudden crush of activity—a boy with a pair of canes wobbling across the lot, a tall man in shorts holding the door for an older couple leaving—seemed to invite them to join in. Or was it the Institute itself, that idea of a relaxing, high-minded summer, that appealed to her? Waiting for a break in traffic, Emily peered down the hill and over the spiked iron fence at the tiny practice cabins, plain as outhouses and spaced neatly as graves, imagining some bright teenager's days, the chaste dedication to her instrument and the great dead. As they passed, she thumbed down her window, hoping to catch a lithe phrase of oboe or a cello's deep sigh. There was nothing.

"Emily, look," Arlene said, incredulous. "The Putt-Putt."

Its orange-and-white fence was still there, but everything back to the concrete-block restrooms was leveled, a FOR LEASE sign out front.

"Kenneth will be so disappointed."

"You'd think they could make money with the Institute right here."

"Obviously not," Emily said.

She knew everything here: the Christmas shop; the hot laundromat where they still did their sheets and towels; the grade school now used for storage. They slowed for the walkway by the brick entrance of the Institute, an empty police car left by the maintenance hut as a decoy, then cruised alongside the lush fairways of the club (apparently they were having no trouble getting water). Henry had enjoyed the course. On six there was a pond, and he would always leave his tee shot right, mucking through the reeds beside the cart path. Once he'd discovered a snake and come running out with his nine-iron. She hadn't swung a club all last year. She and Kenneth would have to get out for their traditional round. It would be the only time they'd have alone.

And there was the Wagon Wheel, with its rusted ladder of signs:

DELI

NEWSPAPERS

ICE

FILM

And the We Wan Chu cottages and campground, now with its own website.

"Now I've seen everything," Emily said.

"That was up last year."

Arlene slowed for Manor Drive, and Rufus stood, smearing his nose against the window. The turn convinced him to fold himself down again. He was well off the towel now but Emily let it go.

The drive was entirely in shadow, barely a car wide. The association had put up a 15 MPH sign. The policeman with the trampoline and the Irish setter was home, but not the people with the ugly aboveground pool. The Nevilles were here in force, their driveway lined with minivans and SUVs, the garage open to show their old Volkswagen convertible. Two little girls she didn't know rode their bicycles across the yard in their bathing suits and tennis shoes.

Between the houses Emily could see the lake, a Laser heeling near shore.

"Looks breezy out there," she said, but Arlene had slowed for some older children on bikes—Craigs, they looked like, gripping tennis rackets. A blonde girl waved to them, and automatically they waved back, neighbors.

Farther on, a red Cadillac with Florida plates sat in a shaded drive. "The Wisemans are here," Emily said, happy, because last year Herb Wiseman had had a heart attack and they hadn't come up.

"Both of them or just Marjorie?"

"I can't imagine her driving that car, can you?"

"We'll have to go over," Arlene said.

The Lerners' place was for sale, also listed with Mrs. Klinginsmith, and seeing the sign disappointed Emily. She wondered what they were asking.

Rufus was up again, turning around to look at everything.

"He knows," Arlene said.

Emily could see part of the cottage, obscured by the big chestnut next to the garage. "Well," she said, "it hasn't burned down."

Closer, she could see the orange daylilies nestled around the mailbox. Something hung from it—a flyer in a plastic wrapper—and she thought there ought to be a law against delivering them when people weren't home. It was an open invitation.

They turned onto the grass, running over fallen branches. The cottage was fine, even bright. She hadn't seen the new paint job, gray with red shutters and white trim. No wonder the buyers paid their price. A pair of new steel bands held the chimney together, and the old TV antenna was gone. They'd even painted the garage, scraped the moss off the shingles. It looked better than it ever had, almost false. She wondered what Henry would have said.

Rufus scratched at the window.

"Down," Emily said, but he was too excited.

Arlene stopped the car and Emily let him out. He shot around the side of the cottage and squatted, looking back over his shoulder. Another thing to clean up. The towel was covered with hair, one tuft caught in a blotch of drool; the seat was fine, though Arlene went through a pantomime of wiping it with a hand.

"*I* will wash the towel," Emily said, and balled it up.

When Rufus was done, he came back, looped around the two as if calling them to follow, then raced straight for the dock. Arlene ignored him and laid down the tailgate.

"Let's just get the food in for now," Emily said. She found the keys and crunched the brightest one in the kitchen door, propped the greased arm of the screen so it would stay open. The place smelled musty as a well house. Emily leafed among the keys (each taped and labeled in Henry's neat hand) and went out back to turn the water on.

The spiders had been busy, fat as puffballs, their webs festooned with gnats, dotted with cottony eggs. Above the controls, tacked to the wall and bleeding with humidity, was a set of directions Henry had written out for Kenneth. She flipped the switch and the pump complained. The water here was soft and stunk of sulphur. It made her remember swimming in the lake and hanging their suits on the back line, thirty, almost forty years ago, when the children were little. All those summers were gone, but how sharply—just now—she could recall them. She wanted to inhabit them again, those long August days, the croquet and wiffle-ball games and campfires, skiing behind the boat. It was why they came here every year, she supposed, this feeling of eternity and shelter.

She locked the pump house behind her. On her way to the garage, she slipped on a mossy flagstone and barely kept her feet. "Stupid," she said. Every year she forgot how treacherous they were. Think just once she'd remember.

No one had bothered to clean the garage. Henry's junk was everywhere: beer cartons and bushel baskets, coolers and buckets, fishing gear, gas cans for the boat, cases piled with dusty Iron City and Genesee bottles, a steel trash can spiky with kindling. Suspended from the back wall were a saggy life raft and a trio of bare-breasted-mermaid boat bumpers that had embarrassed Kenneth as a teenager. Through the dulled rear window she could see Rufus out at the end of the dock. She wanted to go and sit with him, but Henry's workbench drew her to it.

His tool apron lay at one end as if waiting for him. The rest was a clutter of gnarled work gloves and plastic cups full of screws, coils of yellow nylon rope, a handheld sander, aerosol cans of spray paint and WD-40, nails in wrinkly paper bags, wood putty, a crusted caulking gun, a wasp bomb, old screw-in fuses, ripped sandpaper disks, paint stirrers from the True Value in Mayville, a bent cleat, a can of 3 IN 1 oil, a scarred Maxfli, a dark lightbulb. She resisted the urge to touch any of it, stood there breathing in the smell, enjoying the mess. She'd ask Kenneth if he wanted the tools. He'd probably take them all just so none of them got thrown away. He really was her son.

Inside, Arlene was going through the cupboards. "Where's that bowl we always put the fruit in?"

"The green one."

"Is that the one?"

Emily checked above the dishwasher and to the left of the stove, then the lazy Susan under the counter. "This one."

"I don't remember it being this one. I thought it was orange for some reason."

"Is there much more?" Emily asked.

"No, that's it."

"Do you mind if I go down to the dock for a second before we eat?"

"Go ahead. There's not room in here for both of us anyway."

The wind was blowing in, raising cat's-paws on the water. Under the chestnut it was cool, but once she stepped onto the dock her face warmed. The lake was down several feet, and weedy. Pearly clam shells winked up at her from the bottom. Rufus was lying down and raised his head to see who was coming. In its slip the Starcraft sloshed and knocked, its lines creaking. The handsome salmon cover Henry had bought was streaked with gull droppings. The buyers had their own boat, so Mrs. Klinginsmith had arranged for Smith Boys down in Ashville to buy it as salvage. At that point Emily didn't argue. It was nearly thirty years old, and the Evinrude regularly stranded them. Funny how much she could part with now—how little, really.

She reached the broad ell of the dock and stepped around Rufus to sit on the bench. He got up and flopped down at her feet. She bent and petted him, absently scratched behind his ears.

"You're glad to be out of the car, I bet. Yes."

He looked up at her as if she'd said something vitally important. His eyes were misted with cataracts; lately he'd been bumping into doorways. She didn't know what she would do if he became incontinent.

"You're fine," she said. "You're all right."

On the next dock a wooden duck caught the wind, its wings slowly spinning in opposite directions like a deranged clock. She leaned back and looked off to the far shore. It had been so dry that some of the trees had already started to turn, not a brilliant red but a muted, diseased shade.

She wondered if they would die or come back next year, then realized she would never know. She remembered a toppled redwood they'd seen out in California, ages ago, on some more ambitious trip when the children were little. The rings were different sizes; the thinnest indicated drought years. Maybe this year would be like that, next year a better one.

She looked out at the waves as if they might provide an answer. Rufus sat up and pushed his wet muzzle under her hand. He'd missed his breakfast, and now that he was out of the car, he was hungry.

"I know," she said, "you've been very patient."

Next year had to be better. Practically.

In all her concentration she had stopped petting Rufus. He'd turned away from her to face the lake, so when he tipped his head up to question her, he looked cross-eyed. His tongue flopped out to one side, and she wondered how it was possible to be that open to the world, that willing, still.

"You *are* a doofus," she said.

She felt his ridged skull under her nails, the grain of his hair. The sun was out but the wind was up, making the duck's wings pinwheel and slice like propellers. Her own hair stabbed at her cheeks.

"Come on," she said, and got up, and together they walked back toward the cottage. Arlene would need help with lunch.

2

"There it is!" Lise said for the kids' benefit. As if obeying, Ken glanced away from the road.

Below, a mile away, the water spread wide and silver beside them in the long afternoon light, a boat cutting a black fantailed wake. Trees flashed up to block the view, a wall then a gap, a gap. They caught another opening, a vineyard letting them see all the way across, a fat calendar shot.

"Wake up," Lise said, "you're missing it!"

Ken checked them in the mirror. They were groggy with sleep. Ella's new braces made her pout. She stretched her arms above her head and groaned. "Yeah, yeah."

"Yippee Skippy," Sam deadpanned.

"Start getting your shoes on," Lise said, though they had another twenty minutes in the car.

Ken marveled at how calm she could be. It wasn't just his mother (his father, the cottage, the whole trip), and it wasn't the job, though he was prepared to hear his mother laugh at the irony of him processing other people's pictures all day, say it served him right for leaving Merck. That would set Lise off, and then forget it.

It was everything. While he knew it was temporary, all the way from Boston he'd been thinking of money. On their way out of town they'd stopped at an ATM and he discovered their checking account had a negative balance. He didn't understand. He'd been keeping a close eye on their bills. He was sure he'd left a good cushion.

"I use the card for food shopping," Lise told him. "That's probably it."

"Yeah," he said, "that would do it."

"We have to eat."

"I know," he said, controlled, "it's fine," aware of Sam and Ella listening in the backseat, his failures apparent.

It wasn't the way he wanted to start the trip. He'd had to transfer five hundred from savings, and now he couldn't get the current balance out of his head. His next check from the lab wasn't due till the first of the month.

Part of it was the cottage, obviously. All July he'd been thinking of his father, the confines of his life, whether he'd been happy or not. The hardest part was understanding why he was with his mother, the two of them were such complete opposites.

"I don't know how he did it," he said. "How many years?"

Lise laughed but did the math. "Forty-eight?"

"I wouldn't have lasted five minutes with her."

The irony of it was that he and his father were so much alike, a fact Ken had fought off as long as he could and that, privately, Meg never tired of citing. Once, stoned over the phone, she'd teased him with it—

"God, you turned into him!" Only his sense of how hurt she would be prevented him from coming back, not at all joking, "And you turned into her."

Lise could have had a week at the cape with her family but agreed to come this one last time. Now, as they crossed the Veterans Bridge, trying to spot the Stow Ferry—there, loading cars on the Bemus Point side by the old casino—she was making gentle disclaimers. She knew how important this week was to his mother.

"Listen," Lise said, "I know you're going to disappear when we get there."

"I will not."

"Yes you will, you'll go off looking for shots."

He shook his head because he knew it was true. Not that he'd find any.

"Just don't leave me alone with her, all right?"

"Arlene'll be there."

"What about Meg?"

"She probably won't get in till around dinnertime."

"Interesting how she's always the last one to show up and we're always the first."

"What can I say," he said. "I'm the good son."

"You'd never know it from the way she treats you."

"I can take it."

"You shouldn't have to."

He shrugged. She wasn't so bad. She was his mother, it wasn't like he had a choice.

They made it across the bridge and he got off 17 and waited at the stop sign for traffic to clear (the sign was bent and scratched as if brushed by a truck, the gouges rusted; he'd need his wide angle to get it, but already he could see how dull the print would look, how sixties). Behind him, Ella and Sam sat peering out the window at Hogan's Hut, the combination gas station, general store and ice-cream place they sometimes stopped at on the way in. He'd wanted to give them a special treat after nine hours in the car, had planned on it since Binghamton, but it was just too late. He turned and gunned the 4Runner, paying attention to his shifts, checking the bikes through the sunroof, watching Hogan's Hut dwindle in the mirror, and, bless them, the kids let him off the hook.

This was the easy part. Once Meg arrived with her kids it would be bedlam, and their mother wasn't used to the noise. All week he would be stuck in the middle of them just as he had been as a child, trying to defuse or at least delay the inevitable, and then he would be accused of taking the wrong side, when all he wanted was peace. He couldn't see how his father had managed an entire life of this. He would just have to make it through the week, counting down the hours like he did when he was a boy.

When Meg was at camp one year, he spent every Tuesday and Thursday at the Putt-Putt, his father dropping him off and picking him up. All day they gave out prizes; his pockets were thick with discount tickets. For lunch he ate Milky Ways. The time flew by, the speakers playing "Hold Your Head Up" and "Uncle Albert/Admiral Halsey," #1 and 2 week after week. Between songs, notes from the practice cabins drifted across the road, squealy reeds and the dark farts of horns. By summer's end he'd mastered the course, pared his score down to the low thirties, even won a tournament. His mother had a faded picture of him smiling in front of the windmill with his trophy (still in Pittsburgh, in the attic room he'd moved to). He'd been so proud, felt so lucky. "I wouldn't have known it was you," Lise said when she saw it. He could have said the same thing. The boy holding up the trophy was gone.

He wondered if he would ever be happy like that again. Happy for Ella and Sam perhaps, but that was a different kind of happiness.

At B.U. he'd been thrilled to lose himself again in studies of light and long conversations about art and the photographers he loved, but the work he'd done there embarrassed him now, seemed sterile and over-composed, just an extension of his technical skill. The eye Morgan tried to help him find had eluded him. His new stuff wasn't much better, and the setbacks of the last few years had forced him to admit that maybe he didn't have what it took. Love had done it once, his happiness with Lise. Could that come back and surprise him again? And if it didn't, what then? Would he be like his father, quietly dedicated to getting along, so steady and stoic that he seemed inscrutable, disconnected from everything except what was in his head and the newest project on his workbench?

He'd only brought one camera along—the Nikon. The Holga was just plastic, it wasn't real. It was supposed to teach him to rely on his eye or, better, as Morgan said, his gut. By its very simplicity it was supposed to make him see.

What he would see was the cottage. The screenporch, the lake. He'd made it his assignment, as if he were back in grad school. Twenty rolls of black and white, twenty rolls of color. One week of light, weather permitting. At one time that would have been enough to fill him.

"Does everyone have their shoes on?" Lise asked.

"Yes," they said.

"Mom?" Sam asked.

"What?"

"Does a Game Boy count as a video game?"

"Yes," Lise said.

"Ella said it doesn't."

"I did not," Ella said.

"For this trip it does," Lise said.

Sam sighed heavily in protest.

"Listen," Lise said, turning around and warning each of them with a finger. "We're here to visit Grandma, not to play video games. I expect you to be polite and help out. And Sam, I don't want to hear any more sighing out of you. When someone asks you to do something, you do it. All right?"

"Yes," they said.

"Thank you," Lise said, looking forward again. "That goes for you too, buster."

"Aye-aye," Ken said.

A farm stand slid by on their right, flocked with minivans. PIES, a handmade sign said. He suspected there might be a shot in it—the cars parked cockeyed, the cut orchids in a white bucket—but couldn't find it, and he wondered if all vacation spots were the same, numbingly familiar.

"Are we going to have pie for dessert?" Sam asked.

"Would you like pie for dessert?" Lise asked.

"Yes."

"There's another one up here," Ken said, seizing on her mood.

"How about we surprise Grandma with a pie?" Lise said. "What kind should we get?"

"Apple!" Sam volunteered.

"Ella-bella?" Lise said.

"I don't care. Anything but peach."

He pulled in behind another 4Runner, this one from Virginia. Ella stayed in the car and read while the three of them split up among the tables. Sam went straight for the pies, ranked in the slots of an old-fashioned high-rise safe, each wrapped in a plastic bag with a twist tie, a slip of paper like a Chinese fortune listing the ingredients. Sam had to stand on his toes. They seemed expensive to Ken, but after the fiasco at the ATM he didn't want to make an issue of it. His favorite was there, cherry with a lattice crust. Lise had made one for him at Christmas.

"What's peck-tin?" Sam asked.

Ken had to admit he didn't know. Maybe Mom did. Sam looked the apple pies over before grabbing the biggest one with both hands.

They found Lise checking out the produce. Pectin was like jelly; it was the stuff that kept pie filling together, like a thickener. "Are you guys all set?"

He lifted a pint of Grade-A maple syrup to read the price on the bottom.

"I think it's called stalling," she said.

"I think you would be right."

As they waited for the girl to ring up the pie, Lise laid a bouquet of wildflowers on the counter. "For the house."

"A peace offering."

"It can't hurt," she said.

"We got apple," Sam announced in the car, holding the pie in his lap.

"Big whoop," Ella said, but the mood had shifted and they all laughed at her, poked fun at her gloom.

"I guess you don't want a piece," Lise said.

"I didn't say that."

"Mmmm," Ken said, "pectin!"

They got going again, a wraith of dust leaping up and then vanishing behind them as they pulled out, as if it had given up chasing them.

It was only another mile, not enough time to bother asking for a new CD. He'd had five hundred miles to get used to the idea of visiting his mother, but only now, speeding toward her, did it become real, something he would have to deal with, and while he knew he had no choice but to come, he felt tricked and trapped, the past closing around him, thick as humidity. This would be the first time they'd all been together since the funeral.

He didn't have time to process his thoughts. The used-book store floated by on their left like a warning (NEW $2 HARDBACK BARN), and the campgrounds with their plywood cutouts of Yogi Bear welcoming RVs, and the Willow Run Golf Club, a failed farm turned into a par three where his father had taught him not only to make contact but the etiquette of the game before he was allowed on the Chautauqua course. Around the bend squatted the Snug Harbor Lounge, a local dive with a portable sign advertising that night's band, a vintage Firebird for sale gleaming beside it. And then they were spinning alongside the fishery, its complex of square ponds ranked neatly as an ice tray, and from habit he was searching the far edge for herons, stealing glances from the road.

He would take the Holga over there, he thought, shoot the fish in the pump-house well, dark shapes in the water. The expectation of something to do soothed him, making the sign for Manor Drive less of a shock.

"Here we are," he said, and turned in, rolling the 4Runner through the slow curve by habit, the action of his hands practiced.

How well he knew this place, even the trees—the gnarled crab apple in the Nevilles' yard with its contortions he and Meg had been sure sprung from some underground evil; the two big oaks that pinched the road, lifted one lip of asphalt like carpet. He knew every cottage and even the big houses now, how each held that family's unguarded hours, the damp, casual passing of the summer. When they left, those long days would still be here, waiting the winter beneath the snow, the lake beneath its ice like the pike and muskie huddled in the mud, heartbeats slowed to a discrete thump. All the gin-and-tonic card games and chicken-salad sandwiches on the dock would be waiting for them, the arms of the willows swinging in the breeze, but they would not return, and wherever they went next year he would miss this place, would always miss it.

He realized he was panicking and caught his breath.

"Are you all right?" Lise asked.

"I just had this big nostalgia attack all of a sudden."

"Think it's your father, maybe?"

"Maybe. I don't know."

Again he was aware of Ella and Sam listening in. They learned more about their parents on one long car trip than all year at home.

There was the cottage, tucked under the big chestnut, and the mailbox with his mother's daylilies. They'd brought Arlene's car. He aimed the 4Runner off to one side, under the chestnut, so they could both get out. The top of the car rattled the branches.

"The bikes!" Lise cried, and he stood on the brakes and the car stalled, rubbery chestnut pods bonking the roof.

"Goddammit," he said, because he'd been careful with them all day, estimating their height from his own, checking the clearance before hitting the ATM and the gas plazas.

Lise opened her door and stood on the running board.

"What's it look like?"

"I think if you back up you'll be all right."

He started the car with a roar.

"Wait till I get in," she said.

He was aware of the anger that made him clench his entire face to maintain control. This was exactly the kind of shit he hated. He hadn't even wanted to bring the bikes. The kids barely rode them.

His mother and Aunt Arlene came out of the house, Rufus bounding around them. His mother was laughing, saying something.

He rolled down his window.

"Having a little tree trouble, I see," she said.

"I just need to back it up. If you could keep Rufus out of the way."

She stepped back again, displeased with him not seeing it as a joke. "Go ahead," she said, "he's fine."

He looked over his shoulder to find Ella frowning, her head down, as if mortified by his driving.

He eased the clutch up. Branches plucked the spokes, thumped against the roof, then let go with a swish and a sprinkle of leaves.

"All clear?" he called.

"All clear," his mother said, and he turned off the car.

"All right," Lise said for the benefit of the kids, "everyone help bring stuff in."

They set after the task in a squad, Lise doling out the bags, glad to have something to do, leaving him the job of saying hello to his mother.

She came toward him, smiling, and from habit he bent down and wrapped his arms about her bony shoulders. He could not say she looked good, since each time he saw her now her scrawniness shocked him. Instead, he gave her a quick hug and asked, too sincerely, "How are you?"

"A little overwhelmed but hanging in there. How about you?"

"The same."

It was not a lie. There would be a right time to tell her about the job.

"I'm so glad Lisa could come."

"She wouldn't have missed it," he said, and realized how false it sounded. "The paint looks good."

"Of course. Now that we've sold the place, it looks great."

Lise came by with the flowers in one hand and a duffel in the other, his camera bag over her shoulder. His mother accepted the bouquet, protesting, just touching one arm, as if tagging her back. "I'm so glad you could make it."

"Don't be silly, Emily," she said, and headed for the door.

Sam struggled out of a hug from Grandma, while Ella, acting grown up, lingered over hers, consoling his mother, patting her back. They were both all long bones, and their glasses nearly matched. While he and Lise always commented on how much of his mother was in Ella—the moodiness, the love of books—in person the resemblance was almost comical, two sisters separated by sixty years.

Arlene gave him a lipsticked kiss on the cheek, smelling of cigarettes. She leaned in close, conspiratorial.

"I don't know if your mother told you, but we're shooting for a moratorium on video games this year."

"Lise already read them the riot act."

"How'd they take it?"

"Ella was fine with it, as you'd expect. Sam, well . . ."

"I don't think it'll be a problem, as long as it doesn't rain."

"What's the weather supposed to be like?" he asked, but no one knew.

They said hello to Rufus too, Ella kneeling beside him, enveloping him in a hug. He lay in the shade of the chestnut as they unloaded their tennis rackets and sleeping bags, Sam's backpack full of *Star Wars* Legos and Pokémon cards, Ella's crammed with bottles of nail polish and library books. Merck had occasionally sent Ken to their plant in Baltimore, and he'd learned how to fit a week into one carry-on. At some point his children would have to learn to make choices, to sacrifice. He feared, in the future, some crippling repercussions from these early indulgences, and thought that was due to his own childhood being for the most part idyllic, the hard facts of life reaching him only in his mid-twenties, as if until then he'd been swathed in a cocoon of his parents' making, composed of equal parts love and money.

Bringing the bags through the living room, he wanted to stop to look at the familiar sailing pictures on the walls, the ugly orange shag rug, the mobile of Spanish galleons that poked you in the eye. It was like entering a party full of good friends, and the memories each piece of furniture, each object on the mantelpiece stirred up as he passed orbited like overheard conversations. He would have time later, he thought, and envisioned documenting it all with the Holga.

He lugged the bags upstairs where they would be sleeping, in the one long room under the peak of the roof. This floor was also shag-carpeted but in red, white and blue, the dresser drawers and brick chimney where it came through painted to match the bicentennial scheme. The walls were an old sort of pressboard, sky blue, soft as cork and flaking along the seams. He could see the ghosts of his father's hammer blows around the nails. The past was as thick as the air up here—games of spin the bottle and post office, Meg blowing her cigarette smoke out the window, drinking illicit beers while their parents entertained the Lerners and Wisemans on the screenporch. There in front of the mirror on the low wardrobe was the 7UP bottle with the taffy-twisted neck his father won for him at the carnival in Mayville, and there on the cedar chest between the beds, the ashtray he made at camp, beating the square of metal until it took on the shape of the leaf at the bottom of the mold. The TV that hadn't worked in twenty years, the fire truck he'd had as a boy that Ella cut her chin on when she was three. The room was so full of history he had to fend it off, concentrate on getting the kids settled. There would be time—and light, he hoped. He hadn't brought his strobes.

"Can you put the fan on?" Lise called from the bathroom, and he found the switch. The fan was built into the wall at the top of the stairs; it did nothing but make noise, even when he opened the two windows at the far end. The air smelled moldy and faintly, sweetly fecal from the generations of bats that had lived in the walls. At night you could hear them bumping and squeaking, and for a long time Sam had refused to sleep up here. He was still scared of them, but there was no graceful way out now without Ella calling him a baby.

"Can we go down to the dock?" Ella asked. Sam stood right beside her, her client.

"After you put your clothes away. Neatly."

"And help make the beds," Lise called.

"They're already made," Ella said.

"We have to strip off the old sheets and put on new ones."

Ella sighed.

"And no sighing."

"Yes, Mother," Ella said, going along with the joke, but a minute later, trying to fit a contour sheet on, she almost burst into tears. "This stupid sheet won't go on."

Lise came out of the bathroom and looked at the problem. "That's because it's a double."

"How am I supposed to know that?"

"It's nothing to cry about, " Lise said. "Here, this one's queen-size, it should work."

Sam was done shoving his clothes into the dresser and stood there watching them.

"Ken," Lise said, "help him with the other one," and he stopped filling the medicine cabinet with their toiletries.

When they were done, Lise sent the children off to the dock and took over putting their clothes away.

"I swear, everything's a crisis with her. And it's only going to get worse."

"I don't think she's so terrible."

"Just wait," she said, but halfheartedly. They both knew they were lucky with Ella. Sam was the tough one, always would be. Boys were supposed to be easy, but that hadn't been the case with him.

The room was dim. Outside, the golden hour was starting, the light beginning to sweeten. Lise pulled her book from her beach bag, one of the kids' Harry Potters. He unpacked his camera bag, the little he had. He would wait till tomorrow, slip out early and see if he could find something plain to start on. She stretched out on the bed and set her bookmark on the cedar chest.

"Just a few pages," she promised. "It's getting good."

He laid a hand on the small of her back and bent down awkwardly to kiss her. "I'll be downstairs."

His mother and Arlene were on the screenporch, reading the Jamestown paper and watching the lake. The Steelers had crushed the Bills. He hadn't even known they were playing, and suddenly fall seemed that much closer. Arlene said the chance of rain tomorrow was thirty percent. His mother was worried about Meg.

"It's six o'clock," she said. "Don't you think we ought to get dinner started? I imagine these kids are hungry."

"There's no rush," Ken said.

"Well I'm going to need something to eat soon."

"What are we having?"

"We were planning on hamburgers, if you can manage the grill."

"Not a problem," he said, and went out to the garage, the screen slapping shut behind him. He was almost to the door when he slipped on one of the flat stones and fell hard on his bottom. "Son of a bitch," he said, checking his wrist. The edge of one stone had gouged out a pale twist of skin but there was no blood. They were always slick; it had something to do with moss and condensation, the fact that the chestnut kept them in shadow most of the day. He was pissed that they'd tricked him again.

He was still shaking his head at his own stupidity when he opened the garage door and saw the shot. The whole garage was stuffed with his father's junk, and everywhere he looked he saw interesting collisions. He stopped automatically, wanting to run upstairs for the Nikon. The light was wrong, too soft to get the detail he wanted—the extension cord coiled in the enamel basin like some Far Eastern delicacy, the child's life jacket protecting the jug of wiper fluid. But this was exactly the problem, according to Morgan: he had to stop building his shots.

Tomorrow he'd bring just the Holga, leave the details to chance. He turned from the messy workbench and found the shallow grill and a bag of charcoal and dragged both out under the chestnut.

They had an old electric charcoal starter, a loop of wire the size of a spatula on a black plastic handle. He plugged it into an extension cord running from the strip of outlets on his father's workbench and piled the charcoal on top of it. While he waited for the wire to warm, he took an Iron City from the little fridge in the garage and stood there sipping and looking out at Sam and Ella on the dock, Rufus tucked between them. He wondered if they were happy, and thought at least they were happy to be out of the car, away from their parents. He could not help but see them as himself and Meg, sitting there thirty years ago, but what he and Meg would have discussed at that point—she thirteen and ready to leave, he so far behind at nine, snug in his own private world—he could not recall. The water made everything seem possible, as if they could cross it and begin a different life on the other side, shed the past and be those other people they'd dreamed of. Perhaps that was why his work was so dull: his desires had become practical when they needed to be extravagant.

He tipped the bottle and checked the starter, glowing away under the coals, just beginning to smoke. Another five minutes. The Lerners' was for sale, and as he was wondering what they were asking, the balance from the ATM came back and stung him, hovered and flitted off again. He would not be done with it until he looked at their checkbook. He took another sip and realized the beer was already working on him, and he remembered his father doing this, standing out here by himself, tumbler in hand. When it rained, he'd set up directly under the chestnut and the smoke would filter up through the leaves. Before his father, his grandfather Maxwell was in charge of the barbecue. Now it was his turn.

The last sip was mostly air. He flipped the bottle and caught it in his palm like a gunfighter and went to get another. The interior of the little fridge impressed him in its simplicity, the beers he'd bought last year still vigilant, ranked shoulder to shoulder, the freezer compartment clogged with frost. He could see what the print would look like (another thing Morgan warned him against) and shut the door. All he'd had to eat today was an egg-salad sandwich around Albany; he'd have to be careful with these beers. The last time he was drunk he'd gone all maudlin on Lise, thanking her for sticking with him. It had made them both feel pathetic the next day.

"How are the coals coming along?" Arlene called from the kitchen door.

The top of the pyramid was on fire, the centers of the briquets dark. They always took longer than you thought.

"Five, ten minutes."

"Is everyone going to want cheese on theirs?"

"Everyone but Sam."

He unplugged the starter, leveled the coals with the glowing wire, then set it on the concrete apron by the garage. Rufus was smart enough to stay away from it, but he kept checking to make sure it didn't catch anything on fire.

The lake had gone calm, flags limp at the end of the docks. The sun hung just above the treetops, throwing shadows. In the field across the road, a family of rabbits was out, feeding under the apple trees. They stayed close to the bushy edge of the field, brown balls in the dark light, cheeks working as they nibbled the grass. He counted five, one just a baby. This was what he would miss after the cottage was gone, these slow moments.

He decided he shouldn't have had that second beer.

He held a hand over the coals, mostly gray now, then set the circular rack on its post.

Lise was in the kitchen, helping Arlene, who had spilled a potful of snap beans on the floor. Lise gave him a goofy look as he swung through. He warned her with a straight face, and she let him know he was being no fun.

"Are those coals ready yet?" Arlene asked.

The burgers were waiting on a plate. He grabbed a spatula and took them out and slid them on, watching the fat drizzle and flare up. Sam and Ella had come in from the dock and installed themselves on the screenporch. From around the corner he could hear his mother asking them questions. Lise and Arlene were working on the salad. He flipped the burgers, nearly dropping one through, saving it with his hand, wiping his greasy fingers on the grass. The burgers were thick and would take a long time, and he wondered where Meg was, not at all surprised that she was late. They would talk tonight, long after his mother and, grudgingly, Lise had gone to bed, and she would tell him about Jeff and exactly what happened. He hoped so. While it never played out that way, he always thought that together they could solve any problem by talking, the way they'd joined forces as kids, the two of them against the world.

It seemed they'd lost that battle—or maybe it was just him, his disappointment tinting everything. But Meg really was struggling. His own problems were ones he'd knowingly chosen. She'd never had that luxury.

He felt he'd let her down somehow, not been involved or helped out enough. Not that she would have listened to him. For months he didn't hear from her, and then she was calling him practically every day, keeping him on the phone until his ear was sore. All she did was complain about Jeff, or the kids, or her therapist. Some days, she said, I call in sick and just lie in bed and read. I don't get dressed, I don't do anything, I just lie there. And then the next minute she'd be all excited about her promotion and this new program at her work, as if the rest of it didn't exist, until one day she admitted she'd been fired months ago but didn't want to tell him because she knew he'd tell their mother.

She was so fucked up.

He flipped the burgers and dug into one with the corner of the spatula, but it was still raw. The coals were hot enough, he just had to be patient. When he went inside to rinse off the plate the kitchen was empty, everything laid out on the table. He came back out with the cheese. He was tempted to peek again but held off.

It was getting dark, shadows filling in the trees, bats flitting like swallows. From the screenporch came a blast of laughter—Lise—and then his mother saying something, and Arlene, and more laughter, the children in it this time. What they were laughing at he could not imagine, this strange family of his. He stood under the chestnut with the spatula in hand, waiting, like his father.

3

"I can't believe this," her mother said, digging through the napkins in the bag. "I swear, they are such idiots."

Her mother jerked the van left and pulled a U-ey across the oncoming lanes and half onto the gravel and back toward the lights of the Taco Bell. Justin's milk rolled out of the cup holder and fell to the floor, but it wasn't open.

"It's okay," Sarah said, since it was her Mexican pizza they'd forgotten.

"No, it is not okay," her mother said, as if she was the one who messed up. "You need to eat something. We paid for it and we're going to get it, that's the way this thing works, not whatever they're trying to pull."

She didn't apologize while they waited in the drive-thru line again, and when they got up to the window, she said, "My daughter ordered a Mexican pizza?" to the guy in the visor, like it was a crime, and all Sarah could do was look away, hide in the dark of the car. Beside her, Justin was almost done with his Gorditas. Shreds of lettuce stuck to his shirt, a glob of sour cream on Tigger's arm. She wiped it up with a finger and reached between the seats for a napkin.

"I hope you don't do this very often," her mother said. "It's not a very good way to stay in business."

Mom, she wanted to say, it's Taco Bell; no one cares. It was like Mark, getting majorly pissed off about something tiny.

"Sorry about that, ma'am," the guy said, but her mother had the overhead light on to inspect the new bag, to make sure what was in the box was actually Mexican pizza. She clicked the light off and handed it back to Sarah before pulling forward. Sarah sat the warm box on her lap, unopened. She didn't feel like eating it now, she just wanted to be out of there.

It wasn't PMS, her mother was just like this sometimes, and it frightened her, not knowing when this crazy person might show up. Once she was out, there was nothing anyone could do, not even her father, certainly not her. And then five minutes later she would hug you and kiss you on the forehead and say she was sorry, that things had been hard for all of them lately, as if all of them had been screaming and swearing because someone left a towel on the floor.

On the highway, the dark fallen around them again, her mother asked her how her pizza was.

"It's okay," Sarah said.

"What?" her mother said. "I can't hear you. Speak up."

"I said it's okay."

"After all that it better be fantastic, hunh?"

She was always doing this, trying to make things funny after they happened.

Sarah took a few bites and then closed the lid and set the box on the floor with the rest of the mess. The van was like this most of the time now. Before a trip, her father used to take two grocery bags out to the driveway and fill one with trash and one with pop cans. Her mother didn't even think of it, so they rode in a nest of crumpled maps and rolled Doritos bags and used tissues, in the pockets of the doors an army of sticky Rugrats and Darth Mauls.

"Did everyone get enough to eat?" her mother asked an exit later, and Sarah made sure to answer clearly. Justin mumbled, and her mother was on him immediately. Sarah gave him a look: don't be stupid. She pointed to the food on his shirt and he brushed it off without her mother seeing.

He tapped the back of his wrist and she held up two fingers for two more hours. They were still in Ohio, not even to Cleveland. She clasped her hands together and tilted her cheek against them, feigning sleep, then pointed to him. It was already past his bedtime. Sam and Ella wouldn't be waiting up for them this late, only the adults. They would have to go straight to bed, her mother trying to find Justin's toothbrush and then telling him to just use Sarah's.

He didn't want to go to sleep, so they sat there in silence, their faces now shadows, now sliced by light, angles opening and closing like doors. Outside, trucks whined by the other way, headed west. She couldn't decide if she missed Mark. He promised he'd write and then he didn't. He was probably still pissed off about that last time, using it as an excuse. He'd wanted more than she wanted to give him, and then was hurt when she said no.

It wasn't her fault. Everyone said so. Liz and Shannon both thought he was being a jerk. She thought of him at camp, teaching little kids how to do archery. The way they left it, Sarah was sure he would feel justified meeting someone new. She could see her, some blonde with a ponytail and field-hockey legs. Tiffany, her name would be, or Ashley. Something dumb.

Her mother lit a cigarette and opened the window a crack, switched the radio on, veering across the dotted line as she tried to find a station, then correcting. She finally settled on dinosaur rock, keeping it low. She tapped the wheel along with the song, her ashes falling on the carpet. The next rest area was in fifty-three miles. Sarah leaned back in her seat, hoping to go to sleep herself.

The station played too many commercials. Voices caught her short of falling, and she tried to relax her eyes, forget their muscles, see nothing. Her father listened to jazz on trips, long honking solos floating them cross-country. He taught them the names of the greats so they could guess who was playing. John Coltrane, Charlie Parker. There was even one guy who played the flute like her, she could never remember his name. She'd brought hers to practice this week, and to play for Grandma and Aunt Arlene. Next year in school Justin was going to take tenor saxophone so the two of them could play duets. Her father would come and listen to them, maybe tape them so he could listen to them when he was driving to work, or to Grammy's place in the U.P., the long haul through the pines. Thelonious Monk made him smile and play the dashboard like a piano.

He was probably in his apartment right now, watching TV. The one time he'd had her and Justin over for dinner they watched *Austin Powers*. It wasn't as funny as it should have been, probably because the place was strange—the plates she'd never seen, the glasses with the flowers on them, the green couch. But Justin laughed. "Oh, behave!" he said all the next week, and every time she thought of the cramped bathroom, the grocery bag her father was using for a trash can beneath the sink. There was a clump of blond hair in it, and the strip from a maxipad. She hadn't told anyone, as if he had asked her to keep his secret. It made her feel strange and powerful, but just privately, like she was in her own little world away from everybody, a place no one could go.

Maybe he was asleep.

Maybe they'd gone out to a movie or to a nice restaurant, dressed up, and for a minute Sarah saw the blonde woman as beautiful and tall, her hair done like someone on TV, and she wanted to be with them instead of here, in the van smelling like old Taco Bell. "This is my daughter Sarah," her father would say, and the woman would like her because she knew how much Sarah meant to her father. The three of them would be a new, glamorous family. Justin would be stuck with their mother. He'd visit them in the summer for a week and beg to stay.

He was asleep now, his head bent forward on his neck. Sarah wedged Tigger under his chin but it didn't help. She took the sleeping bag between them and pushed it against the far door, then pulled his knees sideways towards her so he leaned back. He smacked his lips and mumbled something, that was all.

"Thank you," her mother said, "that was nice," as if her being nice to him was something unusual.

"You've been pretty quiet," her mother said.

This was how it started. She would want to talk about Mark, and next year.

"I'm tired of being in the car."

"I thought you might be missing Daddy."

It was a tricky question, one her mother had been asking her all summer. Her usual answer was "a little," but that wouldn't work here.

"*I* do," her mother said, encouraging her. "I'm not used to driving the whole way by myself."

Sarah didn't know what to say. It's not your fault. That's what her mother wanted.

"It's worse because this is when he's with us the most, in the summer," her mother tried. "I think when school starts it'll be easier."

She could agree to this and then pretend to go to sleep, it would be so easy. But all she could say was "Maybe." Even that was more than she'd wanted to say. She hated when her mother made her give away her feelings. It felt like they weren't hers anymore, or fake, just what her mother needed.

"I'm going to need your help even more then, with Justin and the house. Will you do that for me?"

This she could promise honestly.

"Thank you," her mother said, way too grateful, like Sarah had done her the biggest favor. "I know I can count on you."

Inside Sarah's head, a buzzer went off, like on one of those game shows. Wrong, she thought, but just sat there in the dark—as if no one could see her ugly, secret little heart.

4

"I'm afraid if I sit here any longer I'll fall asleep," Emily said. "I hope no one minds."

Why did she have to be so dramatic? Lise thought. Of course no one minded.

"You're sure?" Emily asked.

"No, go ahead," said Ken. "I'll wait up for her."

Lise expected this, but to hear him say it so plainly, in front of everyone—it was not that he'd chosen Meg over her, or that she was jealous. It was the fact that he hadn't bothered to discuss it with her, left it unsaid and therefore understood between them. Of course he would want to talk with Meg alone, especially now. And yet she suddenly wanted to stay up with them.

It was greedy, wanting to be part of everything he did, everything that meant anything to him. In the same way she wasn't really jealous of his work, she just wanted to be included. It was exactly what her parents warned against, the curse of the only child. She would hear it all from Ken anyway, tomorrow morning in bed, and that conversation would be richer, being theirs.

Besides, she was tired from the drive, and she wanted to read her book. It had been a long day. She felt like she was still in the car, still moving. She wished she hadn't had that piece of pie. The news was on in ten minutes, but she really didn't care. She was on vacation. Let the rest of the world go on without her.

"I'm going to water Rufus before I hit the hay," Arlene said, taking a cigarette and her lighter from the mantel. She was good about not smoking inside, she just disappeared from time to time. "Unless either of you want to do it."

"That's all right," Ken said.

"Come on, lazybones," Arlene called, and Rufus lifted himself in stages, his front half first, his back end dragging, stiff-legged. She held the door for him, and the screen, then gently closed it behind her. The lawn was dark, and Lise watched as Arlene put her hands out to her sides, afraid of tripping over the croquet wickets. The porch light followed her only so far. The night swallowed all but her ankles and tennis shoes, and then there was just the glow of her cigarette, headed for the dock.

Lise turned from the window back to the bright room. For the first time today, she and Ken were completely alone, but he was reading the paper and didn't seem to notice. With his family around, he was on vacation from her. Maybe it would be good, a break for both of them.

"I think I'm going to head up," she said, closing her book. She wished, ridiculously, in this pause, that he would stop her, take her hand and pull her down to the couch. He was reading opinions, letters to the editor. She turned and made for the stair door.

"I'll be up as soon as they get here. Are there pillows for Sarah and Justin?"

"Yes."

"Thanks for putting the beds together."

"You and Sam did ours," she said, her hand on the knob, because it was like him, overpraising her, as if she needed encouragement. She wanted to tell him not to stay up too late but worried that he'd misread her. Instead, she asked what their plans were for tomorrow.

"The kids'll probably want to go out on the boat. Is there anything special you want to do?"

"I was thinking the flea market. We won't be able to next weekend."

"Good idea."

"As long as you don't bring your camera," she said, then could see he thought she was serious. "I'm just kidding, I don't care if you bring it."

"I wasn't going to."

"Well, you can if you want. You shouldn't listen to me."

He completely ignored this, went off into logistics, how many life jackets they had, and that was what drove her mad, how he chose not to acknowledge her apologies. And she wanted romance? He probably hadn't thought of it at all, with Arlene on the dock and the kids in the same room with them, but there was a lake, a moon, the lawn. Once they'd made love on the tennis courts, the asphalt warm on her back, but that was years ago, before Sam. She couldn't remember the last time they did it outside.

It didn't matter. She had her book.

"So after the flea market we come back and have lunch and then do the boat. I think that's pretty ambitious for our first day."

"Your mom has those chickens for dinner up at the Lighthouse."

"Whoever picks them up should get another milk."

"She's already got a list on the fridge." It was a private joke, how rigid Emily relied on lists, and so a good note to end on, the bond reestablished between them. So often marriage felt like work, and then with no warning they were back in that easy familiarity, the intimacy of things long agreed upon.

"I hope they're okay," Ken said.

"I'm sure they are. She's probably just being Meg."

"Probably." He looked thoughtful. He still had the paper open, and she could see he wanted to get back to it.

"I'm going to read for a little." She waved her book.

"Okay," he said, and let her go.

She opened the door and stepped up into the musty dark of the boxed-in stairs. She tried to be quiet climbing them, a hand on the wall. It was warmer with every step, even with the fan bombing away. They'd left the bathroom light on, and Sam and Ella were sprawled out on the floor in its dim reflection, Sam with his pillow half underneath him, his nightshirt twisted and his belly poking out, Ella with her mouth open and her knees making a tent of her sleeping bag. Sometimes when she watched them sleeping they seemed darling and full of promise, but more often she thought them graceless and ungainly (Sam's hair an explosion, Ella's fingers clenched), and felt all the more tender toward them, as if they needed protection from her own judgments. Here was a picture for Ken, flawed and breathing, not those cold arrangements his professor called art.

She didn't dare say that to him, not the way he'd been lately. Seeing him so desperate worried her. He'd taken what he loved and turned it into work. She believed in him, he knew that, but that wasn't enough. He wanted everyone to say he was wonderful, and that, she thought, would probably never happen.

She took her book into the bathroom with her, laying it on the red crescent mat in front of the toilet, then sat there distracted, scratching at her lifeline, examining the withered grain of her thumb, thinking of the dishes she'd washed, phones answered, lovers touched, her entire life there in her skin. Like anyone. The world turned cosmic when you'd gone too long without sleep. She rubbed her eyes, ground her eyebrows under her fingertips. What was he going to do—what were *they* going to do? The book lay there on the mat between her feet, but suddenly she didn't care about Harry Potter; she was only reading it to see what the kids found in it. Escape. She could use some right now.

The water smelled, a fact she conveniently forgot from year to year. For cooking they used bottled water, long plastic jugs they kept on the counter by the microwave, but for brushing her teeth she was stuck with the tap. The basin was stained. Fartwater, Sam called it, and she swished and spat fast, then covered the taste with a slug of Listerine.

"Uck," she said, and found herself in the mirror. On her chin was the beginning of an Emily-induced zit.

"Isn't *that* nice."

She took her book from the windowsill and navigated the dim room to the head of their bed, then backtracked and found Ella's flashlight from camp, turned it on and stuck it beneath her pillow. She felt grubby after the car but the shower smelled and she'd never get her hair dry. She dumped her shorts and top on the pile by the dresser and pulled on a T-shirt, then sat on the bed and swung her legs under the humid sheets. She settled in, the flashlight nestled in her shoulder, throwing its bull's-eye against the page and beyond, the ceiling alive with an eclipse.

She was sure she'd read this sentence before. Harry was taking the train from platform nine and three-quarters to Hogwarts, then meeting the headmaster Dumbledore for the first time, the picture on his business card disappearing when Harry turned it over. No wonder the kids loved this stuff, there was always another marvelous thing popping up. By the end of the section she was deep in that magical world. She actually had to stop herself from going on to the next chapter. She patted her stomach for her bookmark and set the book reverently on the cedar chest, then thumbed off the flashlight.

At the far end of the room, the fan barreled on. Ella stirred and slurped—her braces made her—and Lise wondered what time it was, and if Meg was okay. Their windows overlooked the garage, stark as film noir in the floodlight above the kitchen door, the barbecue grill sitting beneath the tree. There was no wind, just the lake slapping faintly. She would hear if Meg's van pulled up, the gust of the engine finishing, the croak of the emergency brake.

The pillow smelled of mold, and she wished they'd brought their own. Across from her, the other bed was empty. Meg would be fine, she thought, but couldn't stop imagining the red-and-blue lights of police cruisers blocking the highway, flares throwing a ruby glow over the crash scene, glass scratching under the firemen's boots.

Ken's father's death was expected, had only deepened his isolation from them, lost further in his work. Meg's death would be different, a chance for Lise to intervene. She would comfort him, bring him back to the world. Or he might grow even more remote, curled around his disappointment. She couldn't live with that kind of sadness, that kind of man. His distance already took so much energy to bridge. She could feel it wearing away her spirit, like water cutting into rock.

On the way out they'd passed an auto graveyard, the cars laid out in rows. Ken saw it first (it would be like a playground for him, all those stilled objects, and she almost told him to stop). The damage to some of the cars astonished her. Surely no one could have survived that collision, or that one there, the roof chopped off. Lise was surprised to see a whole row of minivans—sides caved in, windowless, noses smashed flat—each speaking of some family's terror.

"Actually," Ken had said, "I'm surprised there aren't more."

She expected that from him now, the morose, heartless comment. Logical, flat, at the core a pitiless truth he pretended to accept. No, the sad thing, she thought, was how quickly she agreed with him.

5

Arlene swiped at the bench with her hand, only to find it dry. The air fooled her, cool and filled with water. How bright it was in the dark. Overhead, the moon let in light like an eye, its spectral outline to one side. The stars winked, the field deepening the longer she looked up, but it was hard on her neck. She exhaled, found Rufus with her ankle, inhaled and tapped the ash behind her into the water.

She and Henry used to take the canoe out on nights like this, dipping the paddles in silently, a war party sneaking up on the enemy. When they were far enough from shore so the light from the cottage was just a dot, they stopped and let it drift, the only sound their breathing, the paddles dripping, fish breaking the surface. Henry took out the Pall Malls he'd filched from Uncle Perry's jacket and, shielding the kitchen match from shore, they lit up and lay back, keeping the brilliant end below the gunwale, taking the smoke in and breathing it out languorously, the way people did in the movies. One each, and even that was a risk. The butts sputtered when they flipped them overboard. If they timed it right, they would be sitting there in absolute black when the clock tower up at the Institute struck twelve, the solemn tolling of the bell clear and sharp as the moon, seeming to go on far too long and then echoing away to nothing in the hills, the lake still again.

For a while they didn't speak, and then Henry said, "That was a good one."

"It was a great one."

Their voices were tiny in the dark and made everything seem more important. They talked about the war, and what branch Henry should enlist in, and how she would become a nurse and follow him to the South Pacific. They talked about what they were going to do now that the war was over, what college to go to and what kind of jobs they wanted. They talked about Emily, and whether Henry should get married before he finished his degree. But always there was the canoe and the moon and the bell tower chiming midnight.

"I think," Henry said, "that this is my favorite place in the whole world."

"Me too."

If only they could stay here, never get older. But it was already too late.

"Will you come out here with her?" she asked one night, and she knew what it sounded like, but he didn't laugh.

"No, this is just for us." And the way he said it, she didn't have to make him promise.

They'd been out a few times after that, though she knew Emily resented it. Their talks were different, as if she were in the canoe between them.

Tonight Arlene had come out to hear the bells. The canoe was long gone, and their father's mahogany Chris-Craft (the *Lady Belle,* after their mother), and the old dock, but she was sure that at some point back then her body had occupied this same space, breezed through it like a ghost—riding in a boat, or diving, fishing the pilings. She had probably filled every square inch of this shore at some time or other, and a hundred feet out into the lake. But this water was all new, the old moved on to God knows where. Downstream. She thought of the diagram she'd taught her third-graders, the rain falling on the mountains, rolling through the fields to the sea only to evaporate and rain down again from the clouds. It was all the same water, cycling over and over, yet it seemed the lake no longer knew her.

Last fall when Henry was in the hospital, she visited every day. Once, when Emily had left the room, he gestured for her to come closer. She took his hand and bent down to hear him better.

"Arlie," he said, and it was an effort.

"Yes, Henry."

"Be patient with her."

She could have asked him who he meant. "I always am."

"I know," he said, and found the strength to lift his other hand and sandwich hers, as if he were comforting her. She thought he had meant to thank her for putting up with Emily all these years, but instead it felt as if he was charging her to take care of Emily, passing Emily along as if she was a child. It was unfair: she'd never wanted Emily, only him. She'd wanted him to acknowledge that bond that existed before any other and that she thought was stronger—having been in love just once—than any since. But it seemed he'd forgotten how they'd been, or could not tell her, and it would have hurt her even more deeply to press the issue, beg him like a woman jilted.

She remembered, even if everyone else was gone, and there, as if proof, came the first peal from the bell tower. And then the second, chilly, drifting away over the lake. She sat there listening without a cigarette, holding herself against the cold, while far out on the water she lay back, happy, waiting for him to say something.

6

Justin refused to wake up, so Ken had to carry him. Meg grabbed the sleeping bags and asked Sarah to bring the pillows. Yes, and Tigger. The rest would just have to wait till tomorrow.

She'd been driving so long her only goal now was getting inside the house, getting the kids down, then collapsing herself. Her eyes hurt, and her back, even her hands, cramped from gripping the wheel, but they'd made it, and with no tickets, no major fights. It seemed a great accomplishment.

The grass was wet and lumpy beneath her feet—she was stepping on chestnuts. She was surprised to find Arlene holding the screendoor for them; usually she was asleep by this time. She was not surprised that her mother had already gone to bed. She'd hear about it first thing tomorrow, how worried she'd been (but not enough to stay up).

Inside, the light hurt her eyes, and then when she headed upstairs she couldn't see, and had to stop, and Ken bumped into her from behind.

The fan was running and the air smelled the same, instantly snatched her back thirty years, turned her into a thirteen-year-old with her period, hiding up here on a beautiful day. Sam and Ella were by the chimney, and she laid out Justin's bag right beside them, unzipped it so Ken could set him down. Sarah was there with his pillow, and Meg slid it under his head. She pulled off Justin's shoes and socks, Sarah pushed Tigger into his arms, and she folded the flap over him.

Lise was asleep in one bed, the other queen was for her. It seemed a waste of space, all that room. Jeff had left her nearly a year ago, and she still wasn't used to sleeping alone.

"You can take care of yourself, can't you?" she asked Sarah.

"What about my toothbrush?"

"Do you really, absolutely need it?"

"I guess not."

"It's not going to kill you to skip brushing this once," Meg explained, but Sarah put on her wounded face, as if she were bullying her. "Which bag is it in?"

"My purple one."

"Get ready for bed," she ordered, and went downstairs and through the living room and out the screenporch and across the lawn to the van.

She thumbed the button for the back hatch, but she'd locked it at the rest stop and had to dig in her pockets for her keys and then hold them up to the moon to find the right one, and then when she opened the hatch the bags fell out onto the grass. She threw Sarah's purple one aside and shoved the others in, reached up and slammed the hatch down before they could escape again, then headed for the house, sure that all this time Ken and Arlene were watching her.

"Here," she said to Sarah in the bathroom, and Sarah thanked her mously, as if she might yell at her. "Don't give me that face, all right? I've just driven twelve hours by myself so we could be here with your cousins."

Sarah's face changed to one Meg was too familiar with lately, the pinched lips and downcast glare, and while she now regretted saying anything, she couldn't let this pass. "Just stop with the attitude. You keep this up, it's going to be a long week for both of us, and I don't know about you, but that is not what I came here for."

She left her there at the sink, mad at herself. They were both tired. Christ, she was trying to do her a favor. She hadn't driven this far since college, but that meant nothing to Sarah. In Sarah's eyes, every fight they had was between the two of them alone, a bare contest of wills fought in a stone ring on some sand-swept plain like in her sword and sorcery books. In Sarah's eyes, Meg was sure, she was always the one who attacked first, as if she carefully plotted each ambush, leaving Sarah no choice but to defend herself.

Downstairs, Ken had brought all the bags in, which meant she'd have to take them upstairs or hear about it tomorrow morning. She did not want to start things with her mother like that. Already she would have to explain why she was so late, and though she'd had five hundred miles to come up with an answer, she didn't have one. The truth would not do. She was prepared to tell her mother about the divorce—expected, maybe even welcome news, after all the back-and-forth—but she couldn't say she spent the morning in a pointless, informal three-hour meeting, and that it had ended nastily, with Jeff's lawyer threatening to bring up not just her years in therapy but her rehab, and that later her own lawyer—the woman she was paying good money to fight for her—advised her to take the settlement and give Jeff the visitation he wanted, and that she had cried in a stall in the women's room, her face hot in her hands, because she knew she would lose the house and they would have to move, and the kids would have to start over in another school district because they couldn't afford Silver Hills anymore. Her mother did not need to know all that.

Ken helped her take the bags up while Arlene stood at the bottom of the stairs, supervising. He looked good, still trim, his hair receding but not gone dry and flyaway like their father's. As a girl she'd envied Ken his natural wave, his eyelashes, yet he'd never been vain. He seemed, in his own stumbling, oblivious way, incredibly lucky. She supposed it would always be like that: there were people who things just worked out for, and there were people for who things didn't, no matter how hard they tried.

"I'm going to turn in," Arlene said when they were finished. "I just wanted to make sure you got in okay."

"Thanks."

"All right, sweet dreams," Arlene said, and she and Ken echoed her.

They went into the kitchen so they wouldn't wake anyone up. Ken turned off the outside spotlight, and the van disappeared. "You want a soda or something?" he asked, opening the fridge.

"No, I should be getting to bed. It's a long drive by yourself."

"I'm sure. How are things?"

He asked it so casually, closing the door, that she was tempted to say okay, they're fine.

"Awful," she said. "It doesn't matter. Did you tell Mom about the job?"

He answered by tipping his head to one side, a kind of shrug.

"You're such a chicken. You were waiting for me so it wouldn't look that bad."

"No." He was so transparent, so helpless. And she was the one they all felt sorry for, judged, held up as the troubled child.

A whole week with them. For a second the years she vacationed with Jeff's family up in the U.P. seemed a breeze, but that was untrue. Their squabbles were the same except she was outside of them, instead of at the eye. And eventually—it was her one real talent—she'd found her way to the center of them too, and then been cast out. Here they still accepted her, if with a condescending pity, binding advice. They were all she had now.

"What's the plan for tomorrow?" she asked.

"We're going to do the flea market and then go tubing after lunch."

"What time is everyone getting up?"

"I'm getting up around six to catch the light."

"Just be quiet."

The kids would be up early, and it was late. Together they battened down the house, turning off the lights one by one until they couldn't see each other. She bumped a table and Rufus barked in their mother's room, making her laugh.

"I forgot about him," she whispered. "How's he doing?"

"He gets tired if he plays too long. His back."

They were quiet going up. Her feet remembered the stairs, her hands naturally found the banister around the top, closed over it like the rail of a ship. She expected to find Sarah reading by flashlight, but she was already sleeping. Justin was long gone, Tigger lying on the carpet, rejected. Beside them, Sam and Ella could have been their missing twins, and she thought how much harder the next few years would be for Justin and Sarah, how they would want to trade places with their cousins, go off to Boston and leave their crazy mother behind to deal with her mess. She wouldn't blame them; she'd do the same if she could.

She told Ken to go ahead and use the bathroom, she had to find her toiletry bag, then sat there on the bed with it in her lap, waiting for him to finish. She'd gotten up early to dress for the meeting, which now seemed to have taken place weeks ago. But no, that was today, Jeff walking past her in the hall without a word, his lawyer blocking her like a bodyguard. And then her own lawyer lecturing her on watching her temper, as if she had no right to be angry after what happened, as if she were the one in the wrong. And then the bathroom, weeping into her hands, dabbing at her makeup with toilet paper. All today. The trip itself had been a reprieve, but now the hours, the hundreds of miles she'd driven disappeared, every lane change and rest stop forgotten, and her life settled upon her again.

She'd always survived her disasters, gone on—wiser, she hoped, certain she wouldn't make the same mistakes again. This was different, not completely her fault, and the consequences weren't hers alone, though in the end she would be held responsible for them.

She wasn't just being melodramatic. She thought it was amusing that she could pinpoint it, being so close. Taking everything into consideration, it was fair to say that today had been the worst day of her life. The only good thing, she thought, was that it was almost over.

Sunday

1

Sam was the first one up, even before Justin, sleeping right beside him. The room was gray like when it rained and there was no clock, just the mirror on the dresser throwing back the dull squares of the windows, the leaves of a tree. Someone had turned off the fan. The air outside his sleeping bag was cold on his arms. Sarah was there, and he watched her breathing, her hair covering one cheek. He wanted to brush it away and touch her face.

He wanted them all to wake up and play with him—croquet maybe, that wasn't too loud—but he knew Ella would be angry and then his mother would yell at him for getting up too early. The room was too dark for his Game Boy and he didn't feel like reading. He stepped over Justin and went into the bathroom and closed the door. He didn't hear anything as he peed, so he turned his hips to change his aim and the water drummed until he was done. He didn't flush because that would wake people up; he just put the seat down, and the lid, so no one would see it. The window by the sink was frosty with water; he swiped at it to see if it was on the inside, and his fingers came away dripping. The world blurred, turned runny. In the side yard, a blackbird was hunting, poking his bill into the grass. At least someone was up.

Aunt Margaret was in the other bed next to his parents, wearing a T-shirt, her arms over her head like she was giving up. She was pretty like Sarah, with the same red hair that looked fake, and he made sure not to go too close. On the cedar chest next to the bed she'd left some money by a glass of water—change on top of a lot of bills—and he thought they would probably have to go to the stupid flea market like every Sunday. All he wanted to do was ride the inner tube. His mother wouldn't let him go for a plane ride, and they never let him buy any decent Hot Wheels. It was just old screwdrivers and stuff, ugly plates and rusty frying pans. It would take all morning—and watch, it would be raining by the time they got back.

He went to get some pants and discovered another pile of change on top of the dresser. It was probably Sarah's, since her pocket watch was in the middle of it. It was almost six. He pretended not to look at the money while he zipped up and pulled on a shirt. There were a lot of quarters. He got his socks on and then searched the floor for his shoes. When he found them he brought them back to the dresser.

He liked the watch, how small it was. There wasn't room for all the numbers. It had a strap you snapped around your belt loop so you could pull it out of your pocket easier. He imagined whipping it out at recess and Travis Martin wanting to take a look at it. But he couldn't take it. Sarah would miss it.

She might miss one of the quarters. A nickel would be easy, but a dime was worth twice that, even if he didn't like dimes. He checked his parents and Aunt Margaret on one side, Ella and Sarah and Justin on the other, and then, with a finger, as if by accident, knocked a dime over the side.

He knelt down to put his shoes on and pinched the dime up out of the carpeting and secretly slipped it into the pocket of his shorts. Tying his shoes, he checked everyone again. No one had seen him, he was sure. He found his Game Boy and headed for the stairs, stopping at the top to look at them all one last time. He could've gotten a nickel too.

Downstairs, Grandma was up, making coffee at the stove. Rufus left her to come over and sniff him, and Sam had to push his head away.

"Look who it is," she said. "Sam Sam the Dinosaur Man, all bright-eyed and bushy-tailed. Are you ready for a Grandma breakfast?"

"Okay."

"What kind of toast do you want with your eggs? We have a choice this morning."

He waited at the kitchen table while she soft-boiled the eggs, the steam rising up over the stove. At home he'd watch TV now, hoping for the Red Sox score so he could tell his father when he came down, but the TV here didn't get ESPN, and Grandma didn't like them watching it anyway. He turned on his Game Boy and waited for Pokémon Red to load.

"You're not planning on playing that thing the whole time you're here," she asked.

"No." He'd wanted to take it out on the porch and play with the sound down so it wouldn't count against his hour; now that was impossible. He turned it off.

"Thank you. I'm sure you can find plenty of other things to do. Your mother tells me you're a reader." She looked to him as if she expected an answer.

"Yes."

"What kinds of books do you like to read?"

"Matt Christopher."

"And what does Matt Christopher write about?"

"Baseball."

"Am I to take it there's a whole series of these books?"

"Yes."

"Have you read them all?"

"I've only read the first three. The library has like fifteen."

"Would you be interested in these books as a Christmas present?"

"Sure."

"What else are you up to? What was the beach like? Your father said you took the ferry to Block Island."

"Yeah," he said, "we rode bikes out to this cool lighthouse," wondering if his father had told her about him getting caught taking the Butterfinger from the snack bar. His mother slapped his hands and he cried, then his father hugged him and told him they still loved him and it was all right.

"What's Block Island like? I've never been myself."

While he told her, she served him his eggs and toast and poured him a glass of orange juice even though he was supposed to have a glass of milk first. He crumbled the toast into the soupy yolk and started eating, and she came and sat down across from him, moving the flowers his mother bought out of the way so she could see. Rufus lay down facing him in case he dropped anything.

Grandma asked about Ella's braces and their school, what teachers they would have this year. She asked if his mother was working, and who watched them after school. She asked if his father liked his work. Sam said he didn't know a lot about his new job.

"Really," she said, "your father has a new job?"

"Yeah. He develops pictures. At a lab, I don't know where."

"I guess I'll just have to ask him then. How are your eggs?"

"Great."

"Do you want some more juice?"

"Yes, please."

She poured him another glass and came back. She asked him about Grammy and Grampa Sanner and how they were doing, and whether or not they might be coming for Thanksgiving. What about Christmas? She asked if Ella had any boyfriends yet or, slyly, if he had any girlfriends.

The whole time she was talking to him, Sam felt special, singled out, so when his father came downstairs with his camera bag and said good morning, it felt like a spell had been broken. Rufus got up to sniff him, and Sam covered his Game Boy with a magazine. He remembered the dime in his pocket, and the ferry, how his mother had asked if he knew what happened to thieves. They go to prison, she said. Do you want to go to prison?

His father said he didn't want any breakfast. "Not yet. I'm going to try to catch some of that light."

"Sam and I were just discussing your new job."

"Is that right?" his father said, and looked at Sam like he was surprised, and he wondered if he was in trouble.

"It's the first I've heard of it. You'll have to fill me in later."

"I will. Right now I've got to go get that light."

"I understand," Grandma said, and let him go. Rufus stood at the door, wagging his tail as he watched him cross the yard.

She turned back to Sam and smiled, and Sam smiled too, happy to have her all to himself again.

"Now," she said, "tell me what else is new with you."

2

He expected getting out of the house would feel like a jailbreak, but walking down the road in the cool, heavy air, Ken thought it was the opposite; he knew that this escape was temporary, that he'd have to come back and tell his mother everything.

It wasn't Sam's fault, and he hoped he wouldn't hold it against him. Sam had enough troubles.

She would accuse him of shutting her out or, worse, of misleading her, letting her believe he was teaching at B.U. (when in fact he'd only filled in for Morgan the week he was out in Berkeley for the opening of his show). He'd have to admit he wasn't working part-time at Merck either, that that had just been an old project they needed him to reconstruct, and not because he was indispensable but because he'd mislabeled his negatives. Instead of the twin professional and academic successes he knew she wanted from him, he'd have to admit that he was making $8.50 an hour developing overexposed birthday party and graduation photos.

After that, the conversation would spread and accelerate, sweep like an avalanche across his life, dredging up the ridiculous choices he'd made and their consequences—for the children, she'd say, as if he'd let Ella and Sam down, doomed them to shame and starvation. He knew she thought he was a fool and feared the world would crush him, and yet her worry never felt protective, more like a lack of faith in him. He'd just have to sit there and listen to her tear him down, without his father to soften the blows, to reassure him that she was only concerned about him, that they all knew what a tough profession he was in.

Crows called, mocking. The canopy of trees blocked out the sky so only a low band of white light filtered in from the lake, sneaking between the houses. Squirrels were out. One froze, then skittered up the far side of a tree as if Ken were a hunter. In the driveways, the Volvo wagons and Cadillacs sat with rocklike patience, windshields beaded with dew, and he remembered the ludicrous bulk of his father's 98, waiting, he supposed, in their dim garage in Pittsburgh, the concrete beneath it stained with the blood of its predecessors. He saw the backyard with its old basketball pole, and the steel garbage cans tucked under the porch stairs. That's what he should be shooting—their dented, mottled sides and knocking handles, the porch rail his father fashioned from pipe. He'd have to visit before his mother sold the house.

He had the Holga and a small tripod in his bag. The light was grainy, too much water in the air, as if it might rain. He'd do a few rolls of black and white. Already the prospect bored him. The Holga was too simple, took too many tools out of his hands. Morgan had made Ken promise to leave it alone, not swaddle the box in black gaffer's tape to stop the light leaks. The plastic lenses were notorious for their distortion. Even if you thought you had a shot, you had no idea how the prints would come out. "That's the whole idea," Morgan said.

He knew how it was supposed to work, he just didn't think it would. But he agreed that he had to do something. Looking over Morgan's shoulder as he picked through his portfolio (rejected, again), he saw how polished and mediocre he'd become. The images told him nothing. Anyone could have taken these stark trees and benches and street signs—an undergrad or retiree with an eye for light—and anyone could have printed them so crisply they would look striking on a wall, but they were empty, all composition; as Morgan said, no gut.

"Talent is great," Morgan said. "Talent and technique are absolutely necessary, but they're not enough. At some point you're going to have to fish or cut bait."

It seemed to Ken an ultimatum, a test of their student-mentor friendship, and so here he was, creeping between the sleeping cottages at first light, hoping to save himself with what was meant to be a child's toy, heading for the fishery. It was no comfort that around the world, as the sun seemed to move westward, thousands of photographers were doing the same thing, dragging themselves out of bed to see the world in its freshness. He should have at least gotten a coffee.

Maybe, his mother would say, you weren't cut out to be that kind of photographer. She'd said this before, and now, in his doubt, he was inclined to agree with her. Maybe he should put his pretensions away and take baby pictures, portraits of normal families for Christmas cards. That would make her happy.

He passed the Cartwrights' and the A-frame owned by the new people from Erie and turned up the crumbling access road, the woods dark on both sides. At the far end where it T-boned the marina road, a van hauling a bass boat rattled past, chains clanking. His father had loved to fish, loved to sit in the reeds in the early morning, the water calm as oil. In one of Ken's favorite pictures of him he was clamping lead sinkers onto his line with his teeth, a cigarette burning on the edge of his workbench. Maybe tomorrow he'd take Sam out before breakfast, just the two of them. He thought of a whole book of fishing shots, the total subculture—men and their sons, their boats and gear—done in that flat style like Bill Owens's *Suburbia*.

It was precisely this kind of abstract thinking that got him into trouble. The Holga was supposed to make him feel the shot, not just see it.

And he'd never taken Sam fishing, not once.

He turned onto the marina road and the trees opened up, giving him a half-mile view across the raised plain of the fishery to the highway. Vapor rose off the ponds, caught in the pasty gray tree line like gun smoke, a Michael Kenna effect, majestic and fake. He wanted something homely and real. He hoped there would be herons, and that the Holga could get him close enough.

He hadn't expected anyone to be in yet, but a game-service pickup stood by the front doors of the main building, and from experience he knew he should get permission before he started shooting.

The inside was alive with the thrum of compressors and the bubbly rush of water through pipes. It was warm, and smelled not of fish but mud, the richness of silt. Posters identifying the different species hung on the cinder-block walls. In the center of the poured floor was a well in which several fish nosed the curved sides. He was admiring the speckled skin of a pike, its ice-cream spoon of a snout, when a ranger in blue came in.

Ken pushed his bag back on his shoulder and extended a hand. "Hi," he said, "I'm a photographer," and gave him his pitch, showed him a photocopied release form.

It was no problem.

Outside again, walking between the blank tablets of the pools, he wondered why that wasn't enough for his mother.

There were no herons that he could see, only some sleepy gulls nestled against the banks, their legs tucked under them. The light was fine, not soft but not dramatic yet, a nice in-between, promising the rich middle grays he liked. Water bugs zipped across the surface, leaving rippling silver trails. There, he thought—not even a thought, really, just the recognition, in a blink, of something interesting. He didn't stop to think about what the print would look like. He set his bag on the ground and scrounged around for a roll of Tri-X, loaded the Holga and got to work.

3

Just waking up made her tired, her brain incredibly heavy, a cloud filled with rain. Ken and Lise were already gone, their made bed a challenge. Meg groped for her watch, hoping the hour was unreasonable. Her wrist bumped her water but it didn't spill.

Nine o'clock.

"Fuck," she exhaled, and let her head fall back into the pillow.

She could have easily slept another hour but she didn't want her mother getting on her case, not the first day. There was no rush, they'd get into it eventually—probably today, after she told her. She could hear her mother's measured response, just short of an I-told-you-so, and then the pause, her mother waiting for her to say she was wrong, that all of this was her fault for not being the daughter she wanted, for defying her as a teenager, dropping out of college, leaving home. She was supposed to admit she'd earned her mother's disapproval, that after twenty years she'd finally realized her mother was right and she was ready to change her life, maybe even move back to Pittsburgh with the kids so they could be closer. From there, who knew where it would go—her ungratefulness, her mess of a life.

This was what she was waking up for.

The air was dry up here, her nose glued shut. The room was familiar without being welcoming—the same banished furniture of her grandparents that haunted her childhood, except, like the cedar chest and dresser, it seemed to have been miniaturized. The angles of the ceiling reminded her of months spent listening to AM radio and writing in her diary, the lonely stretches of vacation relieved only by camp, and then, more crushing, returning with her footlocker full of mildewed clothes and mementos: the decoupaged rock, the macramé ankle bracelet, the second-place ribbon for the breaststroke.

She remembered her father calling up the stairs, "Are you going to come outside with us?" and herself sitting on the rug, the sunlight a slice across her knee. She watched the motes drift as if suspended, sea horses shifting with the current. "Margaret?" She said nothing. "Okay," her father said, "but you know you're welcome to."

He had to say that.

So many times he'd taken her side, yet it didn't matter because in the end he always gave in to her mother. He was a weak ally, and ultimately—again, a teenager, brave and unforgiving—she shamed him with it, and the two of them were never the same, like Jeff after her rehab. She would never understand why men were so brittle. For all their posturing they didn't know how to fight, how to win or lose without letting it wreck them.

Ken's funky 7UP bottle, the broken TV. It was amazing how all this crap had survived when so many other things closer to her had been destroyed. It didn't seem fair. But if she'd hidden up here for thirty years, she'd be fine too, covered with dust but miraculously intact, her belief in love untested.

The boys were long gone, but Sarah was still asleep. Since turning thirteen she despised getting up for school. Ella lay beside her, reading one of Sarah's fantasy trilogies. Though they were only a couple of months apart, Ella idolized Sarah, trailed in her wake the same way Ken had tagged after her.

Ella smiled when she saw her, and Meg knelt down and gave her a clumsy hug. She was shy and polite, like Ken. It was a shame she had his long jaw, not Lise's pretty chin. And thin, a breastless thirteen. Sarah already had a boyfriend and was turning heads at the mall—husbands in their thirties, their eyes like rifles. Meg wondered if this plainness was worse, if Ken was worried for her.

"How are your braces?" she whispered.

"They're okay." Ella opened up to show her.

"I remember when I got mine, my teeth hurt for a week. These look like a different kind though. Mine had a key the orthodontist turned every time I visited. He used to have to hold my face like this and turn it."

"Ow."

"Yeah—ow. But look." She smiled, giving her both profiles, and Ella was kind enough not to mention the subtle yellow Meg had noticed a few weeks ago. Jeff's dental no longer covered them, so she hadn't had them cleaned in a while. The kids' checkups were nervewracking enough. "Yours will look even better when you're done."

"They better. Will Sarah have to have them?"

"So far, no—knock wood." She tapped Ella's part with a knuckle. "But it looks like Justin will."

She left her to her book and used the bathroom. Sitting on the john, she could see only the top half of her face in the mirror, a tired Kilroy. She settled her hair with her hands and looked at the ruts under her eyes. In two weeks she would officially be divorced. She was too old to be starting over again, but that was exactly what she would have to do.

There was a knock on the door.

"Try downstairs," she said.

They knocked again.

"Yes?"

"I need to brush my teeth," Sam said, in that blank voice of his.

"Just a minute," she said, and sighed at the lack of privacy. She knew it was uncharitable of her, but sometimes it seemed to her that Sam wasn't all there. There was something odd about him, the way he stood there looking with his mouth open, his eyes stuck, as if he couldn't actually see you. Glazed, like a sleepwalker. Even when he was doing things, he seemed to be in his own little world, playing with toys designed for younger children. But a lot of boys were like that. She wondered if they'd ever had him tested.

She wrapped a towel around her waist before she opened the door, then gave him a hug. He suffered it, stepped back when she let go.

"And how are you?"

"Good," he said.

"Did you find Justin?"

"Yeah."

"Are you two playing something?"

"Yeah."

He was like a man, she thought, defying her with silence. At least Sarah let her know what a pain she was.

She couldn't resist needling him as he placed his toothbrush bristles up on the sink and squeezed the tube with both hands.

"What are you playing?"

"Croquet."

"Who's winning?"

"I am."

"Are you tired of me asking you questions?"

This struck him as funny, and he stopped brushing to smile at her.

"No," he said through the foam. He seemed so genuinely tickled that she wondered if his blankness was unconscious, not Sarah's practiced act. She would have to ask Lise—politically, of course—and then get the real story from Ken.

He spat but didn't rinse, stuck the brush in the chrome holder.

"Are you all done?" she asked. "Because I have to take my shower."

"I'm all done," he echoed, and headed downstairs.

"Yikes," she said when she had the door closed and the water going.

The plastic insert of the shower head was stained the color of rust. In the middle of shampooing her hair, the water turned freezing and she ducked away, shielding her front. The house—she'd forgotten its tricks. The hot came back and she hurried to rinse off before it disappeared again. A whole week like this. It was bad enough that the water smelled.

She got out, shivering, fists clenched, only to discover the towels were all wet. For a minute she thought it was a joke, a gag Sam had played on her, but then she checked the cupboard, and there was the threadbare collection she knew from her girlhood, the obsolete burnt-orange and dark avocado sets, the striped beach towels bleached white, the patterned wash-cloths. The cupboard smelled of mothballs and latex paint with an under-current of strong cheese, even a dead mouse, all of it scenting the towels.

She noticed she was taking her time, being thorough, as if getting ready for a wedding or a formal dinner. A press conference, she thought. She should have prepared a statement. She could read it off notecards in front of them, then deflect their questions.

As she was rolling her deodorant on, Sarah opened the door, groggy in her nightshirt.

"I gotta go."

"Can you wait?"

"No," she said, hesitating.

"Go then," Meg said, "you're already here," and moved over so she could squeeze by. "When you're done I want you to take a shower and get some breakfast."

"What about Ella?"

"I'm not in charge of Ella." She could almost hear Sarah answer in her head: You're not in charge of me either. "We're going to the flea market."

"Great," Sarah said, deadpan, tinkling.

"You can stay here if you want."

"Who else is going?"

"I don't know. I haven't been downstairs yet."

She ceded the bathroom to her, and the cold hit her skin. She unzipped her green bag and grabbed some underwear off the top. She wasn't sure how warm it was outside, so she hedged and went with jeans.

There were no outlets in the bathroom. She had to hunt behind the low wardrobe for one, then blow-dry her hair kneeling in front of the mirror. Doubled, Ken's 7UP bottle seemed even stranger, sadder. Whose idea was it to bend the neck like that, and why was it considered a prize, something to be won? And yet the bottle with its deep green glass and old-style writing—both long obsolete, the domain of collectors—contained more of her feelings for the world than the ugly rug or the ridiculous dresser or even the decent-looking wardrobe. The heat roared and stiffened her hair, and as she turned her head (seeing Ella still reading) she noted all the other junk up here—the daybed and the chairless ottoman, the clothes tree that looked like a stork, the dusty beanbag chair—and wondered what they were going to do with all of it. The only thing she wanted was the set of tumblers they used for orange juice in the morning and that her father drank his scotch from at night. Each had an antique car embossed on it, a Buick or an Olds with an anonymous couple in goggles and dusters sitting on what appeared to be an upholstered loveseat. The glasses weren't rare or even good-looking but, like Ken's bottle, were charged, brought back the years and meals like a talisman, the laughter in kitchens.

Sarah came out of the bathroom and lay down again.

"Take your shower and get dressed," Meg said in her direction, but didn't press it. It was her vacation too. She dropped her flip-flops on the rug and pointed her toes into them. "You're responsible for your own breakfast," she said, but only Ella looked up.

Downstairs she was relieved to find her mother wasn't there. The boys were on the couch in the living room playing their Game Boys, and through the corner window she could see Lise reading on the porch. She decided to walk past the door normally; when she did, nothing happened.

The coffeemaker still had a few cups in it. Getting a mug from the cupboard, she noticed some of her father's glasses, stacked upside down on the red-checked contact paper so bugs and dust didn't settle in them. She counted four. She thought there were six and stood on tiptoe to look in back, then checked the top rack of the dishwasher—always a horror, the aqua rubber of the prongs worn off.

She could have sworn there were six. Buick, Olds, Reo, Cadillac, Stanley and something else. She'd have to ask her mother, though that meant tipping her hand.

She took her coffee out on the porch. Lise was polite enough to get up and give her a hug, and Meg thought she'd gained weight.

"You look good," she said.

"What time did you get in last night?"

"Not that late. Eleven-something."

Lise apologized for not waiting up, and Meg said she understood. Ken was off with his cameras somewhere. Her mother and Arlene had taken Rufus over to the ponds. Everything was going okay at home, everyone was healthy. She liked her new job, and Ken was looking for something better. Meg said things were rough but they were getting through them, and Lise said she was sorry.

"It's just as well," Meg said.

She sounded just like her mother over the phone, shrugging off seventeen years like a thin windbreaker. It's awful, she could have said, but Lise's "sorry" already covered whatever she might say. She couldn't expect her to know what it felt like watching TV in bed by herself and then turning the light off and not being sleepy, lying there and knowing tomorrow would be the same. A confession would only embarrass both of them.

"Sarah has a boyfriend."

"Really."

"Mark. Very hot."

"Is he nice?"

"We rarely see him. He's like a cat who comes prowling around at night. Don't worry, you'll have your own pretty soon."

"I can't wait."

Far out, a boat smashed past, the engine coming to them late, like a plane's. Meg sipped her coffee and felt the blood spread into her limbs, her sinuses open with a twinge. They sat looking out through the big screened panels at the gray band of the lake.

"One thing," Lise said. "I told Sam he's allowed one hour of video games a day, and that includes his Game Boy."

"I'll tell Justin."

"Thanks."

"No problem. It's a good excuse, actually." If nothing else, they shared the bond of motherhood, the practical application of power. There was something adult and businesslike about their relationship, separate and matter-of-fact, while she and Ken were joined by the inexplicable ties of childhood, a dependence that came from the lifelong effort of defining each other.

They were leaving for the flea market at ten, or whenever Ken returned.

"He starts to work and he loses track," Lise said.

She ducked back into her book and the sun came out, spangling the water, coloring the trees. The cottages on the far shore shone white as limestone. Meg followed a sailboat tilting in the wind off Midway, then, bored, looked to Lise, reading intently—Harry Potter, which she thought of as a kid's book. This was what her mother and Arlene did, Meg thought: sat here and watched the lake all day as if they had nothing else to do. She was more like her father; she needed some project to work on, some complicated repair job, if only to keep busy. Maybe that was her problem. Her life was her project now, and work alone wouldn't fix it.

The danger of vacation, she thought, was having too much time to think.

She contemplated another cup of coffee but knew it would send her into a spin, crack her into fragments, thoughts zipping off in all directions, too many of them dangerous. She needed something to eat, and went inside to see if there was anything that would appeal to Sarah.

The fridge was the opposite of hers: so empty she could see through the racks, and clean. The eggs were probably fair game, the cheese bread she assumed her mother was saving. Milk, a small tub of margarine, cold cuts, a head of lettuce. The door was heavy with ancient, iffy condiments, some of which (like the purple horseradish) belonged to her father. The cupboard was half full of canned soup and taped-up boxes of pasta, packets of gravy mix, only the most nonperishable stuff—like a survivalist's kitchen—but on the top shelf stood a row of cereal boxes. Her mother had remembered, because one was an unopened box of Cap'n Crunch, her favorite.

It was so unexpected, this gift, so unlike her mother (who hated Cap'n Crunch, ridiculed the very idea of it), that for a second Meg wondered if she'd bought it because she felt sorry for her. But for her to remember, that was enough.

She poured herself a bowl and took it out on the dock, holding it away from her as she walked so it didn't spill. A green-headed mallard paddled under the boards as she crossed above. With every step, the planks gave a little, swayed like a shaky bridge. The wind was up, and she wished she'd brought her sunglasses. She settled herself on the bench and dug in before the cereal got soggy, feeling the sugar energize the muscles of her jaw, a tingling release of enzymes. The rush reminded her of getting high.

She held the bowl close to her chin and scooped up a spoonful, painfully sweet on her teeth, and suddenly thought of Jeff. It was nearly a year, and yet he could still paralyze her, make her mind turn inward and begin chewing at herself like Rufus with a hot spot. Jeff had left because she was old and Stacey was young; because she had a temper and Stacey was a pushover; because she was dull and Stacey was exciting. All true and simple enough (Stacey was twenty-eight and played squash, wore a size four), but the more she brooded on these facts, the more she was convinced there was another, deeper reason he wasn't telling her, and never would, some secret shortcoming of hers that made it impossible for any-one to ever love her fully. She had sensed this as a child, learned it, per-haps, from her mother, with all the conditions she put on her, carried it like a cross and then a mark of honor through adolescence until, in her mid-twenties, she began to search in earnest for someone who could prove her wrong. She'd found Jeff, and he'd fooled her into believing she was worthy of that kind of love.

The boards jiggled beneath her feet, and she turned to see Rufus padding toward her, her mother in her quilted jacket and clip-on sunglasses stepping onto the dock. Still defenseless from the memory of Jeff, Meg felt as if she'd sneaked up on her.

She stood, squinting, as Rufus pranced around her knees, his claws scrabbling on the boards. She was almost finished, so she set the bowl down, and he sloshed away at it.

"Don't give that to him," her mother said, but took her in her arms, kept her hands after they'd separated. "I'm so glad you could come."

"It wasn't a choice."

"I know things aren't easy with just yourself."

"I'm used to it. How are you?" she countered.

"Good," her mother said. She took her hands back and sat down. "We're not getting as much rain as I'd like, but it hasn't been too bad."

"Getting out to the club much?"

"I try to get over for a dip around lunchtime. Afternoons it's a zoo, as you can imagine." She laid a hand on her arm. "I'm so happy you could make it. I see you found your cereal." Rufus was done and licking his nose.

"I can't believe you remembered."

"For years it was all you'd eat. I saw it in the store yesterday and I just thought. Is it still utterly dreadful?"

"Absolutely."

"I've caught up with Justin, but haven't seen hide nor hair of Sarah."

Meg explained her new sleeping habits, and predictably her mother reminded her of her own as a girl, as if they were the same person, the world and time identical for all of them.

"How late did you all get in?" her mother asked.

"About eleven."

"You could have called. I thought you said you'd be here in time for dinner."

"I should have told you," she said. "Jeff scheduled a meeting yesterday morning with the lawyers, very last-minute."

Her mother sat up straight for the news, her face grave, and Meg thought that she was taking this personally, seeing it as her failure as well.

"Basically we were going over the paperwork," she said, when Rufus wheeled around, wagging his tail. The dock shook, and they both turned to see Justin and Sam racing across the boards toward them.

"We'll finish this later?" her mother asked, as if Meg might try to avoid it, and it was funny, her mother reading her like that, because that was exactly what she'd been thinking.

"Yes," Meg said, just as the boys thundered up, Game Boys in hand.

They were breathing hard. Both of them wanted to talk.

"Sarah and Ella say they don't have to go to the flea market," Justin reported.

"And?" Meg said.

"Do we have to?"

"Yes."

"Why?"

"Because all you'd do is stay here and play your Game Boys. Aunt Lisa's rule is one hour a day. How long have you been playing for?"

"Half an hour," Justin lied.

She took the Game Boy from him, and Sam slid his into his pocket. "You too." He stepped forward like a prisoner and handed it over. "When you come back from the flea market you can have your other half hour, all right?"

"I don't want to go," Justin said.

"But you like the flea market," she reminded him. "Remember the man with all the Hot Wheels?"

"We never get to buy any," Sam said.

"You talk to your father about that."

"Why don't *they* have to go?" Justin said.

"Because *they* can take care of themselves."

"I can take care of myself." But he realized it was a weak argument. "Do we have to?"

"Yes, you have to," she said. "And no pouting. We're going to have a wonderful time."

4

The first thing Ken noticed was that it wasn't there. His mind was set on getting gas; the pump-shaped caution had popped on when he started the car. It could go another thirty miles, Lise insisted, but he didn't want to push it. Meg and his mother and Justin were ahead of them in the van. He was just following, remarking on the familiar scenery. They came up past the golf course and by the diner and then the main gate of the Institute, decked out with hanging baskets of flowers, but when he glanced over to show Sam the Putt-Putt, to say maybe they could go tonight, all that was left was the orange-and-white fence. The snack bar was gone, demolished, and the soda machines and the windmill, the hooded fluorescents that made the air shake at dusk and the speakers that blared "Travelin' Band" and "Mercy, Mercy Me." Vanished, nothing now but high grass. A saggy roll of chain-link fence blocked off the parking lot, a FOR LEASE sign prominent.

"Whoa," he said, easing the 4Runner up the curve by Andriaccio's, and Lise laid a hand on his leg as if to comfort him. She had a way of anticipating his feelings, and he wanted to say, Wait, I haven't even started processing this. The hand stayed there, stroking him, consoling.

"Your mother and I noticed it coming up," Arlene said from the backseat.

"No one told me."

"I wonder what they did with all the balls," Sam said.

"It's a chain," Ken explained. "They probably have a big warehouse somewhere that sends supplies out to other ones around the country."

"You'd think they could make money here," Arlene said. "With the Institute right across the street."

"That's an older crowd," Ken said. "And there's Molly World now, and that new place in Lakewood with the driving range." He didn't say that when he was a boy the course was deserted, just him and a few other goony kids happy to be off by themselves, the teenager behind the counter bored and listening to a different radio station. The paint was flaking off the fence even then. They didn't bother to scrape it, just slapped another coat on top. So someone had finally pulled the plug on it.

The idea that he could go back and shoot the lot rose and fell away again, replaced by the vain wish that he'd brought his Nikon along last year, documented all the dumb obstacles—the concrete triangles and inchworm hills, the clattering loop-the-loops and gopher holes. Close work, maybe with a fishbowl to give it that nostalgic, gritty carnival look. Too late.

"I'm surprised the Institute hasn't bought up the property," Lise said. "With all their parking problems."

"Maybe they have," he said.

"Can we go miniature golfing?" Sam asked.

"Sure," Ken said. "Maybe tomorrow."

The CD protected him—early Bill Evans, real Sunday-paper music. He aimed the 4Runner down the long hill by the cemetery, the snowball trees bright between the graves. A bare-chested boy with a backwards cap and work boots was cutting the grass, slouched down and riding the mower like a Harley. The chaff was wet and stuck to the headstones.

"Think he'd be cold," he said, and Lise patted him and withdrew her hand.

She'd be expecting him to be thinking of his father, and he had been, seeing him under the shadowed grass in his suit, the box making a space like a cave. Ken could see no further, refused to, his eye flying out in front of the windshield, grabbing the first thing of interest—the plastic-sheeted greenhouses of Haff Acres Farm, and then its signs for pies, corn, the usual roadside menu.

"Corn on the cob," he said, drawling it out, "and Lighthouse chicken," just as they passed the market with its silly half-scale beacon on top.

Lise pinned him with a look, but he deflected it, distracted himself with the gas gauge.

The counter at the Putt-Putt had been covered with astroturf and the putters laid out by size, their rubber grips the color of hot-water bottles. By each tee stood a pole with a slanted metal plate on it (painted orange) for players to fill out their scorecards. When he made a hole in one and his ball was the color that was lit up on the special board, he sprinted for the snack bar to collect his winnings.

He'd never thought of his father like this, in a flood of images. It took a conscious effort to remember him, to bring back a moment the two of them spent together, tromping out in the snow to cut down the Christmas tree at his grandfather White's farm, or looking in on him in the upstairs office at home as he silently paid the bills. What that meant he was careful not to answer, let it float free to be picked up again and examined the rest of his life. He did not doubt his love for his father, or his father's for him, only the strange way memory presented it, mixed as it was with all this other garbage. Their bond was not automatic, a reflex, but, like his father, measured and reliable, bracing as medicine.

They were closing in on Mayville. Ahead on the left was a combination filling station and convenience mart, the Gas-n-Go. He posted up by the yellow line and let Meg go on, waited for a camper to pass, then turned in.

"Are they open?" Lise asked, because it was Sunday and the pumps were free, but there was a blaze orange sign in the window. He remembered the tank was on his side and pulled it up close.

There was another world outside of the car, away from them, and air. He stood there gripping the steel handle, watching the numbers turn as the cars passed, and wondered what it would be like to live here year-round, the wind blowing over the icy lake, combing the hollow reeds, rattling the windows. He could see himself feeding a fire, eating soup and crackers, piling extra blankets on the bed. In the mornings he would go out and work in the snow and the Scandinavian light. He would be patient, do a study of clouds, like Stieglitz dug in at Lake George. His life would be quiet and dignified, every second concentrated, aimed.

The pump clunked off, and he squeezed out a round number, slapped the latch down and replaced the nozzle. A white pickup pulled in as he crossed to the front doors, searching his pockets for a twenty. There was no one at the register, so he waited, scanning the tabloids with their overexposed candid shots and grainy long lenses. And people got paid for that crap, good money too.

He looked around the store, walking to the end of the short rows in case the clerk was busy shelving, but didn't see anyone. In the middle of one aisle sat an unopened bag of Cheetos like a pillow. A radio was going behind the counter, and a closed-circuit TV showing the pumps— the man from the pickup filling his tank. (He could see a whole series of these stills, each with its own story.) By the register sat a tall cup of coffee, a half-full ashtray beside it. He shook his head, crinkled his face like it might be a joke.

The rest rooms were in the far corner, in a low hall at the end of a wall of coolers. He knocked on both doors. "Hello?" he called. "I need to pay for some gas."

When he came out, the man from the pickup was standing at the counter. Ken shrugged. "There doesn't seem to be anyone around."

"That's strange," the man said. He had a cowboy hat and graying muttonchops, and Ken wondered if he was local. He didn't have that honking, almost midwestern accent he associated with western New York State.

"You check the bathroom?"

"I knocked on both of them."

"You got me," the man said.

They went out front again, each of them taking a side, and Ken saw the truck; according to its license-plate holder, it was from Sayre, Pennsylvania—not far. Lise stared at him from the 4Runner and he waved that he would explain later. Behind the store three plastic buckets that had contained potato salad were drying next to the fence around the dumpster, a hose coiled on the wall, the end still dripping on the concrete. The ice machine was unlocked.

They tried inside again. Both restrooms were empty. He left the Cheetos where they lay, stepping over them.

"*Someone* was here." Ken pointed out the coffee by the ashtray.

"I wish I had time for this," the man said, and took out his wallet. He folded two twenties and wedged them into the keys of the cash register. Meg and his mother would be parking by now, wondering what happened to them. It seemed reasonable, so Ken did the same with his twenty and followed the man out.

"What was that all about?" Lise asked.

"It was bizarre. There was nobody there."

"Nobody?"

"The place was deserted."

"Maybe there was an emergency," Arlene guessed.

"Maybe they had to drive the tow truck to an accident," Sam said.

"I don't think a place like this has a tow truck, buddy," Ken said.

"So how did you pay?" Lise asked.

"I just left a twenty."

"That's good."

"It was weird. There was a cup of coffee right by the register, like someone was drinking it and then just disappeared."

"They probably just stepped out," Lise said, but couldn't come up with a believable reason. "Maybe they quit."

"It's a mystery," he said.

He started the car and punched the button so the tripometer read zero—usually a pleasing feeling—and pulled out onto the road. He glanced back at the gas station, expecting to see movement, a flash of uniform, an embarrassed teenager peering out from behind the wiper fluid, but there was nothing, just the posters in the windows, the sign on the door saying OPEN.

It was so unexpected that it shoved the Putt-Putt and his father from his mind, sent him dashing off after possibilities, chasing after the weird feeling of being in there by himself, the whole store, for a moment, his. As they came into Mayville and the lake spread wide beside them, he was still trying to figure out what had happened. He needed to think and didn't look when Arlene pointed out the *Chautauqua Belle* leaving its slip.

He thought he knew what it was. While he was in there, he hadn't been tempted to steal anything, though the opportunity—and the shared acknowledgment of it—crackled between him and the man in the hat like a live wire. No, he wanted more than that: to set up shop and capture the store in all its plain strangeness shot by shot, shelf by shelf, while it was still unaware of him. To catch it, as it had caught him, by surprise. And while thinking that and doing it were two different things, he felt as if now, having experienced that ripeness, he might be able to recognize it the next time it happened.

Finally he understood what Morgan was talking about. The next time, he promised himself, he'd be ready.

5

Lise knew Emily would make a big deal of them being late, that she would be waiting for them in the dusty parking lot, clutching her purse. Where in the world did you run off to? she'd ask, as if she'd missed out on some grand adventure. Then Ken would go into the mystery of no one being at the gas station, and they'd have to hear about it the rest of the day, like CNN broadcasting the same headlines every thirty minutes.

Well isn't that interesting, she'd say.

Or, That's rather peculiar, isn't it?

Or, That's not standard operating procedure, I should hope.

Or later, bringing the prized piece out for reinspection, It's absolutely baffling to me, absolutely baffling.

She needed to put herself at the center of things she wasn't even connected to. Some of that was how lonely she was now, Lise allowed, but she'd always been that way, at least when it came to Ken.

He'd briefed her about Sam tipping his mother about the job. He didn't know how much Emily knew, but enough, and Lise could see he dreaded telling her, like a child ashamed of something he'd done. Lise wanted to say it didn't matter, that Ken shouldn't care what Emily thought after she'd consistently bad-mouthed any chance of his success, but she knew Ken better than that, so she promised to stay out of it, let him explain the situation, knowing—as he did—that she would only get into it with Emily.

She could be at home, getting work done, or at the beach, laid out on a towel. This wasn't a vacation.

Riding through the leafy edge of Mayville with its body shops and fenced-off electrical substation, she noticed herself dropping into that passive trance she used to make time move faster, to let the outside world slide by untouched. As the sole focus of her parents, she'd learned early to draw a curtain around herself, to save a certain privacy even in their midst, and that talent had never deserted her. She wished she'd brought her book, but that would be rude, and definitely held against her. This afternoon she'd be safe on the boat, and before supper she'd volunteer to run out and pick up the chickens. That left only those few hours before bed unguarded, and for that she had Harry Potter.

It was only the first day.

A half mile from the airport, cars were parked cockeyed on the grass on both sides of the road, like at a disaster. There was Meg's van, nosed in between two ancient station wagons. They were late, and Ken decided to pass on the easy, faraway spots and headed straight for the entrance (to catch up, Lise thought).

"I don't know," she said.

"The first secret of parking," he said, "is you've got to be positive."

It was a conceit of his, his luck behind the wheel, and more often than not he would find a spot right by the door of a restaurant or theater when the place was packed, and then say mockingly, "They must have known I was coming." But as they neared the entrance, they saw the lot was for exhibitors only, roped off.

"Shut down," he said, doing his usual play-by-play. They had to go even farther on the other side to find a spot, and then when they were walking back, a truck pulled out right by the entrance, and Ken groaned as if he should have known.

She knew he was upset about the Putt-Putt, but also that he wouldn't want to talk about it now, so she left it alone, tried not to watch him for signs. Tonight they'd find time to be alone. Things would be better, she thought, if they made love. It always seemed to cheer her, to put things in perspective.

The airport was a worn strip of asphalt between two cornfields, a prefab hangar at one end with a wind sock on top. The plane that gave rides buzzed over, and when it was gone, the air was full of sputters and puffs, pneumatic exhalations like the *Chautauqua Belle*'s. It sounded like a distant battle. Closer, they saw the far part of the field had been given over to antique steam engines, their pulleys and flywheels cycling. Some of the boilers were taller than the leather-aproned old men tending them. With each chuff, a tiny cloud leapt up, drifted over the runway and dissipated.

"Check it out," Ken said, but Sam was unimpressed.

"I want to go on the plane," he said.

"You're not going on the plane," she said flatly, so he'd know it was final.

"I never get to do anything."

"That's right," she said, because he wasn't serious, just testing her. She held his hand, staying on the outside as they walked along the gravel berm.

"Can I buy something?" Sam asked.

"Like what?"

"I don't know."

"Not Hot Wheels," she said. "You have more than enough at home."

"How about this," Ken suggested. "I'll give you a dollar to spend on anything you want."

"Except Hot Wheels," Lise said.

"That seems more than generous to me," Arlene chipped in.

They waited for him to say "Okay," but he did it so glumly that she wanted Ken to take the dollar back, and then she had to prompt Sam to say thank you.

Emily and Meg and Justin were waiting for them by an old Mister Softee truck selling hot dogs, a scarred nightstand set up for mustard and onions, already disgusting, flies feeding on blobs of relish. Behind them, display tables of merchandise spread the length of the runway, row on row of junk.

"What happened to you folks?" Emily asked, incredulous. "I looked in the mirror and all of a sudden you were gone."

"We had to get gas," Ken said.

"All this time?"

Why are you even interested, Lise thought. Arlene seemed to agree, curling off to one side and lighting up, waving the match out, bored with the subject. Lise envied how freely she disregarded Emily, and thought of the two of them in Pittsburgh, living alone just blocks apart. It was that kind of self-reliance she aspired to that Ken would never understand.

He told Emily about the station being empty, and immediately she questioned him like a detective. Had anything been knocked over? Were there signs of a struggle?

"Do you think we should call the police?" Emily said, stricken, and Lise had to corral a laugh. Emily ignored her, appealed directly to Ken. "I'm serious."

"I think whoever it was probably went off to do something and got caught up," Ken said. "We can check on the way back if you want."

"Please, let's," his mother said—as if it had anything to do with her.

That settled, they turned to the first row and headed down the left side. They would do the whole thing in order, like a serious trip to the supermarket. It was junk. Savaged luggage, stacked sets of tires, leaning bookcases. The grass between the tables was matted and dusty, littered with crushed cups. Lise vaguely wondered what time it was and how long going up and down the rows would take them. The drive back, then lunch.

Already the boys were out ahead of them, skipping the flatware and the collectible glass, the costume jewelry and Mardi Gras beads, buzzing from one side of the aisle to the other so she had to peer through the crowd to keep Sam's Red Sox T-shirt in sight. She paired off with Meg, the two of them leapfrogging along, Ken and Emily dragging behind them, Arlene off on her own.

"This pattern reminds me of your aunt June's old breakfast set," Emily was lecturing, and Lise sped up.

Laid out on the tables, the items seemed random and sad—dented beer trays and broken pocket watches, browned and fragile dress patterns, board games missing pieces, greasy skillets. It was as if someone had emptied out a house long abandoned, the good stuff already gone—exactly what they were supposed to be doing this week.

The next table was interesting though, Meg poring over a tray of amber rings and pendants, insects frozen inside the hardened sap. "That's pretty," Meg said, pointing to an intricate Victorian setting, and Lise agreed, prodding her to try it on. She looked up and found Sam and Justin across the aisle, flipping through plastic baskets of baseball cards.

"How's this look?" Meg asked, holding her hand out as if to be kissed.

"Almost," Lise said, and noticed she wasn't wearing her wedding ring anymore, an untanned line of skin where it had been. So were they divorced? In spring they seemed headed that way, but Ken hadn't said anything.

Tagging after her, Lise tried to imagine how she would feel if Ken left her, but couldn't. Ken wasn't Jeff. She would be more likely to leave him, take Ella and Sam and start over somewhere, maybe her parents', north of Boston. Not that she'd ever consider it seriously. It was more of a daydream, an empty wish when she was tired, and her own inability to picture herself leaving Ken made her pity Meg more, especially since in a way she'd brought it on herself. She couldn't see how it would be a good thing for anyone but Jeff, and even he had misgivings, she supposed, leaving Sarah and Justin. And while that was awful, she couldn't blame him. She wouldn't want to have to live with Meg.

Cracked books that smelled like mold, scuffed record albums she'd owned as a teenager. Knives, baby clothes, 8-tracks, campaign buttons dating back to Al Smith. They detoured around a table of fishing gear that snagged Ken and Emily, then turned at the end of the row. Sam and Justin had given up on the baseball cards and were digging through a box of rubber insects, menacing each other with giant flies and centipedes.

"In real life he's terrified of them," Lise confided.

"Justin too," Meg said. "And Sarah's fearless."

"Not Ella, she's the ultimate scaredy-cat."

"I wonder how they're doing."

They wandered, sauntered, stood flat-footed. The plane came in and they watched it land, wings tilting, and then when they'd lost themselves in someone's collection of typewriters or old can openers, it took off again, the racket making them look up. The steam engines coughed and ratcheted. She saw a Tiffany lamp she liked but knew she couldn't afford, a child's rocker. Meg was losing interest too; they walked down the dry middle of the aisles, keeping the boys in sight.

They were almost to the head of the next-to-last row when Ken and Emily caught them from behind.

"Will you look what I found," Emily said, holding out two fist-sized ceramic pigs in vests, waiter's towels folded over their arms. Meg looked to Ken, mystified. "They're the salt and pepper shakers we used to have! Don't you remember?"

"Not really," Meg said.

"You remember. We used to keep them on the windowsill of the breakfast nook. They used to have a napkin holder in the shape of a barn. They were a wedding gift from your aunt Lucille. Oh, your father despised them, but you kids loved them. You used to call them Salty and Peppy."

"Oh my God," Meg said, "you're right. Whatever happened to them?"

"I'm sure they broke years ago, they're cheap little things, but here they are. Isn't that wild? Aren't they darling?"

"They're something all right," Lise said when Emily passed them to her.

"They're fun," Emily said.

An entire week, she thought. She wouldn't be able to do it.

Arlene came over to see what they were looking at. To Lise's relief, she seemed unimpressed, turning one over like a bruised tomato before handing it back.

Together they faced the last row, the steam engines huffing and popping beyond the far tables—all taken up by one vendor whose specialty was used tools. Set out on the tops in precise, mazelike designs, largest to smallest, were hundreds of hammers and wrenches and screwdrivers, pliers and vise grips and drills.

"Incredible," Ken said, and she could see he wished he had his camera. He stood there taking it in, as if to memorize it.

"Makes you wonder who they belonged to," Arlene said.

"They're probably from estate sales," Emily said. "Brokers will buy up lots to get a few antique pieces and then sell the rest for next to nothing."

"Where'd you learn that?" Meg asked.

"Since your father died I've learned more about that side of things than I care to admit."

That was sad, Lise thought, but in a strange way it sounded like bragging.

The boys dodged through a group of old ladies, and Meg told them to slow down. They were coming to show off their purchases. Sam led, holding up an R2-D2 for everyone to see. Lise could have sworn she'd seen it before, then remembered: it was a prize from a Happy Meal. It couldn't have cost more than a penny to make.

"Don't we have a thousand of those at home?" she asked, and he stopped bouncing.

"No," he said doubtfully.

"I'm sure we do."

"You said I could buy anything."

"Who is this again?" Emily asked, sweeping in to save him, and then gaped, fascinated by his explanation. "Justin, what did you get?"

He'd chosen a C-3PO so they could play together, and Lise felt foolish and cruel. The plane buzzed overhead, a speck, and she wished she were in it, the wind deafening, taking away her thoughts. She could be so small. Emily seemed to provoke it in her.

Ken was done with the hardware; it was time to go. The kids wanted hot dogs from the Mister Softee truck, but Emily said there was perfectly good salami waiting at home. Arlene had a last cigarette on their way to the car, flicking it into the road, where it rolled, smoking, across the yellow line. Lise climbed in and buckled up. The clock on the dash said they'd wasted the morning, yet it didn't feel like a success to her.

"You okay?" Ken asked.

"It's nothing," she answered under her breath, putting him off till later. He would hover, concerned, until she absolved him.

On the way back they passed an Amish family selling pies by the roadside, their horse hitched to a telephone pole, the daughter in a plain bonnet. Traffic was surprisingly heavy through Mayville—the church crowd, she figured, going out for brunch at Webb's. They were caught in a pack leaving town, and then it was stop-and-go, bumper to bumper.

There were police cars all around the gas station, and a state trooper standing in the middle of the highway directing traffic. Another was spooling out yellow tape, wrapping it around the pumps to block off the front doors.

"I guess something did happen," Ken said, and while it was obvious, Lise couldn't quite believe it. She'd completely misread the situation, and Emily, with her penchant for melodrama, had been right. While the proof was inescapable, Lise refused to accept it.

"I better stop and tell them what I saw," Ken said.

"Yes," she managed.

Ahead of them, in the back of Meg's van, Emily was pointing frantically, as if they might miss it.

"We know," Lise said.

6

"I'm not supposed to know," Sarah said, lying on her back and looking up at the ceiling like it was the sky. "So, you know . . ."

"I wouldn't," Ella said, happy that Sarah trusted her with something so big. "How old is she?"

"My mom's age, I guess."

"Whoa." Ella couldn't imagine her dad having his own apartment and a blonde girlfriend—or Uncle Jeff for that matter. She couldn't see Uncle Jeff anywhere without Aunt Margaret and Sarah and Justin. The four of them were a team, like when their families played wiffle ball. She didn't say it to Sarah, but it felt like he was missing, like he might show up today while they were out on the boat. Sometimes he would do that because he had to work. They'd come back from tubing and he'd be sitting on the dock drinking beer, wearing sunglasses and a baseball cap backwards, his little sports car by the garage. He'd make chocolate-chip pancakes and play chess with them when it rained, and at night he was the one who showed them how to build a fire. Now Ella wondered if that was the real reason he was late all those times.

"Does he ever visit you guys?"

"What do you mean?"

"Like does he ever come over and just hang out?"

"No, it's all written down on the calendar. My mom's still mad at him."

"Well, yeah," Ella said.

"She's gotten really weird, I don't know. Like even weirder."

"Like how?"

There was no one home except them and Rufus, but Sarah glanced toward the stairs before leaning over and whispering, "She always screamed at us, okay? Now when she does it, she starts crying like right away, and then she'll hold on to you while she's crying." She lay back on her pillow. "I mean, it's weird."

"Yeah," Ella agreed. She tried to be nonchalant, but hearing another person's secrets was new to her. In school, the few friends she had were like her. Not like Sarah, who was smart and beautiful too. At her school, someone like Sarah didn't hang out with someone like her. Sarah was the kind of girl boys talked about on the bus right in front of you like you were invisible. "Sarah Carlisle," they'd say, trying to top each other like it was a game, and then the rest of them would groan. They didn't even have to know her, her name would be famous. No boy would ever say "Ella Maxwell" except to get a laugh.

"I don't know," Sarah said. "I guess she's just sad, but . . . You can't be sad all the time. She lost her job. She'd turn her alarm off and I'd have to make Justin breakfast. And then when she did go to work she'd come home and go right to bed." She rolled over so the two of them were facing each other, lying on their sides. "One week we had takeout the whole week because she didn't feel like cooking."

Ella had never heard any of this from her mother, and she believed every word. Aunt Margaret walked around the house in her bathrobe. Aunt Margaret forgot to buy groceries. Sarah told it all plainly, and Ella wondered if she could be that brave if her mother went crazy (but she wouldn't have to do everything like Sarah, she had her dad). She wished she had a secret she could give her in return, but her life was dull, nothing ever happened to her. Except this, she thought, this sudden closeness between them, and how it made her feel, but she couldn't tell her that.

She didn't have to. Sarah reached over and took her in her arms, a quick squeeze of a hug.

"Thank you," she said. "I don't mean to dump all this stuff on you."

"It's okay," Ella said, surprised by the firmness of her, the musk of her hair.

"They'll be home soon," Sarah said. "We should get up."

Ella didn't want to but agreed. She watched Sarah walk across the carpet in her nightshirt, then close the door to the bathroom. Even her feet were pretty, her calves strong as a ballerina's. With anyone else she would have been jealous, but with Sarah there was no reason to be.

She thought that she'd never met anyone whose looks matched their inner beauty so perfectly. The shower came on, and Ella lay there, her book no longer interesting, listening to the water splash, Sarah's secrets warm and safe inside her.

7

The Institute was free on Sundays, and this was the only chance they'd have, so after lunch Arlene and Emily left Margaret in charge of the children and hopped in the car. It had been sitting in the sun with the windows up. The interior was stale and smelled faintly of dog, but Arlene didn't mention it. After the racket of the boys, she was just glad to have some quiet. She'd spent thirty-five years listening to children, and while she would keep each of their smiling faces and eager spirits with her (and did, of a winter's day, occasionally page through a thick album of class pictures that showed the tall young woman slowly grow old and bent while the children stayed the same), very early the music had gone out of their voices.

This was the difference between the lake and the city: once they got going, it was too cool to keep the windows open. At home she'd be blasting the air conditioner and wouldn't see these cornfields butted up against the road like a fence, or the ponytailed girl in her convertible making a call from the box outside the Wagon Wheel. Though they had nothing to do with her, these random scenes pleased her, and Arlene thought it didn't make sense. She felt closer to life away from her own. That was why people traveled, she thought, but they wanted majesty, natural wonders and scenic views. She was happy enough to watch other people. On the golf course, a foursome retreated from a green, the last man flipping his ball in the air and catching it, and for the moment she was satisfied.

"I'm going to miss coming up," she said.

"So will I," Emily said.

"Do you think we might rent a place next year?"

"Possibly. I know I can't stay in the city all summer."

"We could stay on the grounds," Arlene offered. She'd wanted to since she was a little girl, enchanted with the stately mansard of the Athenaeum, the pink and green cottages and their gingerbread eaves and scalloped shingling, the neat lawns and dazzling gardens. One of her earliest memories was her mother guiding her hand to toss a penny in the hotel's indoor fountain.

"Can you imagine?" Emily said. "We'd fit right in with all the other old biddies. I can just see us hustling off to the amphitheater after dinner to hear some professor from SUNY Buffalo enlighten us on God and Public Policy."

"Or the opera," Arlene countered. "Or the symphony. Or the theater."

"What about the children? We couldn't get a place big enough— if we could get in at all. I know Don and Martha Shepard tried to buy a place and were basically told there weren't any, and that had to have been five years ago. I'm sure it's worse now."

"We'd have to look into it."

"Now wouldn't be the season."

"I'll give Mrs. Klinginsmith a call tomorrow and see what she thinks," Arlene said.

She'd never said to Emily that the cottage wasn't hers to sell, that by rights it still belonged to the Maxwell family, of which she was the eldest living member, but she suspected Emily knew how she felt. Not that Emily had ever asked for her input or apologized for her decision. That wasn't Emily. In the same way, Arlene never pressed her claim, naturally accepted Henry's choice, thoughtless as it was.

The main gate was busy, a guard in white gloves manning the crosswalk as a gaggle of older ladies waddled past, aimed for the turnstiles. They moved as a group and seemed to have dressed as one, all sporting a uniform of floppy sunbonnets and sunglasses tinted the purple of jellyfish, flowered blouses and pastel polyester slacks and what seemed to be nurse's shoes. Probably a wing of a local senior center, overdue for a dose of fresh air and culture. Arlene thought she and Emily weren't so different, drawn by habit and the lure of free admission.

At home she'd be back from cleaning up after coffee at church and halfway through the *Times,* saving the puzzle for last, struggling with an acrostic her mother would have finished in a snap. A day like today she'd lock the apartment and walk to the park where couples would be playing tennis, young mothers shepherding their toddlers through the playground. She'd find a bench in the shade and read, looking up when an ambulance screamed by or something happened in the pickup baseball game, happy to be the still center of so much motion. Back in her apartment, the illusion drained away, and when the weather was bad there was nowhere to go. She was bored with the Frick Museum, the Scaife Gallery. Some days she didn't speak to anyone except Emily, over the phone. The mail disappointed her, nothing but second-class junk, offers for credit cards with her name misspelled. She read the *Post-Gazette* and watched the local news, became, like her mother, intimate with the public life of the city, tracing the intrigues of business and city government as if she were involved. She became—again, like her mother—a dedicated baseball fan, listening to the Pirates on the kitchen radio as she cleaned. She knew the Steelers needed a new quarterback, and that debating with the checkout girl at the Giant Eagle exactly how they should go about getting one was a pleasant break from the monotony of her own thoughts. So was this. It had been the one thing she could count on. She'd been coming here over sixty years.

When she'd first come, the whole family had taken a clicking trolley along the shore, boys and dogs chasing after it. Henry wore mustard knickers and a short, wide tie, his hair brilliantined, grooved. Her church dress was linen, and the breeze off the lake was delicious. All the girls wore white gloves.

Now they followed the cars in front of them through the gravel lot—an acre of glinting windshields—and up a dusty cut, jouncing over a grassy field with traffic cones laid out like a driver's test.

"Look where we are," Emily said, but Arlene was trying to mind the teenager in his Institute uniform of white shirt and black slacks waving her into the space. It wasn't until she'd muscled the shift into park that she saw they were right behind the Putt-Putt.

On their way to the gate they stopped to take a look. Not even the concrete remained, the slabs dug up and smashed, chips lying under the pines. In one corner an orange-and-white barrel the size of a wine vat listed, its bull's-eye drifted with needles, a pop can stuck dead center.

"There's a picture," Emily said.

American and one Irish, one American and one French, as if they were miniature embassies. The railings were too beautiful for flower boxes, and it appeared the entire block had agreed on hanging baskets of red geraniums. The crowd had thinned out, milling. A man in a Hawaiian shirt was videotaping everything for posterity.

"Imagine the upkeep on these," Emily said. "They probably have to paint them every other year."

"How much do you think they go for?" Arlene asked.

"I have no idea," Emily said.

"It's been such a good year for roses."

"With the heat. I doubt very seriously any of these would be for sale. The condos are what they're trying to get rid of. I think they overbuilt. People don't want condos when they're at Chautauqua. They would have served themselves better if they'd built more cottages."

"There's one for you." It was lemon with pink eaves and gobs of scrollwork, trumpet vines twining up a coach light. "I think it would be fun for a week."

"You're not going to let go of this, are you?"

"How much could it cost to rent one?"

"Two thousand. Twenty-five hundred."

"Split four ways, that's not outrageous."

"I don't think Kenneth *or* Margaret have that kind of money."

"Maybe we could foot the bill," Arlene suggested, and when Emily didn't respond, added, "It wouldn't be summer without us coming here."

"I understand what you're saying," Emily said. "If worse comes to worse, we'll get ourselves a room at the Saint Elmo with all the other spinsters and widow ladies."

She said it so dryly it could have been a joke or a promise.

"I think I prefer the Athenaeum."

"We couldn't afford it. It's where they put up church bigwigs and special guests now. My mother stayed there when Gershwin was here. She said he would walk into the lobby after composing all day in one of those god-awful huts and sit down at the piano and just go to town. He'd take requests, and he knew everything—not that that's surprising. What *is* surprising is that she said he had a wonderful voice. I always think of him as rather quiet, and Ira as the more public one, but it turns out he was very outgoing."

Like most of Emily's tidbits, this seemed to have no point except to impress Arlene, who'd heard it at least ten times before, usually on the porch of the Athenaeum itself, among company. She decided not to pursue her own point for now, but let it flutter untouched between them.

As they wandered deeper into the grounds, the brick path gave way to lumpy asphalt that looked strangely out of place, as if it were temporary, the remnant of some construction project. The cottages were less showy back here, more utilitarian, tucked under the shadows of peeling oaks. Instead of cushioned wicker, the porch furniture was ugly resin, and Arlene thought they could surely afford this.

On the plaza the Crafts Alliance was having its weekly festival, makeshift booths lining the four sides. After having spent the morning at the flea market, she was in no mood to shop, but Emily seemed interested, so she followed dutifully, giving her opinion on scarves and earrings, geode paperweights and sand paintings, windchimes made from nylon fishing line and someone's tarnished, discarded silver. On the grass, two little boys were throwing a Frisbee ineptly, with no parents in view. As she and Emily moved from booth to booth, Arlene kept an eye on them, until finally the boys' father showed up with ice-cream cones.

"Should we get something for the children?" Emily asked.

"Do you think they really need anything?"

"The girls might like these," she said, meaning the beaten silver rings a shaggy man in a denim jacket had laid out in black velvet trays. Unlike much of the jewelry there, these were noticeably handmade; the man had a red beard and his hands were tough as roots. Emily found two plain bands that were nearly identical. "They're only nine dollars," she said ("Two for fifteen," the man bettered her), and looked to her as if for permission, and Arlene said Yes, that would be nice for them, but then they'd have to get the boys something, and boys were impossible.

They were. There was nothing here that would interest a ten-year-old boy. There were not very many things in the world that would interest a ten-year-old boy, Arlene thought, plumbing her memory. Sports equipment and video games, possibly frogs and snakes, but those only for a moment. There were years when she confiscated hundreds of comic books, dozens of yo-yos, a drawerful of the big McDonald's straws they used to shoot spitballs, but not once had she caught a boy with a scented candle or a crocheted pot holder. "This is a waste of time," she said, but in the name of justice Emily persisted. They walked all the way around the plaza before giving in and buying cheap, prepackaged kites from the gift shop by the cafeteria, and then had to drag them around all afternoon.

Such a minor inconvenience could not stop her from falling under the spell of Chautauqua once they started walking again. Girls with violin cases strapped to their backs like soldiers rode by on bikes, late for practice. She knew each street and grove intimately, the way her children knew the rides at Kennywood Park. Like them, she had her favorites. The amphitheater with its Doric columns. The Italianate bell tower, its red tile roof, the clock demurely striking the quarter hour with a single sweet peal. Children's Beach and Palestine Park, the diorama of the Holy Land fashioned like a giant sandcastle. Ivied Smith Library, where she'd spent hours in the cool children's room, the light caught in the varnished floor. That was what was the same—the light, the way it angled across tree trunks and fell on lawns, bounced off flowers. On certain streets, at a certain angle, it could be 1938, 1946 again, and there was something reassuring about that.

Not that she wished for those years back, or regretted the present. Regretted the years that had passed. Yes, that was it. She lit a cigarette.

"You're awfully subdued," Emily noted.

She couldn't say that she was weighing her life, tallying up what was lost, missed, forgotten. The mood had come on her suddenly, would pass like a summer storm.

"Just thinking," she said.

"My feet are killing me," Emily said.

"Mine too."

From Heinz Beach, if their eyes had been what they once were, they could have seen their dock among their neighbors' on Prendergast Point. Instead, they admired the grand summer house that ketchup had built, the four inlaid chimneys and whimsical carpenter's lace. That was enough sightseeing for one afternoon, thank you, and they hobbled back to the Athenaeum.

They ended up, as planned, on the porch at three-fifteen, right as high tea began, just beating the lecture crowd leaving the Hall of Philosophy. Around them, the tables filled up; clumps of people filtered along the walkways, debating fine points, heads bent in discussion. The sight pleased the teacher in Arlene. This was the same crowd she'd seen for years coming out of Heinz Hall or the Benedum Center after the symphony, except here they were wearing sandals and Bermuda shorts. She belonged to them, irrevocably, in the same way she belonged to Emily, but the realization, instead of comforting her, hurt. They did not know her beyond the simple image of the woman who sat next to them at *The Nutcracker* or the oratorio, the deacon who helped their children on with their acolyte's robes, the teacher who shook their hands at the end of open house. Like Emily, they were not the least bit interested in her. They passed, even now, intent on one another, as if involved in lives far deeper and more complex than hers would ever be.

"By the way," Emily said, "I want you to have the TV in the living room. The tube's practically new."

For a second Arlene didn't know what to say, then thanked her too effusively. She hardly watched TV as it was.

"Would you excuse me?" she asked, and Emily let her go.

She knew where the rest rooms were, to the right off the lobby. As she stepped inside, into the dull, artificial light, directly in front of her rose the fountain her mother had helped her toss a penny in. After all these years it still burbled, the water dribbling down to a pool, the bottom of which was tiled a light blue and spotted darkly with coins. She tried to envision her mother holding her wrist, the two of them together flinging the penny, her fingers opening, letting go. What had she wished for—or had her mother wished for her? Had Henry been given a penny? She could not remember, and she did not want to know if any of their wishes had come true. Her own had and had not across her life, and she would not be dwelling on this if Henry were alive, if the cottage were not being sold. Her life was her own, no one else's, and she had done the best she could.

She'd brought her purse and so she opened it and unsnapped her wallet. She had a fair amount of change. She stirred it with a finger until she found a nice shiny penny and plucked it out, but stopped before tossing it in, trying to get her wish perfect in her mind.

That I will always come back here.

Like a child, she closed her eyes.

8

Three times Justin told his mother he didn't want to swim off the dock. He sat on her bed, head down, while she stood over him, already wearing her suit and her flip-flops. The polish on her toenails was chipped like a broken dish.

"But you *love* to swim. Last week I couldn't get you out of the pool. Help me, I don't know what the problem is here."

The problem was the water. It wasn't like the water at the pool, blue and chemical-tasting, the light making patterns on the bottom. The water here was green and brown and you couldn't see what was underneath. And it smelled bad, like the basement after it rained. It reminded Justin of water caught in old pop bottles you'd find buried in the high grass behind the playground. You'd step on one and think it was a ball but it wasn't. Inside would be what looked like root beer except it had old grass in it, and dead bees floating on top.

"I just don't want to," he said.

"It's not a request. I can't watch all of you unless you're in one place, so put your suit on. You don't have to go in if you don't want to."

"Why do I have to put my suit on if I'm not going in?"

"Everyone else is going to have their suit on."

"Why can't I just wear my clothes?"

"Stop," she said. "This isn't a discussion. I don't know why you're getting all winky on me, but I do not need this right now. Get your suit on and come downstairs with the rest of us. And bring a towel for yourself."

She left him sitting there and banged down the stairs. For a moment he didn't move, then he stood up and opened the bottom drawer of the dresser for his suit. He went into the bathroom to pull it on and discovered he needed to pee. The toilet kind of smelled like the lake. When he came out he remembered the towel, and then he couldn't find his water shoes and went around the room looking under the beds.

"*Jus*-tin!" his mother called up the stairs.

"I'm *com*ing," he called.

"You watch your tone of voice."

"I can't find my water shoes!"

"They're right down here, I already got them for you."

"God," he said to himself, the way his father used to when his mother called them in to dinner from watching TV. At least they weren't going out on the boat. Then everyone would know he was a chicken. It wasn't that he was afraid of the water, but what was underneath, the pale hands reaching up to drag him down. He knew there was no such thing, that it was something he'd seen on TV, but when he was in the water his imagination tricked him, made every weed feel like the brush of wrinkled fingers.

"What do you say?" his mother asked as he was slipping his water shoes on, and he was so busy he didn't understand the question.

"Thank you," she said.

"Thank you," he said.

"Very heartfelt. Now get going, slow Joe."

They were all waiting for him in the yard, knocking the croquet balls around, their towels flung over their shoulders.

"About time," Sarah said, lifting her sunglasses. She had a new suit that showed off her boobs. He'd already gotten in trouble for making fun of it at the pool, his mother sitting down with him all serious and telling him how everyone was sensitive about the way they looked. Not me, he wanted to say, but then she said, "You know how it feels in gym when you're the last one picked," and even if it wasn't true (sometimes Michael Schulz was the last one), he understood what she meant. But no one called Sarah gay because she had boobs, or laughed at her when she tried to dribble a basketball. It was different. When his friends said anything about her ("*She's* your sister?" Michael Schulz said), he told them to shut up.

"Here we go!" his mother said, herding them ahead of her with both arms.

Rufus ran onto the dock, looking back at Sam, who had his tennis ball. Justin cut through the girls to join him. Weeds and lily pads floated in the shallows. Once he'd seen a dead fish bobbing by the rocks, but today the only nasty thing was a muddy milk jug. As they walked out, the dock bounced, and a pair of ducks took off, flew a couple of docks down toward the point and landed again. Rufus didn't even see them.

"Can he go in?" Sam asked when they reached the end.

"Yes, but not for long," his mother said. "You have to remember, he's old."

Sam threw the ball, and Rufus launched himself off the dock. He did a belly flop, hitting the water with a smack, making them all laugh. He paddled out, his head turning like a periscope until he saw the ball.

Sarah laid her towel out and went down the ladder slowly, afraid to get wet, testing the water with a toe.

"Jump in," their mother said. "It's easier."

Sarah lowered herself step-by-step, hunching her shoulders against the cold. The water only came up to her waist. She kept her hands flat over the surface like it was quicksand.

"How is it?" Ella asked.

"Freezing!"

Rufus paddled around Sarah as if she might steal the ball from him. There was no way for him to get back onto the dock. He had to swim all the way in past the motorboat, his lips puffing around the tennis ball, and then climb the slick rocks. Justin and Sam walked along above him, scooted out of the way as he dropped the ball and shook. He was breathing hard and his tongue stuck out to one side.

Justin got the ball—all slimy—but when they reached the bench, his mother looked up from her book and said, "I think that's enough for now."

"Sam got to throw one."

"That's because I love Sam more than I love you," she said. "Go swim for a while. Maybe when you get out he'll be rested."

"I don't want to go swimming."

"Not this again," she said. "Is there something in there you're afraid of?"

"No," he lied. "I just don't like the mud."

"How's the mud?" she called to Sarah and Ella, practicing hand-stands, holding each other's legs straight.

"Muddy!" Sarah said.

"I'm going in," Sam said, and scrambled down the ladder. Rufus stood at the top, watching him.

"Aren't you going to swim with your cousins?" his mother asked.

"You said I didn't have to," Justin said.

"For Christ's sake, don't go in then," his mother said, "I don't care." She put up her book like a shield, and he lay down on his towel, facing away from her.

Rufus came over; his breath smelled like dead fish.

"Go away," Justin said.

Last year he would be crying now, but he'd learned to stop himself. It only made her madder.

Lying flat, he didn't feel the wind so much. The wood of the dock smelled hot and dry. A blue dragonfly landed on top of the piling next to him, then took off, flying crooked, the sun in his wings. Up by the bell tower he could see a lot of little sailboats. Out in the middle, motorboats crisscrossed, headed up and down the lake, making noise like stock cars. Rufus wouldn't sit down, and every time he moved to follow Sam, the dock shook.

"I'm sorry," his mother said. "If you don't want to go in, that's fine. No one should make you do things you don't want to."

He didn't roll over or turn his head, just lay there, knowing she was looking at him, waiting for him to say it was okay. He wouldn't. Silence was his only weapon against her.

Sam and the girls were having a splash battle, Ella shrieking, "Get him!" Rufus barked, wanting to be part of it.

"Can I throw the ball for him now?" Justin asked.

"Not yet," his mother said. She looked at her watch. "You can throw the ball in half an hour."

"What time is it?" he asked, and she sighed and told him.

If he were living with his father, he thought, it wouldn't be like this. His father took his side the same way his mother always took Sarah's. And he was like his father. His father liked to stay home and do nothing; his mother liked to go places and do things. His father watched *The Simpsons* with him; his mother thought it was rude. It only made sense to Justin that Sarah should live with their mother and he should live with their father. Whenever they visited him, his father never asked Justin if he'd like that, but Justin knew that one of these times he would. And Justin would say yes.

He was sure half an hour was up when Rufus got up and ran off and the dock shook hard.

"Look who it is," his mother shouted, because it was Uncle Ken and Aunt Lisa wearing their suits, carrying the inner tube between them. They set it down by the motorboat and Uncle Ken unsnapped the cover.

"Who's ready for some inner-tubing?" Aunt Lisa asked, and everyone splashed for the ladder. Rufus waited at the top, wagging his tail.

"Is a half hour up yet?" Justin asked.

"You really want to throw that ball," his mother said, only half joking, like he might have changed his mind. She gave it to him. "Just once and that's it."

He showed the ball to Rufus, who jumped by his side. In gym, kids imitated the way he threw to make fun of him, so he tossed it underhand, Rufus diving after it. Rufus was so close to it he lunged, showing his teeth, and got a mouthful of water, came up hacking. "He almost caught it!" Justin hollered, pointing, but Sarah and Ella and Sam were drying off and his mother was helping Aunt Lisa with the boat cover. Rufus swam for the shore. In the boat, Uncle Ken stopped to watch him paddle past. "Good boy!" Justin called, but Uncle Ken didn't look at him.

While they were waiting for Uncle Ken to say they could get in, Rufus came running out on the dock with the ball. He didn't look tired. "Drop it," his mother said, and took it away from him. "All done."

"Okay," Uncle Ken said, "everybody grab a life jacket."

Justin hung back, thinking they might not have enough, but then Aunt Lisa threw him one. His mother didn't have one, and he tried to give her his.

"That's yours," she said. "I'm staying here and reading my book."

He held it, unsure what to do. She looked at him, waiting, then, when he looked back, hoping she would save him, sighed like she was mad at him.

"I don't want to go," he said softly, hoping no one else could hear him.

"Not this again. What is the problem?" She said it loud enough for Sarah and Aunt Lisa to look over and then look away. "I don't understand where all this is coming from. Can you tell me?"

"I just don't want to."

"That's not good enough. This is what we're here to do. If you're not going to go in the water, we might as well stay home."

That would have been okay with him, but he knew better than to say so.

"You coming with us, Just?" Uncle Ken called, and his mother yanked his life jacket on over his head, pulling his hair.

"Ow."

"Shush. Uncle Ken doesn't have to take you guys out. He's doing it because it's a nice thing to do for everybody, so don't give him a hard time."

"But—"

"But nothing. Everyone's going. You'll have fun. Now quit giving me a hard time." She prodded him to the edge of the dock, where Aunt Lisa reached up and closed her hands around his arms. He took a step into empty air, and then his foot found the edge of the boat (he could see himself slipping between the boat and the dock, knocking his head, drifting down through the dark water, the weeds wrapping around him) and then he was stumbling, falling into Aunt Lisa and across the seats, the rubber-smelling inner tube against his face, bending his neck. He was in, sitting backwards, his life jacket strangling him.

"Smooth move," Sam said.

"Shut up," Sarah said, defending him.

"Okay," Aunt Lisa said, "settle down."

"Have fun," his mother said, holding Rufus by the collar, her book in her hand.

"We will," Uncle Ken said.

They had to paddle out because the propeller might get stuck in the weeds. Uncle Ken and Aunt Lisa each took a side, splashing. The water slid by right beside him. Sam put his hand in, making a wake. Justin had seen people fishing here and imagined the fish swimming beneath them, their eyes wide open. On the bottom there were old bottles stuck in the mud, snapping turtles waiting to bite your leg like a drumstick.

Uncle Ken gave Ella his paddle and sat in the driver's seat. "Keep us into the wind," he ordered. He turned the key and the engine rumbled, then stopped. He tried it again and the same thing happened. Four, five times. "Come on," Uncle Ken said, angry, and Justin thought maybe they wouldn't have to go. The thought became a wish, the way after visiting his father he wished his father would come back and play *Star Wars* Monopoly with them and sing when he made breakfast.

The wind was pushing them toward the next dock, and Uncle Ken had to grab the paddle from Ella and help row them out again. He was sweating when he finally got the engine to start, and his face was red. "*That's* what I'm talking about," he said, like he'd beaten it.

Aunt Lisa put the paddles away and they aimed for the middle of the lake, the front bouncing, the wind making Justin squint. Beside him, Sam sat with his legs crossed, his feet propped on the hole of the inner tube. The engine drew a white line on the blue water. It was so loud they couldn't talk, just sat back in the sun and let their hair blow all over. Cold drops jumped into the boat and landed on Justin's arms. His stomach felt weird, like it did when a plane took off, sliding loose inside him. Looking back at the shore, he thought that he couldn't swim half that far.

Aunt Lisa had a throwaway camera she was taking everyone's picture with. They couldn't hear, but by waving her hands she got all four of them together for a group shot. Justin worried that he would look scared in it and put on a big smile.

They turned around the marina and into a cove no one was fishing in and stopped, rocking in the water. Uncle Ken didn't turn the boat off. He came back between the seats and clipped the inner tube onto the tow rope and threw it in so it wouldn't mess up the engine. The tube floated behind them on the dark water. To Justin it looked a long way away.

All you had to do was hang on. You could let go anytime you wanted.

Sam was the only one who wanted to go first.

"If you want to stop," Uncle Ken said, "make a thumbs-down like this."

Sam jumped in and swam to the tube in his life jacket. He waved and Justin waved back. Aunt Lisa came back to sit with him so she could see Sam. She made a big deal about getting a picture of him.

"Okay," she said, and Uncle Ken started off, standing up and looking behind them as he drove.

The yellow rope pulled tight and the inner tube rode on top of the water. They went faster and the tube bounced Sam around. He held on, smiling at them. Uncle Ken turned the boat in a circle, and the tube skidded sideways, Sam's legs kicking into the air when it hit a wave. He cut the boat the other way and the tube shot across their wake, skating on one edge. Sam hung on.

"Not too fast," Aunt Lisa warned, and the engine slowed. Sam gave them a thumbs-up.

What would happen, Justin thought, if you fell off and another boat couldn't see you and ran you over? What if you hit the water wrong and broke your neck? What if the rope got caught around your wrist and snapped it?

They went around again, the boat tipping so he was sitting higher than Aunt Lisa and had to hold on to the edge, then they straightened out and slowed and Sam made a thumbs-down.

"Who's ready for a turn?" Uncle Ken asked.

Sarah was.

"That was so awesome," Sam said while she was swimming out. "You gotta try it."

Compared to Sam, Sarah looked big on the tube. Her legs didn't flop around as much. She wanted Uncle Ken to go faster, and he did until Aunt Lisa said that was fast enough.

Ella fell off twice during her turn, but when she climbed the ladder she traded high fives with Sarah and Sam.

"All right, Justin," Aunt Lisa said.

"Come on, Just," Sarah said, "it's easy," and then everyone was cheering him on. They'd all done it and had fun, and it did look easy. He knew waiting would make him look bad, so he stood up and Aunt Lisa helped him take off his water shoes and climb onto the seat and then held one hand as he stood on the slippery edge.

The water was darker out here. It was impossible to tell what was under it. He pictured a car sitting on the bottom with a dead guy in it, floated up against the ceiling, his face pressed to the window.

"Just jump," Sarah said.

And he wanted to—he wanted to be able to—but his legs wouldn't move and he held on tighter to Aunt Lisa's hand.

"If you don't want to, that's fine," she said.

"I'll go again," Sam volunteered.

"I'm gonna go," Justin said.

"Then go," Sam said.

"He's going to," Ella scolded.

"A little less pressure, huh guys?" Uncle Ken said.

They were waiting for him now, and he wondered why he'd stood up on the edge, why he'd gotten into the boat, why he'd put on his suit in the first place. He couldn't go back in the boat or he would hear about it not just the rest of the week but the rest of his life. It would turn into a story, like the time he shoved the peas up his nose when he was a baby, or the time he fell on the escalator at the airport and grabbed the fat lady's leg. At dinner someone would start the story and then everyone would pitch in. At Christmas or next summer he'd hear it. Everyone would laugh, and he would have to laugh too.

All he had to do was let go of Aunt Lisa and lean forward. The life jacket would hold him up—but what if it didn't work? Maybe it was old. What if it filled up with water and he couldn't get it off in time?

He let go and started to fall back, then waved his arms and fell forward.

"All right!" Sam shouted, and then he was going over, the water coming closer.

He hit it and went under—freezing, the cold making him groan—then popped up because of the life jacket, gasping to catch his breath.

"Way to go!" Sarah called. Aunt Lisa was laughing and clapping. The side of the boat seemed too high. His first reaction was to head back to the ladder, but someone had pulled it up.

"Good job," Uncle Ken said. "Now stay away from the propeller while you're swimming out."

He swam stiffly in the life jacket, looking at nothing but the tube. The water was colder in spots, then warm as pee. He would not think of what was under him, the man in the car, the fish looking up, watching him, a shadow with kicking legs. That's what drew sharks to you.

The closer he got to the tube, the harder he swam, so that when he reached it he barely had the strength to drag himself up on top. They were all watching him. The rubber wasn't slippery like he thought it would be. It stuck to his knees and arms so he couldn't just slide into position. He felt better out of the water, but the boat still seemed a long way away. He grabbed the handles and lay down flat with his legs spread out like Sam and gave Aunt Lisa a thumbs-up. She gave him one back. He was disappointed—she'd forgotten to take his picture. He wanted proof that he'd done this.

Uncle Ken had to wait for another boat towing a girl on water skis to go by, then revved the engine and the rope pulled tight, jerking him forward. He kept his head up to see where he was going and concentrated on holding on. The tube made a hollow, ringing sound as it skimmed along, like the inside of a basketball. Uncle Ken went faster, and water shot up through the hole and tickled Justin's stomach, but he just held on tighter.

He laughed. It really was easy—easier even than swimming. If there was only a way at the end where he could float over to the ladder and get back on. It didn't matter; he liked flying along like this, water spraying up from the rope when it hit a wave. The tube jumped another wave and he bounced up like when he went sled riding, his legs flopping like Sam's, and he was laughing again. His mother was right. He couldn't believe he'd almost missed the most fun thing because he'd been a chicken.

Uncle Ken turned hard, and Justin saw the girl on water skis come past in front of them. The tube slid sideways, swinging out on the rope, and Justin could see the side of the boat. He thought the tube would swing back but it kept going, whipping him over the wake of the other boat. The tube bumped once, twice, then flew up in the air.

Justin could feel it tipping and held on. It flipped, went over, then hit with a smack, filling one ear, and he was underwater, upside down and being dragged, the water pushing at him, prying his fingers from the handles. He couldn't hold on any longer, and let go, still under, drowning, the sound of the engine pulsing away, dissolving to nothing.

His jacket saved him. He popped up in time to see the tube racing off, spinning into the air and splashing back down. He coughed and snot ran out his nose and he pinched it away, wiped his lip, panting. Uncle Ken was turning the boat, and Justin looked around to find the girl, afraid she might run him over, but they were way down at the end of the cove.

Beneath him, his feet hit a cold spot, and he raised his knees. Uncle Ken was still turning in a big circle. They seemed far away to Justin, and he began swimming toward them, the jacket getting in the way. The boat curved around and came straight at him. He stopped swimming and waved his arms above his head in case they didn't see him.

Uncle Ken slowed the boat and turned it sideways, and Aunt Lisa hung the ladder over the side.

"You okay?" she called.

"Yeah," he said. "Can I try again?"

"Sure."

"Go ahead, Just," Sarah cheered.

He swam around the back of the boat, staying away from the engine, and followed the rope to the tube. It was easier getting on the second time. This time Aunt Lisa did take a picture of him giving her a thumbs-up, and then Uncle Ken started off, the rope lifting out of the water. The tube thumped and rang, shuddered across the waves. Justin held on, thinking of how he would tell his father.

9

"The chickens are under Maxwell," Emily instructed. "And ask if they're taking orders for cheese bread. Where are you going for the corn?"

"Haff Acres, I thought," Kenneth said.

"I'm not sure they haven't closed down. If not them, then Red Brick Farm. Get half Silver Queen and half Butter and Sugar if they both look good. That way we can see which we like better."

"What else do we need for tomorrow besides hamburger and buns?"

"We have regular relish but not the yellow hamburger relish you like. Get an onion for people who want onions on their hot dogs. And we need another gallon of milk. Better make it two at the rate we're going."

"It's on the list," Kenneth said. "How are we on beer?"

"There should be some in the garage unless you've drunk it all. So they didn't say anything?"

"They said they weren't making anything public yet."

"We should be watching the news," Emily said. "I'm surprised no one tried to interview you."

"There was nobody there. I guess they're trying to find this other guy, but I don't think he saw any more than I did. Anything else?"

"Yes, get some new crackers. These have seen better days." She dumped them in the sink with a clunk, stuffed the wax-paper sleeves back in the box and, out of habit, neatly closed the tabbed flaps. She noted with dismay that the trash needed to be taken out again—she could have sworn she'd just put a new bag in—and then she saw that someone (one of the children, obviously) had thrown half a sandwich in with the paper trash.

She pulled the sandwich out only to find a scattering of potato chips, a soggy pickle stuck to a used tissue. "Could you *please* remind the children that all food garbage goes in the disposal. It's not like the old days when pickup was free."

"I'll tell them."

"It's probably the boys. Remind me, tomorrow's garbage day. Oh, and if they have those Greek olives, the salty ones. That might be nice for before dinner."

"That it?"

"I can't think of anything else," she said. "Use your best judgment. We're shooting for no leftovers. Here, let me give you some money."

"That's all right."

"No, really."

She had her wallet on the mantel with the boat keys and old flashlights and the nut dish filled with matches and batteries and gum bands, all the other junk. She took out two new twenties and handed them to him. He thanked her and folded them away, and while she was happy to help, she wished he'd argued a little harder. Lisa was waiting for him outside, steering clear of her, which was just as well after how she'd treated her at Christmas. Emily watched him back their huge SUV out of the driveway (the money must have come from Lisa's parents) and then head off, not bothering to wave.

No one was on the dock, and the empty bench tempted her. Sarah and Ella were out walking Rufus, Margaret was on the porch watching the boys play croquet. She hadn't seen Arlene since they came back from the Institute; maybe she was taking a nap, or reading. The quiet pleased Emily, and having everyone there—even Lisa, because she was with Kenneth. She went back to cutting slices from a block of extra-sharp cheddar, nibbling as she arranged them daisylike around the plate. A glass of red wine would be nice, but all the bottles in the cheap lattice rack were probably vinegar by now.

It reminded her of how much she would have to throw away. The food. The dishes. It was easier to think of them as categories. If she stopped to think of the insulated plastic Snyder's potato-chip mug they'd had since the sixties, she would balk, remembering one of the children drinking orange pop from it at some lawn party, or Henry pouring a beer so it foamed over. The cupboard was filled with glasses, orphans from the house in Pittsburgh or curiosities gleaned from the flea market. Jelly glasses with the Flintstones fading away to colored shapes. Beer cups from Pitt Stadium and Three Rivers. Maybe the children would feel something for them and take them, the way she hadn't been able to resist their old salt and pepper shakers.

The silver. The heavy butter knife that said U.S.N. on the handle. It had traveled the world only to find a home here. The pink plastic spoon that turned purple in hot oatmeal. These things had delighted them once— still did, she thought. It seemed a waste to throw them away. It was foolish, she knew. She'd become too sentimental, an old lady and her plates.

The cheese crumbled on her tongue, grainy and tart. She wanted a drink, something to keep her company while she worked on the hors d'oeuvres. There was Henry's beer, but the thought of it bubbling inside her made her open the cupboard over the microwave. In the back, behind a box of chicken noodle soup, hid the fifth of Cutty Sark Henry kept for late nights and campfires.

She chose one of his tumblers, a Model A on the side. They'd been gas-station giveaways. As if to infuriate her sensible nature, Henry had driven miles out of their way to collect the whole set. Esso or Atlantic or Boron, she didn't remember which. What she did remember was Henry dropping one on the hearth, the scotch splashing over his slippers, staining the suede.

"Easy come," he said, but she could see he was upset.

She filled it to the running boards, rolled the scent under her nose. She went to the window over the sink and held it up to the light, long now and mote-struck, casting shadows under the chestnut, firing an amber glow in her hand. The glass could have been crystal. Scotch never went bad. It was magic that way. It only took a sip to convince her to bring the bottle home with her.

She returned to the cutting board, setting the glass down on the counter, then held on as a shiver rode up her back like a breaking wave.

She decided she should drink scotch more often. And to be careful with that knife she was holding.

The dip was solidifying in the fridge in an old sherbet tub. She worked on the green and red peppers, the broccoli and carrots and celery, until her fingers were sore.

One of the girls should be doing this, she thought. In her day—

Yes, well. Her mother's kitchen was gone, the hours of instruction and drudgery, her mother teaching her the value of work. She'd learned. She wished she could say the same of her children.

She took a good-sized drink and had to breathe out the fumes. The glass was suddenly empty in her hand.

"Well, well," she said, a saying of her father's.

She poured one up to the door handle. Her uncle Magnus had actually had a Model A. She must have ridden in it at some point, but she couldn't picture herself in the backseat, holding a ribboned hat on, her hair streaming behind. The one on the glass was from 1921, nearly eighty years ago. Uncle Magnus died when she was thirteen or fourteen. The subtraction evaporated. She was obsolete, the product of another century, like her grandparents. Everything she had loved was gone, everything she knew was useless, all the songs and dances, the trendy recipes, like an old lady whose clothes had long gone out of style. But that's what she was, that least desirable of things: an old lady. She'd never thought it possible.

The vegetables were done. All they needed were the crackers for the cheese. Around her the house was quiet. She thought she wanted music, but before she could take a step in the direction of the tape player (one of the boys might use it), she stopped to listen to the murmur of a powerboat far out on the lake, leaves rustling like static. The very air of the house had a frequency, vacant and electric at the same time, not a hum but a wire of concentrated nonsound threaded through her ears.

In the distance, a dog barked—not Rufus, but it reminded her that he needed his dinner. She stooped for his bowl and almost fell over.

"Easy now," she said, as if she were a horse.

That was another thing she remembered: the man who sharpened scissors coming around in his horse-drawn cart, ringing a bell.

She spilled the awkward bag of kibble across the counter and onto the floor.

"Clumsy." Her mother had called her that. Something to do with the gravy boat overturning, the tablecloth a lake, and then her father coming after her, upstairs in the dark where she was hiding, saying it wasn't her fault, it could have happened to anyone. It was a holiday, but whether it was Christmas or Thanksgiving she couldn't say.

She scooped up the food and topped off the bowl, set it on the floor and washed her hands. She didn't see how he ate the stuff day after day.

The scotch was going down easy now, and she thought she'd better watch it. She added three ice cubes to the glass and covered them, the Model A fully submerged. She looked around the kitchen again as if she'd forgotten something but couldn't find what it was.

Margaret looked up from her magazine when she came outside. The boys were on the dock.

"Do they want to go fishing?" Emily asked. "We have all of your father's stuff in the garage."

"They're playing their Game Boys. They think they're being sneaky."

"I see. How much time do they have left?"

Margaret tilted her wrist. "Eleven minutes, twenty seconds."

"Did you want a drink?"

"I really shouldn't."

"Why's that?"

"Do you really want to know?" Margaret said, and it was not a challenge, not defiant, the way she could be.

Since the separation she seemed defeated to Emily, and while it was easier to talk to her, it was unnerving. She'd always had more spirit than Kenneth. Emily had never worried about her making her way in the world, and now it seemed she'd been wrong.

"Yes, I want to know."

"Do you?"

"We were going to talk before," Emily remembered.

"We *are* talking," Margaret contradicted her. She looked to the boys. "What I wanted to tell you before is that the divorce is going through next week."

"Next week." Even though she'd been preparing for this moment for years, Emily thought she needed more time. It wasn't as if anything had changed. Jeff had not been strong enough to say no to marrying her and then had not been strong enough to put up with her. "I'm sorry."

"You don't sound surprised."

"Should I be?"

"No," Margaret said, as if she didn't mean to argue. "If you want to say I told you so, you can."

"I would never."

"Even if you did."

"Even if I did."

"There's one problem though."

"What's that?"

"You remember the accident where I smashed up my knee?"

"Yes," Emily said, not following her.

"When I was recovering from that, I went through rehab."

"I remember," Emily said. "You had that physical therapist you liked."

"Not that. I'm talking about the other kind of rehab, for drinking. Nobody knows about this. I don't want to go into a lot of details, but I felt—and Jeff felt—that I was having a problem, so I went to this rehab clinic in Pontiac. Remember when I had the surgery on my knee?"

"Yes," Emily said. It must have been the scotch, because she could hardly catch up to this news, make any sense of it. Margaret in a hospital? Her first thought was what Henry's reaction would be.

"I did have the surgery, but I also went through rehab right after that."

Emily held a hand up for her to slow down, to stop assaulting her. She shook her head to clear it.

"What has this got to do with the divorce?"

"It has to do with the settlement."

"But that has nothing to do with anything."

"Neither does Jeff screwing around on me. My lawyer calls it a draw. She says if I'd told her about it, it wouldn't have been a problem, we still could have won."

"Won what? What do you win in a divorce?"

"Nothing, apparently, while he gets to run off with his little girl-friend."

"I'm sorry." Though Emily had suspected, she'd never heard of a girlfriend.

"You know what he said about her? He said she was *fun*. Is that great? He said I depressed him. He said when he looked at me, he felt tired. You want to know the worst thing? He said he only stayed with me because he felt sorry for me. Not for the kids. He said he was worried about what would happen to me after he left, like I'm some kind of mental patient."

Emily wanted to ask if she'd discussed this with her therapist, if she was still seeing her. She knew they hadn't been getting along. Margaret was shaking her head, looking up at the porch ceiling.

"We're going to lose the house. I don't make enough to cover the mortgage, so we're going to have to move. Do you know how that makes me feel? It's bad enough they're losing their father—and they love him, they don't care about Stacey or any of that crap, they still love him. So I'm the villain again because I don't make any money. This year I'll make twenty-three thousand dollars. That's a joke. You can't live in Silver Hills on that, it can't be done, so we're going to have to move. I know Sarah's never going to forgive me."

"She will."

"No, she won't. And Justin barely says anything as it is. I know he misses his father but he's keeping it all inside the way I used to."

No, Emily thought, you always let everyone know how you feel, then silence any criticism. But Margaret rarely opened up to her like this, so she knew things were bad. Drinking, and her half-crocked on scotch.

"I figure with the settlement I can keep up the mortgage for another two years, but Sarah's only going to be sixteen then, right in the middle of high school, and I hate doing that to her. It's probably better to do it now, before she starts."

"Do you need my help?" Emily asked. "Because I can help, you know."

"It's not that. I just wanted to tell you what's happening. I wasn't sure how you'd take it."

Emily knew that at the middle of this—nearly stated, barely veiled—lay their years of misunderstanding, each charging the other with being coldhearted, too rigid to give in and accept the other's true nature. She could choose to protest her innocence again, but that would lead to yet another battle. At heart Margaret had to know all of this was not her fault; that, like any mother, she had wanted the best for her, but, uncharitable thought, Emily wondered why, at this late date, Margaret worried about her reaction. She'd never stood in judgment of her, despite what Margaret thought.

"I think it's sad," she said. "And I do want to help."

"Thank you," Margaret said. "I know you must be disappointed."

"Why?"

"Having a divorcée for a daughter."

"I'm not disappointed," Emily said. "I feel bad for you and the children, that's all. I think you're doing the right thing."

Something beeped—the alarm on Margaret's watch, insistent. Margaret pinched it off. "You do?"

"I don't know all the details—and I don't need to—but yes. I trust you know what you're doing."

"Wait, let me get that on tape."

"I'm serious. I may disagree with how you do things sometimes, but I try to respect your judgment."

"Like you respected Ken going back to school."

"That was a different case. I'm sure this is something you've thought through."

"But I haven't. How can I know what it's going to be like? I can barely keep track of what's going on day to day."

"But," Emily said, searching, "I know you'd only do this if you thought it was absolutely necessary. I think that's the difference between you and Kenneth. I'm not saying he's irresponsible. The situations are different. He had any number of options, including the option of doing nothing at all, which might have been the way to go, in my opinion. You didn't have those choices, or felt you didn't have them. And I think you made the right choice from the few you had. There, did you get that on tape?"

"There wasn't a choice," Margaret said. "At least it wasn't mine. Everything's turning out exactly how Jeff wants it. That's what makes me so mad."

Emily couldn't help her with this and merely nodded along with the litany of betrayals. She had seen how Margaret badgered him in front of others, and how patient he'd been with her. Perhaps she'd misread him, his patience in reality boredom or distance, some anesthetizing cocktail of the two. When he played with the children or palled around with Henry, he was wild and loud, but in Margaret's presence he turned docile, invisible, waiting, it seemed, to escape. Emily had marked this difference in him years ago. Apparently Margaret, blind to her own abrasiveness and need for control, had missed it. At this point, there was no reason for Emily to enlighten her. It was enough to listen.

"Thank you," Margaret said again, and they stood up to hug each other.

"I'd better put out the vegetables and dip if we're going to eat by six."

"I've got to talk to those boys."

"I think you're brave to be doing this," Emily said. "If there's anything you need . . ."

"Thanks," Margaret said.

In the kitchen, a fly perched on the block of cheese she'd forgotten to put away. Rehab, Emily thought. An alcoholic. She set her empty glass down and wrapped the cheese in plastic and stuck it in the fridge. Rufus's food sat untouched, and she wondered where the girls were. The scotch bottle stood on the chopping block. She was sober from their talk, the beginnings of a headache seeped behind one eye. She put the bottle back in the cupboard and tossed her ice cubes in the sink. The fly had moved to the tap, walking on it like a diving board. She waved a hand and it circled away.

Divorced, with two kids still in school. Justin was ten.

What a mess.

It was not a judgment, just a statement of fact. A sadness. And probably, somehow, partly her fault. She was not blind. Margaret shared the worst aspects of her personality, the same impatience and inexplicable rage she had inherited from her mother. From the very beginning Margaret had baffled Henry, and he had withdrawn. Emily had fought her on a daily basis, giving Margaret the weapons and training she would later use on Jeff. It was no surprise to Emily that he had grown tired of bearing that kind of anger. Thank God Henry had been stronger.

The dip was cold and stuck like icing to the lid of the tub. Emily used a spatula to dish it into a bowl, then placed the bowl at the center of the platter. The red peppers and broccoli and cauliflower made the tray look unintentionally Christmasy.

She took it outside and balanced it on the wrought-iron table between the two aluminum rockers. Margaret was out on the dock, talking to the boys. Emily looked around to make sure there were enough tables for drinks. She wanted everything to be ready so they could eat at a decent hour.

"Napkins," she said to herself, and went back in.

10

"Let's just keep going," Lise said hopefully. "We've got gas."

She wanted Ken to laugh but he was waiting for the person in front of him to turn. His mind was so far away sometimes—probably on the gas station, or the Putt-Putt, the heroic moment of his childhood. She knew that sometime this week he'd end up there, leaving her to deal with everything.

"What about the kids?" he asked.

"They'll be fine. Your mother thinks she can raise them better than we can anyway."

"Where would we go?"

"Anywhere. Where do you want to go?"

"Iceland," Ken said.

"Iceland."

"Very stark, lots of light."

"So you could work even more. How romantic."

"They've got hot tubs."

"Forget it," she said. "We'll go back. Your mother's dying to discuss the Mystery of the Gas Station with you."

"She is a little too excited about it," he admitted.

"A little bit," she said, pinching her thumb and one finger together.

The problem with Emily, Lise thought, was that she didn't have anything going on in her life. Lise could never figure out what she did in that big house all day. Having spent much of her childhood alone, Lise knew how slowly the hours could go, and the pain of waiting for someone to rescue you from your own harsh thoughts. That someone had been—still was—her mother, which only made Emily's coldness seem more foreign.

"I wonder if they found that other guy," Ken said.

"You said yourself, he wouldn't have seen anything different." She said it dully, nearly mumbling, so he'd know she was tired of the subject.

"How'd you like Ella tubing? I didn't think she'd get back on that last time."

"She's trying to impress Sarah."

"You think?"

"This is nothing. Wait till she has a real crush on some boy. I remember one that was so bad I couldn't eat."

"And who was this on?"

"Josh Marcowitz was his name. He was a swimmer, and I couldn't eat for three days. Finally my mother sat down and made me eat a bowl of oatmeal."

"What happened?"

"I ate it."

"I meant with him."

"Nothing. He had a girlfriend. I remember waiting for him to come out of math class just so I could walk by him. I must have lost five pounds."

"Did he even know your name?"

"It wasn't that big of a school."

"Whatever happened to him?"

"He's probably a lawyer or something. You jealous?"

"Of course," he said.

"Good," she said, and that one he laughed at, shaking his head as if she was crazy.

The drive was too short to pretend they were really getting away. It was enough to be together and alone, their own little vacation, and she let her hand rest on his leg as he drove. He reciprocated between shifts. They passed the abandoned stand of Red Brick Farm and the busy one of Haff Acres (CENTER OF THE UNIVERSE, their banner claimed), where they would get the corn on their way back. She was tired from the sun and her nose felt tender. They had barely been here a whole day.

"Will you make love to me tonight?" she asked.

"Where?"

"I don't care where."

"How about on the dock?" he said.

"That would be fine. Even here in the car would be fine."

"I wonder if there's a drive-in around here."

"See?" she said. "Now you're thinking."

11

Sarah saw him while Ella was letting Rufus poop in the grassy ditch by the fishponds. She stopped on the hot, tarred road, her arms crossed, and watched him turn the riding mower in squares around his front lawn—or maybe it wasn't his, maybe he was getting paid, saving money for a car or something. An ugly van hauling a boat rumbled past, startling her, and she went back to watching him.

He wasn't old enough to be in college, Sarah thought, but wasn't sure. He was taller than Mark and looked too big for the mower, his knees poking up. He had on work boots and cutoffs and a flannel shirt with the sleeves torn off, open to show his chest. Over his backwards baseball cap he wore a pair of headphones. He was far enough away that she couldn't tell what color his hair was.

She wished she had on sunglasses so he couldn't see where she was looking. She wished she'd worn the white sleeveless top she'd just gotten for her birthday instead of her cruddy T-shirt. Her hair still wasn't quite dry from the shower.

Rufus was done. She wanted to tell Ella they should go back the way they came, make up some excuse like she was tired or they were late for dinner.

"He is so nasty," Ella said. "He peed on his own leg."

"He's just old."

"And stinky, oh my god."

"Just because he's wet. He's a good boy."

A wall of pine trees lined the side of the road, and it was cool in its shadow. The buzz of the mower floated over the fishponds, filling the air. Ella didn't seem to notice him, so when he turned away from them, Sarah nudged her, making eyes in his direction.

Ella just shrugged like he was nothing special.

"Can you even see him with those glasses?"

"Please."

"What?" Sarah said. "No way. He is so hot."

"Whatever," Ella said.

He turned at the end of the lawn and came back, blowing cut grass onto the road. When he saw them, Sarah had to concentrate on how to walk. He was tan and his boots weren't tied. The hair sticking out from under his cap was dark blond and wispy, one lock by his sideburn curly. The noise made her blink. He smiled at them—at her, Sarah thought—and as naturally as she could, she smiled back, just a little. She didn't want to give everything away.

The mower rolled by, the hot air tickling her ankles, and she had to squash the urge to run. Rufus was afraid and trotted into the middle of the road until Ella got him by the collar. Once they were safely past, Sarah turned to her, her whole face open with triumph, but Ella just rolled her eyes. Sarah looked back; he was almost to the driveway, so she had to snap her head around, and then she felt his eyes on her back, on her dumb running shorts and her spotty tan, her ratty sneakers.

"Is he looking?"

"How would I know?" Ella said.

"You could look, for one thing."

She did, stiffly. "I can't tell."

"Why do you have to be so blind?"

"F you," Ella said.

"I didn't mean that. He's just so . . . Did you see his eyes?"

"I was trying to keep Doofus from getting run over."

"Okay, Nurse Hathaway."

"Dude!"

"Dude yourself."

They took the shortcut through the tennis courts, the sun shooting through the trees, lying over the nets, spotting the weathered park bench. Rufus scooted ahead of them, sniffing the ground, his tail whisking. The white flowers on the bushes were like perfume. She wished they could stay here instead of going home.

"My dad told me to sign us up for tomorrow," Ella said by the bulletin board with its little roof, then couldn't get the pen to write. Finally she got it going on her palm.

Sarah watched Rufus nose through the brush, hoping for a ball. She'd been waiting a month for the letter Mark promised her. Not even a postcard. Having a great time, miss you.

She wondered what his name was.

She imagined going out with him every weekend, sitting with him in the movies, meeting everyone at Denny's, kissing him good night. She pictured his friends, and her new ones at his school. She could see her mother's face when she told her she was moving here.

"Hello?" Ella said, bringing her back to the world.

"What?"

"You didn't even hear me. I said we should get back."

"I heard," Sarah said, but Ella imitated her and made her laugh at herself.

Rufus didn't want to stop looking, and Sarah had to whistle for him. The trees closed over them and they followed the path through the shadows, coming out by the basketball hoop no one used, the asphalt cracked, broken pieces like shale everywhere. Mark would expect things to be the same when school started. She'd have to tell him before that.

They walked down the middle of Manor Drive, Rufus scouting out ahead of them.

"I bet he's a jock," Ella said, "a total airhead."

"It's not like I want to copy his homework."

"What do you want to do with him?"

Sarah made a face.

"Ew! He was all sweaty too."

"Yeah," she agreed, as if she could work on that.

Rufus stopped and looked back at them like they should catch up, then waddled on.

"Doesn't it look like he's limping?" Sarah asked.

"He's old."

"I mean really limping."

"He's really old."

A bunch of little kids were running around the Nevilles' crab apple tree. There was still sun out on the lake, but the wind made it cool.

"What kind of guys do you like?" Sarah asked.

"I don't know," Ella said. "All kinds. Why?"

"Maybe he has a friend."

"No thank you."

"Come on, don't be like that."

"Like what?"

"I don't know, just . . . Can't you just be happy for me?"

"I am happy for you," Ella said, but the way she said it made it clear she wasn't.

"Look," Sarah said, "I promise I won't forget about you. I know how that feels, okay? What do you think it's like with my dad? It's still going to be me and you most of the time. There's no one else here I want to hang out with."

"I guess that's a compliment."

"You know what I mean."

Ella said she did, but Sarah could tell she was hurt, the way Liz was when they went to a dance together and the guys only tried to hit on her. It wasn't her fault that she was pretty, but Sarah wanted to apologize anyway. "You have to be aware of your effect on people," her mother lectured her. And while she was right, Sarah wished she wasn't. She hated when other girls didn't like her just because of the way she looked. Sometimes she wished she was ugly or just plain.

Justin and Sam were riding their bikes in front of the house, so they cut across the Wisemans' yard for the porch. Rufus stopped to mark his territory and they passed him on opposite sides, not talking. Her mother and Grandma sat on the porch with their drinks.

"Help yourself to the veggies and dip," Grandma said. "It looks like we won't be eating till late."

"Wash your hands first," her mother instructed.

Inside it was dark with all the lights off. Ella took the kitchen sink and she took the bathroom. She flipped on the light and closed the door, turned on the hot water, and let it run. For a while she stood there before the mirror, soaping her hands, glad to finally be alone. She set the soap back in the holder and held her hands under the faucet, and she discovered she had lied to Ella. Ella, her mother, her father, Mark—everything fell away when she thought of him. There was only the lake and the two of them, his house, the dark lawn and the sunset painting the sky. When everyone left, they would still be here.

She dried her hands and opened the door, turned off the light. Ella had beaten her outside and she took the chair next to her, the plastic cushion settling with a hiss. The red pepper she bit into was juicy, the dip sharp. She didn't know she was so hungry.

"How was your walk?" Grandma asked.

Ella looked to her as if they had a secret. Sarah dared her—go ahead and tell—and took a carrot stick.

"It was good," Ella said. "Rufus pooped."

12

"Doesn't everything look wonderful?" his mother said in the kitchen—to no one, to everyone.

In the living room, alone with Ken, Lise mimicked her, throwing one hand extravagantly in the air and fluttering her eyelashes like a silent film star. She'd only had half a beer, and he thought he'd have to watch her.

"And coleslaw!" his mother was saying for Sam and Justin's benefit. "And sliced tomatoes—oh my. I think I'll have a little bit of everything, how does that sound?"

Lise mimed surprise, wagging her head, until Ken gathered her in a hug, smothering her routine.

"But she's so funny," Lise whispered.

"Stop."

His mother came out with her plate and gave them an odd look, as if their hugging was strange, then headed for the porch. Lise pretended to strangle him, shaking him by his neck, the side of her bottle chilly on his skin.

"Thank you, all done now," he said, and broke her hold.

In the kitchen Meg was checking the corn and the air was wet. Sam fixed his plate, shying away from any vegetables, just chicken and cheese bread for him. Justin was brave enough to take a spoonful of coleslaw. Ella and Sarah waited, shaking their wicker plate holders like tambourines. Ken fitted a paper plate into a holder and gave it to Lise, then got himself one. Lise tapped his arm and nodded toward the back door. Outside, Arlene stood alone under the chestnut, smoking and looking at the rabbits across the road, the low, pink light gilding the tree trunks. She dropped the butt and ground it out but stayed there, folded her arms and kept watching.

"Not *too* creepy," Lise said.

"*You* never watch the rabbits," he challenged.

He didn't say that he'd done the same thing yesterday. It was a conceit of hers that his whole family was crazy, the bloodline diseased like in some cheesy old Poe movie, and he was the most normal of the bunch. It was supposed to be a joke, but, having had to actually deal with them over the years, he had come close to believing it himself. He trusted there were reasons for his mother's harsh optimism and his aunt's aloofness, somewhere in their history, but often he had to admit that they came off as eccentric old ladies. That he could almost believe it—he who knew better—convinced him that Lise did, the joke transparent.

Lise drained her beer and got another from the garage, Arlene noting her as she passed.

"Dad?" Ella asked.

"What, hon?"

"Are we going miniature golfing?"

"I don't think so. It's kinda late."

"Okay," she said, so sweetly that now he wanted to take them. "Maybe tomorrow."

"I think it's supposed to rain tomorrow," Meg said.

"Please no," Lise said, coming back in.

"Is that right?" he asked, thinking he wouldn't have any light to shoot with. He wouldn't be able to take Sam fishing.

"That's what Arlene said."

For lack of anything better, it became the main dinner conversation. The radio said there was a 70 percent chance of morning showers, 90 percent by afternoon. Temperatures would be cooler. So forget the Holga. Ken thought if they ate fast and left the dishes for later, they could squeeze in miniature golf, but no one seemed in a hurry except the boys, typically impatient with any interruption of their fun.

The chicken was lukewarm and greasy, and the coleslaw had a chemical tang. The corn was the one triumph, both kinds perfect, the kernels bursting. The kids took too much butter, poured salt on the floor. In the corner, beside the glider, Rufus sat drooling, alert for the littlest spill. He curled his tongue sideways to clean up a piece of chicken Justin knocked off his plate, then pounced again when Sam fumbled an ear. It rolled over the boards, leaving a smear of butter.

"Rufus, no!" his mother said, and Rufus froze, uncertain, the corn within reach of his muzzle.

Sam sat there with his plate tipped in his lap, as if waiting for someone to save him. He was too old to be so helpless.

"Don't just look at it," Ken said, "pick it up."

He must have said it too hard, because Lise scolded him, "It was an *accident*."

She helped Sam wipe the floor, then held the screen door for him, and the two of them went into the kitchen, dinner continuing on the porch as if nothing had happened.

"So no more word on this morning's incident?" his mother asked.

"The police didn't call while we were out, did they?"

"It's all rather curious, I think."

"It seemed routine while I was there," he said. "I gave them my statement and they took it down."

Lise and Sam returned, Sam without his plate, Lise with a soda. He sat, head hanging, arms folded, and Ken could see he'd been crying. Sometimes he cried for her attention or her sympathy—to deflect her from something he'd done—and Ken wondered if that's what was happening. He hadn't actually yelled at him, just told him to do something (which he didn't do). Suddenly he was the bad guy. He took a swig of his beer, as if that might erase it.

"There's lots of corn left," Meg prompted, but Lise waved her off. Sam was done.

"Can I ask you what questions they asked?" his mother covered.

"Just what I saw, that was about it. I think they were trying to put together a time line."

He didn't tell her about the surveillance tape that showed him and the other man like a pair of criminals, the two of them jerkily searching the aisles, disappearing into the little hallway by the rest rooms, leaving their money at the register. Is that you? they asked, but first—and this he definitely would not tell her—they reminded him of his right to refuse to answer their questions and to have an attorney present. There was an intensity in the room that he wanted to shoot: the washed chalkboard on wheels, the constellations of silver tacks on the corkboard above the tray of mugs. The detective, whose name he'd forgotten immediately but whose frayed collar tabs he could still picture, looked at him as if admitting the man on the video was him was crucial to the investigation. Ken didn't point out that he was wearing the same clothes, just fingered the stilled image and said, "That's me, and that's him." And you didn't see anyone else? The entire time you were there? Tell me again about the coffee. The bag on the floor. Did you see anything else out of place? They went over it three times before writing it up, and while Ken signed it, photocopied his driver's license, blowing it up so the state seal showed.

"What do they think happened?"

"They wouldn't tell *him,*" Meg said.

"My guess," Ken said, aware that the children had stopped chewing to listen, "is that either the cashier robbed the place and made it look like a robbery, or someone else robbed the place and really did scare off the cashier."

"We'll have to get a *Post-Journal* tomorrow," his mother said. "They'd carry something like this, wouldn't they?"

"It should be in the police blotter," Arlene said.

"That might just be for Jamestown," Meg said. "This would be Mayville."

"I don't think the *Mayville Sentinel* handles things like this anymore," his mother said. "They're more of a tourist guide now."

"Can I be all done?" Justin asked, and showed Meg his plate—not clean but a better job than Sam's.

The girls were slow eaters, and then Sarah had three pieces of corn, her plate balanced on her clenched knees. Her dimples reminded Ken of Meg at that age. Like Meg, like his mother, she was the pretty one in the family, the same straight nose and sharp jaw of his mother's softened, not as stark, and he had to quell his natural inclination to see her face as a work of art, the planes changing while he fiddled with his lights.

They all helped to clear the plates, bunching up at the screen door. Lise commandeered the sink and he pitched in, hoping to break out of the doghouse. Meg and Arlene let them handle the dishes, going outside for a smoke. They waved at the bugs, stood watching the light fade over the lake. He dried the bigger items, interrogating the sky for any sign of rain.

"Isn't it red sky at night?"

"That's what I thought," Lise agreed. "But I thought the kids were going to do the dishes too, so . . ."

"Tomorrow," he promised.

"Yeah, yeah." She really didn't care.

It was almost dark when they finished, the sky violet, the evening star low over the horizon. His mother had lit a citronella candle on the porch.

"We have pie for all those who want dessert," she announced, but only the boys took her up on it.

"Maybe later," Meg said.

The adults had coffee. The kids stayed inside, the boys in the living room, the girls upstairs. On the porch, the candle flickered and the roof shuddered. Bats flapped raggedly between the trees, fireflies rose from the bushes. A boat went by with its running lights on. After it passed, they could hear the lake washing over the stones.

"This is why I come here," his mother said, and no one refuted her. She put her cup down. "I guess this is as good a time as any. I want to talk to all of you about the house." She paused dramatically, and he could sense Lise stiffening beside him. "You're of course under no obligation to take anything, and to be honest, most of it is junk. I'm as sentimental as the next person, but there's no sense taking something if you're not going to use it. I don't want you to feel like something's going to go to waste if you don't take it. I've arranged for the Goodwill people to come next week, so anything we don't want will eventually find a home.

"Now, some of the things here are mine, like the gateleg table, and obviously I'm going to hang on to those—you'll get them eventually—but most of the stuff is up for grabs. There will be some things that more than one of you are going to want. I think the best thing to do in that case is for each of you to put together a wish list of the things you want the most and rank them in order of importance to you."

As she spoke, Ken thought of his father's golf clubs (though he was too tall to use them), and the twisted 7UP bottle on the low wardrobe (for Sam). The wardrobe itself was cheap, and he'd never liked the varnish, too dark. The cedar chest was a possibility, not that there was room in the car. His eye flitted through the rooms, and then the garage, the cave his father hid in, alone with his treasure. The barbecue starter, yes, and the little fridge, avocado and ugly with bumper stickers. No one else would want them. At least he could save something of the cottage.

"So if you could give me your lists tomorrow that would be a help," his mother said.

"How many things can we put on the list?" Meg asked.

"Five should be enough, I'd think. There really isn't that much here. Oh, and Arlene *is* taking the TV, so that's out. The other appliances are staying with the house—not that you'd want them."

"It's like a silent auction," Arlene said, amused.

"And please," his mother said, holding her arms wide, "look around this week. It's all got to go."

Little things, he thought. All the crap on the mantel. Marbles, tees, ball marks, penlights. Decks of cards he knew the backs of intimately, softened by a family of hands and years of humidity. One summer they played hearts every night, the scorecard on the refrigerator keeping track (he'd cried then, quit because he was so far behind). Bridge, gin, Michigan rummy. His father was a quiet player, a conservative bidder, never letting you see what he had when he lost. Like me, Ken thought, then worried that he was flattering himself. His father was a better man than he was, more secure, far more capable. His father wouldn't be surprised that, faced with deciding what he wanted most, he was thinking of childish trinkets.

The cedar chest, then. That was a serious choice, and Lise would go for it.

To their right, a spotlight suddenly cut on, and the Lerners' house jumped out of the dark, the split-rail fence and boarded-up porch flattened like an O. Winston Link locomotive, followed by an electronic voice reporting "Intruder alert, intruder alert" over a monotonous high-pitched chirping.

"What the hell?" Meg said, standing and holding her ears.

"It's their alarm," his mother hollered.

It was supposed to turn off in a minute, but they couldn't wait that long and ended up going inside and closing the door.

"Intruder alert," the voice went on, menacing in its evenness, "intruder alert, intruder alert." The chirping, barely noticeable to begin with, soon grew piercing. The boys stuck their fingers in their ears and rolled around on the carpet. The girls glared as if it were someone's fault.

"It's probably a squirrel or something," his mother said, already on the phone to the police. His father had left the number of the security company around here someplace but she had no idea where.

The police would have to come and check out the house.

"All this excitement in one day," Arlene said.

"I can live without it," his mother said.

They huddled inside as if under fire. When the alarm finally stopped, an echo hung in the air, then the buzz of locusts. "Intruder alert," Sam mimicked, and Lise stopped him with one finger.

Outside, the Lerners' was dark again, the dock and the lake invisible, but the quiet tone was broken, the evening's stillness ruined.

They retreated inside again, the light and the drawn blinds making the living room seem even smaller than it was. Lise and Meg pulled out their books and kicked the boys off the couch. His mother found her library mystery and took his father's chair by the light in the corner as if it had naturally passed to her. Arlene announced she was taking Rufus for his constitutional. He wished he'd brought something to read, some project to work on. He was no good at vacation, couldn't relax into it the way his father had his retirement, raking leaves, poking around the basement like a ghost.

If it rained, he could sleep in. What they'd do with the rest of the day he didn't know. Go to a movie? Lise would have to get out of the house. Maybe they could do the Book Barn, waste the afternoon picking through the shelves of cracked paperbacks. Or the old casino with its warped dance floor and basement full of video games—Lise's idea of hell. There were only so many choices, and the kids didn't go in for antiques.

It was almost the boys' bedtime. He'd get them down, then have a piece of pie as a reward. The girls could take care of themselves, and his mother would go to bed early. He hadn't forgotten Lise wanting to make love on the dock. There was an old army blanket in the bathroom cupboard upstairs. He went up and liberated it. The girls were lying on their sleeping bags reading and didn't bother with him. He left it at the foot of the stairs so the closed door hid it.

It was too late for another beer, so he chose a soda, the light from the fridge making the little food they had seem meager and desperate, a bachelor's rations. Meg came in with an unlit cigarette, said, "Hey," and with a shake of her head beckoned him to follow her out the back door.

She lit up before filling him in. "I told Mom, so I thought you ought to know. Next week we're finalizing the divorce."

She gave him an apologetic smile in the dark, a shrug, and he held her. Her arm around him, her chin on his shoulder, she took a hit of her cigarette. Even now she had to come on tough, breaking, backing away. They could be in high school, hanging out by the smokestack, waiting for the bell to ring.

"I'm sorry I didn't tell you earlier, but I thought . . ."

"That's okay. How was Mom?"

"Good. I was surprised."

"Good," he echoed, but discovered he was hurt. He'd always kept her secrets. He was the one who needed to be close, they both knew. Spring she'd stopped calling, and twice he'd given in and dialed her number.

"The real thing is, I told her about my rehab."

"No." Meaning the accident too.

"Not everything," she assured him.

"Why?"

"I don't know, just to explain things. If she asks you, you don't know anything."

"That's fine with me," he said, but he wasn't sure.

"You can congratulate me. Or not."

"I'm sorry."

"I'm not. Not really. Things weren't so great. You know."

"I know," he said.

He'd heard most of it over the phone, believing her even when her accusations seemed crazy. He didn't think Jeff would intentionally hurt the kids by depriving them of his time, or that his pursuit of another woman was proof that he'd become mentally unstable. A husband himself, he naturally had a different view of what happened, and the resulting guilt kept him from advising her completely honestly. That she wouldn't have listened to him anyway—that she and Jeff didn't love each other anymore—didn't matter. He had somehow let her down. While he knew it was stupid, he wanted to apologize for the fact that he was still married.

"So what are you going to do?" he asked.

"Hell if I know. Try and keep the house until the kids are through school, then get the hell out of there."

"I think that's smart."

"I don't see any other choice. The problem is I can't afford it."

"I was going to say . . ." He and Lise were looking at the same thing, eventually. So far he'd been able to say no to her parents, but that wouldn't last. "Mom might be able to help you out."

"I don't want to ask her. I just don't."

It had been a point of pride, since his parents hadn't approved of her leaving college, or leaving Pittsburgh. They hadn't liked Jeff at first either, and Meg was convinced that while their mother loved her, she didn't like her very much.

"I hate to ask," she said, "but could you and Lise maybe help? Just enough to tide me over."

"I wish I could." He didn't want to go into the details. He didn't have to; she knew he was back to making hourly wages. They hadn't been able to save anything since he left Merck, and he offered her this as comfort.

"Shit," she said, and sent the butt looping into the Lerners' yard, where it glowed like a dull eye. "I hate asking her for money."

"When did you ever ask Mom for money?"

"How do you think we could afford to buy the house in the first place? I asked Dad. Jeff wasn't making that much at Philco."

Of all the intimate things she'd said to him, Ken filed only this admission away, added it to the image of his sister and his view of himself. Much of his life, he'd considered himself intelligent, and yet every so often a glaring oversight like this proved that he assumed more than he knew, not only about the world—whose workings would remain closed, forever a mystery—but even those closest to him. He'd wanted her to be noble and daring to balance his meekness. He thought he shouldn't be disappointed to find she was just like him.

He apologized and she thanked him. If nothing else, their parents had taught them to be polite. She kissed his cheek and then led him inside. When he entered the living room, Lise pinned him with a look that said she was jealous. His mother had put on the classical station from Jamestown, so low that he didn't hear it until he sat down and chose an old *New Yorker*. The pages were tacky with humidity. The boys still had another ten minutes. They were battling with their Pokémon cards. Apparently they'd already been warned about making noise, because they whispered their characters' names: "*Vileplume! Charmander!*" He had no idea what special powers each of these had, the same way his father only vaguely knew the names of the superheroes Ken followed as a child. Green Arrow and Green Lantern, the Silver Surfer. Even now they seemed more adult than Pikachu and Squirtle.

"How's Harry?" he asked.

"He's all right," Lise said, as if she was deep into the book and didn't want to talk.

He found an article about the building of the Tacoma Narrows Bridge, but with the music—big strings and a clamoring piano—he couldn't concentrate. Meg had taken the chair by the fireplace, her hair shielding her face. He was glad they'd talked, but unsatisfied, too. For some reason he'd expected more, and he wondered if she realized how often he'd thought of her this last year, alone out there and falling apart. He'd done nothing, called every week, twenty minutes, half an hour at best. He'd wanted to come out for Easter but Lise had made plans with her parents. He remembered thinking of Meg while the children darted across the yard with their baskets. They reminded him of when they were little, outside St. James, Meg dragging him around by the wrist, making sure he got his fill. He wanted to do something like that for her.

The clock on the mantel let him set the magazine aside.

"Okay, spudlers," he said, "time to head that way."

Since they weren't watching TV, there were no protests. They rubber-banded their cards and went up.

"Brush teeth," Lise reminded.

Upstairs, the girls were giggling over something. The boys couldn't resist picking on them, but he hurried them past like a prison guard. The air was thick, and he turned the fan on.

Their conversation whirled in his head, filled with unstated implications. It sounded like Meg was giving up, admitting defeat. This latest turn made sense, another of her unfinished plans. He hoped their mother had been gentle with her, and thought that he would probably never know, not honestly.

The boys left blue slugs of toothpaste on the basin. He expected Sam to bug him for a story but he and Justin were busy with their cards. "Lights out in one hour," he commanded from the top of the stairs, "boys *and* girls." They obeyed by ignoring him, by not whining. Before he opened the door at the bottom, he tucked the folded blanket under one arm.

"The boys are down," he announced to the living room, and Lise thanked him. He could hear Rufus drinking in the kitchen, his chain clanking against the metal bowl. He screened the blanket from his mother with his body as he crossed the fireplace, slid it around front as he turned into the kitchen. He had no explanation for Arlene, who looked up, holding the fridge open, just breezed by her and outside like he was going to get a beer.

In the dark, he was pleased with his little espionage until he slipped on the stone by the garage door. He flailed an arm out for balance and whacked the frame. He saved himself but dropped the blanket in the wet grass.

"Motherfucker!" he said, fingers stinging. One knuckle was bleeding, sweet to the taste.

He was just picking up the blanket when a car pulled in the drive, its lights nailing him to the garage. They dimmed, the night turning green, deep blue, and he saw it was the police. For a moment he wondered if they'd jump out with their guns drawn, thinking he was a burglar. He waved and tossed the blanket in the garage, shut the door and walked to the cruiser.

He was surprised to find only one officer in the car, a heavyset guy in his mid-twenties with thick glasses and an undershirt peeking out from his uniform. As a teenager Ken had acquired his stoner friends' disdain for the police, but that had mellowed with age, and now more often they seemed to him helpless and not very bright, especially the young ones, like this guy. He was from the sheriff's department, not the state cops he'd talked to this afternoon. He asked Ken if he'd noticed anyone around the Lerners' before the alarm went off, then walked around the outside, shining his light in the windows.

His mother stepped out on the porch, holding the door.

"Ask him if he knows anything about the gas station," she ordered him, then went back in.

"Nothing," the deputy reported after one circuit. "It's routine, we have to check them when they pop like that. I don't remember this one being a problem."

He had a miniature clipboard mounted on his dash and pulled it out to write something Ken needed to sign in a space marked COMPLAINANT.

"Say," Ken said, handing it back with the pen, "did they find out anything more about that gas station up in Mayville?"

"She's still missing as far as I know."

"The clerk?"

"I've got a picture of her somewhere." He ducked in the car and came out with a MISSING flyer, the center a photocopy of a snapshot. The girl was light-haired and smiling, subtly bucktoothed; the picture looked like it came from a yearbook. TRACY ANN CALER, it said underneath, with her date of birth and other particulars. Ken did the math automatically. She was nineteen.

"Looks like whoever robbed the place took her with them."

"Oh my God," Ken said. "I was one of the people they interviewed. I must have walked in right after it happened."

"It's a big deal. They're bringing in the FBI."

"It didn't look like there was any violence."

"That's one of the things they're looking at."

"Oh my God," Ken said again.

"Yeah," the policeman said. "You think a place like this is safe, a little town like Mayville. It's not."

He told Ken to give them a call if the alarm went off again, then backed out of the drive, his lights playing over the Lerners', dazzling the reflectors on their mailbox.

Ken waited, listening as the car dwindled and the wind in the trees closed over it. He sucked his knuckle but the blood had stopped. The cop had said "them." It must have been more than one person to do it in daylight on a Sunday morning. Nineteen, he thought, and for an instant saw a flash of teeth and clothesline cutting into thin wrists. He tried not to think of Ella, or Sarah. The trunk of a car, the basement of a farmhouse out in the middle of nowhere. Driving out, he'd been comforted by how much country there was, how insignificant, finally, the cities were. Now he pictured her stashed back in the hills far off the interstate, some hunting cabin, the men talking in another room, brothers maybe. It was hard to see it as anything but a bad movie. He tried to imagine what her parents must be going through.

He shook his head and walked toward the porch as if he could flee the news, leave it out here. His mother would want to know everything, and then they would never hear the end of it. Already he could see the story taking its place in their family history—"that was the summer that girl was kidnaped"—and his own role, wandering into the convenience mart, unaware. In all of her stories, he was clueless, forever innocent.

She would find out eventually, he figured.

The light was orange inside, a product of the lamp shades, relics from the sixties.

"Well?" his mother asked.

"False alarm."

"We know that. Did he venture a guess why?"

"He just did a walkaround. He said he didn't remember the house ever being a problem."

"It may be a new system, since they're selling the place. What about the gas station?"

"He said the FBI's supposed to be coming in."

"They think it's serious then."

"The clerk's still missing, that's about all he could say."

"So they think it's an inside job."

"He didn't say."

"Well," his mother announced to the room at large, as if the one word implied a much deeper meaning. "It appears we have a mystery."

"Excuse me," Lise said, too proper, and got up and headed for the bathroom.

"Was the clerk a man or a woman?" Meg asked.

"Good question," his mother said.

"He didn't say."

"He was just full of information, wasn't he?" his mother said. "So, what do we absolutely know for certain?"

While she propounded her theories, Ken was aware of Lise's absence. She'd taken her book with her, was undoubtedly reading on the pot, the door locked, hiding the same way she accused him of abandoning her. It seemed, after so many years together, that their tactics were all bald, their moves few. He supposed his own were even more feeble, and that she indulged him as much out of habit as love. Maybe at some point it was the same thing. He tolerated his mother's familiar condescension while Lise, having grown up differently, could not. His mother's martyrdom, her pompousness—all of these had fallen to him, but not her implacable certainty, and because he recognized these qualities in her, he was forever apologizing, questioning his own motives and means. He shouldn't have mentioned the clerk. He hadn't meant to tell her anything.

The discussion waned, and then when Arlene returned with Rufus, rekindled. He tried to establish simple kidnaping; otherwise, why bring in the FBI? The toilet flushed behind the door, as if in rebuttal. Only Meg noticed it. While his mother and Arlene were rehashing the latest police-union snafu in Pittsburgh, Lise snuck out of the bathroom and upstairs, Meg's eyes following her, then finding him.

"Well," their mother finally said, "this is all fascinating but I need my beauty sleep. Don't forget your lists for tomorrow."

"Right," Ken said, because he'd completely forgotten.

A last check on the weather—rain, Arlene insisted—and she waved her book at them and closed her door. He felt drained, as if a long game had ended. He thought he wanted a beer, but Lise came down the stairs in her bulky Tufts sweatshirt and took his arm, pressed against him to let him know she was braless, smiling at his surprise.

"We're going to take a walk," she announced.

"Have fun," Meg said.

Outside, he detoured around to the garage for the blanket, this time careful of the stones. The moon off the lake peeked in the windows, his father's junk nothing but black mounds. The light in the little fridge didn't work and the necks clinked together, the crimped caps biting his fingers.

"You're so sneaky," she said, and carried the beers for him.

The dock shifted beneath their feet. It was clear and the lake was calm, the lights of Midway's boathouse drawn on the dark water like flames. He wondered if Tracy Ann Caler had done this this summer, if she had a boyfriend, maybe a guy she went with through high school. He imagined the Lerners' alarm going off again, the floods on the roof freezing them like convicts tunneling under a wall. He wished they could take the boat out in the middle and just drift, lay the seats flat and gaze up at the stars. They didn't have to make love.

It was nothing to worry about, just the usual paranoia his family brought out in him. He missed Boston, even his damn job, the daily imperative of something to do.

He spread the blanket in front of the bench and they folded down onto it. He didn't know what to do with his bottle cap, so she shoved them both in her pocket. They kissed, and he could taste the beer, but hot now. Tracy Ann. Trace. She pressed his shoulder and he lay down. He solved the copper button of her jeans while she worked on his shirt. She wasn't wearing anything there either.

"It's been a while," she said.

"I know."

They didn't talk. They knew each other, and sometimes, after being apart so long, they found out why they were together in the first place, discovered nerves and muscles they couldn't remember using and stretched them till they ached. They returned to each other.

It made him lie still, stricken, sticky, his mind wiped clean. It made her laugh, made her jump up.

"Come on!" she said, tugging his arm.

"What?" He was putty, and gave in, balked only when he saw she was leading him to the ladder. "No."

"Yes. I'll go first."

She did, groaning, her shoulders white against the dark water. She reached her arms up. "Come on."

The wind blew through his body.

"You're crazy."

"And you're not."

"Yeah," he said, climbing down, the water shocking on his ankles, freezing his thighs, "but mine's hereditary."

13

Meg wished she'd left a window open, but she couldn't lower one now without turning the van on, so she leaned her seat back and lit up, the dope in the bowl crackling, warming her lungs. The smoke roiled like storm clouds, filming the windshield, then dissipated. This was her reward for telling her mother about the divorce, and she wouldn't second-guess it. She had so few pleasures left. Let her have this one without guilt.

They would talk again, Meg was sure, but the worst was over. She would have to listen to her mother's opinions and deflect her questions all week, but she'd done the hard part. She would not freak out about the money yet. She needed to let things settle, let her mother come to her. There was time.

She flicked the lighter again but the bowl was spent. She tapped it into the ashtray and lay back, looking up at the chestnut, the leaves black and overlapped, joining into a huge shadow with scalloped edges, a monster leaning over the garage. The tree had been here when she was a girl, the garage too, with its musty smell, its eaves full of squirrels. There were probably things in the garage her father hadn't moved since she was born, and the thought made her realize how odd it was that they were all here, gathered, out of all the possible places in the world, by this little lake in the middle of nowhere. It seemed wildly arbitrary, like planets suddenly lining up, electrons switching molecules.

Her mother wanted a list of five things she wanted, like it was a game show, a lottery. What *she* wanted—she could admit it now, alone and stoned—was to be young again, to try it all over: love, family, everything. That wasn't what her mother was offering, just furniture, mementos, souvenirs of another life. It was all gone, she thought. With the cottage, they could pretend it wasn't, but it was, as sure as Jeff would never come back to her or Sarah would never love her like a child again. Time destroyed everything.

"Poof," she said, the fingers of one hand extending all at once, a slow explosion.

She desperately wanted a drink but fought it off. At first she'd thought marijuana maintenance was an AA joke, but it had become her saving grace. Not that she could tell anyone about it.

Her father's glasses, that's what she would put first.

The house itself. She could hole up here, send the kids to the local schools. They'd love that, huh? All three of them alone then, with no friends.

Like any whim, it dissolved when it hit reality. Her choices were simple: stay and make the best of it, or leave and start all over again.

She licked her lips, the taste like a rich spice on her tongue, overwhelming. She had gum in the glove compartment. When she thumbed the button, a tiny light came on behind the maps and repair bills. The foot well was a nest of Taco Bell garbage, the van a fucking mess—another mark against her. She hadn't had time to deal with it. Tomorrow, she thought, already arguing against such a waste of vacation. It was going to rain anyway.

The gum was old and hard to get going but then spread its sweetness through her mouth, behind the castlelike battlements of her teeth, under her tongue. The Wrigley family came to Chautauqua. There was a real Mr. Hershey too, and she saw them walking in some formal garden of a mansion, a gravel path between rosebushes, two turn-of-the-century tycoons with canes and swallowtail jackets. That should have been her life. Instead she was getting stoned in a piece-of-shit minivan, her husband probably boffing his little girlfriend this minute.

"Asshole."

It was like a mantra, holding off any real thought of him. And he *was* an asshole.

She sat back and felt the gum squishing, resisting her teeth. From the dock came laughter, and then footsteps, the planks shaking. The seat was low enough to hide her; she poked her head up, her nose resting on the thinly padded sill of the window.

It was just Ken and Lise. Ken had a pair of beer bottles, and Lise had her arms crossed over a folded blanket. They stopped in the yard and kissed deliberately, silhouetted in the frame of the Wisemans' oaks, the lake silver behind them, a Hallmark card, and though she wanted to duck down so she'd be hidden, she watched them until they finished and walked hand in hand to the kitchen door and inside. He still relied on Lise, still needed her in the simplest way. She wanted someone who needed her like that. Even Justin had learned to go to Sarah when she wasn't feeling well.

They'd kissed right in front of her, and she felt jealous the way she'd been as a teenager, hurt that she wasn't the one in love, the loved one. She was too old for this shit.

"Exactly," she said. That was the problem right there.

She found the lever and flipped the seat up, quietly got out and walked to the dock. Halfway to the boat, she noticed wet footprints—not shoes but toes and heels, the insteps missing. By the ladder they were almost solid. They'd been skinny-dipping. She would have gone if they'd asked her.

They didn't want her there.

"Duh," she said, like Sarah.

She thought of shucking her clothes and diving in, but it was too shallow, and there was no point doing it alone. She did enough things alone.

She turned and headed back toward shore, the lights of the house drawing her on. Five things. Her mind emptied after the glasses. There were five of them, but her mother would think she was making fun of her, ridiculing something she held dear. It was her father's memory they were all paying tribute to. Something of his, she thought, something he loved.

The boat was gone, and the TV. Ken would get his tools. She'd inherited his love of scotch, that should count.

Maybe the glasses would be enough. She would come up with some obvious choices to placate her mother. A dresser, an end table. She'd ask Sarah and Justin if they wanted anything.

The door to the garage was open, and she closed it. She took the kids' suits and towels off the line and brought them inside, still damp. Only one lamp was on in the living room, and the radio was off, Rufus escaped to her mother's room, crashed on one of the braided rugs. Upstairs the sink was running, Ken and Lise getting ready for bed. It wasn't even eleven yet.

What would they say if she went out to a bar, got in the car and hit the Snug Harbor Lounge, came home plowed and shouting? She could

let herself get picked up—but here the fantasy ended, turned into a ser-
mon, that AA training kicking in, and the memory of several ridiculous
nights, rooms like nightmares, men she would have never slept with sober,
drives home she didn't remember, torturous mornings listening to Jeff's
accusations, some of them true. Easy does it, you bet.

She looked in the fridge and then remembered the ice cream,
stopping to spit her gum out before she served herself. Spooning it into a
dish, she noticed her mother's goofy salt and pepper shakers and thought
they were being asked to do the same thing—reclaim some lost part of
themselves and pretend it had never left.

It wouldn't work. It couldn't; the world just wasn't like that.

She took her ice cream into the living room and sat on the couch.
The water had stopped upstairs, leaving only her spoon tapping against
the dish. When she was done, she rinsed her bowl and spoon and fit them
into the dishwasher, gave the counter a light wipe-down, locked the doors
and turned out the lights—all calmly, precise, her steps measured as a valet's.
For the first time all day, she felt useful, human again.

14

The rain woke Sam up, thumping like something running across the roof.
A pressure insistent as a pinch told him he had to pee, the water flogging
the roof only confirmed it. Justin was asleep with his mouth open. The
girls were lumps. Someone had turned the fan off. He left his warm sleeping bag, guided by the night-light beside the bathroom door.

The heat lamp in the ceiling made everything red, like he was in
an oven. He sat on the toilet, staring at the glass knobs of the vanity, the
light making everything look strange, his toes barely touching the cold
floor. It was so quiet he could hear what he was doing through the rain,
the stream interrupted by one plop, then another.

When he couldn't get anything else out, he wiped himself the way his father showed him, folding the paper in squares, then did an extra one to make sure. At home when he left streaks in his underwear they lectured him, his mother pretending she wasn't mad, but once he'd overheard her emptying his hamper, stopping dead and saying very clearly, "Not *again.*" He'd hidden in the basement with his Nintendo, and later his father had talked with him, shown him the trick of folding the paper over. Sam didn't tell him it didn't always work. Sometimes when it didn't, he buried his underwear in the bathroom garbage can. Sometimes to be safe he didn't wear any.

Silently he put the lid down, then turned to the window. He was sure he would see someone standing in the dark side yard, a man in a suit and tie like Grandpa at the funeral, not moving, just standing there looking up at him.

There was nothing, just the grass, the leaves waving and slick with rain.

He shut the light off and opened the door at the same time. There was someone in front of him.

He froze, waited for the shadow to fall on him, consume him whole.

A hand reached out of the dark and gently touched his head, as if to soothe him.

"It's just me," said Aunt Margaret. "Go to sleep."

She passed above him like a ship, trailing a warm scent, shutting the door behind her. The edges glowed red. He burrowed into his bag, waiting for her to return, his face aimed at the door, but then he and Ella were in a canoe on this river in the jungle and there were rocks everywhere and something to do with a book and a compass, and yet he was still waiting for Aunt Margaret. Aunt Margaret was beautiful, that's why they were in the canoe. She had put her hand on his head, passed so close he could smell her perfume. In the morning he would remember it like a dream.

Monday

1

Emily had asked Kenneth to remind her last night about the garbage, but it must not have been important enough, because here she was, pursued by Rufus, going through the downstairs emptying out the sticky wastebasket in the bathroom and the woven wicker one under the gateleg table and the nasty kitchen trash as well. He was like his father, he could never take a hint. Or was it just male stubbornness? Men acted so put-upon whenever you asked them to do the littlest task, as if they were taking on chores you were supposed to do.

"*Please* stop following me," she told Rufus, and he slunk under the table, turned twice and sank down with a bony thunk, still looking to her for instructions, or forgiveness.

She dragged the trash out the kitchen door and into the rain. The screen swung shut too fast, and the bag caught on a sharp corner, jerking her back, a cold drop falling down her collar. "Come on, you thing," she said, and tugged. It let go, a white hole appearing in its skin, a balled tissue peeking through. It was bad enough that it was raining without this kind of nonsense.

She needed to get herself organized. She still had to run last night's dishes, and there was that postcard for Louise Pickering she needed to get out today, otherwise it wouldn't arrive until she was back home, and that was no fun.

On her way to the garage, she recognized the shearing squeal of a power saw and the gunlike report of hammer blows echoing from the Smiths' new addition. It was larger than the cottage and blotted out what had been a lovely view from the road. The permit had been a bitter fight among the homeowners' association. It was one more reason the Lerners were leaving, and a small but nagging factor in her own decision to sell. Manor Drive wasn't what it was when Henry had first brought her here.

She had her old tennies on so she was careful on the stones, and opened the door all the way before pulling the bag through. She pushed the wheeled garbage can and found there was something in it. A bungee cord threaded through the handle on top protected it from raccoons. She unhooked the cord and popped the lid to find a bag from last year, dark liquid pooled in the folds; the winelike smell made her turn away and clap the lid down. She swallowed a large breath, set the lid aside, muscled the new bag up and in, then clamped the top on again.

She had to step outside a second. "Good God," she said, ignoring the drops falling all around her. Kenneth was probably still asleep. The children would be down any second, needing breakfast. She could make corn cakes from last night's leftovers. The idea appealed to her. Though they had the rest of the week, she didn't see how they would eat everything in the fridge.

She unlocked the garage door and rolled it up, creaking in its steel track, then tugged the handle of the can. It was more bulky than heavy, and easy to roll, at least until she cleared the concrete apron and bumped onto the sodden grass. Her tennies were smooth and she had to take baby steps. Rufus watched her, dry behind the kitchen door.

The Wisemans had their can out, which reassured her. She rolled hers around the mailbox, out onto the hard, glossy road, then backed it into the grass and left it there, her hands suddenly unburdened, her first task of the day crossed off. How strange that she still took satisfaction from such mundane things. They just had to be done all over again—but not this one. This really was the last time she would take the can to the curb.

There would be time to get maudlin later. Back in Pittsburgh there was nothing but time. Again, the notion of inviting Margaret and the children to come and live in the house with her flashed and died without residue. Stupid, not what Margaret wanted. They would be at each other's throats in no time.

The idea that she had been in real trouble and hadn't told her hurt. It was just one of a list of things Emily needed to say to her. With the rain, she might not get the chance.

What a gray, dismal day, the lake choppy and mouse-colored beneath the trees, mist out on the water. She hurried back to the kitchen as fast as her tennies let her. Rufus pranced behind the screen door.

"What is it?" she asked, wiping her shoes on the mat. "I already fed you. Go lie down."

Before she got the dishwasher going, she went into the living room and listened to see if anyone was in the shower. The box of detergent was a green foil brick, clumped from the humidity. She had to bash it with the heel of her hand to fill the compartment. When she turned the machine on, it stalled, then kicked in with a solid knock.

There was enough corn to make cakes for everybody, and syrup in the cupboard. She turned on the light over the cutting board. With the day so dark and the steamy thrum of the machine, it made the kitchen seem cozy. Living alone, she'd come to appreciate these brief, untroubled moments, fleeting as moods, delicate as spells. At home she cultivated them with the radio, with trips to the window, a cup of tea with cream, a favorite Dorothy Sayers, but more often they surprised her like this, needed only to be recognized for the treasure they were.

She was suddenly inordinately proud of putting the garbage out by herself—realizing at the same time what an absurd figure she must have seemed. It wasn't yet seven. The trash didn't get picked up until noon.

She held off turning on the radio until she'd sliced all the corn from the cobs, the thin white juice like milk on the cutting board. The flattened slabs and rows of kernels made her think of stuck-together puzzle pieces. If it rained like this all day, they would have to break out the board games, erect a card table and start one of the giant puzzles—Turner's London Bridge in fog, a field of tulips under a windmill. The Jamestown station would have the weather. She moved the few steps to the radio by reflex, wiping her hands on a dish towel.

She was just in time, an intrusive, unmusical tone noting the hour. A ticker-tape clicking introduced the lead story.

"So far police have no leads in the case of a Sherman woman," the announcer gravely enunciated, "abducted yesterday from a Mayville convenience mart."

The dish towel still in hand, Emily held both sides of the radio, leaned close to the louvered speaker hole, but the man told her nothing of value. Local and state officials were working together on the investigation, and then there was something about a crash on the Southern Tier, traffic backed up for miles, a driver taken by LifeFlight helicopter.

She made sure to get the weather—intermittent rain today and tomorrow, Wednesday a mix of sun and clouds with a chance of showers. Basically they weren't sure.

Maybe there was something on TV. She zipped into the living room, Rufus right behind her.

The set took forever to warm, and then the only channel she could get had a national wake-up show on, a man and woman sitting in plush armchairs surrounded by flowers. As if summoned, the boys thundered down the stairs. She clicked it off so they wouldn't put on a video.

"All right," she said. "Who wants corn cakes?"

"Me!" Justin said.

"What's in them?" Sam asked, looking worried.

"Liver," she said, "and brussels sprouts."

"No."

"What do you think is in them?"

"I don't know."

"Here," she said, "if you don't like them, we can give them to Rufus, how's that?"

"Okay," Sam said, and she wasn't sure if he was serious or joking. He was an odd little thing. She knew Kenneth worried about him. There'd been that trouble at school, and then the guidance counselor suggesting he be tested, and Lisa refusing, a whole soap opera that went nowhere.

But the woman. That was the danger in the morning, other people's business impinging on yours, cluttering up your mind. In the kitchen, she remembered word for word what the radio had said. Abducted. And Kenneth the first to discover her gone. The police would probably want to talk to him again. They would have to get a paper, find out who she was.

The dishwasher ground on, cycling higher. The window above the sink was beginning to steam up. Outside, the Wisemans' oaks flailed; on their dock, the Indians flag stood rigid in the wind, the lake pitching with whitecaps, dishwater gray. It was a day to stay inside, to cuddle up under a blanket and read by a warm light. Who knew with Chautauqua weather. It could be sunny by lunchtime.

While the griddle warmed, she stirred the batter. Arlene came in, wearing the same sweater as last night, and asked if she needed any help. Emily freed her to go have her first cigarette of the day, standing like an exile under the chestnut. The butter sizzled, filling the kitchen with a sharp, salty smell. She wished there were bacon for the boys. She'd tell Kenneth to get some, but she knew she'd forget, and started another list. Milk, bacon.

The butter had disappeared, only a lick of smoke curling up. She spooned the batter onto the hot griddle and stood there, spatula in hand, not yet watching the edges, just standing there, time passing around her. She wouldn't miss the old Westinghouse with its untrustworthy burners, the clock that hadn't worked since the mid-seventies, the broiler that cut out without warning. She loved food but despised cooking. It was something Henry—having never been expected to feed anyone—never understood in her.

This was different, a gift, though she supposed she did still worry about meals. At home the clock nagged her, said she needed to eat something even when she wasn't hungry. Maybe it was the lake, or summer, but she was ravenous.

Arlene opened the door, letting in a cold rush of wind. She returned her lighter to the windowsill; she had another on the screenporch for easy access.

"I found out what happened," Emily said.

"What happened to whom?"

"At the gas station yesterday."

She checked the cakes; they were ready. While she started another pair, she told Arlene what she'd heard on the radio.

"Interesting" was all Arlene said, as if she didn't care.

"I thought it was, someone out there kidnaping people in broad daylight."

"I'm sure there's a whole story behind it they're not telling." Arlene rooted in the fridge for her orange juice.

"I'm sure," Emily agreed, but somehow Arlene had made any speculation unappetizing, killed it with her teacher's deadening objectivity.

Emily called the boys in before the second set was done, trapping Arlene at the counter. "Would you mind pouring them some milk?" she asked, busy microwaving the syrup.

"Can I have juice?" Sam asked.

"After you finish your milk. Did you want some?" she asked Arlene. "Otherwise I'm going to fridge the rest of this. I don't imagine anyone else will be up for a while."

"That's fine," Arlene said, and left. Emily turned down the burner and spooned two for herself.

"Are there any onions in them?" Sam asked.

"No, there are no onions in them."

"I don't like them."

"Then don't eat them," she said, exasperated. He'd barely touched his plate, just a wedge missing. Justin was tucking in as if to prove him wrong. If she didn't know better, she would have said Sam belonged to Margaret and Justin to Kenneth.

"Can I be excused?" Sam asked.

"Drink your milk, then clear your place."

He chugged half the glass.

"Whoa," she said, "whoa. That is not how a gentleman acts. And Justin Carlisle, this is not a race. I know you both want to go play your Nintendo, but while you're at the table, you will act accordingly. Now let's try that again."

They suffered her, their impatience and ungainly restraint the same she knew from her own children and, from the other side, her own childhood. Perhaps that was why children were so reassuring: no matter how the world changed, you could count on them being the same.

"Can I be excused?" Sam asked.

"Wait for your cousin," she instructed, and he sighed.

Finally she released them, telling them to wash their hands before touching anything.

The dishes, meanwhile, had finished their cycle but were still too hot to put away. She did the breakfast dishes by hand, wiping down the sink and draping the dishcloth over the spigot. The griddle she dried immediately so it wouldn't rust. Putting it away, she remembered her mother's, perpetually greased, attracting fat black ants that skittered over the linoleum. Some morning—maybe a rainy day like today—her mother had taught her how to fry bacon, how not to be afraid of the popping grease (saving it in a can kept next to the timer), and then eggs over easy, the way her father liked them. She couldn't have been more than ten. Every morning before school she cooked his breakfast. In high school she tried to disguise the smell with Evening in Paris, opening the window on the bus until her neighbors complained. Every morning before going to work her father kissed her cheek and thanked her, said what a good cook she was. And then, every night, her mother put her to shame with lavish dinners that probably took ten years off their lives, the gravy boat a staple, real cream with dessert. That way of life seemed unthinkable now, antique, and yet it had been hers, was still the guide and yardstick she relied on. She wondered if the children would remember her the same way, these strange corn cakes hopelessly old-fashioned.

Of course. She would be their past. Time was not a circle or a line but a kitchen, a lamp, an armchair.

She would look at the children's lists today and make her decisions. She would see how much would be kept and how much jettisoned. Oh, most of it would fit in at any Goodwill, but there were pieces she was secretly rooting for, combinations she'd appraised like a matchmaker. She wanted Margaret to have the cedar chest (and someday hand it down to Sarah). The wardrobe upstairs had always been Kenneth's, and the dresser in the guest room Arlene's (and the night table that went with it; it would be silly to break up the set). Lisa would want nothing, and that was fine with Emily. She would no longer allow herself to be perplexed by her daughter-in-law's mystifying coolness toward her. After all these years, Emily had built up a protective indifference of her own. Some people would never be sympathetic, and to struggle against that fact was foolish, maybe even dangerous, but surely wasteful.

She tidied up the kitchen, then, satisfied, draped the dish towel over the handle of the oven to dry. She gave Rufus a treat and looked out the window again, the drops on the glass—the glass itself, the dust-specked sill and its tarnished lock—filling her with a dread sense of confinement. She would go absolutely bats with the kids in the house all day. Maybe she and Arlene could take a trip to the Book Barn, have lunch somewhere.

In the living room, the boys were playing their Game Boys but had courteously turned the sound down. She took her book to the couch and tried to read, distracted by their cries. They huddled over the plastic tablets like monks, all concentration, while she couldn't go two paragraphs without looking up.

Taken in broad daylight, from a public place. Certainly they would have a video camera there, like at the bank. She couldn't get over it. Kenneth would be able to tell her something.

She wanted a newspaper. At home she'd stopped delivery for the week, and the thought of the empty vestibule, the front door, the motionless furniture, made her wonder what the children would want from that house. Kenneth was her executor, and she worried that Lisa would convince him not to take anything of hers. Margaret would get everything and then neglect it; at Easter her house was a pigsty, mounds of laundry in the corners of the children's rooms, an inch of dust under the beds.

She would have to add a newspaper to Kenneth's grocery list. There was something else eluding her, flittering just beyond the reach of her consciousness.

"'I understand your confusion, Counselor,'" she read a second time, but the scene in the Lord Magistrate's chambers seemed faraway and stale. It was too early to be reading, she'd end up with a headache by lunchtime. The rain was tough on her sinuses. She needed to write that postcard to Louise, maybe that was it. She set the book aside. Curled at her feet, Rufus looked up as if she were going to move. He rose creakily, anticipating her, and she leaned back.

"Where are *you* going?" she asked. "It's too wet for a walk."

He laid his head lightly on her knee to be petted, as if he understood her.

"Yes," she cooed, "you're stuck here like the rest of us."

2

There was no sense getting up. Above them, the rain tapped at the roof, fingers absently drumming a table. Warm in her corner, Lise pressed against Ken's back and listened to its steady tread.

"Let's stay in bed all day."

"This bed?" he asked, because the mattress was hard and the bottom sheet always slipped off.

"Any bed."

"What about the kids?"

"They can get their own bed."

Her fingers twirled the bristly hair of his stomach, her pinkie circling his innie. When she fished lower, he rolled over, turned to her.

"Meg's right there," he whispered.

"And I'm right here."

She pushed her breasts against him, her greatest weapons. In college she'd let him take pictures of them—not her, just them, disembodied—artsy geometric silhouettes in shaded grays and stark black and white. In the prints they looked like moons, eclipses. In their first apartment on Marlborough Street, he hung them over their bed. By then she'd gotten used to him stalking her around the house, shooting her obsessively—sleeping, getting dressed, using the bathroom. She lost her self-consciousness so that even in the rawest shots there was an intimacy she felt lucky to be the subject of. She was even prouder of those pictures now, and of the girl who'd trusted him, as if they proved and documented not only her beauty but her courage.

"We can't," he said, and while it was true—Ella and Sarah were still in their bags—Lise was disappointed.

All she wanted was for him to flirt with her, make a game of the possibilities. Last night had been so nice. She hated to think they might go back to the way things had been. Their skinny-dipping had seemed a promise of something larger, or maybe she was looking for a change and had latched on to the first hopeful sign.

"I know," she said, and rolled away, flat on her back, her breasts spreading, falling into her armpits.

"Now you're mad."

"I am not mad. Why would I be mad?"

"I don't know, but you are."

She wasn't, she just wanted them to connect again, to be the young lovers who played with his lights and lenses and didn't care if they made any money as long as they had fun. Their life together, begun so openly, so focused on each other, now seemed to depend on Ken's success. Sometimes she wished he would quit, and then she felt selfish and vowed to support him that much more. It would not be her fault if he failed.

Downstairs, the dishwasher kicked into another cycle. Before, she'd smelled butter frying—Emily making breakfast for the boys.

"I'm going to get up," she said. "My feet are sweaty."

"You don't want to read your book?"

"I can read downstairs."

"Don't go," he said, and held her.

It was all she wanted, and she gave in to him, let him slide his knee between hers. The smell of his skin meant home to her, the same way their shared warmth made even these rough sheets familiar. This communion meant so much to her, and yet he barely seemed to notice. Sometimes she imagined that he didn't love her, that he was just playing along for her sake, giving the absolute minimum to keep her happy. How much easier it would be if she didn't care.

She bit at his shoulder in fun. "What's the plan for today?"

"Is there a movie the kids want to see? Doesn't Will Smith have something out?"

"You don't want to take them."

"No," he admitted, "but the boys can't go by themselves."

"The girls can watch them."

"They're not going to want to do that."

"Tough," she said.

"You got some sun yesterday."

"I know." She pressed a finger to her nose. The skin felt thin and tender, as if it might rip. "I'll put some aloe on it. Isn't there anything else to do?"

"The casino."

"Like they don't play enough video games as it is."

Her back hurt, so she shifted, Ken turning with her, both of them facing the powder-blue wall. Long ago the roof had leaked so there was the ghost of a stain, like a tide line. Emily had wanted $325,000 for the place but had never told Ken what she'd gotten for it. Probably what she asked. In four years Ella would be off to college, and they had no way of paying for it. Her parents had offered to help but secretly she hoped Ken would refuse. They'd taken enough from them. Emily had never given them a penny.

Ken cupped one breast, fiddling with the nipple. She chased his hand, then caught it and held it warm against her belly. One of the girls got up and went to the bathroom.

"Is that Ella?" she asked, and he raised up to check.

"Yep."

"What time is it?"

"Does it matter?"

"I'm sure your mother's wondering where everyone is."

"It's vacation," he said. "You're supposed to sleep in."

They lay there with the rain thumping, but she'd started to think, her mind weaving all over the place. Ella left the bathroom and lay down again. The toilet ran for a while and then simmered to nothing.

"I'm awake," Lise said.

"Read your book."

"I don't want to."

"Go back to sleep."

"I can't."

He could, it seemed. Yesterday he'd been up before dawn, leaving her cold and alone, and now when she needed to get up he wanted her to stay with him. It seemed they were never on the same schedule.

He wasn't asleep, just dozing, burrowed into her shoulder. The stain on the wall looked like reaching fingers; they slid down the wall and then stopped, magically evaporated. She didn't hear the dishwasher anymore and wondered if she could take her shower.

"I'm getting up."

"All right," he said, groggy, not arguing.

"Here I go."

"I'll go," he offered, but weakly, an empty gesture.

"No," she said, "you sleep."

She pushed off the covers and got out and the cold seized her. In the bathroom she twisted on the heat lamp, the timer ticking behind the dial. She turned on the water and waited for it to warm, closing the glass door against the spray and the smell. *He* should be getting up, she thought, not her. Something in her conscience, some mother's or daughter's sense of obligation drove her, made it impossible to lie there while others were working, taking care of the children. Then why, standing there naked and tired, the musty steam opening her pores, did she feel so guilty?

3

There was nothing to do. They couldn't go for a bike ride or take Rufus for a walk, so there was no way to go by his house, if it was his. Ella pretended to be disappointed for Sarah, and she was, a little. Stalking him was something they did together, Sarah frantic for her advice, her opinion. Not used to being included, Ella felt like she was part of the romance, like the goofy best friend in a movie. He might win Sarah's heart but only with her help, and she and Sarah would always share something deeper.

Her mother wanted them to get dressed and get their breakfast, like she was in a hurry to go somewhere. Downstairs the adults ("the dolts," Sarah called them) were making plans.

"Your father has generously offered to take you all to the movies," her mother threatened.

Oh boy, she almost said, but knew not to. Vacation made her mother crazy. From the day they started packing until all the laundry was done, she was totally psycho. The best thing to do was keep quiet and stay out of the way, one of the few talents Ella was proud of.

When her mother had closed the door at the bottom of the stairs, Aunt Margaret got up and padded to the bathroom, her hair spiked and wild, her eyes barely open. Sarah shook her head, embarrassed, but Ella watched her cautiously, as if she might slip and reveal her mystery—a flash of tattoo, a hidden scar. Sarah said some nights when she drank she would come into her room and lie down on her bed and cry. She'd say things about Uncle Jeff that Sarah knew weren't true. Now she seemed like she might be drunk, or had been last night. It was nearly ten, late to be waking up. She closed the door and Sarah groaned.

"She's so . . . uh!"

Ella gave her room to continue, but she dropped her chin into her pillow, sticking her lower lip out, thinking, and Ella thought of her own mother and their battles over TV, the dishes, being nice to Sam. Compared to Sarah's parents, they seemed childish, not problems at all.

"Why can't we just stay here?" Sarah asked. Instantly Ella was against her father's idea, even though she could think of at least two movies she wanted to see. It might get nice later, and they could always go to the movies at home.

"It's so annoying. They don't even ask you if you want to do something."

"I know," Sarah said. "Then they get mad because they think they're doing you a favor." She rolled on her back and held her arms straight up, mummylike, toward the ceiling, then let them crash back down. "What do you think he's doing right this minute?"

Ella had no clue what boys did at ten in the morning on a crummy day. Watch TV? Play computer games? She couldn't see him doing either, just eating, working out, walking around in his suit of muscles.

"What do you think his name is?" Sarah asked, torturing herself for the pleasure of it.

Dave, she thought, or Dan. Something dumb.

In the bathroom the shower blasted on, the water drilling the stall. Secretly, Ella was pleased. It meant they'd have to wait until Sarah's mother was done. It meant another fifteen minutes alone with her. On a day like today, she'd take whatever she could get.

4

Emily expected her to be upset about the kidnaping, as if they were related to the woman. Caught by surprise—in her room with an afghan over her lap, lost in her book—Arlene could only respond with a puzzled shrug. She thought it would be enough to signal her lack of interest, but Emily lingered in the doorway. Until now, Arlene hadn't realized how much she was enjoying the quiet of the room, the thin light reflecting off of the lawn and through the window, the wind pushing the trees. She could stay here all day and be content, put on some tea before lunch, listen for the whistle. She had grown so used to being alone.

"You have to wonder if there's a boyfriend involved," Emily speculated, "or an ex of some sort. These things don't happen at random."

Arlene would not be drawn into a discussion and chose her only escape, a noncommittal "I'm sure we'll find out."

"Do you think?"

"Eventually," Arlene said, not looking up from her book.

"I'm not so sure. A lot of these missing-persons cases go unsolved, young people especially. Of course who knows how many of them are runaways. I would be very surprised if we learn anything by the end of the week."

"I said eventually," Arlene said. "If they're bringing in the FBI, they probably have something to go on. They wouldn't bring them in unless they had evidence this is a federal case. A lot of those missing persons you're talking about are children involved in custody battles. This was a grown woman, if what you're telling me is correct."

"That's why I'm betting on the boyfriend."

"And the federal connection would be . . . ?" She could hear the teacher in her tone, coaxing logic out of a confused student, asking for supporting facts. She knew from experience what the criteria were.

"Drugs," Emily said.

"That sounds like a guess." But probably right.

"Do you have a better one?"

"No," Arlene admitted. "I don't have to have one, do I?"

"I just thought you might be interested. I'm sorry I bothered you."

"You're not bothering me, and it is interesting. I'm just trying to read my book, that's all."

"Do you have your list?"

It didn't register, this wild shift.

"Of things you want," Emily said.

"I'm already getting the TV."

"That doesn't count."

"I haven't really thought about it."

"Do, please. I need them as soon as possible. I was hoping we could go over them tonight."

Arlene agreed to have hers this afternoon. No, she didn't want the door closed, but Emily pulled it most of the way.

Arlene sighed and tipped up her book again, crossed her legs under the afghan. She read a sentence and then the gray light from outside made her look up. The trees were calm now, a few leaves stuck in the lawn showing their pale bellies.

One of the criteria was drugs and another was interstate transit, taking someone across state lines against his or her will. She pictured Eugene Ingram sitting in his seat, and then his terrible handwriting, only his name easily legible. When he disappeared two men from the FBI interviewed her in the teacher's lounge. Arlene told them what she knew. Eugene was absent a great deal and sometimes didn't bother to hand in assignments. His aunt had come to an open house early in the year and had been pleasant enough (in reality she was bored, but so were most of the parents, doing their duty), and Arlene had not talked to her since. The FBI didn't say that the aunt and uncle were missing as well. She'd had to read that later in the paper.

And eventually everyone at school found out what happened to Eugene Ingram. His uncle had been dealing dope and some local gang members decided to rob him. They kidnaped Eugene along with the aunt and uncle and kept them in an abandoned house down in Homewood. They tortured them to find out where the money was, and then, according to the *Post-Gazette,* killed them execution-style.

She'd had students before who ended up dead—it was not the safest neighborhood—but much later, when they were in high school or beyond, dropped out or graduated to a harder life than she would ever know. Eugene was in the third grade and still had that annoying clown in him that some boys have in place of personality. He thought farts were funny and had trouble with math. After she heard what had happened to him (from the eleven o'clock news, a minute's information), she tried to remember something he'd said to her, some moment of closeness the two of them had shared. She had a number to choose from—Eugene taping his Polaroid to the board by the door, Eugene reading his Thanksgiving essay in front of the class, Eugene singing in the third- and fourth-grade concert—but in the end she kept returning to the time he'd cut his chin at recess.

He'd been playing on the Big Toy and another boy had pushed him off, and he came to her holding his chin.

"Let's take a look," she said, and when he removed his hands, she could see there was blood and that he would need stitches. She asked Mrs. Casey to take over and escorted him straight to the nurse. "It doesn't hurt," he insisted on the way to the doors. It must have seemed like punishment to him, her dragging him along (he must have thought she was angry with him, or maybe he was thinking of his aunt and uncle), because all the way down the hall he repeated it, tears coming, planting his feet, his sneakers slipping on the marble, "It doesn't hurt, it doesn't!"

Her book lay open on her lap. She hadn't thought of Eugene Ingram in years. It had to have been the mid-eighties, long gone. Her hold on him was fleeting, like the book's on her attention, and maybe that was for the good. Later the neighborhood was worse, and the city had trouble finding teachers, with the result that she kept her job longer than she'd meant to. Some of the children she'd taught had probably gone on to college, and some were probably dead. The majority were no doubt somewhere in between, off to jobs or not, in love or alone, happy or unhappy or, like her, some muddled combination of the two. Marvin Liberty and his lisp, Crystal Worthington, who laughed at everything and made her a leather change purse. There was no way of knowing. She thought that if she began wondering what had happened to each and every one of them, she would never stop.

So, though she couldn't explain all this to Emily, there was no reason to make wild guesses. Eventually they would find out, whether they wanted to or not.

5

Before the children could go to the movies they needed their lunch.

They were not going to eat in the living room, Emily decided, that much was certain. Somehow they would crowd onto the porch.

Soup would be too much, and messy, though it was cold enough, sweater weather. She had water on for tea. She thought the children could all have cold cuts, but Sam didn't like cold cuts, or any kind of sandwich for that matter, because she tried to offer him a PB & J and was summarily rejected. The hot dogs were for dinner, she explained. Then they ran out of potato chips. There was leftover chicken, which was fine for her, but Kenneth didn't like leftovers, and she could tell Arlene wasn't thrilled with the idea. Margaret and Lisa were hiding somewhere upstairs. None of the children touched the coleslaw or the sliced tomatoes except Ella. Emily really did see so much of herself in her—the willowy arms, the restless intelligence. Then Justin knocked the fork for the pickles onto the floor and she got cross with him and he stood there terrified with his plate clutched in both hands until she told him to go. She wiped up the green juice with a paper towel and went to the silverware drawer. Kenneth and Arlene were milling around, waiting for the kids to finish.

She had the glasses out for milk when Sam asked if they could have their plastic bottles of Kool-Aid that were taking up the bottom shelf, and Kenneth said yes. They all wanted the pink, and then they had trouble twisting the plastic tops off. The bottoms of the bottles were rounded so they couldn't set them down, meaning in essence that they had to guzzle them or hold on to them the entire meal. She was sure she would find some of them half full on their sides and seeping sticky pink fluid.

Arlene fixed a meager plate.

"There's enough for everyone," Emily urged her.

"This is more than enough for me," Arlene said.

"It's a regular smorgasbord, isn't it?" she asked Kenneth, who waited, plate in hand.

"It looks great," he said, "thanks," and pleased her by taking some of everything, even the tomatoes, which she knew he didn't like.

That left Margaret and Lisa.

She walked through the living room—a mess, the boys' *Star Wars* toys strewn across the carpet like a plane crash—and called up the stairs, "Lunch is ready."

"Okay," Margaret hollered back.

Emily waited for her footsteps but heard nothing.

"I'm afraid it's buffet-style," she called. "It's all laid out in the kitchen."

"I heard you the first time," Margaret shouted.

"Fine," Emily said, walking away.

She fitted her paper plate into a holder and forked up a morsel of dark meat, a slice of salami, a spoonful of coleslaw. Her plate looked suspiciously like Arlene's, but she had reason. Making lunch—handling the food, selecting and then arranging it for everyone—had naturally ruined her appetite. It would be nice, she thought, if for once someone else served her.

6

"My Kadabra just learned recover," Justin said.

"So what," said Sam.

"What level is *your* Kadabra?"

"Fifty-eight," Sam said, and when Justin didn't say anything, did his Nelson: "Ha ha!"

"I've got a Dewgong," Justin tried.

"Yeah? Well I've got an Articuno. And a Zapdos. And a Moltres."

"Don't you guys ever talk about anything else?" Ella asked from the front seat.

"No, they don't," Sarah said.

"Be quiet," Sam said, tipping his Game Boy so he could see the screen.

"Sam," Uncle Ken warned him, but he was driving. They were going to see *X-Men*. "Is your hour almost up yet?"

"Almost."

Justin turned his off and set it in the perfect-sized slot in the armrest. Outside, pine trees and creepy-looking houses went by, and cars driving with their lights on. Raindrops hit the windshield with a loud plastic tapping. When he'd said he liked the Maxwells' 4Runner better than their van, his mother had told him it wasn't safe, that it was too tall and because of that it could tip, and now he imagined them rolling over and over into a ditch with a stream in it, landing upside down so the brown water ran cold through the broken windows and over the ceiling and out the back hatch. Everyone except him would be hurt and hanging in their seat belts, and he'd have to crawl out and run to the nearest house and ask an old lady if he could use the phone. He didn't know their number at the lake house, but he could show the police how to go after they'd saved everyone. His mother would call his father. So, his father would say, sounds like you were the big hero.

His father would want to see him the day they got back, or maybe he'd get in his Camaro and drive straight here. Maybe Sarah would have a broken arm and he'd want to see her, or maybe *he* would have a broken arm, maybe he saved them all with a broken arm. That was better.

"Magmar grew to level forty," Sam said.

"Who cares?" Ella said.

Justin didn't have a Magmar. It made him want to play, to catch up, but they were almost there. They'd already gone by the place where they went for ice cream. He didn't see anyone inside, just a yellow light. He hoped they'd be able to get candy at the movie, but he didn't want to ask. He didn't have any money.

"Here we are, right on schedule," Uncle Ken said, and in a minute Justin could see the sign over Ella's shoulder, all the different movies lit up and the rain falling through the blue neon. Sam turned his volume on, the plinky music filling the car.

"Sound," Uncle Ken said, and Sam turned it off. "And we're not bringing our Game Boys in with us."

They had to wait for the other cars to park, and then there was a long line for tickets. The girls were going to *Charlie's Angels* all by themselves, which Sam said wasn't fair. Justin stood off to the side with them while Sam and Uncle Ken went up to the window. The sidewalk by the doors was dry, a straight line between the brown and the white. The rain shone on spots of old gum.

They waited. More cars were turning in. Parents stopped and dropped kids off and went around and out the same way. Two older kids were messing around, pushing each other, and the one wearing a Pirates cap backward said, "Fuck you." Justin looked to see if Uncle Ken heard them. He was next in line.

Sam came running over to Justin. "It's sold out."

"What else is there?"

"Nothing. *Rugrats in Paris.*"

Uncle Ken gave the girls their tickets and some money and they disappeared. "I'm sorry," he said. "We chose the next best thing. I hope that's all right."

"No, I wanted to see that," Justin said. "It has good commercials."

"Are we going to get candy?" Sam asked inside.

"You can each get one thing," Uncle Ken said.

Justin got Sour Patch Kids and Sam got Gummi Bears so they could trade. Uncle Ken didn't get anything, which was weird. His father always got a large popcorn and a jumbo soda to share with everyone. Justin looked around for Sarah but they must have already gone in. If there was a fire, he wouldn't be able to find her.

Their theater was all the way at the end, and almost empty, just some little kids with their mothers. They had good seats, right in the middle. The dumb trivia questions were running, with the scrambled names. Sam went to the movies a lot, because he knew all of them. Uncle Ken sat on the far end, looking everywhere except the screen. Justin was done with his Sour Patch Kids before the lights went out. He found the red EXIT signs and figured out which one was closest to him. It would be easy. There weren't that many people.

The previews looked good. "I want to see that," Sam said to everything. *The Grinch* was the best, except it wasn't coming out until Thanksgiving. And then the lights went completely out and the movie started.

Justin wasn't afraid of the dark; it was just that no one was sitting on one side of him. At school Michael Schulz told him about a kid who went to the movies by himself and when his mother went to pick him up, he wasn't there. They found him sitting in the theater he was supposed to be in, all by himself. He looked okay from behind, except when they came around the front of him, they saw that someone had stabbed him right through the back of the seat. It was just a story, Justin knew, but he couldn't stop himself from picturing it happening. Even now he looked over his shoulder to make sure no one was sitting there.

Once the movie got started he stopped worrying. He only remembered the story when a scene was really bright and he could see the rows of seats in front of him, or a scene was so dark that all he could see was the exit lights. Most of the time he was fine.

7

"God, get me out of there," Meg said when they were on the road. "If she mentions the Lindbergh baby one more time I'm going to scream. And I don't care if we go to McDonald's, I'm not eating that chicken again."

"There's always cold cuts," Lise reminded her.

"And sliced tomatoes. Does she think we won't recognize them from yesterday?"

"Don't forget the coleslaw."

"It's the kids I feel sorry for," Meg said, stopping and looking both ways. She was a notoriously bad driver, and Lise leaned back to give her a better view. "It's hard enough getting Justin to eat regular food."

"Justin's better than Sam."

While they talked, Lise tried to ignore the raft of torn cigarette packs and fast-food wrappers her sneakers rested on, the Chap Stick that had melted into the change tray under the emergency brake, coating the coins like Vaseline, a fur of dust beginning to accumulate. Even through the stale air of the heater, the car smelled like old dope—no surprise. Lise was not the most organized person herself, but had grown used to Ken's maniacal tidiness, and there were times when she couldn't believe he and Meg were brother and sister. Too often Meg seemed strange to her, alien and almost comic in how completely she played the black sheep, her problems piled up like a guest's on a talk show. She was such a magnet for bad luck that Lise would honestly be surprised to hear something had gone right for her.

She was grateful to Meg for getting her out of the house, away from Emily. It was a bad habit of her mother's to judge everyone against her perfect parents. Lise needed to guard against it, to see her own position more coldly.

She could. Sometimes she was dissatisfied, and when she said anything, Ken made her feel like she expected too much. She felt caught in an opera, wanted daily to be ravaged by passion, and then, doing the dishes, picking up after the kids, thought it was just her age. She wasn't the only woman bored at forty, wondering what had gone wrong.

The rain turned the highway into a black mirror, taillights caught in spangled drops on the windshield, then swept away.

"What's the weather supposed to be like tomorrow?" Lise asked.

"The same."

"Don't tell me that."

"Wednesday too."

"No," Lise said. "Someone kidnap me, please."

"You can't let her get to you."

"How am I supposed to do that?"

"Just keep doing what you're doing. You haven't said two words to her since we've been here."

"Is it that noticeable?"

Meg laughed. "Only to everybody."

"I don't know how you do it."

"The same way you do it with your folks—just ignore them."

"No, they drive me crazy too."

They went on like this, skimming the surface. They could have had the same conversation last year or a decade ago—it was a relic, like Emily's lunch. Out of politeness, Lise stayed away from the two most tempting subjects, Meg's rehab and Jeff. She wished Meg would breach them first, but as the cottages and wet cornfields slipped past, and then, like a highlight, the Book Barn (packed), Lise realized that wouldn't happen. And why should she, she thought. She wasn't eager to discuss what she and Ken were going through, or her fears about money (which she couldn't even talk to Ken about without making him feel bad). The silence reminded her of how little she knew Meg. There were no magic words that would bring them closer, no instantaneous heart-to-heart talks. Meg would not ask her out of the blue what she was thinking or how she felt. It seemed like a missed connection, but missed so long ago and so consistently that Lise wondered why it bothered her now.

The miniature golf went by on their right, streams gushing down the papier-mâché rocks in the rain. The movie theater was jammed, and she was glad that Ken had volunteered to take the kids.

"Where do you want to eat?" Meg asked.

"I don't care. Not McDonald's. Somewhere we can sit down."

"How's Chinese?"

"I know the place you mean. Sure."

It was cheap, a family buffet, chafing dishes over Sterno, yellowed reviews framed in the hallway. Better than the chicken, she figured.

But the place was closed, killed by a brand-new Denny's across the road. Its windows were dark, blinded by butcher paper, a big FOR LEASE sign on the door proclaiming their failure. Meg slowed and they gawked as if passing an accident, then drove on.

"There's a Red Lobster by the mall," Meg suggested.

"What the hell," Lise said. "We've got to go to Wal-Mart anyway."

Finding a parking spot was a chore, and then when they got inside, they found the vestibule crowded. Where did all these old people come from, Lise wondered. It was a small town, and fading, from the look of the mall. The hostess told them there was a ten-minute wait, maybe less, so they stood by the bubbling lobster tank, Lise feeling conspicuous with her peeling nose.

It was a safe place, she thought. No one would be abducted from a Red Lobster.

Meg leaned over and whispered, "We're the youngest people in here."

It was true. The padded bench along the wall was all seniors, the men in obsolete suits and wide ties, the women's hair sugar-white and stiff as fiberglass.

"It must be their day out," Lise muttered, hoping none of them could hear. She was no judge of age, but they had to be in their late seventies, maybe their eighties. Emily was in her early seventies, not so far from them. In ten years Lise would be fifty, an age that seemed impossible.

It was not a subject to dwell on, not on a day like today, and she looked hopefully to the hostess's empty lectern. The walls were done up with nets and oars and lobster pots, a codified lack of imagination. Every time someone opened the doors, a wet gust rushed in.

"Do you want to try someplace else?" Meg asked.

"No, we're here. I'm just getting creeped out thinking how old we are."

"We're not old."

"I feel old," Lise said. "In two weeks Ella's going into high school."

"So's Sarah, but I don't feel old. I feel a lot of things, but not old."

Lise wanted to ask Meg what she meant by this, but felt she didn't have the right. As if to trade a confession of her own, she said, "I feel like I could have done more."

"Everyone feels like that," Meg said, but so offhand that Lise saw she would not be drawn into a discussion, not here in the lobby.

The hostess moved the old people as a group, then, without the merest attempt at sincerity, thanked Lise and Meg for being so patient and hurried them to a booth, the table still bearing the beaded trail of a washcloth. Once she'd gone, Lise swabbed the surface with her paper napkin and left it by the edge for the waitress to take. The old people were seated far across the room, and most of the booths around them were empty.

"So why did we have to wait?" she asked.

It didn't matter. The idea was to kill time, to pass the afternoon away from Emily and Ken and the kids, and it was working. They talked about nothing, about movies and dry cleaning, about politics and carpeting. Lise felt like ordering a margarita but out of consideration for Meg had a Diet Pepsi. The menu was vast and bland, as if designed by a child. Everything came with fries and coleslaw.

"Oh God," Meg said. "Coleslaw."

Lise knew most if not all of the fish would be frozen and that the crab would be fake, the rubbery stuff made in Japan. She wondered if Meg ever got good seafood, living in the middle of the country. If Lise needed a reason to be proud of New England, it was places like this.

The chowder was paste, but that didn't matter either. She didn't care about the food—or the air-conditioning, the room chilly as a morgue. None of it mattered, yet she could feel herself turning hypercritical, destroying anything set before her, the littlest stupidities turning corrosive. She couldn't figure out why and, worse, couldn't stop herself from doing it.

"Sometimes I feel," she said, "like I'm sick of everything. Now you can't tell me everyone feels that way."

"Of course they do. Why do you think we have all those shooting sprees? What do you think road rage is?"

"That's hardly a majority of the country."

"Those are the worst cases, but think of all the domestic violence. Those are people who are sick of everything and take it out on the people closest to them."

Lise wanted to read meaning into it at the same time she refuted her argument. "But the majority of people, I think you'd agree, are happy with their lives. Otherwise they'd change them."

"How? How would you change *your* life?"

Lise thought first of Ella, and then Sam. She wouldn't change Ken, she just wanted him to be closer to her again. But herself, the way she lived her own life, she had no idea.

"I don't know," she said.

"Because you can't," Meg said. "You can't just wake up one morning and decide you're not going to live your old life. You can pretend to, but it doesn't work. You're always going to come back to who you are. Some people don't like that, but that's the way it is."

Lise recognized the rehab platitudes in her speech, and wondered how they applied to Jeff leaving.

"I guess I don't want to change my life, I just want to make it better."

"That's possible," Meg allowed. "All you have to do is figure out what you want, then work like hell to get it."

"Sounds easy."

"It's easier than trying to fix what you've already ruined. Or so my therapist tells me."

The waitress came with their entrees and took Lise's unfinished cup. When she'd cleared off, Meg said, "Right now I'm probably going through the worst time of my life, and you know what the biggest thing I'm worried about is?"

"What?"

"Money. Isn't that terrible? I have all this other stuff to deal with, but before I can even start thinking about it, I've got to take care of the money."

Lise could counter with their own money troubles but thought it was not the same. This was Ken's worst fear, the impossible job of paying bills suddenly far too large and having no one to turn to, the numbers accumulating month after month, their savings dwindling to nothing and then sinking into the negative, the bank sending threatening letters.

She tried to pinpoint the worst time in her own life and couldn't. Her life had been easy—not perfect, but free from any deep loss. Her parents were still alive, her children were healthy, Ken loved her in his own distracted way. To ask for more than that would be greedy.

Even her unhappiness was unearned, and she thought this was more proof that there was nothing wrong with her life but something wrong with her.

Meg was going on about how they might lose the house, and while Lise sympathized with how awful that was, and honestly felt for her, she did not want to hear any more about her tragedies. She knew them anyway. She wanted Meg to be distant again, a mystery. She wanted them to be like the rest of the couples spread around them, chatting meaninglessly, laughing over their heaping plates, happy to be out on the town.

8

Beside Ella, Sarah watched with her arms crossed over her stomach like she was trying to stay warm. The reflected light of the movie shone on her throat and lips, a dot on the tip of her nose, a bright wash across her broad forehead. Ella could see her breathing, the stripes of her shirt lifting slightly, the different blues black and white in the dark, and then everything shifted as she reached for her Reese's cups, and Ella pretended to be fascinated with Drew Barrymore walking down a long hallway with a candelabra.

Sarah aimed the orange package at her, but Ella waved her off. They rearranged themselves, slouched down against the armrests. Sarah raised the Reese's cup to her mouth and took a tiny bite, showing her teeth, breaking off a ridged edge of chocolate, and Ella thought all she had to do was lean over and kiss her.

That would be the end, she thought. Sarah would push her away, spit at her, never talk to her again.

She could let her hand accidentally fall on Sarah's. She'd say she just wanted a Reese's cup, and Sarah would believe her.

She couldn't believe Sarah didn't already know. Since last night, Ella could feel the secret rising to her cheeks in every conversation. This morning they'd dressed together, and at the last second Ella had turned away, not out of decency but the fear she would be overwhelmed by the sight. She had to watch where her eyes landed, and how she held herself when Sarah was in the room. They were alone together all the time, and Ella thought she couldn't hold on much longer. It would be easier if she could just avoid her, but that wasn't going to happen.

She felt doomed, her fate sealed like the queen in her book, waiting for her ordained murderer in her tower room in her castle in the middle of the forest, except she was the murderer too, and the fortune-teller. Sarah was her cousin, and gorgeous, while she was a geek. No one at school secretly wrote her initials on their book covers and then blacked them out, or stole glances at her in science lab. No one even looked at her. And Sarah was in love with Dan or Dave or whatever his name was.

All great loves were impossible, she thought. There was Guinevere—but she'd been punished.

It was all wrong, there wasn't a single thing right with it, but all day and all through the hours she lay awake, it was all she could think of. Every song on the radio was about her, and her book, even this idiotic movie. She couldn't stop, even if she wanted to.

She didn't want Sarah to hate her. That was the thing she was afraid of. If she never confessed, that would never happen. She could be with her all day and all night, sleeping right beside her. She could hear her secrets and be her friend, her geeky cousin. Sometimes she thought that would be enough, but it wasn't. She wanted Sarah to be in love with her as helplessly as she was with Sarah. She wanted to bite her on the neck like a vampire, leave her teeth marks like a sign. You're mine, she wanted to say.

Beside her, Sarah took another tiny bite of her Reese's cup, her front teeth glinting liquid for an instant. Ella didn't understand how she could eat it so slowly. She wasn't nearly as patient. Like most people, she just shoved the whole thing in her mouth.

9

The racket coming from the Smiths' addition reminded Emily of Henry working in the basement, the ring of the table saw reaching her at the cutting board. Each of his machines had its own sound. Standing at the stove, she could locate him beneath her feet by the roar of the belt sander or the buzz of the router, the wobbly shuttle of the lathe. "Dinner's ready," she'd shout down the stairs during a lull, and he'd scrub his hands at his sink down there and then come up, smelling of burnt sawdust and Lava soap, blinking like a mole. After dinner he retreated to his burrow, only to pop up at eight o'clock sharp for prime time. He had a radio Kenneth had given him one year for his birthday (still down there, presiding over his spotless workbench, his tools hung like merchandise from the pegboard, filling their prescribed outlines), and while she did the dishes he turned to the station that played Tommy Dorsey and Artie Shaw, the music they'd fallen in love to, and when she was finished she stood at the top of the stairs and listened as if he were serenading her. Because he was singing down there, his voice a murmur as he moved from one machine to another, trailing off in the middle of a verse, rising for a chorus.

> *So be sure that it's true*
> *When you say I love you*
> *It's a sin to tell a lie*

Those were the heirlooms, the pieces he'd made down there. The stuff up here was junk mostly, ruined by humidity, the veneer peeled off. Still, she'd been so happy to find their old salt and pepper shakers the other day, as if she'd saved some small part of them and how things used to be.

She didn't care. At her age she was allowed to be sentimental. She would never become one of those women who loaded every horizontal surface with china knickknacks, but since Henry had died she found herself dusting the things on his dresser more often, and going through their photo albums, trying to find a nice shot of the two of them to set on top of the piano. That was natural, she thought. She needed to look back. And it hadn't been crippling. It hadn't stopped her from getting things done. She could count on her mother's Prussian industriousness to buoy her, keep her even-keeled. Even now, on vacation, she roamed the house, looking for something to put in order—gathering up the coasters, straightening a stack of magazines.

In the kitchen, putting on water for tea, she chanced to look out at the road, the rain jumping white off the blacktop, and saw that the garbage was still there. She was sure today was the day. Maybe they'd changed their schedule; it had been two years. Maybe they were late because of the rain.

At that moment, an ancient boat of a station wagon rolled up and stopped beside the mailbox, the car facing the wrong way, and the man in the front seat leaned out and with a practiced motion flipped down the door and slipped the mail in with one hand. She waited until he passed the Lerners' before sticking an umbrella out the screen door.

"Sorry," she told Rufus, who thought he might get a walk. He turned around and stumped out of the kitchen, grumping.

It was colder than she thought, fat drops thumping Arlene's car; twigs brought down by the rain speckled the hood. The grass seemed a brighter green, despite the fact that it was overcast. To her delight she found a toad sitting stone-still in the pebbly grit by the side of the road.

"Well, look at you," she said, bending down. He was the color of wet sand, with dark markings and lidded eyes, and she could see his heart beating. "All right, I'll leave you alone."

The road itself was decorated with drowned worms, their white bodies like watery chalk marks. The gardener in Emily pitied the waste.

She checked for cars, then turned her back to the road and opened the mailbox.

There was a letter—junk mail, it looked like—and a local free sheet. A small red ant was walking the edge of the letter. Another was running along the metal floor of the box. There were more crawling on the door and a dark concentration on the wall—hundreds of them swarming on one spot, some fleeing the sudden light, streaming for the safety of the far end.

Emily slapped the door shut and looked up and down the road as if it were a joke, as if someone might be spying on her. It was only on her way back to the kitchen that her mind thawed from the shock of it and turned determined. She'd dealt with her share of aphids and potato bugs and, one summer, a plague of Japanese beetles. Henry had laughed at her ruthlessness, the way she defended her garden like a mother protecting her young.

She'd forgotten the card for Louise. Completely forgotten it.

"Damn."

She left the umbrella outside rather than navigate the doorway with it. She thought there was a bucket under the sink, but she ended up using the corn pot, blasting hot water into it while she searched for the Bon Ami. The sweet dish soap would just attract more of them.

She needed both hands for the pot, and had to pause at the corner of the counter and open the door before shouldering through. The water sloshed as she walked. The rain tapped at her, a subtle weight in her hair. There was no one coming so she set the pot down in the road. She saw how she wanted to do this. She would need paper towels, but not until this part was done, and it came to her—too late—that Henry probably had a spray in the garage. God knew how old it would be, and she didn't trust sprays anyway. This was better.

She grasped the tab that opened the door, yanked it down and backed away. The ants were more disorganized, scattering, their antennas feeling the air. She bent down and lifted the pot, the cloudy water steaming like soup.

Her first throw half missed, the water splashing in the grass. What did hit trickled out around the door, which was filled with swimming ants. The mail itself remained inside, a soggy island; she reached in and pinched it out, let it fall to the road with a slap. It was raining harder, she could feel it on her face, dripping down her brow. Her second throw was better and brought a waterfall, and a possible cause—a popsicle stick. Ants caught in the backwash waved their legs as they went over the lip. On the ground, a struggling knot of them dissolved under her shoe. She threw the rest of the water and stomped back and forth, being thorough, scuffing her soles on their bodies.

There were still some in the box, and now they were escaping, racing along the outside, under the hinged flag and over the red reflector. She had them on the run. She needed more water, and a flashlight to see inside, and paper towels. She felt a strange sense of triumph, as if she'd met a great challenge. But how absurd it seemed to her, how ridiculous she must appear to someone else, battling a bunch of ants. Racing back to the kitchen with the pot, she thought that anyone watching her would think she was a crazy woman. The very idea made her laugh.

10

Ken fell asleep in the movie, as he knew he would, so the cold air and the rain—trailing like snow through the high lights—seemed refreshing and necessary. The sky was a blue filter, the world a cheap horror flick, all mist and black trees.

He saw a boy standing by the ticket booth and wanted to tell him to wait for his parents inside. How easy it would be, one person driving, another to drag him in. They could pretend the choke hold was just rough-housing.

It was the girls' turn to be in the backseat together, and he had to ask Sam to sit up front. The first time, Sam pretended not to hear him, and when he repeated it, an edge crept into his voice that he hadn't really meant. For a while after they got out of the lot, the car was quiet.

Behind him, Justin turned on his Game Boy. The girls replayed their favorite scenes, chopping the air and making kung-fu sounds.

Sam stared out his window, ignoring Ken when he looked over.

"You've got to listen to me, buddy," Ken said softly, but Sam just sulked, clammed up the way Ken himself did when Lise wanted to fight. He'd come by it honestly, he thought, and pictured his father's serene face at the dinner table. He was the last one done even though he said almost nothing. He seemed to eat in slow motion, to set his fork down between every bite. Once Ken had tried to outlast him only to have his mother scold him. He knew his father was just being polite, that he'd grown up in a household where it was considered greedy to reach for the food, rude to rush through supper. In his mildness, his father seemed to embody the very idea of manners. Ken had never heard him seriously complain about anything, not Vietnam or Nixon or the IRS or even his health at the end, as if a Zenlike acceptance was proof of his wisdom. But to a child his self-possession could seem an illusion, the usual adult insistence on infallibility. For years he seemed backwards to Ken, out of touch, but later his calm seemed ideal, his silence not empty but dignified. Ken still could not figure him out.

"Can I please play my Game Boy?" Sam asked.

He'd gone far past his hour, but Ken didn't want another battle.

"Till we get home, but that's it for today."

"Okay."

It came on with an electronic tweet, and reflexively Ken said, "Sound." He drove, Sam beside him, bent over the little screen, unreachable.

In the movie, the father was the same way, so lost in his job at the amusement park that he completely missed Paris and the kids' adventures. The film was typical, Ken thought, telling children that their parents were selfish and that they deserved better—a Disneyfied guilt he didn't remember from the movies he grew up on.

His father would have never taken them to the movies by himself. Maybe to the drive-in on a Saturday night, the whole family going, his mother making popcorn at home to take in a cookie tin. He could envision his father at the wheel, a seed of light trapped in his glasses, an indistinct picture flashing on the screen. Ken had passed the place ten years ago, and even then it was overgrown with weeds, the fence around it falling down. Now it was supposed to be part of a mall, the field of speaker poles harvested and paved over. It was like the Putt-Putt, another lost monument to his imaginary happy childhood. That time had solidified, become history, and yet he could bring back conversations at the dinner table, Meg jumping from her seat and running upstairs, slamming her door while her napkin uncurled on top of her mashed potatoes.

"Do *you* know what her problem is?" his father asked, as if he had no clue—as if there were an answer—and then his mother (after hesitating, waiting to see if he'd do it) would get up and remove the napkin from Meg's plate and rigidly cross the living room to the stairs and go up them slowly. Meg never came back down, and so this turned into a wordless ritual, quicker each time, less upsetting. The solution was to send Meg away to boarding school. After that, their dinners were uneventful.

He could never think of sending Ella or Sam away from him—as if that made him a better father. He was too aware of his own shortcomings to criticize or even compare himself to anyone. He resented the movie, that its clumsy moralizing could make him rethink his own complicated

life, yet provided no real help. He didn't need Tracy Ann Caler to remind him of how precious his children were.

They came over the rise that looked down on the bridge, and
wind buffeted the 4Runner, turned the wheel in his hands. Up the lake,
the clouds held a greenish tinge. It began raining harder—loud—and he
had to click the wipers to high and lean forward so he could see. A splash
of taillights flared. Rather than brake and risk hydroplaning, he took his
foot off the gas. Hard drops battered the windshield, knocked the roof
like marbles.

"Whoa," Sam said.

Ken downshifted, keeping his eye on the lights. He was afraid they
were going too fast, that the car was too large to stop if the guy ahead of
him locked them up. He could pull off, but then his lights might be a
target. The rain had to weaken eventually. He put the defrost on but all it
did was dry out his eyes. He noticed that the girls had stopped talking, the
silence a kind of alarm.

Though he couldn't pick out any landmarks, he knew they were
coming downhill into the dip before going over 17 and past Hogan's Hut.
If he could see the turn for Hogan's Hut, he'd take it and they could wait
out the storm there. He imagined what it was like out on the lake. There
were sure to be a few fishermen stuck in remote coves, bundled up in
ponchos with only beer to keep them warm.

He realized he needed to blink, and did.

The car in front of him braked, and he braked. They were crawling
along, doing less than twenty. He could see a second car ahead matching
them. Another materialized, brighter. The double yellow line reappeared,
and a black strip of sky. The rain softened, slackened, and the wipers were
beating crazily. He turned them down. In the distance, a wave of thunder
broke and rolled over the hills. Beside him, Sam thumbed on his Game
Boy. The girls went back to reciting the best lines.

He sat back and relaxed, the tension draining from his arms, bleeding through his fingers into the wheel. The cars ahead sped up, shedding
mist. The road turned in a long curve, bottomed and climbed the far side
of the dip. They were right where he'd thought they were, nearly to 17. It
was still raining, but he could see now. They crossed the overpass and
Hogan's Hut floated by on their right, its pumps lit against the gloom, a
red Pegasus flying in a white circle. He thought of Tracy Ann Caler stand-

ing behind the counter, sipping her coffee and listening to the radio. She must have had no idea what was happening.

He thought he could have done something, but short of going back in time to warn her, he couldn't imagine what that might have been. He could not have done that any more than he could revisit his father in the hospital and tell him he'd done a good job. The wish was pointless; it was just how he felt now. He wondered if his feelings for his father would change in the coming years, though his father himself would be absent from the process.

As they passed the Book Barn he looked for Meg's minivan but didn't see it. Willow Run was deserted, a light on in the dumpy clubhouse. In overgrown yards sat scabby cottages losing their asbestos brick in patches, and then, heralded by a giant billboard, a lone model home, its yard neat as a green. The wrecks were more interesting. While they must have been here through his childhood, and in better shape, he didn't remember them. The country seemed old to him, long gone to seed, like the Pittsburgh his father knew, a city of natty bankers and brawny steel-workers. It was a trick of memory, giving the past a solidity the present could only imitate.

Part of it was vacation. The days were shapeless and bland, like today, taking the kids to the movies. It was just the rain, and having nothing to do. In Boston he'd be in his darkroom, satisfied to work in the quiet red light. Part of it was his father, he couldn't deny it. For all its changes, Chautauqua seemed to belong to the past, brought those lost summers and everything in them closer.

He and Lise still had to do their list. The thought of it annoyed him, wiped his mind clean. The idea of choosing a literal memento stumped him. He wanted all of it, none of it. It seemed more of a gesture than anything.

The Snug Harbor Lounge had snagged a good-sized crowd, pickup trucks and an El Camino with a tarp parked on the grass.

"Can we go by the fishponds?" Ella asked, and he took the first turn.

The road was rough, a lumpy quilt of frost heaves and plugged potholes. They weren't quite high enough to see the surface of the water. He pictured it stippled, a moil of black and white textured like the face of a planet. There was no point. He didn't have the film or the light or the lens. He could cheat with the Nikon, but it would look mushy, and setting up would take forever. In back, the girls were laughing, and he shelved the thought before it could bother him, set it beside the list. Lise was right; he needed to take a break. He needed more than the Holga. He needed a whole new way of seeing. That wasn't going to happen in a week.

Morgan was always talking about things being organic, coming from the subject rather than being forced on it. Maybe he'd try to find that feeling he'd had at the Gas-n-Go. There was always the garage.

Sam was still entranced by his Game Boy when they pulled up. His mother hadn't taken the garbage can in. Arlene's car was tucked under the chestnut, but Meg's was gone. There were another two hours before dinner. He took the spot closest to the back door.

"Be careful getting out because the grass is going to be slippery," he announced, then waited to make sure their doors were closed.

They piled inside the house, leaving him alone with the rain and the empty gray lake. A branch from the Wisemans' oak lay across the dock, its leaves riffling in the wind. Suddenly he was tired, having delivered them, his mind fending off all thoughts, as if, now that the drive was over, he was shutting down. He wanted to lie on the couch, nothing else. He dragged the branch off the dock and left it in the grass.

Inside, the kids were explaining the movies to his mother and Arlene, Rufus wagging his tail and nosing between their legs, begging for attention. He hung up his windbreaker and set the keys in a nut dish on the mantel—right beside an old Acushnet his father had put a smile in, who knew how long ago. The ball's dimples were overlaid with crazing as if it were porcelain. In the bottom of the dish was a steel ball mark, the three cloverlike rings of Ballantine ale. Purity, Body, Flavor. He could see it cupped in his father's large palm along with his keys and tees and change, could see his father set it down and stand back so Ken could read the green. "Take your time," his father counseled, and Ken double-checked, made sure of the break. On those long, walking mornings, the two of them said little. His father had wanted to teach him patience. Ken wasn't sure he'd learned. He pinched the ball mark up and slipped it in his pocket, pretending to inspect the logs on the hearth. It wasn't all pretending. Maybe he would build a fire later—another thing his father had taught him.

His mother was asking the kids if they'd had fun. They crowded around her like a queen. "And did you all thank your Uncle Ken for taking you to the movies?"

"Thank you, Uncle Ken!" they hollered, Sam pawing him obnoxiously, and he wished he had a picture of it.

"You're quite welcome," he said.

11

In the Wal-Mart Meg came upon her own future.

She and Lise had split the list. Lise had gone off to look for more Kool-Aid Koolers. Meg was trolling the automotive and hardware departments, searching for outboard oil, when a woman in a bright two-tone uniform popped out from around a corner and asked if she needed any help.

The first thing she noticed was the woman's skin, rucked and papery around her mouth, nearly pleated. She wasn't old. Her long, dark hair was full and real, maybe the gray touched up a little. She was Meg's age, but gaunt and drawn, her face dried and shriveled, seams deep as scars, that hollowed-out shell of the recovering alcoholic Meg had seen again and again in rehab, two- and three-time losers come back for another try at sobriety, worn down from the struggle. The booze weight came off, leaving just the weathered skin, stringy as beef jerky. Her eyes were watery and too large.

"I'm looking for motor-engine oil," Meg said. "I mean, outboard engine. For a boat."

It didn't seem to register, but then a flare of recognition lit the woman's face, as if her synapses needed the extra second to catch up.

"That is gonna be . . . right . . ." She raised one finger and led the way to the next aisle, Meg reluctantly following—like Scrooge, she thought, but this spirit was already showing her what lay in store for her. She would eat up her savings to make the house payments, and without a degree this was the kind of job she'd end up getting.

"Here!" the woman said cheerfully. "Anything else I can help you with today?"

"No thank you," Meg said, and then lingered there, fingering the plastic bottles as if choosing between brands. They only needed enough for the week.

She beat Lise to the checkout and paid, then stood by the gumball machines waiting, sure she'd see the woman again.

She didn't. Lise returned with a flat of blue Koolers and they escaped.

"It must be the water around here," Lise said in the car. "Every time I go into that place there are more weird-looking people."

"I know," Meg said.

But the first thing she did when they got back was to go upstairs and close the bathroom door, turn on the light and lean over the sink and look at herself in the mirror.

12

Sam didn't like the downstairs bathroom because too many people could hear you. He went upstairs, but Aunt Margaret was in there, and then while he was waiting for her, he noticed Sarah's watch on the dresser. He moved away from it in case Aunt Margaret would think he wanted it. Their car was right under the windows. He could jump on it to escape and not break his legs.

He didn't say anything when Aunt Margaret came out, went invisible standing by the curtains. She saw him and stepped back, a hand on her heart.

"Jesus," she said, "don't scare me like that. Next time say something, okay?"

The bathroom smelled and the toilet was warm, and he thought that he was sitting right where she was. It made him feel strange, like he'd seen her naked.

When he was done he flushed and put the lid down like his mother said to. He came out and looked around the room to make sure no one was hiding on him. He went to the dresser and picked up the watch, followed the stuttering orbit of its second hand. He cupped it against his ear, listened to it tick. He liked how small it was, how alive. Sarah didn't even wear it. He hung it from his belt loop to see what it would look like. Downstairs, someone passed the door, and he put the watch back down on the dresser where he found it and turned away.

No one came up. He stood in front of the dresser with his arms behind his back, looking down at the watch, the second hand clicking between the numbers. He watched it go around exactly a minute, then went downstairs.

13

At five the dip came out and the children attacked, dropping chips for Rufus, who was too stiff to ferret them from under the chairs. The boys ducked down and swept them free, and Rufus licked the floor until Emily told him to stop. Arlene stayed out of the way, tucked into one corner of the glider with her gin and tonic, the wind nipping through her sweater. Rain beaded the screens, tiny bright windows. The flags on the docks were soaked. The storm showed no sign of letting up, or letting go its grip on their conversation.

The front wasn't supposed to move until Wednesday, which was fine with Arlene. She'd spent a delicious afternoon with her book, at one point drifting off under the afghan, and now the clamor of the children seemed an imposition. She could retreat to her room, but that would be antisocial, and she felt she'd already segregated herself enough. She hoped it wasn't noticeable.

She genuinely liked spending time with her grandnieces and -nephews. In a way they were a substitute for her students, an echo of or link to her life's work. But there were certain things about that world she didn't miss, and noisy boys were one of them. Girls, in her experience, weren't a problem. She couldn't help but see the children through professional eyes, and she worried that it distanced her from them. When Margaret and Kenneth were little, they'd all lived in Pittsburgh and saw one another weekly, so they were familiar. This was different. At most they saw one another one week of the summer and one major holiday. Arlene sent them birthday cards and bought them savings bonds, but occasionally she realized that she knew little about them personally. For their part, they seemed wary of her, if not mistrustful. It was Emily's attention they wanted, Emily they asked to play Monopoly. She supposed it was the lot of an aunt, a great-aunt, but couldn't help feeling slighted, her simplest feelings hurt.

"Did I tell you about my toad?" Emily asked the porch at large. "Well," she said, and launched into the story.

She told it as if she'd discovered gold by the road. The boys wanted to catch the toad. They went out in the rain and looked at the edge of the grass, came back and spilled more chips.

"That's enough," Lisa decreed, and Sam took a last handful.

Without the chips, the porch suddenly lost its attraction, and the children disappeared inside, Kenneth letting them get by before emerging with a beer. Arlene wanted another gin and tonic but thought she shouldn't with Margaret sitting there.

"Now that we're all here," Emily said, as if calling them to order, "I'd like to canvass everyone and see how we're doing with our lists."

No one volunteered. Arlene hadn't had time to do hers but could ad-lib in a pinch. She'd never pressed her Maxwell claims on the cottage, knowing they wouldn't be honored, and now she felt even more of an outsider, included only out of propriety. Like Emily, she waited for Kenneth or Margaret to start.

Kenneth turned to Margaret as if looking for permission. Margaret nodded for him to take the floor.

Finally he said, "If we're supposed to put them in order, our first choice would be the cedar chest."

That was that, Arlene thought.

"That's fine," Emily said, "but I really need you to write your choices down. I don't want this to turn into a group discussion. Do you think you can have that for me sometime tonight?"

"I haven't gotten around to mine either," Margaret said.

"Does everyone need a little more time?" When none of them answered, Emily said, "Please, by bedtime. I'd like to take care of this."

Released, Arlene went into the kitchen and poured herself another drink. She took the last Lucky from the pack on the windowsill. The chestnut was dripping, so she tucked herself into a corner of the garage door, under the gutter, and lit up. It was freezing for August. The downspout gurgled, water bubbling out onto the lawn.

She imagined what her mother would have thought of her daughter-in-law breaking up the cottage. It wasn't that the furniture was so carefully chosen that it would be a shame to separate it, but that each piece had been salvaged from other houses sold long ago and carried the air of a place well remembered and of people dearly missed. Opening the cedar chest, Arlene would see it as it had been, butted up against the foot of the bed in her grandmother McElheny's guest room, redolent of her grandfather's army blanket from World War I. The room with its iron bed and gilded cross on the wall would lead her into the upstairs hall, past the mirror that surprised her at night and to the top of the stairs. Below, the rest of the house awaited her, every room decorated the way it had been when she was seven. In the backyard, through their grandmother's sunny kitchen, Henry might be throwing a ball to himself or sitting in the cherry tree, whittling a stick. Kenneth couldn't remember that, and certainly not Ella.

They would remember this place, she thought—and her, or so she hoped.

Of her great-aunt Martha she could recall her solid frame and dark dresses, a clasp purse with a gold chain, her feet wedged into tiny shoes so that when she came home from church she pulled them off in the living room and kneaded her toes. One Christmas she backed into a table and knocked the eggnog over, Henry saving their mother's punch bowl, a sweet flood covering his good shoes. Martha had laughed as she apologized for the size of her behind, and no one held the accident against her. When

Arlene thought of her, she saw a good-natured, down-to-earth lady in middle age with a winning sense of humor. She'd take that if it were offered.

The lime in her gin and tonic was bitter, not quite ripe, a guillo-tined seed floating among the ice. She considered having another but vetoed the idea as unwise. She peeked around the corner of the garage to see if the rabbits were feeding, and a fat drop splashed off her nose. When she leaned back, Margaret was coming out to join her.

That was one thing: they'd always smoked together. It wasn't much of a legacy, she supposed. She'd tried to support Margaret, aware that at times it was a losing cause. She knew the weight of disapproval, the pain of plans that unraveled. Everyone had wanted more for her. At first she resented their presumption, then tried to impress them by excelling, and, when her teaching awards didn't move them, finally learned to accept the fact that in their eyes she would never be a success. She wished there was somewhere to put her drink down. Instead she took a hit of her cigarette to cover her breath.

"So," Margaret said, "what's on your list?"

"Not much. The cedar chest."

"That makes three of us. I guess Ken gets it then."

"You don't know that," she said.

"You know it and I know it. What else do you have?"

For a moment Arlene hesitated, as if Margaret would steal this information. There was nothing she really wanted. Emily had claimed the gateleg table. Her mind swooped through the cottage, taking in the furni-ture, ricocheting off the walls. Nothing in the living room, nothing upstairs. The lamps were horrors; only patterned fabric dated faster than lamp shades. Her dresser, perhaps.

"I think you're all right on that one," Margaret said.

"I don't know why I'm included in this. In ten years you'll just have to do it again."

"Don't say that."

"It's true."

"Hell," Margaret said, "I don't know where I'm going to be in two years, let alone ten."

Ambushed, Arlene could only nod at the confession. Months ago, in the breathless humidity of Phipps Conservatory, stopped before a gaudy offering of orchids, Emily had speculated grimly on the odds of Margaret and Jeff reconciling. Arlene disagreed. Now Margaret proved her wrong beyond a doubt, and yet she felt relieved and oddly gratified that she'd told her personally.

"I'm sorry," Arlene said.

"It's best." Margaret crushed her cigarette underfoot. "Anyway, it's not like I have a choice."

Arlene wanted another cigarette, wanted to stay and talk, but they were done. The rain drummed the garage. They hustled across the spongy grass to the kitchen door. Inside, Lisa was shaping hamburgers and arranging them on a plate. Margaret asked if she needed help, and Lisa put her in charge of the children's french fries. Arlene saw there wasn't room for her and kept moving, into the living room where the boys were watching cartoons. Through the window, she could see Emily and Kenneth on the porch, Emily holding forth on something.

On her way past the set she turned it down, but when she closed the door to her room she could still hear it. The room was too cramped for a chair, so she sat down on the bed and looked at her hands, limp in her lap. She turned them over and examined the backs, the veins woven through the delicate bones, as if they were alien, not a part of her.

In all the world, the people in this house were the only people she had left. In a week she'd be back in her apartment, surrounded by memories, the sun climbing the wall above the couch as the day waned, painting it pink before gray filled the corners. They would not be back here next year. It made sense that she should choose something to remember it by. Ten years could be a long time. She sat there with the cartoons going in the other room and thought about what she wanted.

14

Sarah had to get out of the house, just bounce, go, get away from every-one—her mother mostly, telling her she needed to help and then yelling at her when she said there was nothing left to do (she'd checked, Uncle Ken said so).

"There's lots you can do. You can pour milk for everybody. We need napkins and silverware, and I don't see any ketchup or mustard on the table. You can ask whoever's on the porch if anyone's interested in having onions on their hot dogs."

"I am," Aunt Lisa chipped in from the sink, her accomplice.

"There," her mother said, "you can chop an onion and put it in a dish for everyone. After you're done with that, ask me and I'll give you another job. Don't ever think there's nothing to do."

"Where's a knife?"

"Where do you think one is, Sarah? In the drawer with all the other knives, right where they always are. Look, if you're going to be like that, then just go. That's not being helpful."

"I *am,* Mom."

"That's not how it sounds to me." She pulled the drawer out with a clank, and then when Sarah had found a knife, closed it for her. "Use the cutting board on the dishwasher, it's clean. You remember how to cut an onion."

"Yes."

In half, so you had a flat side that didn't roll around, then half of that if it was too big for your knife. You cut it longways first, making rain-bows, and then when you cut it the other way the inside pieces came out already chopped.

"Do you want to use the sink?" Aunt Lisa asked.

"That's okay."

She'd cry anyway; the purple were the worst. She was careful peeling it and didn't break the skin. She leaned back as she made the first crisp cut—crooked, but her mother wasn't looking. It was a big one, so she quartered it. To do the slices right she had to see. She held them together, her fingers stiff, the blade crunching, then hitting wood. White juice slicked the cutting board, and the hot scent made her turn her face away. A familiar sharpness tickled her nose, pinched her sinuses until the air seemed to leave them. She sucked a cool breath through her mouth, but it was too late, her eyes were burning, filling, tears catching in the lashes, breaking free and wetting her cheeks. She squeezed her eyes shut and breathed. It did nothing.

She could barely see to cube the rest of it, but that was the only way—fast. Sniffling, she drew the blade through the four quarters, all thought of neatness forgotten, blinking to keep from cutting herself. Why did her mother have to be so mean? It had nothing to do with her. Her whole life Sarah had watched her go off on people, and still she didn't understand it. Her only defense was that she'd done nothing wrong, but she'd grown tired of being yelled at, and at some point (she couldn't remember when) had begun to hate her, so in truth she wasn't innocent. Now, instead of coolly appealing to her own blamelessness, she felt a hot combination of shame and anger, a stinging helplessness. The feeling would pass as quickly as these tears, but unlike them, it was real.

She finished sloppily, hacking at the last pieces where they fell. She scraped it all into a bowl and set it on the table, washed her hands and dried her eyes with a paper towel. They burned as if she'd been swimming.

"Thank you," her mother said, as if things were square between them.

"What else?" Sarah asked.

"Silverware."

She counted out nine sets, spoons included, whether they needed them or not, and grabbed a stack of paper napkins. Salt and pepper shakers, mayonnaise, ketchup, mustard, brown mustard, relish, hamburger relish, three different kinds of pickles.

"Why don't you tear up some lettuce," her mother said, and when she was done with that, said that people might like tomato. "You'll need a sharper knife for that."

I know that.

Sarah had patience. She would outlast her. She couldn't go anywhere in the rain anyway. She thought of writing Mark a letter, but he still owed her one. The tomato fell in see-through wheels. She washed the seeds off the board, scrubbed it with a sponge.

The burgers were almost ready when the smoke alarm went off, peeping from the ceiling. Aunt Lisa used a broom to knock it down, then pulled the battery out.

Sarah poured the milk without being told. Were any of the adults going to have milk?

"I'm not," her mother said.

She had to go out onto the porch to ask. None of them were.

"What else can I do?" Sarah asked as sweetly as she could.

Her mother looked her work over. "We'll need serving spoons for the coleslaw and the potato salad, otherwise I think we're set."

It couldn't be easy. There were no big spoons in the drawer. She had to get them from the dishwasher. While she was reaching in, her mother said, "Rufus needs to be fed."

It's Justin's job, she wanted to say, but didn't. That would be cheating. This was just between the two of them.

15

In the middle of dinner, Rufus threw up. He'd been sniffing the children's plates, padding across the porch floor whenever anything fell. Emily had just told him to stop begging when he paused beside Kenneth's rocker and coughed, stretched his neck and hung his head like a horse, then silently upchucked a yellow pile.

"Ewww!" the boys accused, pointing.

"Take him outside," Arlene ordered, and Kenneth jumped up, plate in hand, and got him by the collar.

"Bad dog!" Sam scolded.

"He's all right," Emily said, "he is not a bad dog," because she knew what the problem was. He wasn't used to people food, and the children had been feeding him chips all afternoon. She could see undigested pellets of his dry food in the pile.

Kenneth put him out, and Rufus stood at the door looking in at them.

"It's all right," Emily comforted him, and left her plate. "I will take care of it," she told Kenneth. "You sit and eat your dinner."

Arlene stood.

"I've got it," Emily insisted.

"I'm not eating out here now," Arlene said, as if there was no question.

"Oh please," Emily said, but when she came out with the paper towels, everyone had fled to the living room. Rufus stood at the door, watching her sop up the mess.

"Really," Emily said. "You'd think it was toxic."

She swabbed the boards and deposited the ball in the trash, washed her hands and returned to her seat.

"Feeling better?" she asked Rufus. "I imagine so."

She opened the door for him. He eyed her guiltily, then sniffed the spot she'd cleaned until she told him to lie down.

She had just started on her coleslaw when Ella came out with her plate, and Sarah. They sat down and ate as if nothing had happened.

"Two hardy souls," she remarked.

"It's just barf," Ella said.

"They're being weenies," Sarah agreed.

Emily expected Kenneth and the boys too but someone had turned on the TV. It didn't bother her, and honestly it wouldn't have bothered her to sit out here alone to show her loyalty to Rufus and make a stand for levelheadedness. That Ella and Sarah had come to her rescue was an extra pleasure. She was happy to have such brave allies.

16

Emily could be such a pill sometimes. Arlene knew that people expected it of herself, the crabby old schoolmistress, but every teacher she'd worked with had had a sense of humor. Secret ballots! Arlene was tempted to give her a blank sheet but knew she'd be offended. Henry would have found the whole process ridiculous, would have found a way to be absent when Emily announced the lucky winners.

She still had not come up with anything. She was getting the TV, not that she needed it. The dresser, maybe, but that was somehow unsatisfying. She felt dull from being inside all day, housebound, the stale air drugging her. The rain, so comforting at home, here cast a hazy purposelessness over the day. It did feel like a Monday, the sense of having gotten nothing done, the promise of a long way to go yet.

She tried to read but the TV interrupted her progress, the live dialogue trumping her printed words, hauling her in against her will like a sideshow barker. The living room was full, everyone in sweaters. The cold and dark had driven them inside, and to keep the children entertained they had compromised and chosen a perennial favorite, *The Third Man*. It had become a rainy-day staple, a puzzle of sorts for the children, pointing out the now obvious devices they knew from cartoons. Through the years Arlene had seen it at least ten times, the monotonous zither music part of Chautauqua. The boys were on the floor, absorbed. The actors had to contend with the dishwasher, barreling away in the kitchen. Kenneth was laying a fire, stuffing crumpled newspapers under the grate, the folding screen set aside. Later, for a treat, they would roast marshmallows and make s'mores. She sat in one corner of the couch, Lisa successfully reading beside her, and then Margaret—three monkeys. Emily had pulled a kitchen chair up to the gateleg table and fussed over a puzzle of Buckingham Palace, a lamp pulled close so she could see.

Joseph Cotten was running down a wet alley in Vienna when the lights died. "Hey!" the boys hollered at once, and Lisa shushed them. The TV blinked off, the dishwasher stopped with a dripping. Arlene looked up from her page at the blackness.

"The power's out," Sarah observed, invisible.

"It's not raining that hard," Margaret argued.

"Good old Niagara Mohawk," Emily said.

A match flared in Kenneth's hand. The disembodied sleeves of his sweater appeared, then his face. He touched the flame to the newspaper and the room warmed.

"Nice timing," Lisa said.

None of them moved, as if paralyzed by the lack of light. Arlene was still holding her book open as if she might keep reading. Rufus looked up from his spot on the floor, confused.

In seconds the fire leapt up, the flames reaching into the flue.

"Well," Emily said, "isn't this cozy?"

Outside, a bright light popped on. "Intruder alert," the robotic voice warned, "intruder alert."

"Not again," Arlene said. "Is it going to be like this every night?"

"Call the police," Emily instructed Kenneth, already on his way to the phone.

They were all quiet while he spoke to someone, listened in on his end of the conversation. "Yes, for the second night in a row."

"Intruder alert, intruder alert." The chirping in between seemed louder because there was no other sound. Arlene hoped people up and down the road were bombarding the police with calls. At home, she had to deal with car alarms going off in the parking lot behind her building. She shouldn't have to put up with it here.

Kenneth hung up. "They're going to send someone over."

"You don't sound hopeful," Emily said.

"All they're going to do is look around. It'll go off by the time they get here, but there's no way they can disarm the system, only the security people can do that."

"I think I'll be giving the Lerners a call tomorrow."

"Intruder alert, intruder alert . . ."

Margaret got up and made her way to the kitchen, as if she could escape the racket. The boys theatrically stuck their fingers in their ears. The fire had settled, and Kenneth replaced the screen, throwing a floating net of shadows across the walls.

"Let's sing," he suggested, projecting over the noise. "Ella, how does that *Titanic* song start?"

Ella pleaded ignorance.

"You know. 'Oh, they built the ship *Titanic* to sail the ocean blue, and they said it was a ship that the' . . . something could never go through."

Both boys popped up on their knees and raised their hands, as if in class. It was a camp song, they all knew it. Ella was just being shy. Arlene and Henry had sung it sixty years ago around a fire taller than their father, sparks sailing into the night sky.

"It's 'waves,'" Justin said.

"Ohhhhhhh, theyyyyy," Kenneth wound up and nodded the rest of them in, clapping:

> *built the ship* Titanic *to sail the ocean blue*
> *and they said it was a ship that the waves could never go through*
> *but the Lord's almighty hand*
> *said the ship would never land*
> *It was sa-ad when the grea-eat ship went down*
> *All together!*
> *It was sad*
> *It was sad*
> *It was sad when the gre-eat ship went down*
> *to the bottom of the se-ee-ee-ea*
> *It was sad when the great ship went down*

The verses were harder to remember, but Arlene recalled lines and images as if from a favorite movie: "Mrs. Astor turned around / just to see her husband drown," and the one the boys shouted loud, "Uncles and aunts / Little children lost their pants / It was sad when the great ship went down." Margaret sang from the doorway, Emily from her chair. Lisa knew the song from the children. They laughed as they stumbled through the endless middle. Kenneth had cleverly chosen the longest song they knew, and before the final verse ("Oh the moral of the story / as you can plainly see"), the alarm outside stopped. They sang even louder, spurred by their success, and gave themselves a hand when they were done, the girls persisting with a coda Arlene had never heard before:

> *Too bad*
> *So sad*
> *It sank*
> *The end*
> *Amen*
> *Go to bed*
> *Wake up dead*
> *With a hole in your head.*

"Very nice," Emily said. "I take it that's new."

"Not that new," Margaret informed her.

Outside, the only sound was the gutters dripping. The fire whistled and cracked.

"What shall we sing next?" Emily asked.

"Lion hunt!" Justin cried.

"There were three jolly fishermen!" Sam begged.

Ella wanted "The Lord Said to Noah," which Sarah immediately seconded.

Kenneth stood by the fire, deciding, then started: "In a cabin in the woods."

"Little old man by the window stood," they all followed. "Saw a rabbit hopping by, knocking at his door."

The gestures, the rhythms—Arlene was surprised how completely she knew them after all these years, how familiar and soothing the firelight was, something she hadn't known she'd missed. Peeking at the glowing faces around her, knowing how much Henry would have loved this, she felt she was one of them, part of them. The list, the TV, the dresser—she realized now why it had seemed so ridiculous. This was all she wanted.

17

"Be careful on the stairs there," Emily warned the children. "And you'll take care of the fire?" she asked Ken—needlessly, Lise thought.

She knew it was unfair, bristling at everything Emily said, and that the strength and, even more, the tenacity of her disdain baffled Ken, as if, lacking immediate provocation, she should be civil with Emily. He was like her father, she thought, wanting things to be pleasant, withdrawing into his den at the slightest hint of a disturbance between Lise and her mother, then poking his head out later to see if the storm had passed.

The kids thumped above them, the bathroom door shutting, water running. Ken had moved to the couch to watch the fire with her. They held hands, Arlene quiet in the far corner like a chaperone. Meg toasted a last marshmallow. Outside, the rain fell steadily, endlessly, making Lise think of tomorrow, new excuses to go out, errands that needed to be run. The Book Barn, but she still had Harry Potter, and with the power out she wasn't getting any of that read.

When the lights went out, she thought they'd pop back on—if not instantly then within a few minutes, however long it took Niagara Mohawk to realize something had gone wrong. After the first half hour she imagined a falling tree limb clawing down live wires, or a bad car accident toppling a pole, sparks on the road and broken glass. Now she resigned herself to the darkness, gave in to the strangeness of the event. The blackout had actually saved the evening. It was early, before ten, yet it felt like midnight. Upstairs the water had stopped, and they could hear the logs sizzling and the juicy rumble of Rufus's stomach.

"I think I'll put him out," Meg said.

"Good idea." Ken patted Lise's hand, then let go. "I'll check on the kids."

He left her alone with Arlene, wrapped in shadows at the other end of the couch. Lise thought the silence between them was growing uncomfortable when she realized the breathy whistle she was hearing was Arlene sleeping. She leaned over and verified it and had to catch a laugh.

She pointed her out to Ken when he came down.

"Arlene," he said, "go to bed," as if talking to a child, and helped her up and through the door to her room.

"Where's Meg?" he asked when he came back.

"Probably having a cigarette." Her worry was that he wanted to talk with Meg, have one of their long heart-to-hearts by the fire. She patted the couch and he sat down and took her hand again, rubbed it with a thumb.

"Last night was nice," she said.

"It's a little cold out tonight."

"Too cold?" she teased.

"Too wet."

"There's always the car."

He laughed as if this was ridiculous, and shifted, leaning into her. "This is nice right here."

"It's not very private."

"Meg might be persuaded to leave us in peace."

"I don't want you to have to ask her."

"I'm sure she wouldn't mind."

"I would," Lise said. "I'd be embarrassed."

He said nothing to this, which was his way of saying he disagreed— as if, given the time and silence to contemplate what she'd said, she'd see how foolish it sounded. He wasn't really interested, or only in being right. He'd turned what should have been romantic into a question of logistics, possibilities, what was and wasn't convenient.

"Forget it," she said. "This is fine."

"Obviously it isn't," he said, and didn't he sound exactly like his mother now.

They were fighting, but he held on to her hand. He would make her pull away, make her the villain in this, as if he'd done nothing wrong. Why did everything between them have to be her fault, she wondered, and was about to ask him outright when Meg came back in with Rufus and sat down by the fire.

"I can smell him from here," Ken said across the room, taking the easiest way out.

"It's pouring," Meg said.

Lise took her hand back. "I'm going to go up," she said, and stood, and he gave her a look that said she was being unreasonable. She decided not to give him any more proof. "I'll see you up there," she said, and left him and Meg to each other.

On the stairs, she clenched her teeth, biting back an imaginary conversation. It was the first time they'd really talked all day.

18

"So," Ken said, sitting down beside her, "how's it going? I haven't seen much of you."

"All right," Meg said, but subdued, as if tired. The flames smoothed the lines around her eyes, and he could see her as the teenager he knew, the tough girl. Though he'd never told her, he'd taken pride in having a wild sister, her parade of boyfriends in hopped-up cars giving him a kind of secondhand cool. She'd seemed indestructible then.

"Did you do your list?" he joked, and she laughed for him.

"She never changes."

"You don't think so?"

"A little, with Dad," she allowed. "She calls more often. I'm sure she's lonely all by herself."

"How are you?"

"All by myself? Going a little crazy. I was telling Lise, all I can think of is the money, but it's everything. You're married fifteen years and then—boom. On top of all the other shit."

"How's that?"

"Good," she said, but accompanied it by a dip and a twist of her head, as if working out a kink in her neck.

"I can't stop worrying about money either. You'd think by now we'd be doing all right."

"Lise's folks can help you out."

"That's what I'm worried about."

"You should be glad," she said, and then, as if closing the subject, "It's just money."

He and Lise had savings bonds for the kids, and two mutual funds for their college, and though Lise would never let him touch them, he wondered if five thousand might help. She ran her hand over Rufus's coat.

"Hey," she said, "remember the time we stole the Smiths' canoe?"

"You stole the canoe, I was just along for the ride."

"And the light came on and Jimmy Smith came running down their dock, and you dropped your paddle?"

There was the time she ran over the lawn chair with her Jeep. The time Arlene broke the tire swing. The time Duchess jumped through the screen door. He relaxed into the rhythm of their shared memories, glad not to talk about where their lives were headed. It reminded him of how they used to talk at night up here, her voice reaching him from the other bed until their mother climbed the stairs and said it was time to go to sleep. Tonight was just another installment of that ongoing, lifelong conversation.

"It's weird," she said, "to think this is it. Last year I thought we shouldn't be here—"

"It's what he wanted."

"It's what *she* wanted. It was terrible. All I could think of the whole time was him in that hospital. She just didn't want us there because it would have been harder on her. Well, tough. This year I'm thinking, Where are we going to go next year? I'm not going to be able to afford anywhere nice. I don't understand why she thinks she has to sell it."

"She wouldn't come up by herself."

"She's not going to be by herself. Arlene will be with her. Arlene loves it up here."

She was getting loud, and Ken glanced at his mother's door. "She needs the money."

"How much money does she need? Do you know how much she got for it?"

"She was asking three-twenty-five."

"She probably got at least three hundred. What does she need with that kind of money?"

Though she'd justified herself countless times over the phone, his mother had never told him precisely why, only that he and Meg weren't in any position to take it over and she had no business dumping it on them. The taxes alone would kill them. He'd believed her, just as, now, he believed Meg.

"Have you talked to her?" he asked.

"You think she'd listen to me? She thinks I'm not smart enough to deal with something as important as real estate. And you know who made all their investments—Dad. He made all their money, and now she's the big financial genius. It drives me nuts. Until last year I handled all of our money, and did quite well with it."

"'And did quite well with it,'" he mimicked.

"I know—I'm starting to talk like her. I hear myself saying something to Sarah and think, Oh shit."

"It's like a horror movie, you're turning into her."

"Then why does she still hate my ass?"

"She doesn't hate you."

"Just what I stand for, whatever that is. Anyway, it sucks." She looked around her on the floor for her cigarettes and surprised him by standing up. In the old days she would have just lit one here, tossed the butt in the fire. "Come on," she said, and led him through the kitchen and outside into the rain and then into the garage, damp and smelling dangerously of gasoline.

"We shouldn't leave the fire."

"You still get high?" she asked, and packed a pipe.

"Are you allowed to do that?"

"It's medicinal," she said, and handed it to him.

He knew the etiquette from high school, from attics and basements and cars, concerts like milestones, and then college, apartments with mended, mismatched furniture, TVs you turned on with vise grips. Flick the wheel, tip the lighter and the flame bends, sectioned like candy corn. Breathe in the burning flower, leaves vaporized like a jungle under napalm, the brain a map of lost colonies. One hit and he was back there, this weird minute of the future a vision, his sister an old ghost come to warn him of something.

"It's been a long time," he said, and passed it back.

The dark rear of the garage was built of lines and angles he hadn't noticed before. He thought of Tracy Ann Caler, and how little room it took to hide a body, and was surprised to find himself thinking like a murderer.

He coughed and couldn't stop, as if he were allergic.

Meg popped the fridge and handed him a beer. It was cool in his palm, the foil label scratchy. He twisted the top off and it left a hot spot on his skin. She gave him the pipe again and he realized he'd only had one hit. It seemed he'd been high for hours.

"What is this shit?"

"It's supposed to be Thai. Guy in AA hooked me up with it."

"It's pretty good."

"It works."

"How do you do it?" he asked—before he could take it back. He'd never asked her before, and now to do it so offhand seemed wrong, as if he were trespassing.

"Not drinking? By not drinking. It's not like there's a patch."

"It must be hard."

"It's not like it's my whole life. I do other things too."

"Sorry," he said.

"I'm sorry, I'm just sick of talking about it. It's not you personally, though it's kind of tough with that beer there."

"You gave it to me," he protested.

"That's what I get for being nice."

He took a swig and the bubbles spread across his tongue and fizzed, a wheat field of white balloons, water rising over a thatched welcome mat, dropping in the walled lock of a canal.

"I bet you're sick of talking about Jeff too." It came out like a thought, uncensored.

"He was a shit. He was sleeping with this little bimbo at work even before I went into rehab. It's all a big soap opera."

"I'm sorry," he said, and stepped on her foot as he went to hold her.

"Thank you, and ow. Yeah, a little blonde with boobs. There's nothing more humiliating than being dumped for a cliché. Of course the kids don't know. They think it's all my fault."

"I'm sure they don't."

"Believe me, they do. Dad's the fun one, Mom's the bitch. That's how it works."

He thought of himself and Lise, and his mother and father, and couldn't deny it.

"That's all right," she said, but then didn't explain why. "Let's go see how your fire's doing."

Later she told him, laughing, that she had come to the conclusion that she was too chicken to kill herself long before she ever met Jeff. And later still, sobered, deciding a final time to go to bed, she said she'd been through times like this before and lived. She waved everything off as if it were an unpleasant smell, nothing serious.

He hugged her and sent her upstairs, then banked the fire alone, breaking apart the brittle, glowing logs with the poker, unsure why he'd doubted her power. She was used to trouble, was attracted to it the same way he chased after success. She was just better at getting what she wanted. But this didn't relieve him of the feeling that he had somehow let her down, had not been a good brother to her.

It was late, and his eyes felt bathed in vinegar, dusted with salt. The light of the fire didn't reach the stairs. He walked like Frankenstein in the dark, his arms out to fend off the invisible, and then when he found the door, he had to crawl up, his hands feeling each carpeted step ahead of him.

The kids were asleep, the watery reflection of a flashlight coming from the cracked bathroom door. Ella was curled tight, Sam flat on his back. He tucked the flap of Justin's bag over the stuffed Tigger in his arms.

He couldn't see Lise, just a shape under the covers, a shadow on the pillow. It was past two, and he didn't want her to know how late they'd talked. By the foot of their bed, he slowly emptied his pockets, placing each item quietly on the low wardrobe's hard top, a thief in reverse. Among the clinking change was the Ballantine ball mark, its thin edge a dull razor. He could barely see the three intertwined circles in the dark, but the cosmic thought came to him that they were like the three of them, Meg and himself and his mother, joined forever.

His father was separate from them, lost.

Only for now, he thought, and then was afraid he was just trying to comfort himself. He would live the rest of his life without him. Thirty, forty years. There would be days, weeks, when he wouldn't think of him, not even fleetingly, and this seemed wrong.

Meg wasn't done in the bathroom, so he stood there waiting in the dark, the mirror giving back his shirt, his arms at his sides. The roof tapped, and he hoped it wouldn't rain tomorrow. He wanted to shoot the Putt-Putt, and the Gas-n-Go, its short aisles lit by jittery fluorescents. He could use the Nikon, that wouldn't be cheating.

The door opened, letting out a dim wedge of light that fell over the children.

"All yours," Meg said. "I left you the flashlight."

"Thanks," he said.

He was quick, trying not to run the water too much, sitting down so he could pee quietly. When he came out, Meg was already in bed. He turned the light off and set it on the cedar chest, stripped to his boxers and got in, the sheets producing goose bumps, a rush across his front. He needed to warm up before he pressed against Lise, and lay there rigid as a mummy, eyes shut.

He thought of his father lying like this in Homewood Cemetery under the ground and the stones and the dark, starred sky. He thought of Tracy Ann Caler's family, awake, waiting, any second, for the phone to ring. He wondered if there was a way he could help search for her.

"Sweet dreams," Meg said from the dark, as she had when they were kids.

Then, it had been offered literally, an invitation to another, better world at the end of the day. Now it seemed just an affectionate habit that had stuck, little protection against the lives that went on inside of them, real or imagined. And yet, then and now, he thought, she was the one who wished it first, for him, and truly meant it. His sister.

"Sweet dreams," he said.

19

What she had done to earn this was a mystery. Ella didn't recognize anyone at the party, or the room she was in, the long powder-blue couch, and she seemed to be drinking champagne, her hair frosted blond, stiff bangs hanging in her eyes. Her teeth were perfect, her braces gone. Laughter, music, a brick wall and a window behind her and the guy in the black suit with red socks talking. There were so many people dancing she couldn't hear what anyone was saying, and then Sarah was there, sitting down right beside her, so close she could see the sparkle eye shadow they'd tried the other day, and Ella wanted to say, Let's get out of here, this is crazy, wanted to stop

Sarah because she could feel Sarah was going to lean in and kiss her, wanted to kiss her, had wanted to kiss her for so long, and now it was almost happening and Ella didn't know what to do. It would happen, it had to, she just had to wait for it. It didn't make sense, she couldn't figure out why Sarah was in love with her, but she was happy anyway. It was exciting, and frightening. Here it was, Sarah was leaning in, her face inches from hers, her eyes closing, her eye shadow bright. Ella knew she would let Sarah kiss her—had known all along, couldn't stop—and then anything could happen.

20

Emily woke to Rufus yipping, voices and a red light flashing in the folds of the curtains. Her first reaction was that the police were outside taking care of the Lerners' alarm. It took her a confused minute to realize it was the clock on her bureau blinking, telling her urgently, again and again, that it was exactly midnight. Beyond the wall, the dishwasher surged.

"Oh for God's sake," she said, and kicked free of the covers and took her bathrobe down from the hook. She didn't know what time to reset the clock for, guessed three A.M. and turned it to the wall, then hit herself with the door as she opened it.

"Honestly now."

Rufus trotted along beside her. The TV was on in the middle of *The Third Man,* someone walking up a dark staircase. She clicked it and the VCR off, and the lights by the couch and in the kitchen. The outside light was fine. The dishwasher she let run.

"All right," she said, and closed her door and hung up her robe and climbed back under the warm covers. In the corner Rufus circled his spot before folding himself down. He sighed once, disgruntled, and then the night was quiet again.

Tuesday

1

The rain had not abated. The radio said the front had stalled over the Great Lakes; they could expect the same for the next forty-eight hours.

"Well I'm not staying here all day," Emily said over her eggs.

It was a bold statement, Arlene thought, seeing as she didn't have a car. To her, the idea of hunkering down until the storm blew over was appealing, a chair pulled close to the fire, and hot chocolate, but it was too early to get into it with Emily. She'd been in a snit since discovering their garbage capsized, corncobs and paper plates strewn across the road.

"What are the children going to do?"

"That," Emily said, "is up to their parents. I'm sure they're quite capable of entertaining themselves." She tipped her head toward the living room where the boys were playing their Game Boys in their pajamas. No one else was up yet, and it was well past nine.

Emily proposed lunch somewhere, just the two of them. "Somewhere fun. It's so dreary in this house. I have some things I need to do around here, but I want to say I'll be done with them by noontime."

"What were you thinking of?"

"I don't know. Not Webb's, we're saving Webb's for Friday night."

"Naturally."

"You know what I was thinking, and stop me if this sounds a little odd, but I was thinking the Lenhart might be a fun place. I have no idea how the food is—it's probably awful—but I'd like to see the dining room. It's supposed to be completely restored. It always had that view Henry loved so much, with the ferry right there. I'm sure the bridge ruins it, but I'd like to see it again."

"That sounds fine," Arlene said.

They were of the same generation, and she couldn't help falling for the same nostalgia. For her, it went even deeper than Henry and the war years, when the big bands played the casino dances. Her grandmother had stayed at the Lenhart as a little girl. There was an old photograph of her on the long porch there, standing at the top of the stairs, holding her father's hand, the entire picture bleached as if by sunlight.

"I'll call and see if we can reserve a window table," Emily said. "We can take the ferry over and then go up to the cheese place afterward. I think we're running low on the sharp, and I'd like to take some home."

"I could use some too," Arlene admitted.

"It's decided then."

Emily cleared her place and rinsed her bowl in the sink, fitted it into the empty dishwasher and began wiping down the cutting board—all with a brisk industry, without pause, as if she was in a hurry. She scrubbed the sink, squeezed out the green pad she was using, then rinsed and filled Rufus's water dish.

"Do you need a hand with anything?" Arlene asked.

"No, but thank you for offering. All I need from you is your list."

"I'm not finished with it yet."

"Well, take a few minutes and finish it. Whatever I have by lunchtime is what I'm going to go by."

So that was it, Arlene thought. She should have known nothing was that simple with Emily. So many times, as a teacher, she'd reached a stubborn child by discovering what they loved, distracted them from the hard process of learning with pretty window dressing.

But she wasn't a child, and after Henry, Arlene thought there was very little she had to learn.

"I'll have it for you," she said.

"I'm not going to nag people about it anymore."

"Is that a promise?" Arlene said, and then, when Emily gave her a put-upon look, reassured her, "I'll get it done."

2

The dream wasn't real, as she'd feared (it had been too easy, too good), and Ella scolded herself for believing it could have been true. She was so stupid, thinking that could ever happen to her, and for wanting it to. Her life wasn't like that.

She expected to change, to wake up and discover she no longer felt the same way—to find she was free of whatever spell had possessed her. But every day it was still there, and stronger, if that was possible, the passing time making her frantic even though there was nothing she could do about it. For the first time she understood what her mother meant by her nerves not being able to take it anymore. Every minute seemed desperate, like she might seriously go insane, break into pieces, scream.

The worst thing about it was knowing how much better of a person Sarah was, and how pathetic she was herself. Ella felt like she was lying all the time, every second they spent together. Sarah would be so creeped out if she knew Ella was watching her sleep—as creeped out as Ella was that she was thinking about another girl.

She wasn't like that, or she'd never been before. She didn't want to be.

But Sarah's face. Her thin eyelids, the delicate tip of her nose. The place where her upper lip flattened and turned lush on its way to the corner. Just her name—Sarah!—so much prettier than her own. Sarah was smart, and funny, and kind. She would probably try to be nice about it, not laugh at her. She would try to understand.

Ella rolled over and faced away from her. There was so much going on inside her head, yet the rest of the world was infuriatingly the same. Her parents and Aunt Margaret were asleep, lumps of dirty clothes at the foot of their beds. The light through the curtains was white and stopped before it reached the ceiling. Rain again. The carpet was like frayed yarn, a mix of red, white and blue. She couldn't believe anyone would choose something so ugly.

She caught herself gnawing at the corner of a thumbnail, as if struggling with an impossible question, and made herself stop. It was so stupid. Sarah was her cousin, she'd known her since they were little.

She couldn't answer why she was suddenly in love with her. There was no reason, just as there was no reason why in three days she'd turned into a lesbian.

She'd had crushes on boys, her eyes following them in the halls or the cafeteria, their names jumping out of conversations, their favorite shirts becoming hers, but she'd never done anything about them. At the Friday-night dances she hung out with Torie and Kim and Caitlin, the four of them a group. For all their speculation about who liked who, none of them had actually kissed anyone.

She didn't feel this way about any of them, but none of them were pretty like Sarah. She never checked them out, only their clothes.

Maybe this was how it happened, she thought. It wasn't like an adept becoming a sorceress, where you had to practice under a mentor, serve an apprenticeship. You just were. For some reason, she couldn't believe it.

Maybe it was from the way she touched herself in the shower, that secret love of herself spreading out, finding someone more beautiful to practice on. Maybe she was afraid of guys, like Torie making sex sound scary, or Mrs. Greco in health.

She got up, purposely not looking at Sarah, and went into the bathroom. She locked the door behind her, turned on the shower and took off her PJs. She decided not to think. Instead, she watched the clouds of steam billow up, stirred by mysterious currents beneath the ceiling, leaving a slick sheen on the walls. The water warmed one side of her, left the other goose-bumped. Under the spray she scrubbed herself clean, careful where she touched.

3

"What time did you come to bed?" Lise asked, and she knew exactly how it sounded.

Meg had gone down to breakfast. The girls were showered and dressed, their wet towels dropped on the floor. For the first time in ages they were alone.

"Not too late. One, one-thirty."

"More like two-thirty. What did you two talk about for so long?"

"The usual. You know."

"No, I don't know. I was up here by myself."

"She said she's getting the divorce."

"I knew that."

"I didn't," he said, as if he'd really been surprised. Sometimes he played dumb, a turtle pulling in its limbs, hoping she'd leave him alone. It was a child's trick, it only worked if you indulged it.

"What else?"

"We talked about Dad a lot, and the cottage. The good old days."

"There were no good old days for her, I thought."

"There were. Anyway, she's not too happy about Mom selling the place."

"I don't think anyone is," Lise said, and wondered if she was. Relieved, maybe. But she could see how they'd miss it. She liked the lake, the dock, the tennis courts hidden in the woods. It would actually be a nice place to go by themselves. "Arlene's not pleased, I know that."

"It's too late," Ken said. "The time to say something was February."

"No one wanted to upset her. And Arlene can't afford this place, none of us can. The only person who can afford it is your mother. It's her decision."

"I know."

He turtled again, but she would not feel bad for nailing this fact down. He could defend Emily if he wanted, but he had to acknowledge the truth.

"That's what you talked about for four hours."

"That and her rehab, how she's doing."

"You didn't talk about us at all."

"Is there something to talk about about us?"

"Was there?" she asked.

"No," he said automatically. "I told her about my job and how I've been a little frustrated with my work lately."

He'd discussed this with her too, but unwillingly, only because she insisted, after weeks of unhappiness, and then she had to pull everything out of him, so that it seemed more of an interrogation on her part, and he a prisoner giving up his secrets.

He sighed and covered his forehead with a hand, silent but mulling something larger, as if building up to a confession. She would almost welcome one, to change or explain the way they'd been these last months—anything but this good-natured passivity. What troubled her most was the possibility that none of this mattered to him, that he could go on like this indefinitely, pausing to contemplate their problems only when she decided to bring them up.

"She's going through a bad time right now," he said, but with such a lack of emotion that it sounded memorized, banal. "I wish there was some way we could help her."

"Money-wise."

"Any way at all."

"I don't think we're in a position to, money-wise. You're always reminding me—"

"That's what I told her."

"She knows we would if we could."

The door to the stairs shuddered opened, staying the conversation. The footfalls were an adult's, and in a second Meg's head appeared behind the slats of the bannister. Lise noted how mussed she was, her nightshirt holey under one armpit.

Meg made straight for their bed. She had two mugs of coffee, and instructions from Emily to roust them.

"It's that list. She's been obsessing about it ever since we got here.

I think she honestly thinks we're going to fight over things. As far as I'm concerned, she can toss it all in the lake."

Lise raised her mug to the idea, then tipped her chin at the window. "Looks like a Book Barn kind of day."

"The boys are making noise about going to the casino. I haven't said anything to them yet."

"I can take them," Ken said. "I don't think it opens for a while though."

"What about the girls?" Lise asked.

"They're fine. Mom and Arlene are going to the Lenhart for lunch, but there's enough cold cuts and stuff. Sarah can feed herself."

"Ella's fine by herself too," Lise agreed. "So, how long can we look at books?"

"They've got that new addition," Meg said.

"While you're down that way, you can pick up some videos," Ken said.

"You'll be closer than we will," Lise argued.

"There's no way I'm taking the boys there."

No one wanted to choose what they should get, and Meg headed back downstairs. Ken said he'd take his shower first, he had things to do. Lise thought of grabbing him before he could swing himself out, but didn't. The day had already started.

He closed the door to the bathroom, and she spread herself under the cool sheets, pinned like a butterfly by the weight of the covers. She wished he hadn't volunteered so quickly to take the boys. Now she wouldn't see him all day. Meg he would stay up all night to be with. She could see he was uncomfortable, that he thought she was jealous. That wasn't it. She didn't want secrets, just to be included, to not be forgotten. He and Meg formed their own little world, could go for hours recounting their favorite stories, never getting tired, never getting bored. Ten minutes with her and he had nothing to say, gave her the turtle. To Lise, it seemed just one more problem they had to face before they could get to the heart of what was wrong. As always, she had the feeling that they were not done talking.

4

"Charmander is evolving!" Justin read off his screen.

"Whoop-dee," Sam said, too busy with his to look up.

"So I guess you already have a Charmeleon, huh?"

"So I guess you still sleep with stuffed animals, huh?"

"So?" Justin said.

"So that's what babies do." Sam kept playing his game, hunched over, leaning to one side in the middle of a battle, and Justin went back to his, hurt and mad at him, but at the same time afraid he might be right.

5

They asked together, she and Ella, pretending they wanted to be helpful.

Aunt Arlene had already taken him for his walk, Grandma said. It was pouring out, did they know that?

"It's not raining that hard anymore," Ella said.

Sarah had chosen her to argue their case because everyone knew she was smart and responsible (unlike Sarah, even if her grades were straight A's and she made breakfast every morning and helped Justin find clean clothes). It seemed to be working. Ella had answers for everything. The thunder and lightning had passed, and it was warming up. For insurance, Sarah had taken the leash off the doorknob, and Rufus pranced and clamored at her side, his breath hot on her hand.

"Let them take him," Uncle Ken said. "It'll get them out of the house."

"You're not going to wear him out," Grandma asked (it was more of an order), and they shook their heads no, of course not.

"At least take an umbrella," her mother said. "And wear your water shoes—or go barefoot. I don't want you ruining your sneakers."

Barefoot! They hadn't even thought of it. They rolled up the cuffs of their jeans and yanked mothball-smelling ponchos over their heads. Uncle Ken found them two umbrellas and they were set, except now the boys wanted to go too.

Her mother overruled them, and before Justin could start whining, said they could splash in the puddles out front.

"But you have to put on the clothes you wore yesterday. I am not doing any more laundry."

"Mo-om," Justin grumped.

"Can we go?" Ella asked nicely, and with a word they were through the door and into the cool, heavy air smelling of the lake. Rufus nosed the screen open, the stone step of the porch pebbly and slick, the grass wet, freezing their toes. They ran across the yard, leaving everyone behind, laughing at how easy it was.

"You were great," Sarah said, and Ella smiled and rolled her eyes like it was nothing and twirled her umbrella.

Twigs and green whirlybird seeds were all over the road, and worms they had to scoot around. Someone had a fire going, and the smell of it made Sarah hungry for something like soup. Back in the woods, wind rocked the branches. Most of the cottages were dark. Drops of water hung like ice from the power lines. The lake was a sea green, and the boats were covered up, puffed gulls standing on the tall pilings, all facing one way. She and Ella slapped their soles in the shallow puddles and looked at each other, dry under their umbrellas, lucky to be out of the house, free.

Rufus wanted to pee on everything. He yanked Sarah toward every tree and reflector and miniature fence, marking his spots. He was so old he didn't lift his leg, just squatted and squeezed out a weak stream. By the time they got to the shortcut it was just drops, but he kept trying.

"I think he's running out," Ella said.

"Let's hope so," she said, but then at the Loudermilks' mailbox he went so much it foamed.

"That is so nasty," Ella said, turning her face.

"Oh, like you never pee."

"Not outside I don't."

Again, they looked at each other right at the same time, thinking the same thing, and laughed.

"Can you imagine?" Ella said.

"Guys do it all the time and they don't get weirded out about it."

"Those are guys."

Sarah couldn't help but see him at the edge of a mowed field, unzipping his faded jeans in sunlight, his long arms tan—and then stopped herself, not wanting to imagine that far.

"Quick, tell me something else."

"They don't wash their hands either."

"Thank you," Sarah said, "I *have* a brother."

They took the shortcut past the see-through A-frame, nobody home, the furniture waiting for its owners, and she thought she could meet him there, that they could sneak in and make out on the couch the way she and Mark did in the Kramers' pool house, their hair still damp from toweling off, the humidity and bite of chlorine part of their excitement. She had to help him with her top and then wished she hadn't. She made rules, then let him break them—like the time on the chaise longue when they almost got caught by his mom—and she was mad at herself afterwards.

This would be different, more romantic. She could see them in the A-frame, eating by candlelight, a fire behind them, classical music.

"We should have brought his ball," Ella said, and Rufus looked up hopefully, as if she might have one.

"We're not supposed to tire him out."

"He's not tired, look at him."

They turned the corner onto the marina road and the sky opened up, the fishponds spread out on one side, the trees in the distance misted, hazed by rain. Far ahead, a single car ground by on the highway, the swish of its tires faint as a jet speeding high above the clouds. The road was cracked and they walked in the tangled grass, soaking their cuffs. Rufus blazed a trail, sniffing, his snout flecked with seeds from the timothy.

It was hot in the poncho, and Sarah slowed, worried for her hair. The poncho was the doofy bright orange kind crossing guards wore, or football fans. She didn't really expect to see him, she was just hoping.

And then she started thinking about Mark. She knew he wouldn't write, they'd even joked about it. She thought it shouldn't bother her so much.

"Let's look at the fish," Ella said. "That way you can scout out his house before we go by."

"Right," Sarah said, like she'd thought of it.

An official pickup truck with a sticker on the door sat in the hatchery's drive, and the caged light above the entrance was on. From the back came the hum of a pump running. The ponds were raised above the ground, and once they were past the hatchery itself, they crossed the road and climbed a muddy path onto the checkerboard of dikes. Frogs plopped into the water to escape them. Rufus barked, way too late, and across the ponds a heron launched itself, flapping its hinged wings as it banked, giving them the profile of its hooked neck before sailing over the treetops. Sarah imagined the guy on the mower growing up across the road, seeing this every day, playing here. It would be part of him the way the lake was.

The rain made circles on the water, bubbles that floated a moment, then popped. Rufus tracked along the edge, his tail up in the air like he'd found something. In the shallows they could see ghostly fish nosing the surface, expecting to be fed.

As a girl, she'd come here with her father to watch the men cast handfuls of meal from burlap sacks, the slippery fish thrashing and flopping on top of each other to get it. The ponds could be drained, the fish running with the water through pipes, then captured in tanks and released into the lake, just to be caught again. The cycle had seemed unfair to her then, and still did.

She wondered if he fished. Her father didn't. He thought it was a waste of time.

"Looks like someone's home," Ella said, ahead of her, pretending to examine the next pond.

Below, across the road, the coach light was on, a large, dark car in the driveway—his father's probably. The house was small but neat, custard yellow with white shutters, nothing like the ones in Silver Hills. The front door had a half basket with flowers in it. She pulled Rufus along and caught up.

"Nice car," Ella teased.

"It must be his father's."

"And I love the gnome by the birdbath."

"Where?" she asked, just as she saw it, hiding in a patch of ivy.

"Did you see the kitten? On the roof of the garage?"

She tried to be inconspicuous, shielding herself with the umbrella, peeking around the lip. The kitten was the ceramic kind old ladies bought at the garden store for a joke.

"So what?" Sarah said, but she had to laugh too.

She hadn't expected him to be waiting for her on the porch. All she wanted was some sign of him, a promise that she would see him again.

"This is dumb," she said finally, and passed by the last pond, Ella right behind her. They followed a narrow trail down the dike and through a grassy ditch, climbing back up to the road.

The curtains were open, but there was only a light on in one window, a slice of wall, a piece of a table. She let Rufus snoop around the mailbox (no name, just a number), hoping to see someone walk past, but there was nothing. The flowers in the door basket were fake. On the small concrete stoop rested an astroturf mat with a plastic daisy in one corner. A graying wooden fence ran around the backyard, so maybe they had a dog. She kept looking for clues to prove he belonged here, that she wasn't mistaken—the same way she investigated her father's new place, the bland brick town house with its peeling window frames and aluminum storm door like a disguise, his Camaro the only true reflection of him. This felt the same: strange and disappointing, as if the house confirmed the distance between them. She wanted to check in the garage for his lawn mower. She wanted to go knock on the door.

Rufus found a spot and squatted.

"No!" Sarah said, but it was too late. He looked over his shoulder at her as he peed, Ella laughing under her umbrella.

"I don't think he lives here," Sarah said.

"You better hope not."

"Finish up," she told Rufus, and they walked on.

"Maybe he lives next door," Ella said, because there was a Mustang in the driveway, but again she couldn't find any real evidence, just the usual stuff people left outside: a flowerpot, a barbecue grill, a pair of folding chairs. She could play the same game with every house on the road, and none of them would fit him.

"Forget it," she said.

"We tried," Ella said. "Wait till the rain stops, then he'll be out riding his thing around."

She was right, but the day was ruined. Now she was thinking of Mark and what he was doing at camp and why he hadn't written.

They'd nearly reached the path to the tennis courts when a van pulled onto the road from the highway, its lights crossing them, shining off the puddles. The van was ugly and customized like a hot rod, with chrome wheels. It rolled up slow on them, like the guys from Dearborn cruising Superior, windows open, whistling at her and Liz from the backseat. There were two men in it, probably headed for the marina, except they didn't have a trailer. The one driving had a beard and glasses. They both stared at her as if she didn't belong there, let their eyes linger over her.

Before she knew what she was doing, her reflexes (her mother's, really) kicked in, and with the hand holding Rufus's leash, she lifted it up to eye level and gave them the finger.

The van's taillights flared.

"Run!" she cried, and flew by Ella, Rufus bounding alongside as if this was a game. "Come on!" The road hurt her heels, and then, turning, she almost slipped on the grass. She made the break into the woods and cut through the bushes, the path giving mushily under her feet, branches flashing past, grabbing at her umbrella until she dropped it. She struck a hard root and hopped a couple of steps before running again, Rufus confused and then hauling her along. She couldn't hear anything, as if she'd outrun sound. The tennis courts were around the next bend.

"Sarah!" Ella called.

When Sarah slowed and looked back, she saw Ella far behind, her umbrella closed so she could use it as a weapon, and she thought it was wrong to have abandoned her.

"Wait," Ella called, out of breath, and Sarah stopped so she could catch up. The two of them would fight them together.

Ella was wheezing like Liz when she had an asthma attack, and had to bend over. "They're not chasing us."

"Maybe they're coming around the other side."

"I don't think so."

Still, she watched the path.

"Assholes." It was her mother's word, reserved for her father and other drivers.

"What happened?" Ella asked.

"You didn't see me?"

The story gave them a reason to stay there and rest.

"The jerks deserved it," Ella said. "I can think of a lot of people I'd like to give it to."

"Like who?" Sarah asked, and they wasted a few minutes comparing lists. People at school, even some teachers. Rufus grew bored and sat down. Under the trees you could barely feel the rain. Around them, leaves dipped and nodded, and Sarah had the sense that someone was watching from the bushes. She remembered the girl from the gas station Uncle Ken had talked to the police about, and saw the driver shoving her in the back of the van.

"You don't think they could be the ones who kidnaped that lady?"

She could see the idea hit Ella. "I don't know."

It made them both look at the woods differently—very *Blair Witch,* as Liz would say. They couldn't stay there.

"I should go get my umbrella."

"I saw where you tossed it," Ella said. "I didn't think I had time to pick it up."

"Sorry."

"No, it was smart. If they really *were* chasing us."

Sarah gave her the finger and Ella laughed. It sounded loud.

"So we should go get it, right?"

"Right," Ella said.

At first Rufus didn't budge. They made him stand up—stiff, stretching his back legs—then went to retrieve her umbrella, cautious, listening for any sound that didn't belong. Rufus had no clue, walking along like they were at the park, useless. Sarah took the lead because she could see better, Ella checking behind them at every bend. The whole way they stayed close together, a team.

6

This time Ken was careful on the stones, now glazed with rain and smooth as glass. As his own reflection loomed in the black window of the door, the insane idea came to him that he could dig them up and plant them in their backyard—by their garage—so he would always have them to walk on. It was a child's wish, so extravagant and pure that he had to smile as he dismissed it. He could see himself trying to justify it to Lise, see her smirk at his softheartedness. And yet there must have been something to it, because once inside, with the door closed behind him, rain knocking the roof, he imagined prying up the stones and hosing the mud off them, laying them in the carpeted bed of the 4Runner like tiles.

He didn't have time for this. He had the Nikon and two rolls of black and white. He'd told Lise he wanted to look over his father's things for their list, but she knew it was an excuse.

His first worry was seeing. Only a dingy light filtered in through the two windows facing the lake, one of them blotted, crossed by lines of ivy. The still air smelled of mildew and gasoline—a smell unchanged from when he was a boy, as if this place had been waiting for him. He leaned over Ella's bike and flipped the switch by the little refrigerator, but the light in the porcelain fixture screwed to the rafters refused to come on, the dark bulb probably ten years old, rusted firmly in its socket. He found a utility light on the workbench and hung it from a nail. The result was glaring; even turned backwards it flattened everything.

The bench was a mess, and for a moment not only the garish shadows but the profusion of junk stumped him—tools and gas cans and extension cords, saws and scraps of wood, an air mattress folded flat, cases of deposit bottles sorted by color. He recognized a few signature pieces: a plumber's wrench blackened with age, its teeth chipped silver; a Chock full o' Nuts can jammed with dried paintbrushes and stirrers; a peach basket ranked with spice jars full of fasteners, each labeled with masking tape, his father's block lettering identifying deck screws and machine bolts and locknuts. The majority of it was stuff he'd never seen before: a single, pristine masonry bit mummied in its shrink wrap; an unused tube of Liquid Nails for a caulking gun; a coil of copper solder; an unopened roll of nylon rope for the boat. It seemed wrong, all of it heaped up as if dumped there.

At home his father's workbench had been brushed clean, a flexible hose bent ductlike over the circular saw to vacuum the sawdust away as the blade ate through the wood. A push broom leaned in one corner, a dustpan stuck on top of the handle. How many times had he cautioned Ken to clean from the top down? "It's all going to end up on the floor anyway," he said, and made a show of sweeping before hanging up his apron. On the bench, under the steady fluorescent light, rested the simple truck they'd made together, or the airplane, on a folded-over sheet of newspaper, glistening under its drying coat of varnish, and the next morning it would be ready for him. This looked more like his own workbench, their old kitchen table exiled to the basement, piled with tools used and then left out, dead batteries, failed superglue projects.

His eyes skittered over the two giant metal shelves on the far side, loaded with moldering liquor boxes and rusty cans of paint, a gallon of blue wiper fluid. Beside them sat a cracked Coleman cooler, a patio table missing its glass top, a large box for an air conditioner they'd never owned stuffed with orange life jackets he remembered wearing, now probably home to a colony of mice. Hoses, ropes, buckets, lumber—there was just too much. It was like moving. He didn't know where to start.

"Don't try to *see* anything, just start shooting," he could hear Morgan saying.

He was cheating, with the flash, and it would look awful, but there was no way to get this right, not with the Nikon. All he needed was his wide angle, one good light and a fill and he could get everything he wanted—but there, he was thinking too much.

It felt mechanical, every frame too simple, just coverage, documentary at best. The bench was the worst, completely uninteresting, a mess. He did the fridge, open and closed, the two gas cans and the funnel, the scarred front of the metal cabinet. Each scuffing footstep between setups echoed, and with every shot he felt worse, until he straightened up and stopped, let the Nikon rest against him and rubbed his eyes with the heels of his hands.

Sometimes it was like this, after not having worked for a while.

Or when you suck, he thought. When you're just not very good.

He was still spacey from last night, staying up late with Meg. He hadn't been that stoned since college. It was weird being here to begin with, the week a hole in their real lives. Back in Boston it was all waiting for him—their shrinking bank account, his shitty job, Morgan's wise advice.

Meg was going back to even less. As a boy, he'd thought their family was special, somehow blessed. Maybe he'd expected too much or not worked hard enough. It couldn't be just luck or poor choices.

He turned around and searched the walls, hoping something would leap out at him. A wooden rake, an aluminum fishing net, a bamboo pole his father used to rescue kites and balsa-wood gliders from the chestnut. The flash brought out the raw wood, and he wondered how it would print. He'd expected the cottage to give him pictures, to make him feel more, but what he saw through the viewfinder didn't express what he felt about his father. So much of this junk could belong to anyone. The scuffed Husqvarna chain saw, the silly mermaid boat-bumper with its jokey boobs. After Goodwill came, an expensive cleaning service would cart the rest away to the town landfill, leaving the floor clean as his father's workshop.

He spent the second roll on the far end, taking the utility light with him. He remembered these cobwebbed lawn chairs, easily thirty years old, their aluminum tubes pinched and split with metal fatigue, home to spiders. Lime-and-white seats woven with gold threads. He wanted to run inside and grab a roll of color, but knew he'd never get back out.

By now he was counting down the number of frames left, ready to surrender. The last were throwaways, obvious stuff: the kids' bikes, his father's golf bag, the grill. He would have to come back when there was some real light.

He capped the Nikon. His father's golf clubs he didn't need to put on the list, or the barbecue starter. They were his legacy as surely as his father's broad forehead and reticence, his tendency to frown like a bulldog when thinking hard. The tools he gave a cursory inspection. There was a new Makita drill, a good set of socket wrenches—things his father would hate to see go to waste. His father's highest praise for anything was that he'd gotten his money out of it. It was a bitter joke of his mother's that he'd only just had the Olds tuned up when they discovered he was sick. "Six hundred and fifty dollars," she would say, outraged, as if the dealership had failed to cure him. The week before he was scheduled for his first surgery, he drove it constantly, the two of them spinning through the winter countryside around Pittsburgh, cushioned in its plush, heated interior, visiting towns they'd heard of all their lives yet had never seen. Coraopolis, McKees Rocks, Irwin, Zelienople. For a week they got up early and hopped in the car, talked and didn't talk, filled up the tank, squeegeed the windshield, all the time knowing. It was those conversations Ken wanted to hear now, the basic decision making of which road to take, what restaurant to stop at.

The bench's jumble confused him again, too much to process, his father's obsolete car orbiting with the packets of sandpaper disks and tuna cans of roofing nails, all of it tumbling through memory unconnected, meaningless. He turned from the mess and went to the window overlooking the gray lake. The sill was dotted with dead flies, filmed with dust. He stood there ignoring it, peering out through the clouded glass. As a boy, this was his favorite vantage point to watch whoever was on the dock, and now the same sense of secrecy, of spying on something important, fixed him here, the wet planks and greening pilings and the mist over the water locked like a vision, paralyzing his mind and body as if it required absolute concentration on his part to communicate its message.

A drop of water fell from the gutter, bright as a diamond. He blinked, and the vision broke, its meaning lost, if it had ever possessed one. The lake was no mystery, or the rain.

Everyone's father dies, he thought. Everyone goes through this.

In their most honest, vicious arguments, Lise accused him of being unfeeling. Not cold, she'd say, just empty. Sometimes she wondered if there was anyone in there. It was not true, of course, in the broadest sense (she accused him in these same arguments of being oversensitive, a baby), but at times he recognized in himself a holding back, an emotional conservatism he associated not with his father, whose unruffled calm he aspired to, but with his mother, who, faced with any catastrophe, resorted to a rigid order, formulating and crossing off lists until the crisis had passed. He saw in himself her escape into routine, submerging himself, when threatened, in his work.

It was not that he was unfeeling, only that, being a private person, he kept what he felt to himself.

It amazed him how he could be truthful and evasive at the same time, even when he was only thinking. There must be a deeper level, he suspected, a base so selfish and weak that he feared contemplating it.

At heart he knew that was not true. They were just rainy-day thoughts. The weather—the world—could make you feel so small inside yourself, curled up like a snake in an egg.

Out on the lake, a boat trolled along, a man in a slicker standing under the canopy—SHERIFF, it said on the hull. It was Tuesday. Tracy Ann Caler had been missing two whole days. At sixty miles an hour, driving in shifts, they could be in California by now. They could be anywhere.

He turned back to the garage, the flat light making everything seem even more squalid. They could have her in a place like this, he thought, wrapped in that tarp, shoved under the life preservers.

She was probably fine, probably in on it with a boyfriend, legging it west with their nest egg. He hoped so.

He shut the light off and then appreciated the darkness, softening everything, the accidental light from the windows touching on curves and angled surfaces, the crescent heads of wrenches. Yes. Here was rest, and shelter, the quiet he thought of when he imagined his father, happy at his saw, guiding a hand plane along the edge of a freshly cut board, shavings curling up in a white wave over his fist. The rain tapped in the rafters. He could stay here all day, hide like a child. If only he could capture this, but technically it was beyond him.

"Ah, but you felt it, didn't you?" Morgan would say. And he would be right.

Ken checked his watch, as if this time tomorrow he might have the same light. He left everything where it was, his list unchanged. He would be back until he was satisfied. After such a fruitless shoot, it felt like a triumph, a promise. It was strange, he thought, how little it took to stop him from giving up.

7

"Did you eat breakfast?" his mother asked, like he might be in trouble, and for a minute Sam convinced himself that he had. If he said no, she would sigh and march him into the kitchen, and he would have to stop playing his game.

"Uh-huh."

"What did you eat?"

"Grandma eggs."

He was walking in the tall grass when the screen flashed and the wild Kangaskhan he'd been looking for all morning appeared. He had all thirty safari balls, more than enough if it didn't run away.

"I hope you thanked Grandma for making them."

"Uh-huh."

"Did you brush your teeth?"

"Yes."

"Let's smell," she said, beckoning him with a finger and leaning down so he had to stop in midbattle.

She held his chin in her hand. Beside him, Justin looked up like it was weird.

He tried to breathe lightly, hoping he'd brushed well enough last night so his mouth would still be clean.

"No you did not brush your teeth. Why do you lie to me—why? I don't *care* if you've brushed your teeth or not, as long as you tell me the truth. Do you understand? How am I supposed to trust you when you pull stuff like this, huh?"

"I don't know."

"You don't know," she repeated. She reached for his Game Boy, and he had to stop himself from yanking it away like when Ella tried to grab it. She took it from him, then turned it over as if she'd never seen it before. She clicked it off, losing everything he'd won since the last time he saved.

"Hey!" he said, reaching for it, starting to explain, but she held a single finger in front of his face like a knife.

"This is stopping right now. I am not going to have you lying to me. You go upstairs and brush your teeth, and when you come down we're going to have a talk with your father. He *was* going to take you and Justin to the arcade today, but I think you may have blown that deal, I don't know."

It was a giveaway. She knew, just like he knew, that his father would let him go to the arcade. Justin checked them again, worried now, as if it was Sam's fault for messing things up.

"Go," his mother said, pointing to the stairs with his Game Boy, and he did, his whole face twisting, heat steaming behind his eyes. He banged his way up them, letting her know how mean she was being.

"Don't you stomp on the stairs like that!" she shouted.

He caught his foot in midstep and set it down with a violently willed gentleness, finishing the rest of them calm as a robot. It was only when he'd reached the top and turned out of sight that he threw looping punches at the air so hard they knocked him off balance. He kicked Justin's pillow so it wrapped around his ankle, stepped back and kicked it again.

"Are you brushing your teeth?" his mother yelled up.

"Yes!" he called and went to the sink and turned the water on. It smelled, and the holders were gross. He took his brush and squeezed on a green blob of Justin's Crest, then stood there avoiding the boy in the mirror, wondering if she'd ask Grandma if he'd really eaten and what would happen if she found out. It didn't matter. His father would still let him go to the arcade.

Someone was coming upstairs. He hesitated for a second, as if he wasn't supposed to be brushing, then kept going, the white foam clownlike around his mouth.

It was his father, his Game Boy in one hand. "Sam I Am," he said, in a tired tone Sam recognized. His father had his camera around his neck, and Sam wondered if his mother had made him stop too.

"Finish up," his father said, and Sam rinsed and spat. His father put down the lid of the toilet. "Have a seat."

His father leaned back against the edge of the sink, his arms crossed under his camera, and Sam knew not to talk. He looked at the mirror behind his father, the back of his father's head and the bright ceiling near the light.

"Do you understand why your mother's upset with you?"

"Yes."

"Why?"

"Because I didn't brush my teeth."

"Why else?"

"Because I said I did."

"Because you lied about it, that's why she's upset. Do you understand that?" His father moved his face so Sam had to look at him.

"Yes."

"Why didn't you tell the truth?"

"I don't know."

"Is there something difficult about brushing your teeth, or did you just forget?"

"I just forgot."

"You should have just said so. You should have said, 'I forgot.'"

"I didn't want to get in trouble."

His father shook his head. "When you lie, you're going to get in trouble, you ought to know that by now."

Again, he leaned there with his arms folded, saying nothing. The best thing to do, Sam knew, was to wait.

"So what do you think we should do?" his father finally said.

"I don't know."

"I told your mother and Aunt Margaret I'd take you and Justin over to the video arcade later, and I'm going to honor my promise to them. For now, though, I'm taking away your Game Boy." He opened the battery compartment and removed the two double-A's. "You can have it back tomorrow. Next time your mother or I ask you a question, you tell the truth."

"Yes, sir," he was supposed to say.

"Okay," his father said, and stood up and opened his arms for Sam to hug him, and Sam did, looking at himself in the mirror, his hands on his father's back, his cheek against his soft shirt, and it was all right. If it weren't for his mother turning his Game Boy off, everything would have been okay. They were still going to the arcade, like he knew they would.

He'd already played more than an hour anyway, and his father hadn't said anything about breakfast, and Sam thought he'd won.

He'd learned something too. From now on he'd have to remember to save his game after every battle.

8

Emily closed her door and shook the three lists from her pocket and sat sideways on the edge of her bed to go over them. She laid each out in front of her on the spread, trying not to read what they'd written in any order, to ignore them for a moment before starting, though their handwriting gave them away. She felt the same queasy apprehension she knew from opening Christmas gifts or gambling—the sense, through the bubbly anticipation of luck, that something could go horribly wrong. How much easier it would have been for her to select the correct pieces for them and then let them make whatever trades they wanted, but she'd chosen the diplomatic route and now she had to go through with it.

"Oh my," she said, because at a glance she saw that all three had picked the same thing, the cedar chest. For Kenneth and Arlene, it was their first choice. It was Margaret's second, but she was only asking for two things, the other the set of Henry's gas-station glasses that Emily wanted for herself.

The decision was simple. She'd always thought of the chest as Margaret's, to pass on to Sarah, and it would be the only thing Margaret was getting. So. Emily circled it on Margaret's list and crossed it off the others'.

God knew why, Kenneth wanted the little refrigerator in the garage. Henry's golf clubs—that made her happy. Kenneth hadn't played with them last summer, out of respect, and she was pleased that he felt comfortable enough to ask for them now. She would clean them up for him before they went out this week. And Henry's fishing gear. Good. She'd counted on him taking that. It saved her the trouble of lugging it all home. Some of the lures were worth money, and the fancy reels.

Lastly, he asked for the 7UP bottle with the twisted neck. Henry had won it for him at a fair, a ring-toss thing, and how badly he'd wanted it, and for Henry to win it for him. Henry had missed his first three tosses and came up with another dollar. She feared there would be tears, and then the plastic ring leapt and ricocheted, dinging among the glass shoulders until with a last flip it landed solidly, perfectly, on the neck of a bottle. Emily worried the children would break it the next day, it looked so fragile. She was amazed it had lasted this long, that, useless as it was, it had become a beloved relic, even to her. Though it was listed fifth—as if disguised—Emily understood, knowing Kenneth as she did (his moods, the quiet hours he stayed in his room while Margaret and her friends rollicked in the backyard), that it meant more to him than all the other things combined. She thought, sadly, that he should have known it was his to begin with. He really hadn't changed that much from the timid boy he'd been. She'd had to encourage him to speak up, to not let the louder children bully him, but even then he'd been deferential, afraid of offending others, herself included. For all her harping, he'd never overcome it, and that seemed to reflect on her. This was just further confirmation. He should have known he didn't have to ask.

The same with Margaret, she thought, ashamed, and circled the glasses on her list. What kind of mother would deny her children the least thing?

Arlene had listed the TV even though Emily had said it was hers, but also an old, engraved map of the lake that hung in the guest bedroom which she'd completely forgotten—a handsome oak-leaf frame from the twenties adding a rustic touch. And the afghan, to Emily a chocolate-and-butterscotch horror in need of dry cleaning (or perhaps burning). That was it, just four things. She was surprised not to find the dresser and the nightstand. The Goodwill people would be happy at least.

No one had taken the low wardrobe upstairs or the oval mirror with its wavy glass and gilt eagle fiercely peering down. No one wanted the good fireplace tools or the end table the phone sat upon, and these seemed like mistakes, gross oversights. She thought Kenneth would want the new hose by the side of the house, barely a year old. Margaret had forgotten the antique blender she always complimented her on. Emily knew Lisa didn't want anything, that was fine with her, but her own children, and Arlene, who knew the history of each piece. Maybe she could rent a van in Jamestown, drive it down behind Arlene.

She'd known this would happen. Henry would be shaking his head, smiling at her folly, the way she never learned.

"Well," she said vacantly, as if giving in, and gathered the three lists and stood. She folded them together and slid them into the front pocket of her jeans and, looking around the room, imagined it empty, just carpet and walls, even the curtains tossed in the garbage. She and Henry had made love here, maybe listened to the same rain at night. Years, the same trees in the window, the damp. She reached down and touched the bed, ran her palm over the nubbly chenille. It was only a moment before she stopped herself.

9

Sarah had just nabbed her third king when she glanced up and found Aunt Arlene looking at her expectantly, as if she'd forgotten to do something. Panicking, Sarah checked her mouth. Only the very tip of Aunt Arlene's tongue poked out, subtle, like a middle lip.

Sarah slid her tongue out, the tip pinched between her teeth, and peered at Justin to her left, but he was busy with the card he'd drawn from the pile.

Across from her, Ella had her tongue out like Aunt Arlene and was looking at Sam, who was busy wiping Rufus's nose with a tissue.

Sarah turned back to Justin, still fumbling with his discard. He'd lost the first two games already and wasn't happy. He was used to winning at things like chess where there was time to think, but this was different.

Come on, Just, she thought, look at me.

Aunt Arlene and Ella turned from Sam to Justin, stopping to meet eyes with her, conspirators.

Sam threw the balled tissue at the wastebasket and missed, and when he turned back to them he saw everyone and stuck his tongue straight out, a rude strawberry.

She thought she should tell Justin he'd lost, but that wasn't how you played the game.

He put down the king she needed, saying, "I know you want this one," and then, expecting some reaction from her, saw her tongue. He pushed his out hopefully, and they all laughed at him. Even she found herself smiling, going along with the joke.

"It's not fair. You guys are cheating." He was pouting, his eyes reddened, the lower lids brimming.

"Right, we're all cheating," Ella said, though in reality they were all peeking at each others' hands. It was part of the game.

"Don't be a baby," Sam teased him.

"Shut up!"

"Justin," their mother warned from the couch.

"He's making fun of me—"

"Play nicely or don't play at all."

"You've got to stay awake over there," Aunt Arlene said, shuffling. "The trick is not to worry about your own cards. Worry about everyone else's."

He knows how to play, Sarah wanted to say, but Aunt Arlene might think she was giving her lip. She was touchy and Sarah thought she didn't like her very much, the same way Grandma liked Ella better. Part of it was how she looked—she knew that feeling from everyone at school: the other girls, the boys, even the teachers. It was like she was some kind of freak, except she was supposed to be lucky. Her mother was proud of how pretty she was, always telling her to be thankful for her looks, that someday she'd be grateful for them, and Sarah couldn't explain to her how hard it was knowing everyone thought you must be stupid or stuck-up or slutty and were dying to see you mess up.

Aunt Arlene dealt out their hands on the orange velvet ottoman. It was Ella's turn to go first.

"Wait," Justin said, struggling to get his hand together. His hands were too small for the cards, that was one problem.

Sarah had a pair of aces and junk, so she watched Ella and then Aunt Arlene and then Sam pick up and discard, her tongue ready, caged behind her teeth. She hesitated before she picked up, faked, making sure Sam wasn't going to ambush her in the middle of her turn.

She drew the third ace, checked everyone as she slipped it into her hand (not rearranging), then discarded. Ella looked at her, holding her eyes to see what she was hiding, and Sarah gave her a bluff smirk, as if she might or might not have something.

Justin picked up and put down the same jack of clubs, so she concentrated on Ella's face, her eyes reading the new card from the top of the pile, then blinking as she added it to her fan, folded the hand closed and looked them over again.

"Nothing," Sam guessed.

"Let's see what she throws away," Aunt Arlene coached, and glanced at Sarah.

Someone must be close, she thought.

Ella threw the jack of hearts.

"It's not jacks," Sarah said.

Aunt Arlene had to reach from the couch.

Ella's face hadn't changed. Justin scratched at his collarbone, his arm blocking Sarah's view of his hand. He was going for queens. He had three, and she had the other one. She decided to let him win. It wasn't really cheating.

"King of diamonds," Aunt Arlene said, laying it down, and Sam snatched it up.

They all waited for him to punch his tongue out (Sarah eyeing Aunt Arlene, waiting for the delayed move), but he set down the jack of spades.

"Three in a row," Justin noted.

A second check of Sam and Aunt Arlene and then Ella, and Sarah picked up the fourth ace.

Her luck surprised her. She couldn't help but laugh.

"Uh-oh!" Ella cried, and then everyone was watching her face and the five cards in her hand. There was no rule that you had to stick out your tongue before the next person's turn. Part of the strategy was choosing the right time, like an assassin. She fitted the ace into the middle of her hand and dumped the queen.

Ella was staring at her like a gunslinger, sure. Sarah matched her, waiting. Beside her, Justin was so excited he dropped part of his hand. To throw them off, Sarah checked Sam and Aunt Arlene.

Aunt Arlene had her tongue out, just barely, sneaking between her stained teeth.

Ella had hers out, and Sam, grinning like an idiot.

Justin was still gathering up his cards.

She saw that they saw. Losing on purpose would be worse. Short of kicking him there was nothing she could do, so she stuck out her tongue.

"Ha ha," Sam said, doing his Nelson, which Sarah hated.

"No," Justin said, looking around wildly, short of breath, "I won. You're cheating. You're a bunch of cheaters. I don't want to play anymore."

He threw his cards across the ottoman, Aunt Arlene waving at them. He rolled over in a ball, and this time he was crying.

"Go!" their mother said, getting up, and Rufus cowered, his head between his paws. "Justin, go!"

He couldn't stand fast enough, and their mother yanked him by the arm and swung him toward the stairs. "You stay there until you're ready to come down and apologize. That is not appropriate behavior."

She sat down again on the couch, still dangerous, her anger filling the room, and the rest of them were quiet.

"Maybe we should take a break," Aunt Arlene said, collecting the cards, so they did. Ella went back to reading. Sam had one of Justin's *Star Wars* comics. Sarah headed for the stairs.

"I don't want you going up there and disturbing him," her mother told her, meaning she couldn't go and tell him it was all right, that it was just a stupid game and Sam was being a jerk and that her mother shouldn't have yelled at him or grabbed him so hard.

"I just want to get my book," she said.

"Try a different tone."

"I need to get my book."

"That's better." Her mother stood up and came over to her. "I'll get it for you. Which one is it?"

"It's Ella's. It's the one with the dragon on the cover."

Her mother went up, leaving her standing there. When she came back down with the book, she asked Sarah to step into the other room with her—Grandma's room.

"You know," she said, "I appreciate that you're sticking up for your brother. I think that's important. And I know how much you do for him at home, how well you took care of him when I was sick."

You weren't sick, Sarah thought.

"But sweetheart," her mother said, "as much as you want to, you can't fight all of Justin's battles for him. He's going to have to learn how to do things for himself."

Sarah didn't argue with her, didn't say a word.

"Okay," her mother said, "I just wanted to let you know that."

Their talk was over, everything was settled. Sarah was supposed to follow her into the living room. Instead, she stayed there, baffled and angry at what an asshole her mother was being.

It wasn't true, though her mother would never believe it. And it wasn't worth running the risk, here, now, of her mother hitting her or, worse, crying as she held on to her, saying she was sorry, that it was all her fault, meaning—really—that it was her father's. When her mother was drunk or when she was just too depressed to get out of bed, Sarah had learned that the *only* way she and Justin were going to get through this was to fight their battles together. But she couldn't tell her that.

10

It was a reflex, a motion she'd known her entire life—the postcard waiting in her other hand—but as soon as Emily licked the stamp she realized she didn't have to.

"Uck," she said, wiping her fingers across her lips, though there was no taste, really, she just felt foolish.

Sometimes she didn't know where her mind went. She wrote things down on the calendar, then discovered them a day late. Henry was forever chiding her about leaving the oven on or forgetting to let Rufus back in. Even Arlene had started, reminding her to check her purse for her keys whenever they went somewhere together. That exasperating Maxwell practicality. She was sorry, but she didn't have that kind of a mind. She needed her lists.

Self-adhesive stamps. She could remember when a postcard cost two cents and there was no such thing as a zip code. Or computers or cellular telephones, she thought. The world she knew was gone—or still there but obsolete, passed by like Kersey, stranded in the long barrens between exits on the interstate that would always be new to her, though it must be almost fifty years old.

Time had been her friend until her late thirties, then it turned against her.

She would not let a silly stamp send her into a blue mood, not on vacation. The rain was still upon them, but she'd taken care of the lists, the garbagemen had finally come, and now she'd finished the postcard she'd promised Louise. If the mailman took it today it should arrive by Friday, Saturday at the latest—if she got it to the box in time.

In the living room, Rufus was watching Sarah and Justin playing chess on the floor, Ella and Kenneth soldiering away at the border of the puzzle. Arlene and Margaret didn't look up from their books. She supposed Lisa was hiding upstairs. The weather said it would rain again tomorrow, and Emily had no idea what they were going to do then.

Sam was in the kitchen, twisting open one of the plastic bottles of Kool-Aid that filled up their recycle bin, a swampy green the color of antifreeze, pure sugar. It was ten-thirty, and as far as she could tell, his mother hadn't fixed him breakfast yet.

"Did you ask an adult if you could have that?" Emily said.

"No."

"You need to eat breakfast first. Go ask your father to fix you something."

He obeyed wordlessly, clearly unconcerned, and she sighed. She couldn't imagine her acting like that with her grandmother Hedrick. She wouldn't have been able to sit down for a week.

"Rain, rain, go away," she said at the back door, and pushed the wet umbrella through before stepping out. She was careful on the stairs, watching her feet, all the while gripping the postcard in a fist, afraid it would fall, water smearing the ink.

A gust of wind shoved her square in the back like a hand, and she feared for the umbrella, tugged it down about her shoulders.

"Just miserable," she said, squishing across the drive.

The road was empty, her toad nowhere to be seen. She was afraid when she opened the lid she would find today's mail, but then when she pulled the tin flange down, hunched close, protecting the dry inside with her umbrella, she saw instead a seething mass of ants.

She fell back as if stabbed, and the postcard fluttered from her grasp. She fished for it with a swipe of her free hand, but it eluded her, landing facedown on the road. She tried to pinch it up quickly before any real damage was done, in the process grinding it against the wet asphalt.

"Goddammit!"

It was ruined. You could still read it, but the front looked awful, as if someone had stepped on it (and she'd picked this one special from the Institute gift shop, a campy shot of the lake from the sixties, the water swimming-pool blue). She couldn't send this to Louise.

She left the lid open, vainly hoping the rain might disperse some of them, and tromped back toward the kitchen, her face rigid, intent.

"Kenneth!" she called before she was even through the door. "Kenneth!"

11

He'd plotted it like a crime, stealing the opportunity to shoot. He brought along the two gas cans, ostensibly to combine trips, but really to buy himself time, give him an excuse to stop at the Gas-n-Go. He had the Holga loaded, bulky as a revolver in the pocket of his windbreaker. As bad as the garage was, it was a start. As always, Morgan was right. Take it frame by frame, roll by roll, just keep at it until something happens, because it will. It all came down to patience—like anything, Morgan said—and Ken had patience. If nothing else, the last ten years proved that.

At this point there was nothing else he wanted to do with his life. He'd cast his lot, as his mother dramatically put it, and it was too late to change.

There were times, like now, driving with the radio on low, wipers slapping away the rain, when he could see himself thanking a black-tie audience for an award, a great pompous blowup of one of his photos being lowered to the waxed stage behind him, the image he'd seen first now a worldwide icon like Eddie Adams's street execution in Vietnam. In his tuxedo he held up the gold statuette, the medal, and bent to the stemlike microphone. "I'd like to thank my wife Lise," he'd begin, "and my teacher Morgan." His children, his father, his mother. In his daydreams he dedicated the award to his own students, the new generation they could trust with the future of the art. The applause followed him off.

Absurd as it seemed—impossible, since no one wanted his pictures—that fantasy had actually happened to a classmate of his, Davis Larrimore, two years ago. Technically, Larrimore was a mess, but his brother-in-law had an in at *Newsweek* and got him a job with their Seoul bureau. He'd been covering the Hyundai strike when a Molotov cocktail struck a soldier caught between the skirmish lines. A wave of strikers broke forward, and the soldier's comrades deserted him. The frames Larrimore took of the crowd kicking him to death were too disturbing for the cover of *Newsweek,* but by the end of the year the images were everywhere, and they gave Larrimore a Pulitzer. "Right place, right time," Morgan said when Ken bitched about his luck. And anyway, Morgan said with a shrug, that was a completely different kind of photography. Ken just had to work on his own work.

And he had, at that point zealously, sure that his effort would be rewarded and then confused when it wasn't. He'd always been promising, ever since he was a child—advanced placement, high SATs, dean's list—but now, nearing forty, he couldn't call himself promising. If he'd ever had promise, he'd squandered it. The proof was irrefutable. He'd accomplished nothing, and the suspicion that he'd been a fool all along, an impostor, nagged at him, despite Morgan's assurances.

The day was dark, trees waving, a storm blowing in from the north. The Putt-Putt came, and the graveyard, the high grass around the stones flattened by the weight of the rain, wet flags left over from Memorial Day, their stakes marked with bronze stars. His father did not consider him a failure, he was sure, and yet these last months his thoughts seemed to revolve around the idea, picking at it like a scab. Once Ken had shown him his darkroom—neat as his father's workbench—walking him through the developing process. His father was impressed, as he always was, with the technical steps, the calibrated magic of the chemistry, and complimented Ken on the image (from the side, his father in his favorite chair, reading the business section of the *Post-Gazette*). He was sincere, because the print had become a favorite, hanging in the upstairs hall across from the bathroom. Thanksgivings Ken would come across it and admire his own composition, the way the light supernova-ed in the half-glasses balanced on his father's nose, a happy accident.

His father was not ambitious (much to his mother's chagrin, he later found out). He took the bus downtown every morning, dragged his briefcase home at night. Success to him meant having the time to do nothing. Happiness was fishing, or being settled in his chair of a Sunday afternoon in the fall, the leaves raked high in piles, reading the paper while a ball game played. It was this ideal of peace that Meg had despised as complacency and that his mother defended as his right. But of all of them, his father was the least demanding, pleased by their high scores yet understanding when they flubbed a test. If anything, his expectations were too low. If Ken wanted to surprise him with some stunning, unexpected triumph the way Meg had with her rebelliousness, it was too late now. He was down to pleasing himself—or Lise, though honestly he could not imagine her ever being impressed with him again.

He should be more like his father, he thought. That would be the way to honor him, not by mooning after a Pulitzer.

A bolt of static crashed through the radio. He turned it off as if it were interfering with his thoughts. He was driving fast for the rain, timing himself by the dash clock, which seemed crazy, seeing as the challenge was to fill up the hours somehow, make the day pass faster. He had to be back to take the boys to the casino—not that he minded. He'd take another roll or two there with the Holga, work that nostalgic riff, the old pinball machines and sex-appeal testers, the greased cables of the ferry.

The old hotel, the garage, the Putt-Putt, the cemetery—it all belonged to the same faded turn-of-the-century world of Chautauqua, and for an instant he saw an exhibit, a book, a life's work documenting everything here, building up a library from which to choose the most telling images. He liked the idea of a larger project, impossible to fulfill too quickly. Shoot enough and something will come, Morgan said. Maybe that's what he needed.

No, it was ridiculous, grandiose, and noticing how he leapt at the possibility made him feel desperate.

The farm stands were closed, but the Gas-n-Go was open as if nothing had happened, the sides of both islands occupied. In the windows the beer neon glowed. There was no police car parked by the ice machine or the caged propane tanks, just a rusty Suburban, a banged-up truck. He'd expected it to bear some more dire sign.

On the way into Mayville he saw her face stapled to pole after pole, taped to a barbershop window, the door of a darkened sub shop. It was a quiet town, a backwater with a Doric courthouse and two blocks of rotting Victorians anchoring a hilly grid of split-level ranches surrounded by a county of bankrupt dairy farms going back to ragweed and thistle. He didn't think she could still be here, stashed in someone's basement, locked in a dripping barn.

The road curved, turned sharply, and Main Street ran up from the lake like a boat ramp. The Golden Dawn seemed to be the only going concern downtown, but when he pulled into the empty space in front of the True Value, its lights were on, the storefront giving off a cozy glow. The sidewalk was raised above the sloping street and protected by a black railing of pipe; he had to climb a crumbling set of steps before he reached the door.

It chimed behind him, the smell of free popcorn welcoming him inside. Long ago the owner had installed a machine like the one at a theater, making the trip to the store a highlight for Ken as a child. Every summer since he could remember he'd come here with his father, a strictly male pilgrimage, stocking up on fuses, mouse baits, rolls of screening—all the things that had renewed the cottage and now cluttered the garage. His father knew where everything was, ranged the aisles as if he worked there, but Ken couldn't make sense of the store's organization. He wandered the shelves like a lab rat—tempted, every minute, to use the Holga—until in a far corner he ran across a wall of insecticides in tall cans. He read three carefully, weighing their ingredients, finally choosing one with a cartoon of a dead ant on the front.

His mother had been in such a hurry for him to get it that she hadn't given him any money. It was cheap enough, he figured.

The woman at the register rang it up without a word, and Ken recalled his father talking with the owner, a man he presumably knew. Just chitchat, the weather, the level of the lake, but there was a connection there, a neighborly acquaintance that Ken felt none of in this transaction. The woman was older, wearing a Bills sweatshirt, and while there was no one else in the store, she seemed annoyed, as if she was busy with something else. When he thanked her, the words squeaked out as if he hadn't spoken in months.

On the bulletin board by the door was the flyer, and it struck him that his strangled thank-you would have been the extent of his conversation with Tracy Ann Caler if she'd been there. Looking at the bad picture of her, he realized that he'd never met her, never spoken with her, never actually seen her alive. And yet, strangely, that made her even more his. She was his secret as surely as if he'd kidnaped her himself.

The feeling that he was in some way responsible, if only as a witness, would not go away. He'd always considered himself too levelheaded to develop anything resembling an obsession. Perhaps that's what this was, but, unaccustomed to such bizarre thoughts, he'd failed to recognize it. Because it was nuts. She could have been anybody. He didn't know her at all.

Outside, letting the 4Runner defrost, he peered down Main Street at the shallow end of the lake, the old train station turned into a bike shop, the *Chautauqua Belle* in her slip, waiting out the rain. He wondered what it would be like to live here. Quiet. Cold in winter, and pretty in the snow. They could sink their savings into one of those ten-room monstrosities with a massive gas furnace and three staircases. He could see himself running a studio out of the house, taking formal portraits of families posed in their church clothes. In time, he would establish himself, make a name, take out an ad in the Yellow Pages. He'd keep his accounts in the den, crunching his budget on his computer while outside the leaves spun and fluttered down. And all the while, secretly, he would be piecing together Tracy Ann's case, talking to people she knew, photocopying documents, filling a drawer with folders.

"You *are* a psycho," he said, and rubbed his window clean so he could see to back out.

Beyond the Golden Dawn, the streets were deserted. Outside of a shabby two-story brick building, by the curb, sat a flowered couch, on top of it a big console TV, facedown. The apartment must have been upstairs, above the liquor store. He could not imagine who lived there. Someone like Tracy Ann Caler. A town like this would always be a mystery to him—to any outsider. His ideas of small-town life were probably wrong, drawn from Jimmy Stewart movies and episodes of *The Twilight Zone*. Down in Jamestown there was that creep who gave all those teenagers AIDS. The locals said he was an outsider, but that didn't explain why their kids were swapping partners like a barn dance, and some of them were Ella's age. Their neighborhood in Cambridge seemed almost wholesome in comparison.

He checked the clock on the dash, adjusting how much time he could spend at the Gas-n-Go, restoring an extra five minutes he'd taken away earlier. His plan was simple. While he filled the cans at the island with his other hand—without looking—he'd be shooting the front, the pumps, whatever the Holga decided to include. When he went in to pay, he'd circle around back and bend down like he was reaching for a Coke and do the same thing to the aisles, the coffee corner, the rack of maps. If he saw the opportunity, he'd try to do the counter, get the register, all following Morgan's directive, just shoot. The anticipation of working cranked him up, an athlete waiting for a game to start.

Ahead, the Gas-n-Go shone, its yellow sign bright in the rain. He wanted the outside of the inside island so he would have cover to shoot from, and it looked like he would get it, except there was a black Chevy between him and the doors. He pulled in and pulled as far up as he could. Before he lifted the latch for the back, he checked his pocket like a robber, making sure the Holga was there.

There was no one in the Chevy; the driver was inside paying. He swung the cans down to the island, giving himself a view of the front between the pump and the garbage can. He reached into his pocket and dug out the Holga and set it on the concrete. The temptation to line up the shot—or better, to bring the viewfinder to his eye—was excruciating. Instead, with one finger, entirely blind, he pressed the button for the shutter, heard the telltale click.

He forwarded the film as he listened to the gas splash into the first tank. A woman emerged from the doors and headed for the Chevy. He pressed the button, hoping to catch her in midstride.

Forward, and another, forward.

A conversion van with an older couple pulled in at the outside pumps, but, kneeling, he was already shielding the camera from them with his body.

When he was finished with the tanks, he pocketed the camera, carefully screwed the two caps on and hefted the tanks one at a time into the back of the 4Runner. As he closed the hatch, he had the chance to scan the lot, to check the position of the husband, still filling up. Another car was turning in, just a driver, a woman. He waited until she stopped at the very inside pump before crossing to the doors.

In his concentration, he barely noted the flyer taped to the glass at eye level. Inside, he didn't think it was strange that he pretended he hadn't seen it. Logically it wouldn't make a difference to him, someone from out of town. He noted the clerk—a kid no older than Tracy Ann Caler, busy turning on the pump for the woman—and made for the wall of sodas, aware of the cameras trained on his back, wondering if anyone watched the tapes at the end of the day.

There were the tiers of candy bars, the Cheetos and Fritos, the dusty cans of Chef Boyardee ravioli. The lighting wasn't ideal, but again, it didn't matter. He used the glass door of the cooler to see behind him, then looked out at the pumps where the husband was hanging up the nozzle. Ken checked to make sure he wasn't paying with plastic—no, here he came across the lot, innocently counting out his money. Ken squatted, stalling, pretending to search the rows of Cokes. He was right where he needed to be. Six shots left, maybe seven. Enough. He slipped his hand into the pocket where the Holga rested and drew it out like a weapon, then knelt there, breathing, listening for his partner to come through the door.

12

"It doesn't fit there," Ella said. "I already tried."

Sam kept forcing it.

"What are you, stupid? It doesn't go there."

"I don't care," Sam said, and jammed it hard so it fit.

"Stop." She fended him off with an arm and pulled the pieces apart, set the one in the middle.

He pushed her, rocking the table.

"Sam!" she hollered, and shoved him back.

"Cut it out, you two," their mother warned, and before Ella could defend herself, said, "I don't care who started it, it's over. All I want to hear out of you is silence."

13

"Look at them," Lise said, pointing out the window.

Meg saw her mother holding the umbrella for Ken while he sprayed the mailbox. A cone of mist enveloped it, drifted on the wind, and they stepped back into the road.

"There he goes," Meg said, "saving the day."

"My hero."

"*We* couldn't have done that."

"No way," Lise said. "No one could have except her Kenneth."

14

From the ferry the new bridge looked precarious, rising high above them as if on stilts. Fog hung underneath it between the concrete pylons, plumes of frothing runoff pouring down like waterfalls. Arlene watched the tops of the trucks highballing by as Emily fiddled with the knot of her scarf. The wind blew the rain sideways, flogged the Taurus so hard Arlene would have worried if she hadn't crossed in far worse. The ferry hadn't changed in her lifetime, the open deck large enough for nine cars, turretlike guidehouses the size of phone booths at the four corners. A young couple occupied the one nearest them, holding each other as they rode the choppy water. The whole trip took five minutes.

"Okay," Emily said, ready. For some reason, she needed to take her purse.

"Are you sure you want to go out in this?"

"Oh, don't be such an old fart." Emily opened her door and the wind stirred the ashtray so Arlene had to slap it closed.

"Old fart you," Arlene said to no one, then followed her out.

Her first steps were wobbly, though the ferry was rock-solid, the diesel chugging evenly, hauling it along the cable. She slitted her eyes against the wind. Rain stung her cheeks as she veered toward the rail. Emily opened the door to the guidehouse for her, and she ducked in out of the storm, wiping her wet hands on her pants.

"Well, that was fun."

"I'm glad I bundled up," Emily said. "You'd never know it was August."

No, Arlene thought, it was typical of August at Chautauqua, but let it go. Rain snaked down the windows, braided streams twisting like curtains blowing in the wind. They stood and watched Bemus Point draw slowly closer, the old casino and the new docks along the shore, fat cabin cruisers bobbing in the slips—lawyers from Buffalo.

"The casino has seen better days, I'm afraid," Emily said.

"I'm surprised it's still standing. I thought it would have burned to the ground by now."

"It always was a firetrap. Did you ever see them burn the old steamboats off of Celoron Park?" Emily pointed down the lake as if the place were still there, the roller coasters and flying swings standing unpopulated in the rain.

"I've heard about that."

"They used to do it for Labor Day. They'd buy one of these old hulks and anchor it offshore and soak it in kerosene. Terrible for the environment, I'm sure. You couldn't do anything like that today. It would be sitting out there all day where you could see it, and that night when the park was about to close, they'd set it on fire and everyone would watch it burn. It was better than fireworks."

"I wonder why we never saw one," Arlene said.

"They stopped right before the war."

"We were here then."

If it was a mystery, it would remain unsolved. One of Emily's more infuriating talents was bringing up an intriguing subject for no specific reason, dropping it in your lap and then flitting off to something else before it could be fully inspected. It reminded Arlene of her students' propensity for non sequiturs. But they were children, easily distracted. Now, like the teacher she was, Arlene waited, testing her hypothesis, the deck vibrating through her shoes.

"Remind me to get some of that good Lappi at the cheese shop," Emily said. "I know I'm going to forget."

"Lappi," Arlene repeated.

Emily was just trying to make pleasant conversation, and here she was grading her. After all the years they'd been sisters-in-law, they were still new to each other. When Henry was alive, Arlene had been a fifth wheel. Now the two of them were a couple, calling each other to propose a movie (the spate of Jane Austens was a favorite), a day in Shadyside, an expedition to the grocery store. And how much better it was than going alone, even if Emily did wear on her nerves. She felt engaged, part of the world in a way she hadn't before Henry's death. "Arlie," he'd summoned her, and asked her to take care of Emily as if it was a burden, but surely he'd known. He was smart, her brother, probably smarter than her for all her love of knowledge and logical arguments. He understood her.

"And you must remind me," Arlene said, "to remember that horse-radish spread I like."

"That dreadful stuff. Must I?"

"You must," Arlene said, pleased, as if she'd struck a deal in her favor.

The attendant moved to the bow, and they hurried back to the car, braving the rain. The diesel shifted gears, suddenly went quiet, and, floating, they docked, the stopped momentum making them lurch forward in their seats. Waiting for the attendant to unhook the chain, she was tempted to turn the heater on, but didn't. The young couple had one of those new Volkswagen bugs, in an ugly green she supposed was fashionable. She followed them off, a steel plate clanging as the nose of the Taurus rose and then fell.

"A day like today," Emily said, "we should have no trouble parking," and though Arlene thought her optimism—like so many of her pronouncements—groundless, it proved true.

The Lenhart was the same buttercup yellow that had delighted her as a girl, and she thought that maybe they could stay there next year if the Institute was booked solid. The place was built on a different scale, a grandiose robber-baron excess that now seemed quaint and endangered. They walked up the hedge-lined promenade under the dripping oaks and onto the cavernous porch, the rockers herded away from the railing to stay dry.

Before they reached the door, Emily stopped. "I'd like to take in the view, if you don't mind."

"I think that would be nice," Arlene said, though she was cold.

The floor was dirty and peeling. A few boards were new, the wood raw and tattooed with shoe prints.

"That's not kosher," Emily pointed out.

The bridge did ruin the view—had become the view, running like a fence across the lake, blotting out the far shore. Arlene remembered some long-lost weekend dance at the casino, Jimmy Dorsey and his orchestra. Once again she'd been passed over by Henry's friends and had gone to a window of the ballroom where she looked out at the lights of the cottages, wavering like flames on water black as oil. She'd been a silly teenager, terrified that no one would ever love her. No one had, perhaps—certainly not Walter, though she'd hoped. She'd had her chances. It had long since stopped being a need.

"It's criminal, that's what it is," Emily said.

"They could have picked a better design," Arlene agreed. "Bridges can be pretty."

"It appears they were going for the strictly functional."

"They achieved that." Arlene half turned to show she was ready to go.

"It's so disheartening," Emily said, keeping her there. "You look at something like this and you have to wonder what kind of society we're living in."

Arlene's first inclination was to ridicule this as more of Emily's hand-wringing, but in its immense ugliness the bridge seemed to support her claim, as did the woeful state of the casino, even the floor they were standing on. She thought of her school, falling apart around her, and the neighborhood, much of it burned out now, the business district gone.

"Are you hungry?" Emily asked. "I think I'm going to keel over if I don't get something to eat soon."

"Me too."

"Oh, that damned alarm," Emily said as they retraced their steps. "I tried calling the Lerners at home and got their answering machine. Isn't that maddening? I told them to leave us their code so we can turn it off. I'm not going to have that thing waking us up at three A.M. every night."

In the front hall of the Lenhart, they gazed up at the portraits on the walls, staying on the plush runner leading them like a conveyer to the maître d's lectern. The walls had recently been painted, but they hadn't bothered to do the trim in cream the way she remembered. Emily made a dubious face, as if disappointed. They gave their jackets to the coat-check girl, keeping their purses, and just then a draft followed a guest in from outside, chilling them. The maitre d' was young and wore a business suit, probably off from college. The reservation was under Maxwell, a window table.

"Ladies," he said, and led them past a board on an easel advertising Sunday brunch.

The great room was set to accommodate hundreds but was empty save a strip of tables along the windows, most filled by women their age, though at the one next to what seemed to be theirs a baby in a high chair hammered at his tray with a spoon.

"May we have that one instead?" Emily asked, motioning to a table farther along, and the maître d' retrieved the menu he'd just put down. The mother of the child tracked them as they passed.

Finally they were settled, their purses resting on the low window-sill. Their view was much the same as it had been on the porch. The bridge loomed above them, the trucks like flying billboards. The yellow in here was cheerier, lit warmly by chandeliers and wall sconces. The silver was pleasantly heavy, the monogrammed handles nicked and soft-looking from being washed. The menu had the fresh lake perch, her favorite. A waiter in a white coat dropped off an iced butter dish, oversized pats embossed with the hotel's name in script.

"I believe this carpet is new," Emily said.

"I love the potted palms."

"I'm sorry about changing tables, but at this point I am not in the mood."

"This is fine."

"I know it's a terrible thing to say about one's grandchildren, but I swear they are the rudest children at times. And spoiled? I cannot believe what their parents let them get away with. Do you see this or am I making it up, because it seems that way to me."

"All kids are that way," Arlene said, trying not to contradict her. She'd heard this same complaint every year and knew not to join in lest Emily turn on her. "Especially when you get a bunch of them together. They get their own little social scene going, and then you become the intruder, the authority figure telling them what they can't do."

"That's their parents' job, but I haven't seen them doing it. I haven't seen them play with the children once, and this morning Sam didn't get his breakfast until after eleven because his parents couldn't be bothered. I guess I shouldn't let myself worry about these things."

"Well of course you should," Arlene said.

She checked the table for an ashtray and realized with a familiar disappointment that the whole room was nonsmoking. She broke open a roll—ice-cold—and offered the basket to Emily, who was going on about Kenneth and Lisa being burned out from working, their priorities mixed up. She wasn't completely serious, but neither were her criticisms empty.

Arlene couldn't fathom her dislike for them. She'd always seen in Kenneth and Lisa a younger version of Henry and Emily, the wife the real driving force behind the marriage, the husband just going along. Perhaps that wasn't true. She spoke with them so little now, all her information filtered through Emily.

She was saved by the waiter, who gave them his name before taking their drink order. It was a clue to how Emily was feeling, and Arlene was pleased when she asked for a Manhattan. There was something extravagant about mixed drinks at lunch that made her happy. She ordered a perfect Rob Roy, which seemed to momentarily confuse the waiter.

"Well done," Emily said when he was gone. "The look on his face was priceless."

"My great-aunt Martha used to have a perfect Rob Roy whenever we came here. She said it was a proper drink."

"It is. I just haven't heard anyone order one in ages. I can see the bartender flipping through one of those little books. You'll have to give me a sip."

They talked of Pittsburgh, as always, and their changing neighborhoods. They talked of politics and of schools, public versus private, and of Emily's neighbor Marcia, who Arlene knew to see but with whom she'd exchanged maybe ten words all told. Marcia's daughters were in college now, and Emily tracked their academic success as if they were her own children. One of them was doing a semester abroad in England, which led to a long, swooning monologue on the trip Emily and Henry had taken there in the mid-seventies, and the cathedrals they'd seen. Arlene thought of Henry tramping the worn cobbles of Oxford, a place she'd always wanted to see, or huffing up the spiral stairs of some Gothic tower, Emily ahead of him, chattering away. He only half paid attention to her when she was like this. He'd nod or supply an interested "huh" at the right place as a sign for her to go on. It seemed to Arlene, sitting there listening to Emily, that in some way she'd taken his place.

The drinks came, and they both ordered the perch, as if it were a tradition. Emily proposed a toast. "To the Lenhart. Happy days."

"Happy days."

The first sip of her Rob Roy put a chill in her skin, which changed, as if with a flick of a switch, to a syrupy warmth melting over her bones.

"How is it?" Emily asked.

"Perfect. Have a sip."

"That *is* a proper drink. Maybe I'll order one for myself. I'm not driving."

The drinks restored the Lenhart's charm. They both had another after the French-onion soup, vowing it would be their last. The family with the baby left, along with the other earlybirds, leaving only a few scattered couples. Arlene thought this must be what coming in the off-season must be like, the hotel at their disposal. She pictured winter—ice fishing, a sleigh crossing where the ferry ran. That god-awful bridge. The rain on the water made the place cozy. Setting down her Rob Roy, she was fascinated by the outside light caught in her water glass, the ice silvered with veins of air. She was looped.

"I haven't told you about Margaret," Emily said. She looked over her shoulder as if someone might hear, as if this were a real confession, something new she'd just decided to share with her. "I'm worried sick about her. I'm sure she's told you she's getting the divorce."

"Yes."

"That was in the cards long ago, in my opinion. You saw how she treated Jeff."

Arlene wasn't sure she agreed, not knowing either of them well enough, but dipped her head, interested.

"Well, it turns out she's also broke and a recovering alcoholic. And do you know what? I'm not surprised. I know what a terrible thing that is to say, but it's true. Nothing she could do would surprise me at this point."

"You don't mean that."

"I do. She's forty-three years old, for God's sake. You'd think she'd know better, with two children to take care of. It makes me so angry." Emily clenched her fingers above her soup as if she might leap across the table and strangle her.

"But she told you. Isn't that a good sign?"

"I'm sure it's partly our fault," Emily said. "But Kenneth's never had these kinds of problems."

The waiter was approaching from behind Emily, and Arlene looked up to signal her. The perch was too much, the filet covering the rice pilaf. No, they were fine with their drinks.

"It looks very good," Emily said after he retreated. She speared her lemon with a tridentlike fork and squeezed the juice onto her fish, her attack on Margaret forgotten.

The perch was excellent, and for a moment neither of them spoke, the meal needing their full attention. Finally Arlene cleared her throat and steeled herself with a sweet sip of her drink.

"I think Margaret's all right," she said. "It sounds like she needs the divorce."

"You say it like it's a good thing."

"In this case it might be. I mean, how long have they been separated?"

"All right," Emily said, "but how is she supposed to support herself now? Who's going to pay for Sarah's education?"

"I'm sure Jeff will do the right thing."

"Not according to Margaret. According to her he's got this hot little girlfriend he's running around with."

The news stopped Arlene. She could see this all too well, Jeff with his flashy cars and dirty jokes, the way he could make anyone laugh, even Emily. He seemed to Arlene an eternal teenager in the same way—she thought—Margaret must seem to Emily.

"It's not just the divorce," Emily said, "it's everything. It's too much all at once. She needs to spread out her disasters better."

She'd heard Emily say cruel things in the past, but this was too much. She looked at her blankly over her perch, waiting for an explanation, an apology.

"What?" Emily said. "I'm the one who has to clean up after her mess—again. It's always been like this, nothing's changed. Eat." She pointed with her fork, nodding at how good it was. "I can say this because I'm the one with ulcers from worrying about her. I'm the one who stayed up when she came dragging in at four o'clock in the morning. Henry said I was crazy, and he was probably right, but I can't help the way I am. I'll be worrying about her on my deathbed. Both of them. Kenneth's no better. Neither of them has the least idea about money, and I know that's our fault." She sighed as if tired of discussing it, her knife and fork poised, then tucked in again.

The unstated assumption behind all this, Arlene thought, was that she couldn't comprehend what the two of them had put Emily through. There had been a span of years when a litany like this would be followed by "You'll find out when you have kids of your own," but that was long past, though Arlene still filled in the words, felt their dismissal of her as someone without depth or responsibilities. If anything, she had lived her life too stringently, giving too much, asking too little in return. Her students had been enough, and the school, waiting for her every morning, the bright halls swabbed clean, the blackboards ready for the next lesson. It was only when she retired that she began to feel brittle and unloved.

"You're lucky to have them," she said.

She'd surprised Emily, because she had to dab at her lip with her napkin, then reached across the table and laid a hand on Arlene's wrist as if to thank her.

"I know," she said. "I know. Without Henry there's no one to keep my feet on the ground. I start thinking about Margaret's problems, or Kenneth, and I just work myself into a state."

"They're stronger than you think," Arlene said.

"I wish that were true."

"They've gotten this far, haven't they?"

The waiter materialized to ask if everything was all right. Everything was fine.

"I guess I just want them to be happy," Emily said. "And they don't seem terribly happy."

"I guess you just have to hope it's temporary." As soon as the words were out of her mouth she realized they applied to her—and to Emily as well.

"That's what I'm afraid of," Emily agreed.

"Things change." Arlene gestured at the high white ceiling with its fanciful moldings painted gold. "Remember this place after the war? They wanted to tear it down. Now it's a landmark."

"I get the point."

Arlene argued harder when she was drinking, thank God. Emily conceded that Margaret was still young and good-looking, and that Sarah and Justin seemed to have a strong bond. Yes, Kenneth did his best, and Ella was by far the brightest of the four children. At times Arlene thought that Emily didn't listen to her, their conversations a monologue, but here was proof otherwise. Though the children would never know it, she'd successfully defended them, and the glow buoyed her as much as ordering dessert—a Boston cooler, her mother's favorite, still anchoring the menu:

a slice of canteloupe with a scoop of vanilla ice cream. Emily had the Dutch apple pie with a block of sharp cheddar melted on top.

"Lappi," Arlene reminded her.

"That horseradish crap," Emily said. "Did you ever call Mrs. Klinginsmith?"

"Not yet. Why?" She tried not to show her excitement. She hadn't called Mrs. Klinginsmith because she didn't think Emily was interested.

"I was thinking if the Institute's booked we might try here. Depending on the price. I imagine it would be reasonable. They're not exactly swamped."

"No." Then they would come next summer. In her relief, Arlene caught herself wondering—as she had since February—why Emily had bothered to sell the cottage. She didn't understand.

"It's not the Hilton," Emily said, "but it's better than the We Wan Chu."

Arlene gouged a scoop out of her cooler and the ice cream froze her molars. "I'll call her when we get back."

She'd gotten what she wanted, and yet she was still dissatisfied. As much as she loved the Lenhart, she didn't want to stay here. Even the Institute was second best, a compromise. She wanted the cottage, and now Emily was telling her unequivocally that that was not going to happen. Arlene could not reconcile herself to losing it and Henry in the same year, as if her only comforts were being taken away.

The waiter came to clear. Arlene wanted another cup of coffee but Emily was done. Emily figured out the tip and they split the check down the middle, their wrinkled ones piled high on the plastic tray. They took a last look at the lake—at the bridge—and searched for their coat checks. On the way out, everyone thanked them for coming, the maître d' affecting a stiff bow Arlene thought he'd borrowed from the movies.

"We should stop at the front desk and see what their rates are," Emily said, and though Arlene no longer wanted to, she knew Emily thought she was making a concession and it would be rude to say no.

"A single with two beds?" the sideburned boy asked, and after a moment's consultation they agreed—for the sole purpose of getting a base quote—to entertain the notion of rooming together. The figure the clerk gave them brought the idea uncomfortably close to reality.

"Well," Emily said on the porch, "the We Wan Chu is looking better and better."

"I was surprised too."

"I can't imagine what they're charging at the Institute—if we can get in. It was a nice lunch though."

"It was," Arlene said. And it had been, up to a point. Maybe it was the Rob Roys, but she felt rattled, unmoored in the gray afternoon, the rain dripping down through the trees. The idea that this might be the last time she saw the Lenhart sent her into a momentary panic.

"Are you going to be all right to drive?" Emily asked, as if she'd sensed it.

"I'm fine," Arlene insisted.

They were careful on the stairs, holding the cold railing. The ferry was coming in, the diesel plowing a creamy wake. Like the Lenhart, it had been here a hundred years. Before that an enterprising Dutchman had run one hauled by oxen, and before that the Seneca had used canoes, naturally seeking out the easiest place to cross the lake.

It was remarkable how far back her own history went here. Her great-grandmother had stayed at the Lenhart, her grandmother McElheny and her great-aunt Martha, her mother and father, then Henry and herself with them. It did not seem wrong that the hotel had outlived them all. There was nothing sinister about it; it was only her mood, her circumstances joined with the gloom of the day.

She started the car and pulled out before the ferry could unload. She had actually been looking forward to the cheese shop, but now the thought of it held no pleasure for her, seemed just a stop, not a true destination. She peered in her rearview mirror. The yellow monstrosity of the Lenhart filled it, the endless porch and its rockers, the hedge-lined promenade. Again, was it the fading exaltation of the booze on top of her funk, because she felt as if she were seeing past the trappings of the world to some ultimate truth beneath in which her life played almost no part, a game piece, an insignificant marker. Landmark or not, the Lenhart would burn down or fall apart, be demolished like Kenneth's Putt-Putt, and the new bridge too, dynamited before a cheering crowd like the steamboats burning off of Celoron Park, but the point would always be there, permanent, eternal, watching over the lake while the seasons changed.

Everything passed. And that was right, she thought. There was no sense fighting it. There was nothing to be done, and yet the inevitability of life nagged at her, death without resurrection, the end of things.

"Your blinker's on," Emily said.

"Thank you," Arlene said, and silenced it.

15

The new two-dollar room smelled of must and cat pee and there was no order to the shelves. The top rows were too high for anyone but a giant, yet there was no step stool or ladder, only a pair of bake-sale tables like an island in the middle of the room, piled with boxes of encyclopedias marked NOT FOR SALE, as if someone might abscond with them. Everything was cobbled together from cheap pine, the dark knots bleeding sap. The shelves were packed tight, which Lise thought couldn't be good for the books. She inched along, freezing between steps, her head turned sideways to read the spines. One hand kept her place while the other kneaded the muscles of her neck.

The books had come from basements and attics, the rooms of children long since gone, the houses of the recently deceased. It was like a time warp. She recognized titles she'd had to read in high school and college English classes: dozens of soft, dog-eared copies of *Catcher in the Rye* and *The Great Gatsby,* sixties paperbacks of John Updike edged blue or red or cheddar. There were revolutionary best-sellers like *Soul on Ice* and *The Feminine Mystique, Manchild in the Promised Land* and *The Sensuous Woman,* and wedged right next to them an eighties guide to the stock market, a book that showed you how to win at poker, a partial set of Pearl S. Buck the faded color of baby aspirin. There were three copies of *Etiquette* by Emily Post, and church cookbooks in plastic spiral bindings, and *Ripley's Believe It or Not!* anthologies, and a dictionary stamped PROPERTY

OF FREDONIA STATE UNIVERSITY (they could use one for Scrabble, Lise thought) along with the usual book-club offerings from Danielle Steel, John Grisham and Stephen King. There were books on the football stars of 1973 and *The Pentagon Papers,* Rod McKuen, Arthur Hailey, Judith Michaels, A. J. Cronin.

"Junk," she said, and straightened up, her eyes tired, her sinuses tight from the mold and dust.

The shelves ran solid around all four walls, the only light the over-head fluorescents. It wasn't worth the trouble. She hadn't planned on buying anything anyway. The idea was to have fun looking at the books, admiring the odd find. They'd been at it a good hour and a half and they still had to hit the video store.

The original part of the barn was crowded, and she'd lost Meg, probably off in the Mystery section. It was amazing how many books she remembered from last year, as if they'd waited for her. She skipped the room called Old Favorites—squat moss-green hardbacks from the twenties by writers like Gene Stratton-Porter and Grace Livingston Hill, prized by new homeowners looking to decorate their mantels. Literature, Self-help, Romance broken down by imprint. Biography tempted her, and Travel. In Fiction she found an Oprah novel she hadn't gotten around to for ten dollars, but she still had Harry Potter waiting for her back at the cottage.

She couldn't justify the expense. Ken would note that she'd bought something unnecessary, would hold it against her like a willful mistake. She could get that at the library, he'd say.

He was so cheap he squeaked. It had been a joke between them, one he shouldered easily, because he was proud of being sensible about money, like his mother, but Lise was tired of feeling guilty for not squeezing every penny. Their budget, laid out so coldly, had become personal. She was working now, and she could do what she wanted with her money. She never begrudged him what he spent on his darkroom, only the time he stole from them.

And again, she was aware that she was fighting with him even though he wasn't there with her. It had been like this all year, the two of them sharpening their arguments on their own so that when they did fight there was a cutting precision to their jabs, leaving both of them wounded even after they'd reconciled. They knew each other too well, and used that intimacy as a weapon, revealing and then attacking the shortcomings and sore spots, the reasons behind the larger misunderstandings they relied on each other to leave comfortably unplumbed. Sex, money, the children, their families. None of it was a secret, and yet even now she shied from the idea. Their worst fights were either waiting for them or would never happen, all or nothing.

She slid the Oprah novel from the shelf and read the inside flap, aware of the other customers browsing around her. For a second she read without comprehending, unfocused, the sense of the words eluding her. A young mother coping with the death of a child and how she finds strength in a time of crisis. The power of love and faith, the perseverance of the human spirit. It was the kind of book Ken would ridicule as false and sentimental, as if it were common knowledge that the world was not like that. She thought of losing Ella or Sam. It was bad luck to even think it, but the book made her search her mind for a plausible scenario—a car accident, a drowning—and then the aftermath. No mother would be able to go on, and yet everyone had to. If it were her only child, then the grief would be complete, but otherwise there would still be work, laundry to do, meals to plan. She turned the book over and looked at the cover, a painting of a plain ranch house with trees in front, a tomahawk of a folded newspaper waiting on the porch, as if this could happen to anyone.

She kept the book and went to look for Meg, sidling through the line at the front desk, missing the step down into the History section and almost falling. Past Music and Art there was a wall of fantasy paperbacks that made her wish she'd asked Ella to come. Lise didn't know which ones Ella did or didn't have, so there was no point in looking. She could see herself coming back with something Ella already had, and Ken's reaction—and Emily's, her opinion of Lise vindicated once again.

Meg was down on one knee, hunched over the bottom row, a small stack of paperbacks at her feet. "You ready?"

"I think so," Lise said.

"What did you find?"

She showed her the Oprah.

"That's supposed to be good." Meg stood and flashed her her loot, a clutch of Sue Graftons. "I started at H, so now I'm going back to the beginning."

Lise had read them and thought Kinsey was a ringer for Meg—tough and pretty, kind of messy inside, untouchable. Her own person, with all of her faults. It had to be lonely, just her and the children. When Ken had traveled for Merck, doing trade shows or shoots in Baltimore, she couldn't sleep, the bed suddenly too large, the house too quiet. At the airport she would smother him as if he'd come back from a war and their sex the first night would be incredible. Maybe that's what they needed: for him to go away. But Jeff wasn't coming back.

On their way to the register, Lise thought of their conversation at the Red Lobster—Meg's money worries, Sarah and Ella starting high school. Of her friends, only Carmela had as much in common with her, and though they'd been neighbors for eight years, she would never know Ken the way Meg did. She wished they weren't such rivals, that she trusted Meg more, that her problems didn't thrill her with their possibilities for disaster.

The line was short but the owner was slow, writing up each slip by hand, pressing hard on the carbon. He took down the title of every book as if he planned on restocking. With his cardigan and Ben Franklins and his avalanche of a desk, he was supposed to seem homey and warm, Lise thought, but he and his wife had been gouging tourists for years, tweaking the seasonal markup then buying back at half-price, reselling the same tired stock summer after summer at a hundred percent profit. He'd once yelled at Ella for flipping through an art book, afraid she'd ruin his investment.

Lise examined the Oprah book, hoping for imperfections—dog-eared pages, sentences underlined, any excuse to ditch it. There was nothing, even the spine was pristine, as if it hadn't been read. She could borrow it from Carmela or find it at the library. She wouldn't get to it here anyway, with Harry.

"He's taking forever," she said, as if that were a reason, and went to the Fiction section, found the gap she'd created and slid it back where it belonged.

16

The rain had driven everyone down to Lakewood, to the gritty stretch of strip malls around Wal-Mart, the muffler and brake shops, the Rite Aid and Johnny's Texas Hots. Meg noticed the road into Jamestown had been widened to accommodate the boom; traffic inched between the new lights. The wipers jogged her nerves, and the radio. Patience, patience. One two three four five six seven . . . She wished she were alone so she could get stoned.

It wasn't that she didn't trust Lise. She just wasn't sure. Lise judged her, she knew, but Lise judged everybody. She was like her mother, partly afraid of Meg. The idea that she was someone dangerous was amusing, and she traded on it whenever she could, but lighting up now, as they cruised between the discount Christmas stores and tile outlets, would be too much.

At least she hadn't told them *how* she ended up in rehab. Lise wouldn't be riding with her if she had.

Only good had come out of it, she thought, no real permanent damage. She had to block the vision of the crash from her mind, snap it off with a shake of her head. Some days she didn't want to think at all, just exist.

"Red light," Lise informed her.

"Sorry," Meg said, stopping well over the white line. "I was thinking."

Lise didn't ask what about, instead said something about the light being new, a ready-made excuse. It seemed everyone felt sorry for her except Jeff. She wished they didn't. Her counselor was right—it was what she had to fight in herself, lying back in that soft bed of self-pity, as if she'd been the victim all along.

The light changed and she led the line behind her across, braked and turned into the busy lot of the Blockbuster, the driveway riding over the sidewalk. Beside her, Lise glanced at a jacked-up four-by-four in one of the handicapped spaces and clucked her tongue. Meg thought it was probably just some kid dropping off. Unlike the sticklers in rehab, she was inclined to let people slide on little things. If she'd learned nothing else, it was that there was no gain in being right.

"You have the card?" Lise asked as they walked across the lot.

"Right here." It was the cottage's card, still in her father's name. In all her years of renting, no one had ever questioned her. That he was dead would mean nothing to them, as long as they got paid.

Like the Book Barn, the place was teeming, except here most of the people seemed to be local, and younger—girls in windbreakers advertising high school softball teams, guys in faded baseball caps with ridiculous sideburns, two heavy women in their twenties with pink denim jackets and fanny packs. They leapfrogged each other down the wall of new releases, some of which were a good three years old. Above them, monitors suspended from the ceiling blasted clips urging them to rent films that had clearly bombed despite their hot stars. With its noise and motion and its thin red carpeting, the place had the same distracting atmosphere as a casino. At home, Justin would have asked to tag along so he could rent a video game, and Sarah would have refused to go, telling her to look for some teen thing the name of which Meg would never remember, but here the mission was simple: two movies both the kids and the grown-ups could enjoy.

By the letter C, they were discouraged. Most of the boxes described violent, titillating films that neither children nor self-respecting adults wanted to watch. Her mother would not put up with Disney, and Lise said they'd just caught *Mrs. Doubtfire* on TV. There was a solid section, floor to ceiling, of Eddie Murphy's *Dr. Dolittle,* but despite the store's vaunted promise, it was sold out.

"*The Nutty Professor?*" Lise suggested.

"Seen it."

"*Star Trek Next Generation?*"

"At least three times."

"They never have anything."

The selection only got worse as they went down the alphabet. One of the actresses on what Meg could only call soft porn looked strikingly like Jeff's girlfriend Stacey, so much so that she almost picked up the box to make sure it wasn't her, except Lise would see. It couldn't be—Stacey was a senior sales analyst—but inside, Meg jumped at the possibility of finding evidence against her, as if by proving she was a fake Jeff would see that he was wrong and come back to her. The idea belonged to a Julia Roberts comedy, sweetness winning in the end, but there it was, indisputable. She'd believed in fairy tales. Regardless of what her counselor warned, she'd gone through rehab thinking everything would be all right once she graduated, and Jeff had let her. When she called, he was bubbly as a cheerleader, telling her they missed her, they loved her, they only wanted her to get better and come home. The call was the highlight of her week, her one link to the outside world, and when it was time to go, she didn't want to hang up, and stalled.

"I love you," she'd say.

"I love you too."

"Give the kids a big kiss and a hug."

"I will."

There was a pause, an opportunity to say, Okay, good night, but it hung open between them, unused.

"I miss you," she'd say, and they would start all over again. Later, she wondered if he'd been seeing Stacey then, and her righteous paranoia said yes, that he'd been lying all along, probably since the day they met. She knew that wasn't so, but it might as well have been. Their good years together had been stolen from her.

She'd thought seriously of killing Stacey. Though now it seemed absurd, something from a B movie, she had entertained a simple plan—walking up to her in the parking lot at work as if she were visiting Jeff and shooting her before she could get her car door open, standing above her and emptying the gun into her, dropping it onto her body and walking away (not even kicking her face, that would destroy the effect). She didn't think about jail. The plan didn't go that far, only to the goal of killing Stacey. But these were just fantasies. In those days she was too busy keeping herself sane to do anything that involved complex thought.

And now here she was, back in the land of the free, sober and responsible, changed, and—she could admit—terrified of her new life as this alien person. Maybe the women in pink had come through worse, abusive parents giving way to brutal husbands. And who knew what the kids around them would run up against as they graduated and got married and had children of their own. They were so young, joking with each other in the rows, a girl chasing a guy around his friend, whacking him with a box, the guy stopping so she folded into him, both of them laughing. Meg wanted to tell them to stay that way, not to ruin themselves with stupidity and lying, to keep some nobility and hope for when they would need it.

"So much for that," Lise said.

They had reached the skimpy Zs and turned to the store empty-handed, looking over the shelves of older videos broken down by categories, the art on the boxes sun-faded, the colors turning strange shades. She was always surprised by how many she'd seen. Somewhere in here were the classic drunk movies, *The Lost Weekend* and *Leaving Las Vegas,* and thousands of Hollywood affairs and divorces and car crashes, all true and untrue, all returning, in the end, to her.

"Let's try Comedy," Lise said.

"Good idea," Meg said. "I'm in the mood for something mindless."

17

They played double solitaire, facing each other, wrapped in their sleeping bags, settled in for the long afternoon with cans of soda and a bag of potato chips. The upstairs was gray, darkening as if it were winter. Drops dotted the window by the top of the stairs. They lay across their pillows, propped on their elbows, slapping the cards down on the horrible carpet, sometimes hitting each other in a flurry, laughing. And then nothing came. They turned over their threes impatiently, going nowhere. Six of clubs, eight of hearts.

"Jack of diamonds, jack of diamonds," Ella chanted. "Come on, jack of diamonds."

One two three, one two three—

"Here you go," Sarah said, and they flailed away. The end was fast, but Ella put down the last king. They finished and counted up the different backs, not really keeping track. They shuffled and cut again.

"Ready? Go."

Ella thought the rain had stopped, but then it picked up again, racing wild, drumming the roof like hooves. She was happy to be alone with Sarah, to have something both of them could concentrate on. She was convinced that at any second she would blurt out what she hadn't even practiced in her mind, cutting it short before it could form. She would say it flat out, "I love you," or "I'm in love with you," or "I think I'm in love with you"—totally at random, dumping the news on Sarah like it was her problem.

Because she was. She was mad it had happened (as if she'd been tricked), but it had. She thought about her all the time, she wanted to be with her, she couldn't sleep and then when she did she dreamed of her. All the symptoms fit, so there was no point pretending it wasn't love. The question was what to do about it.

The first answer that came to her was to do nothing, just be cousins, spend the week together and say they'd see each other soon, that they'd both write or, better, e-mail, knowing they wouldn't. She could see herself back home, checking her e-mail every ten minutes. Sarah would be back with her boyfriend Mark, or with a new boyfriend. At least she didn't say she loved him; maybe she was afraid of what Ella might think. But Sarah wasn't afraid, Sarah wasn't like that, and she and Mark weren't really serious. It was up to Ella to make a move, and she knew that unless something big happened, she wouldn't. The knowledge shamed her, made her feel weak and digusted with herself, but powerless to change things.

The second answer was to confess how she felt. Sarah might freak on her or they might talk. It was risky, too much thinking involved.

The third was simply to kiss her.

In her highest and lowest moments she preferred the third. It would be fast and honest, final. Her chances were the same anyway.

That was a last resort. Most of the time she navigated the space between the first two, trying to find a casual way of discovering how Sarah felt about being gay without being obvious. "So," she'd say, "what did you think about Ally kissing Ling?" or "I didn't think Ally kissing Ling was a big deal; I mean, she'd already kissed Georgia." Those were the two best lines she had, and she was still looking for an opportunity to use them. Sarah didn't seem to watch the show.

She wouldn't do anything. It was too much of a risk, and this was probably just a crush (she wasn't a lesbian, everyone in her class had been in love with Miss Friedhoffer). If Sarah told her mother, her mother would tell her parents and then it would be this huge thing. It was better if Ella just kept everything inside, private. It wasn't that hard, she thought. She'd had her whole life to practice. It was only three more days.

They played. Sarah won, then she won. It didn't matter to either of them, and Ella liked that. She could be happy just being with her. They didn't have to do anything special. They didn't even have to kiss. It was enough to be her friend. Things would last longer that way.

"What time is it?" Sarah asked.

"I don't know, three-thirty, four o'clock."

Sarah pushed herself up and went to the dresser, taking her deck with her. She moved their nail stuff around, looking for something.

"Have you seen my watch anywhere?"

"Nope."

Sarah leaned across the top of the dresser and looked behind it, then walked around bent over, checking the carpet, holding her hair back from her face with both hands. Ella got up and helped. She thought it might have somehow bounced under the dresser and reached underneath, but all she found was a green plastic letter A with a magnet in it.

"I remember those," Sarah said. "We used to spell things on the refrigerator with them. I wonder where the rest are."

It set them off on a search. Behind the striped beanbag chair beside the chimney sat an old box like the one in the attic at home where they kept their Christmas-tree ornaments. The box had been there since they were little, and probably before, because the toys inside were wooden and old-fashioned, trucks and dollhouse furniture made by Grandpa for her father and Aunt Margaret when they were kids. The cardboard had turned dark over the years, but she could still make out the marks of an orange crayon, a wobbly, unsuccessful star drawn by someone before she was born. Sarah hauled out a Tonka tow truck with a hook you could reel in like a fishing line, and handfuls of small colored blocks, and a naked Barbie with ribbons in her hair. There were Tinkertoy sticks and their biscuitlike connectors and green windmill fins, a set of plastic checkers missing most of the reds.

"Do you remember what we used to do with these?" Sarah asked, and pushed one of the checkers into her own cheek so the ridged rim left a circular print on her skin.

"Yes!" Ella said, and gave herself a matching tattoo.

At the bottom were milky marbles from a set of Chinese checkers and stray Legos and a few miniature pool balls from a table she barely recalled. They had used the cue sticks for swords and someone had gotten in trouble. "They must have thrown the table out."

"I always hated that game," Sarah said. "It wasn't any fun."

"Not like Sorry."

"I remember Sorry!"

"It's right downstairs," Ella said, "right behind the TV."

They agreed that they would have to play tonight.

"And didn't we have like a fire engine?" Sarah asked. "A white one, the hook-and-ladder kind?"

"Maybe. I don't remember."

"I wish I could find my watch," Sarah said, and Ella vowed to herself that she'd be the one to come up with it.

There were no more plastic letters. Someone must have thrown them away. They agreed that it was sad, that they should have kept them. Sarah remembered writing her name on the refrigerator with them. There was a red S. Ella wanted to find that for her too, to give it back to her and make her happy. They piled everything into the box and closed the flaps, but now they had something to do. They pounded downstairs and shuffled through the boxes for Sorry and Monopoly and Life and a new Jumanji they'd played maybe twice, even an old Chutes and Ladders that was almost flat.

"Now *that* is a stupid game," Sarah said, and though she'd liked it better than Candyland, Ella agreed. Sometimes love was giving in to someone. She admired Sarah as she stretched to put the Splat box back and thought it would be easier if she were pretty herself.

But she wasn't. She just wasn't, and there was nothing she could do about it. She could look at herself in the mirror with her glasses off and squint all she wanted, she would never be beautiful like Sarah—the kind of beauty that just a glance could make Ella hold a hand to her heart as if she were dying. It felt like that, a shock and then a withering inside, her strength draining away. Last night Sarah had come to bed from the bathroom in her nightshirt with her hair freshly brushed and drawn to one side, falling along her jawline and down her front, and Ella had clenched her hands and gripped her pillow, crushed by how good she looked, by how faraway in her perfection she seemed—not unapproachable but unreachable, so much better than Ella, as if the two of them were from a different species, like the models on TV. Sometimes she resented Sarah for making her feel this way, but it wasn't Sarah's fault, just the way things were, and she felt foolish, and then Sarah said something or laughed or just looked at her, and Ella forgot everything. It was those moments she waited for, those moments she didn't want to ruin. Like now, the two of them having fun.

In the living room, they poked through the basket of magazines and the drawers of the end tables, finding decks of cards and ugly coasters and old pens, then went over the mantel, the crusted batteries and heavy key rings and dishes of pennies dark as chocolate, the big box of wooden matches.

Sarah slid the box open and held up a match. "Dare me?"

"To do what?" Ella didn't touch the matches at their house except when her parents had her light the candles for Christmas or Thanksgiving, and even then they supervised her the whole time, made sure she ran water over the dead match and left it in the sink through dinner just to be sure.

Sarah scraped one along the box and it caught fire. Ella shrugged, and Sarah tossed the match into the fireplace, where it flickered, still dangerous. "Now you."

"What?"

"You light one."

"Why?"

"Just do it," Sarah said.

Ella did, acting bored. "So what?"

She blew it out before tossing it on the grate. Sarah's was out now too. Both stayed on top of the grate, evidence against them.

"You ever smoke?" Sarah asked.

"Why would I want to?"

"Have you ever tried it?"

"No."

"I have." Sarah hunched closer as if it was a big secret. This was what Ella liked. "I was baby-sitting for these people and they left half a cigarette in the ashtray."

"Eww."

"Yeah, it was pretty gross. I don't know how my mom stands them. Come on, I've got to show you something." She took off up the stairs like it was a game, and Ella raced after her.

Sarah was kneeling by her mother's bed, unzipping her mother's backpack. She dug inside the main part, her whole arm lost.

"What are you looking for?"

"Wait," Sarah said, and then stopped. "Okay, ready? Close your eyes."

"Why?"

"Just close them."

"Okay."

"Now put out your hands."

Ella did. She swayed like she might tip over.

"Keep them shut."

Sarah put something light and made of paper in her hands. It barely weighed anything.

"What do you think it is?"

"A cigarette."

"Nope. Good guess though."

"Some kind of origami?"

Sarah laughed. "Open your eyes."

It was a cigarette, but hand-rolled, a joint right out of her health book. It was the first one she'd ever seen in person. She dropped it as if it were lit, and Sarah laughed at her, throwing herself back on the bed.

"It's not funny," Ella said. The joint was on the floor, caught in the snarled yarn of the carpet. "Is that your mom's?"

"Duh. She's only been stoned every minute since she quit drinking."

Ella sat down beside her on the bed, then lay back so they were both looking at the slope of the ceiling above them.

"That sucks."

"Tell me about it."

"You don't get high, do you?"

Sarah raised up and looked at her like it was a dumb question, then dropped back down. "She says it's safer than drinking. There's a pipe in there too."

Ella wanted to say she was sorry but didn't think Sarah wanted to hear it again. She was mad at Aunt Margaret. She was supposed to be trying to get better. If she got arrested, who would take care of Sarah and Justin? In the middle of this, she realized they were lying next to each other, that all she had to do was roll over and hold her. She froze, aware of how close they were, their shoulders almost touching.

"Yep," Sarah said, "she's pretty amazing. I keep thinking I'm going to come home someday and find her on the kitchen floor or in the bathtub with the water running."

"She's that bad," Ella asked.

"She's better than she used to be. I don't know." Sarah raised her arms up toward the ceiling, then let them drop. "You ever drink whiskey?"

"No."

"Beer?"

"Nope."

At barbecues her dad offered her a swig from his bottle, but she never wanted any.

"I haven't either," Sarah said, and rolled on her side, one elbow jutting out, a hand propping her head. She looked straight at Ella, her smile like a challenge, all sexy teeth, and, as in her dream, Ella thought she might lean forward and kiss her.

"You want to?"

Whatever the question was, her answer was yes.

18

"What are you saying, Mother?"

"I'm not saying anything," Emily protested, and in the flush of her first glass of wine Lise shook her head to keep from laughing. "I just don't understand why anyone would choose to have that done to them."

"You don't," Meg echoed, baiting her.

"I read somewhere that it's tribal," Arlene said, trying, as usual, to turn a personal argument into an abstract discussion. "In some societies it's a coming of age."

"Not Western society," Emily said. "I'm sure it's a middle-class bias of mine and that I'm behind the times—"

"It is and you are," Meg interrupted. Lise was waiting for her to turn around and pull up her sweater so Emily could see the wavy-rayed sun at the small of her back.

"Thank you, but it seems ludicrous to me that we now have a generation of teenagers who look like sideshow freaks because of this. Honestly. It's different from when you kids were growing up. You can always cut your hair or grow it back, but these things are permanent. They're on their faces, for God's sake."

"They'll wash right off," Ken said.

"It's the idea," Emily said, missing his point.

"The boys know they're temporary," Lise put in, "that's why they wanted them. Sam's terrified of needles, so is Justin."

"You don't see girls doing things like this."

The statement was wrong on so many levels that Lise didn't know where to start, and in the seconds it took to process a response, she realized her goal in the whole thing was to stay out of it, let Ken and Meg deal with her. Emily never listened to her anyway. She busied her mouth with draining her wineglass, watched the raindrops gather and fall from the broad leaves of the rhododendren that crowded her end of the porch. It was cool, but they were tired of being inside.

"What is makeup?" Meg asked. "It's the same thing."

"No, I'm sorry, but eye shadow and tattoos are not the same thing."

"I didn't think this was going to be a problem," Ken said, and she could see he was losing his famous patience. It was rare, but he could be rigid when he was attacked directly. "They got them out of a box of Cracker Jack."

"They've been in Cracker Jacks for years," Arlene testified. "My kids used to put them on their hands, that was the cool thing to do."

Lise was ready for a comment from Emily about the debased nature of the inner city, which would lead to a standoff between her and Meg, a drawn-out balancing of moral outrage and practical application, a test of who knew more about the real world. Their sparring bored Lise. Her family were old North Shore Republicans and steered clear of personal politics. Their talk before supper was a lighthearted replaying of the day that naturally turned into making plans for tomorrow, voting on what they would do and who would watch the children, who would be responsible for lunch, the tasks rationally divvied up to avoid hurt feelings. At the beach they would no more discuss the significance and history of tattoos than the consequences of regulating the Internet. Their time was more important, dedicated to the serious matter of relaxing. It seemed to Lise that the Maxwells always had to break things down to principles, except they'd chosen their positions in advance, so their arguments possessed a deadening inevitability. Both sides were right and both sides were wrong, eternally, because of who they were. Honor was at stake, and position. The only compromise was a softening of tone, an apology delivered in private.

Yet there was mercy, too, at times, a nodded concession, a puzzling retreat covered by unexpected silence, a matter for conjecture. Meg said nothing of her tattoo, let Emily's assertions stand. Ken shrugged it off, glad to have peace restored.

Lise needed another wine and used the lull to make her exit, swinging around the screen door. The girls were upstairs, the boys on the floor in the living room, Sam watching Justin play his Game Boy. She was sure he saw her. He purposely didn't look over so she'd know it was her fault he couldn't play his game. She suppressed the desire to stick out her tongue. How many times had she listened to Emily bad-mouth her for letting him have one, and then this garbage?

The wine and finding Rufus alone in the kitchen lifted her above any pettiness. He was slumped down by his empty water dish, his eyes bloody from sleeping.

"Hey, Roof," she said. "Little dry there, huh, buddy?"

She took care of him first, the stream from the spigot ringing in his dish, spritzing her hand. "There you go," she said, squatting to set it in the corner. He looked up, grateful, then bent to it, his tags dinging against the rim.

Arlene's diseased lime sat on the cutting board in a spill of juice. Lise poured herself another sauvignon blanc and took a generous sip, looking out the window at their cars parked under the chestnut. Steak tonight. Ken should get the coals going, she thought. That way they'd have time to watch a movie later. She had a tendency to watch the clock here, as if it might deliver her. Rather than ask time to speed up, she found it was better to slow herself down and let the rest of the world fly by.

Standing at the sink, stalling an extra minute, she felt like a suspect, alien and separate from the others. The first time she came here, her junior year in college, she'd been shy and didn't know what to say to any of them. She spent most of her time finding hiding places and trying to be alone with Ken. Twenty years later, nothing had changed. Like Harry Potter lodging with the Dursleys, she was still a guest, a visitor.

The thought was not new, but the wine made her contemplate its implications seriously, and the view of the lake, intoxicating, locked on her sight like a slide, someone else's rainy vacation, the blackened docks reaching into the water. The scene captivated her, held her, a pregnant paralysis, as if she were about to make a great discovery about not just her life but the true nature of things—how she belonged in all this, how anyone belonged in a world that seemed foreign. There was a mood to the colors, the storm darkening everything. The elements blurred, wavered out of focus, and yet she didn't turn away, stayed connected to the vision and its promise. She became aware of the liquid surface of her eyes, the thump of her heart, and now her vision shifted—like a telescope tilted a few degrees—shortened and fell on the cobwebbed screen, the white windowsill, dust bringing out ripples and eddies of wood grain beneath the paint, knots like islands, the lines on a topographic map. It had the same magnetic power over her, held the same inscrutable meaning for an in-

stant, and then the spell or whatever it was dissipated, and she was leaning against the sink with her wineglass in her hand, Arlene's lime dead
and shriveled on the butcher block, the world's secrets closed to her again,
wholly unavailable. It had been nothing, a momentary buzz, a sip of wine
kicking in, pleasantly destroying a swath of unemployed brain cells, and
yet feeling it slip away from her was a loss.

Rufus slopped at his dish, parched.

"Okay," Lise said, "enough," and he stopped, then stiffly backed
out of the corner. He stood there in the middle of the floor, facing her
expectantly. "I bet you're hungry, huh?"

She called for Sam.

"Yeah?" he called from the other room.

"Come feed the dog." She waited, gave him time. "Now."

He said nothing, but stalked around the corner and past her, intent on fulfilling his mission so he could get back to watching Justin. He
dug the plastic Pitt cup into the bag of kibble. Rufus attended him, switching his tail.

"And remember to close the top all the way. We don't want ants."

He let go a sigh, but, tired of being the bitch, she let it slide. He
worked like a slave under her eyes, every motion forced and defiant at
the same time, the absolute minimum he could do. She had to remind
him to roll the flap of the bag, earning her another sigh. As he rushed out,
dipping a shoulder to dodge the fridge, she couldn't control herself any
longer and chased him with an unfelt "Thank you!"

Rufus looked up, confused, then went back to his food.

She glanced around the counters, did an unsteady pirouette, looking for something she could do—any excuse to keep her there. She thought
of the broccoli in the hydrator, but it was too early to cut it up. Everything
depended on the steaks, on Ken. She wished they needed something from
the store—a loaf of garlic bread, another gallon of milk.

The creak of the screen opening startled her, set her in motion as
if she'd been pushed.

It was just Arlene, finished with her drink, but her presence was
enough to evict Lise from the kitchen, two playing pieces occupying the
same space.

"I think these kids are getting hungry," Lise mentioned in passing.

"Don't talk to me, talk to the chef."

Lise repeated the comment to the porch at large, sticking her head out the door. Ken seemed relieved, levering himself up from the glider, beer in hand. Emily and Meg were on to some other topic and barely registered her.

"Need help?" she asked Ken.

"No, I think I'm all set."

He escaped out the back door to the garage. Arlene was done fixing her drink, so Lise was alone in the kitchen again, even Rufus gone, off begging chips from the kids. Out on the lake, whitecaps foamed and sank, winked on the dark water, all sharply, devoid of any private message, just waves, the effect of weather. That had been it most likely, her isolation mixed with the day. She refreshed her wine from the bottle in the fridge and stood at the sink, watching, ready to flee at the slightest sound.

19

"Not again," her mother objected between bites, like it was a surprise— like it was all a plot against her.

"That's what they said," Aunt Arlene assured her. "A hundred percent chance."

Great, Sarah thought. They'd be stuck in the house again. They could only walk Rufus so many times a day. That was, *if* it was his house. Ella didn't think so, which meant she was dreaming and miserable for nothing. At least after the pain of Christmas break she'd hooked up with Mark. She'd convinced herself she didn't miss him, that he was a jerk. And then, lying down at night, she thought of the couch in his basement and the lava lamp that sent blue bubbles swimming across the walls like fish.

"I'm sorry," Grandma apologized. "I didn't think it would be like this. I was hoping we could squeeze in our golf tomorrow."

Uncle Ken told her it wasn't her fault. They could play Thursday or Friday, he promised.

"If it ever stops," Aunt Lisa said.

Sarah ate, not part of the conversation. She had her dinner balanced in her lap, knees clenched together, pigeon-toed. When she cut her steak the blood circled her plate, staining her potato salad. Beside her, Ella batted at something invisible. A fly had gotten in and was slaloming between the wrought-iron tables, shopping up and down the porch for a place to land, buzzing Justin so he almost spilled his milk.

"Just ignore it," their mother instructed, but Justin kept ducking, though Sarah willed him to sit still, to stop being such a baby. "It's not going to hurt you, it's just a fly."

"I'll get it," Sam volunteered, clanking his plate down on a table to fetch the flyswatter from inside.

"You sit and eat your dinner," Aunt Lisa ordered, pointing, and he sighed.

"All this uproar over a little fly," Aunt Arlene said, trying to be funny.

She wasn't. Sarah felt sorry for whoever her students had been.

Uncle Ken was done—he was the fastest eater—and went inside. When he came back he had the swatter.

"Not while we're eating," Aunt Lisa said, so he propped the door open like it might fly out on its own.

"You know what I was thinking," Grandma announced loudly, so everyone turned to her, and Sarah knew this was trouble. Grandma was great at making plans. "I was thinking if it's going to be cruddy again tomorrow, we might take a day trip up to the falls. As far as I know, the children have never seen them."

"*Niagara* Falls?" her mother said, like it was crazy.

"In the rain?" Aunt Lisa said, and Sarah found herself agreeing, rooting for them, thinking how bizarre it was that they were on the same side. It would be boring, driving all that way just to see something everyone else thought was a big deal but she didn't care about. She knew her mother and Aunt Lisa wouldn't let her and Ella stay here by themselves.

"It should keep the crowds down," Grandma said. "You're going to get wet there anyway with the spray." When no one commented on it, she said, "I'm just throwing it out for consideration. I think at this point people are running out of things to do. I know I am. Of course if no one's interested . . ."

"I'm interested," her mother said, "I'm just trying to catch up to it."

"I think the kids are at an age where they can appreciate it."

Her mother seemed unsure, like there must be a trick.

"I'd like to see them again," Aunt Arlene said. "They're so close."

"From here," Uncle Ken said, "it's less than two hours."

While they discussed how far it was, Sarah caught Ella's eye. Like her, she was bent over her plate, eating, staying out of it, hoping the adults would make the right decision, but a roll of her eyes let Sarah know she was just as thrilled. Her mother was beginning to like the idea, saying it might be fun, and Ella stuck out her tongue as if the steak was grossing her out. Sarah almost laughed at it, had to cough and look away, across the water. They were both thinking the same thing: they were completely and totally screwed.

"Whatever you want to do is fine," Grandma said. "For me, it's a sentimental journey. I'm not interested in it as a natural wonder per se, but I thought you all might feel left out if Arlene and I went by ourselves."

"What else are we going to do if it rains?" her mother asked.

"And it's going to rain," Aunt Arlene said, definite.

"Can we go on the boat?" Sam asked.

"Of course," Grandma said. "You can't go to Niagara Falls and not go on the boat. We'll go down in the caves too, right behind the waterfall. You'll have to wear a slicker."

"What time would we get going?" Uncle Ken asked, and they started making plans. They'd take the van and the 4Runner; they could fit everyone that way. Sarah imagined four hours in the van with Grandma and Aunt Arlene and Justin and her mother.

"Can Ella and me stay here?" she asked.

"No," her mother said, final.

"Then can I sit with Ella?"

Ella seconded it.

Her mother looked to Uncle Ken, who nodded.

"Sure," she said, frowning, as if Sarah had gotten away with something.

"Well, this should be a real adventure," Grandma said, like she was surprised she'd gotten her way.

Aunt Lisa didn't say anything, just ate. Sarah's steak was cold and tough, the fat on the edges the color of old tape. She wanted to be done. Tomorrow was shot, so there was what—Thursday and Friday. Saturday they'd go home. Mark would get back right about the same time. He'd call and say he wanted to get together—or not. In two weeks, school started, her life started again. She wondered if she would see her father before that. He was in the U.P. at her grandparents', probably inside because of the rain, the same as here. She wondered if he took his girlfriend to meet them, the way he insisted Mark come inside before a date and shake his hand. She thought, idiotically, of calling him, and of what she'd say.

I miss you.

So does Justin.

Mom's okay.

On the phone they hardly talked, like they might mess things up worse.

Good, he'd say.

Huh.

That's great, Picklechips, just super. Hang in there, babe—like he might come to save them. That was what Justin thought, no matter how many times she told him it wasn't going to happen. He'd cry and then she'd feel like shit and wouldn't know what to say to him. It was like her father used to say when she was little: just another day in the Carlisle House of Fun.

Another fly had sneaked in and was weaving around the first one, the two of them just missing head-on collisions. Uncle Ken stood up and shut the door, the swatter in his hand, then sat back down and waited for everyone to finish. Sarah took her plate in, holding it high so her mother couldn't see how much she'd eaten. She dropped her fork in the silverware basket, then went into the downstairs bathroom and shut the door, locked it with a metallic clack.

With the light out it was quiet, only the skunky smell of the water to disturb her. She sat there with her eyes closed, biting the corner of her thumbnail, her breath warm on her knuckles. She gnawed one corner, then the other, back and forth over the square points, turning her head. Her teeth slipped and clicked together, making a strange sound in the space above the bathtub, but she didn't open her eyes. With her other hand she reached up and removed the thumb from her lips, took it away. Everything's fine, she thought. There was no need to freak out. Everything was okay, as long as she didn't think.

20

"Whose turn is it to do the dishes?" his mother asked.

She looked around the porch at everyone, and Justin felt like he did at school when he knew Mrs. Foley was going to call on him.

"The boys can do them," Aunt Lisa volunteered.

"I always have to do the dishes," Sam whined—something Justin wouldn't even think of doing. Backtalk, his mother called it. "Ella never has to."

"You haven't done them once since we've been here," Aunt Lisa said. "Now get your tattooed butt in there."

"But—"

"Don't argue," Uncle Ken said, and pointed to the door.

"Don't go in empty-handed," Grandma said, holding out her pie plate and her cup and saucer.

A nod from his mother and Justin cleared her place and followed Sam in.

Aunt Lisa was right behind them, telling them to shove the food garbage down the disposal. He and Sam stood there while she zipped around the kitchen, throwing away paper towels and dropping forks in the sink. Dirty plates were piled on both counters, and on the table with the sliced tomatoes and the open jar of pickles, the container of potato salad.

Aunt Lisa stopped flying around and stared at them. She sighed and shook her head and looked at them like they were idiots.

"*One* of you rinses the dishes and *one* of you puts them in the dishwasher. You figure out who does what. I don't care."

"*I'll* put them in," Sam called.

"Fine, just do it." She turned the water on and kept her hand under it until it was ready.

It wasn't fair, but there was nothing Justin could do. It was like at the video arcade when Sam cut in front of him so he could go on the ski machine first.

The water was hot, steam clouding up around the faucet. The dinner plates were so heavy they bent his wrist. He used a fork to scrape the fat and potato salad into the disposal, then held them under the running water. All Sam had to do was fit them into the dishwasher. Justin's fingers were cucky. Between plates he wiped them on the sides of his pants.

"Turn the light on so you can see what you're doing," Aunt Lisa said. She reached over him and flipped the switch, grabbed a scrubbing pad and swirled it around the plate he was holding. "You've got to get this stuff off, the machine won't do everything for you. Don't be afraid to get wet."

He wasn't. He was afraid of the knives, thin and slippery in the water. He was afraid of dropping a glass and having a piece stick in his thumb. At home he was afraid of their disposal, the blades spinning under the rubber guard. Once he'd dropped a fork in and it had chewed the smooth handle—from then on the scratches snagged the skin of his fingers, and he avoided that fork. He was afraid he'd mess up and get yelled at. He was careful now, cleaning the plates like Aunt Lisa before sliding them onto the counter.

"Can you go any slower?" Sam asked.

"God," Justin said. "You do it then."

"Good luck."

"Less talk, more work," his mother said, delivering a cup and saucer they'd forgotten. "Don't worry about the food, I'll put it away."

Uncle Ken looked in around the corner of the refrigerator. "As soon as you guys are done, we're going to watch a movie."

"They're getting there," Aunt Lisa said, and fitted her cup and saucer in by herself, rearranging things.

"I gotta go to the bathroom," Sam said, and left. The coffee cups piled up on the counter, Aunt Arlene's with lipstick around the rim.

"Where's your helper?" his mother asked. She laughed when he told her. "That's the oldest trick in the book. Your uncle used to pull that one on me all the time. Don't expect him to come back." She leaned over him to see how he was doing, then put the coffee cups in the top. "There's not much left. You know how to start it, right? It's just like ours, you just turn the knob till you hear it go on."

The last thing in were the big serving spoons. His hands felt like they did after swimming. His mother was right, Sam didn't come back. Justin popped the nozzle and squeezed the plastic bottle until the lemony soap filled the little drawer. He closed the door and locked the latch the way Sarah did at home. The knob had an arrow on one side. He turned it until it was even with PREWASH and then a little more. The machine gargled on like a faucet, a rushing of water inside.

He wasn't sure he'd done it right, and stood there watching as if it might stop. When it didn't, he went into the living room where everyone else was. Sam was sitting on the couch with Ella and Sarah, all three of them under a blanket. Justin had to step over Rufus to get to an empty seat. He pulled the blanket over his lap and sat back, his shoulder against Sarah's. At home sometimes she would put her arm around him when they watched TV, but she didn't now. He smelled her smell and that was enough.

"Thank you for doing the dishes, Justin," his mother said so everyone could hear.

"You're welcome," he said.

"Okay," Uncle Ken announced, standing by the VCR, "everybody ready?"

Grandma stopped working on the puzzle and came over to the couch.

"Is there room for your old grandma under there?" she asked, and he lifted the blanket and let her in. "Isn't this nice and cozy," she said. "Snug as a bug in a rug."

It was *Toy Story 2,* where Woody gets stolen by the collector guy. Uncle Ken turned the TV up so they could hear it over the dishwasher. Even Grandma laughed at Woody riding the dog through the yard sale, and then everyone went quiet when the mother put him up on the shelf with Squeaky the Penguin.

"They shelved him," the Slinky Dog said with horror.

"I'm just amazed how far they've come with this animation," Grandma said across him to Uncle Ken so he couldn't hear.

"Who wants popcorn?" Aunt Lisa asked, getting up, and they all hollered, "Me!"

She went into the kitchen and they went back to the movie. At home his father made popcorn with chili powder on it so you had to bolt a soda. At Blockbuster he let them each pick out one candy; he'd even get Reese's Pieces for himself and then share them.

The dishwasher suddenly stopped, making the sound loud. Aunt Lisa stood in the doorway. "We've got a problem," she said.

Uncle Ken jumped up to help, and Grandma, and his mother. They all stopped in the doorway.

"For God's sake," Grandma said.

"It's all right," Uncle Ken said.

"Justin," his mother called him, and he hesitated before going over, afraid of what he'd see, knowing that the others were watching him instead of the movie.

There was foam all over the floor. Fluffy white mounds covered Aunt Lisa's feet, reached all the way to the refrigerator. The dishwasher was so full he couldn't see the plates. His mother put her hand on his shoulder. "What kind of soap did you use?"

"Just soap," Justin said, still not believing it. "The yellow stuff on the sink."

She looked over his head like she was talking to someone else, then looked at him again.

"That's dish soap for when you do them by hand. There's a different kind of soap you have to use for the dishwasher."

"It said right on it—"

"I know," she said. "It's okay. It was an accident."

Still, he wanted to show her. And it did say that—*concentrated dish liquid.* Why did it say it if it wasn't supposed to go in the dishwasher?

"I know," she said, "I know."

"I was meaning to wash this floor anyway," Grandma said, and patted his shoulder.

"A cup of vinegar's supposed to cut the suds," Aunt Lisa said. "You may have to run it a few times to get everything."

"We've got vinegar, I'm pretty sure. The regular kind or cider, or doesn't it matter?"

Uncle Ken was scooping bubbles with a strainer and dumping them in the sink.

"I'll take care of this," his mother said. "You go watch the movie."

"I'm sorry," Justin said, and felt his throat close, choking him.

"Hey, come on," his mother said, smiling, "stop. It wasn't your fault."

He spun out of her hands, cutting around the fridge and hurrying through the living room, his face turned away from Sarah and the others, the light of the TV blinding as he passed and threw open the door to the upstairs.

"Justin," Uncle Ken called, but after he closed the door no one opened it, and upstairs in his sleeping bag, all he heard was the movie coming through the floor, and then, much later, the dishwasher turning on, churning. Sam would laugh and call him a crybaby but he didn't care.

The door opened then, and footsteps slowly climbed the stairs. It was his mother, not Sarah, who he thought it would be. She sat down beside him on the floor and rubbed his back through his sleeping bag before she said anything.

"It wasn't your fault," she said again.

She explained that accidents happened and that was how we learned, that Grandma and everyone knew he was just trying to do something nice. She said it three times after that, touching his cheek so he wanted to scratch it, making him look her in the eyes until he agreed that it wasn't.

But it was.

21

"How is he?" Arlene asked, stopped in the dark.

Margaret found a spot by Henry's workbench and lit up, the cupped flame making her face glow like a moon, then disappear.

"Still despondent."

"I feel bad for him."

"He'll get over it," she said gently, as if that were sad in itself.

She passed the lighter back, and Arlene had to use both hands to take it. When Margaret inhaled, her face warmed, a soft orange. The rain played above them, insistent. Tomorrow they were going to the falls.

Margaret touched a cardboard box on the workbench, a tangled roll of twine. "This place is a total firetrap."

"Usually he was so neat, like our father. Shows you how things pile up."

She remembered the last time Henry was up here, two years ago. He never lifted a hammer, saving his energy to play with the children. She knew there was something wrong from the way his skin hung on his neck, but he didn't feel the need to tell her until the fall, before he went into the hospital. He spent that summer on the dock, or napping, wearing the same gray sweater Emily had knitted him twenty years ago, the cuffs unraveling, dragging in the dip. In the middle of the week, Emily made a special trip to the laundromat with it. When she brought it back, he hauled it on sitting down, Emily helping him find the armholes.

"I remember he used to have everything labeled," Margaret said. "Every screw had its own little place. And this was always cleaned off, in case he needed to fix something. He used to hide out here when he didn't want to deal with us. I don't think he did anything, he just cleaned up."

"He always had some project going on," Arlene said, partly in his defense and partly because it was true.

"I don't know, the more I try to think of him, the less I remember. I can't remember him doing things with us, it was always Mom. I think she made it easy for him not to be involved."

"That was how things were then."

"I don't think so. I had friends whose fathers talked to them. It was the sixties, it wasn't like *Father Knows Best.*"

"Well, that's where we came from," Arlene said. "You have to remember that. I can look back at my mother and father and see where they could have done better, but it doesn't do any good."

"I'm more worried about now. I worry about Justin, and Sarah. I know this is all affecting them, everything I'm going through."

So, Arlene thought, it wasn't about Henry. The two of them smoked in the dark, the air around them cloudy. One of the secrets of teaching was shutting up, letting the student teach herself. Over the years she'd become adept at recognizing these situations, and now she fell into a ritual of counting silently—six, seven—waiting for the inevitable.

"But I'm proud of them," Margaret said, as if she'd thought the argument through. "And I tell them that. I may be a horrible mother—that's all right, I know I've got problems—but I let them know how I feel about them. I know Dad wasn't proud of me, and I know he didn't like me as a person—"

"He loved you very much."

"I know, but he didn't like me very much. I'm sure he wished he had a different kind of daughter."

"That's not true," Arlene said, but her silence afterward turned it into a lie. She was done with her cigarette, and stood there, trapped.

"I'm not trying to say he was a terrible person or that I'm scarred or anything, but I don't think we should pretend that everything was perfect like Mom does." She found a can on the counter and stubbed her butt out in it.

"I don't think anyone's pretending that."

"Maybe she honestly remembers it that way. Maybe she has to. Maybe I'm remembering it worse than it actually was. What do you think, did he like me? I'm sure you two talked."

She couldn't be serious, was Arlene's first thought. She'd said it offhand, but here she was, waiting on her answer. It was like being attacked, forced at gunpoint. Arlene thought there was a confidence on her part that shouldn't be breached, for Henry's sake.

"He didn't," Margaret said, certain, answering her own question. "It's okay, you don't have to say anything."

Arlene thought it was unfair that she'd taken away her only escape.

"He said that you were your own person," Arlene said, aware that in her passion to tell the truth (and shut Margaret up) she'd spoken too loudly. "In our family that was a compliment. He didn't like it, but he respected it. He cared for you very much."

That was all she could honestly say. She hoped it would be enough.

"I didn't like him either," Margaret said. She laughed, just a cough in the dark.

The surprise of it angered Arlene, as if she'd been fooled all these years.

"You don't mean that."

"I know, everyone else thought he was the nicest person. We just never got along. I think he stopped trying after a while, and I think I held that against him, that he'd write me off like that. I know I didn't make it easy for him, but . . ."

Arlene had to restrain herself from shaking her, the ungrateful little thing. Have some compassion, she wanted to say.

Maybe this was the truth for her, maybe this was her confession, what she would have told him if there'd been time, if things had been different. When her father had died, Arlene had had to forget his disappointments in her, his preference for Henry, his dismissal of women in general. No one had been there to tell her she was justified, and she'd been ashamed of thinking of him that way. Perhaps Margaret was asking her for forgiveness.

"I liked you," she said instead. "I always stuck up for you."

"I know."

"You'd be surprised how much he thought of you. He worried about you more than he worried about Kenneth, and with good reason. Do you remember how happy he was at your wedding?"

"That didn't work out, did it?"

"You remember what he said, that toast he gave?"

"Yes."

"Do you think he meant it?"

"Yes."

"Well then," Arlene said. "Don't say he gave up on you. Just because you two didn't get along doesn't mean he didn't love you, or that you didn't love him. He knew how you felt about him."

Arlene wondered if that was true, or true of her own father, a wish spoken out loud.

"Thank you," Margaret said, controlled, so it didn't matter.

They were done, but now, aroused, Arlene wanted to talk more. She'd been a good aunt, a good sister, and as they moved to the door and through it into the rain (the light from the kitchen reflected in the slick stones, drops dimpling the image), she was impressed with herself, surprised by how well she could articulate their situation, as if she'd been secretly mulling it for years.

Inside, in her room, she thought that in a way she had. And yet, alone, the movie playing on the other side of the wall, she remembered her surprise and anger at Margaret's words, though she knew they were heartfelt, not supposed to be a joke. *I didn't like him either.* Arlene pondered her role in Margaret's life, her years as a well-meaning go-between. She'd known all along and not said anything.

It wasn't a secret, not on Margaret's side. Arlene had put it down to a teenager's easy scorn, never thinking it would last past twenty-five. But then there was the college fiasco, the string of menial jobs, phone calls in the middle of the night from distant cities.

Henry was one for making decisions and sticking by them. He'd cut his losses with Margaret, married her off and said good luck. "I hope he knows what he's in for," he'd said of Jeff, and all Arlene could do was frown at him, her disapproval expected, easily shrugged off. It wasn't that Henry didn't like her. He was just tired of her acting like a child, wished she would grow up so he could stop worrying about her, stop bailing her out. He'd hoped that married life would settle her down. Arlene could see him now, shaking his head at this new turn of events, not at all surprised.

She didn't tell Margaret that, and wouldn't.

She needed a cigarette, but she'd just had one and didn't want to go back outside with everyone watching. She'd already walked Rufus once after supper. It was asinine that she couldn't smoke on the porch, with no one there.

Quietly she rose from the edge of her bed and made her way to the door, leaning against it to ease it shut while she turned the lock. She crept to the window and slowly raised the sash, as if she were going to sneak out of the house. The trees were dripping, and from the lake came the slop of waves. She knelt down, her ribs pressing the sill, and stuck her face into the cool air, a drop anointing her forehead. She protected the cigarette, dipping her chin as she lit up, then exhaled so the cloud floated out into the night. The light from the living room windows lay faint and elongated on the wet grass, the TV flaring like a fire, casting shadows.

The view was familiar. During the war she'd opened this window for Henry, out prowling around with his friends after a dance at the casino, getting into mischief. Their parents had a curfew but slept through it, and Henry would show up at two in the morning, smelling yeasty, and she'd have to help him in the window. It was never easy, since he was big and frequently laughed at his own unaccustomed clumsiness. Some nights he'd bug her to come out—Come on, Ar, don't be a stick—and she'd relent, pulling on her sweatshirt and stealing across the lawn, the two of them paddling out into the awesome calm, the stars mirrored in the water.

She had the urge to sneak out now, climb through and come in the front, just to see if anyone would notice—possibly Margaret, sitting in the big chair again, replaying their conversation. She wished she could explain that her father hadn't always been like that, that he'd had his wild times too. They'd all been young once, and made mistakes. Margaret shouldn't blame him for forgetting what it was like.

She should do it, she thought, sit on the sill and swivel her legs out, twist and duck her head under. She'd walk around the house like a burglar, tiptoe in the porch door and peek through the window at them, give the children a thrill.

Silly. It was wet out, and she didn't see well in the dark, never had.

She smoked her cigarette down to the Lucky crest, then held it out for the rain to extinguish, and when that didn't work, spit on the end. She pitched it onto the lawn, then pushed herself up and closed and locked the window, all softly, as if she might get caught, but when she was done, the room oppressively bright around her, she didn't feel as if she'd gotten away with something. No, she thought, it was the exact opposite.

22

1952. The day came back with the date embossed on the matchbooks, her dress, the cake that leaned because the base wasn't strong enough, the ride away from the drunken reception in her uncle Carl's Packard when they were finally alone, both of them reclining in the plush backseat with champagne headaches, eyes closed, while her uncle the teetotaler chauffered, and Henry took her hand. She had been twenty-three, an eager bride. Nearly forty-nine years, Emily thought, and steeled herself for the twinge of missing fifty. She wondered how much she would remember, how much she had already mixed with the trips they took in the sixties, the jerky home movies of the children waving by the inadequate railing, behind them Goat Island and the river swirling blue before it poured broken and foamy over the long drop. There was no thunder, just the whirring of the projector, the image flickering on the screen Henry set up by the fireplace on Pearl Street, popcorn dotting the green carpet she hated and couldn't afford to replace. The children always wanted him to run everything backward.

Beside her Sarah laughed, and the movie drew her attention again, a toy cowboy riding a toy dinosaur like a bronco. For all its technical wizardry it was dull as mush, or maybe it was supposed to elude her. Half the things they laughed at were a mystery, in-jokes from TV shows far beyond her. As simple as the action was, she had lost the story line. The toys seemed to jump from one big production number to another, frantic as a bad musical. She wanted to go to bed, wake up and find it was tomorrow, the rain hanging over the lake. She and Arlene could go to the falls by themselves if no one else was interested.

She was hoping for rain now. She couldn't ask them to give up a sunny day. Arlene would give her a hard time and eventually relent, but the falls would be wall-to-wall tourists, and she had no desire to subject herself to that brand of indignity. She'd lived on memories this far. There would be other summers.

Margaret disappeared upstairs to check on Justin again. The movie had to be over soon. It was past the children's bedtime, fast coming up on her own. Rufus had long since retired to the throw rug in front of her dresser. The soundtrack drowned out the reassuring sprinkle of rain, so perfect for sleeping. She turned to check the window behind her, drops holding the coppery glow of the streetlight by the Wisemans'. It was too bright inside to see farther, only the dark reflection of the drapes, her face, mercifully softened, surprisingly unlined.

Forty-eight years, and even at twenty-three she hadn't been a girl but a young woman accustomed to city living, knocking around that ratty apartment with crazy, leggy Jocelyn as if Pittsburgh were New York, the two of them destined for Broadway, Radio City at the very least. She had pictures from before that, snaps her father had taken of her on their back steps or at her grade school commencement, her peachy cheeks giving her a baby face, her body already blossoming under her gown. "Who's that hot little number?" Henry would say, making fun, and sometimes Emily was jealous, since that Kersey girl was gone, not her anymore. How hard she'd worked to get rid of her, and then she missed her, wished she could return to that quiet life, her mother's house a blur of steam on wash day, the bleached sheets on the clothesline belling like sails, tossing off their pins so she had to hunt for them in the cold grass.

Margaret reappeared and laid her head sideways on her clasped hands—Justin was asleep. This obnoxious cartoon, it was endless. The truly galling thing was that it had been a hit. Emily remembered the commercials playing incessantly those last weeks, the bizarre stereo of several TVs on Henry's floor tuned to the same channel so that the clamor followed her as she walked down the hall and waited at the elevators, meaning the only peace she had was in the cafeteria, taking the corner farthest from the line and eating straight from her tray, the words of the newspaper running through her brain like ticker tape, meaningless figures.

The first time they saw the falls it had been sunny. The spray sent up its perpetual rainbow, as if blessing them. She'd been amazed, though she knew the science behind it as well as he did—the mist a prism bending light into its visible spectrum. How little it was made of.

Henry had been tempted to say something, to compare their love to it, and she kissed him, held her lips to his until she could shush him with a finger. He knew not to ruin it, and they stood there in Canada, married, with money to spend, knowing the motel waited for them at the end of the day.

The children crowed and cackled with laughter, Sam pointing at a toy spaceman sailing through the air, headed for an open window, his eyes bugged wide. The plot was creaking to its slapdash finale, which somehow involved a dog.

She checked her watch surreptitiously, lifting the blanket. It was late, but she was too tired to stay up for the news, and in truth she didn't hold out much hope for the girl, not after three days. Kenneth could fill her in tomorrow. All she wanted to know was what it was going to be like.

She still had a pack of matches from the Bridal Veil Motel secreted in her dresser with the browning report cards and jagged baby teeth, the cardboard cover nicked and discolored, the match heads crumbling like a roll of Henry's Tums she'd run through the dryer. She'd lost the cherished washcloth somehow, gone to spring cleaning or a move, used as a rag in Henry's shop or sent to camp or college with the children. Careless of her, but she'd been so busy then. She had dreamed of sitting like this, no chore that desperately needed her attention.

Finally, the credits arrived. Kenneth and Margaret marshaled the children, making each of them give her a good-night kiss before heading up. Sam squeezed too tight, as if he were wrestling her. The girls were so different from each other, and from their mothers, Sarah affectionate, Ella shy and polite. And then they were gone, the downstairs empty, the ceiling above her thumping.

The bathroom was free. Arlene was hibernating again. Kenneth could close up. She'd have to turn on the radio by her bed and try not to fall asleep. It wouldn't be long, she thought. At ten they'd have the weather.

23

It was too late for pie and way too late to start another movie, but Ken wasn't tired. He'd done nothing today—the convenience store and the casino, but he'd sneaked those rolls in, maybe an hour's worth of work. What he'd done with the rest of the day he wasn't sure. Tomorrow would be lost as well. He'd shoot a roll of his mother in front of the falls, some of the kids, Lise. He'd have to catch up Thursday and Friday, and he worried that he'd run out of time and light. And still he wasn't convinced any of them would come out, the Holga was so prone to leaks. He'd already gone through a whole roll of gaffer's tape trying to black out the cracks.

Meg came down first, and went to check the dishwasher. It needed another run. Without the TV, the machine seemed louder, filling the dim kitchen behind her.

"How's he doing?" Ken asked.

"He's out, the poor kid. I don't think he's having much fun."

"He had a good time at the arcade today."

"I worry about him. He's not like Sarah."

"You mean he's not like you."

"You know who he's like?" she asked.

"Who?"

"I think he's a lot like you. He never says anything."

"That's like Dad, not like me."

"It's the same thing," she said. "Very male, keeping everything secret."

He laughed at this. She was the biggest secret keeper of them all.

"Okay," she said, "I deserved that, but it's true, he does keep everything inside."

"Everyone does, to some extent. Imagine what it would be like if we didn't."

"I don't have to imagine, not after the last year. It's like I've been turned inside out."

"You're all right now though," he asked.

"It's easy here. It's when I'm by myself that it's a problem."

He let it rest there. He wished they had had a fire tonight, but it was too late.

"What about you?" she asked. "You ever have times like that, or is it just me?"

"Of course," he said, "all the time."

He was glad to reassure her. Because it was the truth. He knew Lise considered him oversensitive, but he'd seen her own low moments, nights when, instead of crying, she patiently waited for the TV to reach the news so she could go to bed without him commenting on how early it was, and then when he followed her in she would be asleep, or pretending to be, cut off from him but her turned back sending a message, one he was helpless to translate beyond the fact that she was angry at him for not understanding her (which he didn't). It was normal to have those moments, especially at this time of life, when one was tempted to look back and regret all that had gone wrong, all that was left undone. At times it could be paralyzing, but then there was work to get up for, and the children to get off to school. It seemed almost no help that the only solution was to keep busy, to avoid the question, really, since it never went away. But he couldn't tell Meg that.

"They pass," he said.

"That's good. I'm hoping mine will. It's just been a bad year, with Dad and everything."

Bad *years,* he wanted to say. She'd been like this even before their father, before she and Jeff had fallen apart, before she'd done rehab.

"They will," Ken said.

They heard Lise coming down the stairs and for an instant stopped talking, as if they'd been caught.

"Niagara Falls," Ken filled in, as if he'd thought about it at all.

"Slowly I turned, step by step, inch by inch." Meg's fingers were claws in front of her face. They'd played this game since they were little, a legacy of their father's love of the Three Stooges (their mother had no tolerance for them).

Lise dropped onto the couch beside him with her book. "The girls are still yakking away, but the boys are down."

Out of habit, Ken thanked her.

"So, what time do you want to get going tomorrow?" Lise asked.

"Nine, I think," Meg guessed.

The tone of the room had changed, and he knew that he and Meg could not talk seriously now. Lise laid a hand on his thigh while she read, and he wanted to apologize to Meg. It felt like a kind of contest he was trapped in, and while they were both there, a stalemate. They sat on either side of him like bodyguards, reading. He turned the TV on low, though the news wasn't for another twenty minutes. In the kitchen, the dishwasher rolled on.

24

She got stoned in the garage before putting away the dishes. She liked to go to bed high, to slingshot herself into wild dreams, sleeping as if bludgeoned. It made waking up harder, but all spring she'd forced herself downstairs to get breakfast for Sarah before the early bus, the two of them silently occupying the kitchen—like now, only the clatter of the dishes to keep her company.

She liked this time of night, and being the last one up, beyond the grasp of everyone she'd disappointed, as if the world were fresh again, all things possible in her heart. If it were a clear night, she would go out on the dock and watch the stars, maybe sit on the screenporch in her mother's coat and listen to the locusts drone, no one to interrupt her swerving thoughts, the way they rushed and coupled and then circled back again. To Jeff and the apartment she'd lived in in San Francisco, the night sky there, people stalking the streets at three A.M., the time she'd pitched a brick through the window of a parked car for no reason except she was hammered. And then rehab, the dented steel mirrors in the bathroom and how her face seemed to swell and shrink like a balloon and she thought she would not survive it, that she'd smash the hard plastic cup for her toothbrush and they'd find her bleeding out in a locked stall.

But she'd made it, here she was, living fucking proof. The fact made her laugh, made the simplest motions—reaching up and fitting these bowls into each other—solid and remarkable. She was even taking care of things, being responsible, though the thought sent her plunging again into how she'd fucked up everything with the kids and with Jeff, how it wasn't completely his fault, the men she'd gotten involved with, and the crash, the grit of safety glass under her stockinged feet, the trooper half lifting her into his cruiser, and the defense she clung to, that, ironically, she hadn't been drunk, which later she herself would find beside the point, an easy excuse, leading back to rehab, as if her whole life had landed her there, like a murderer marked from birth for prison.

She was not one of those holy-roller juicers who saw everything as destiny, God's face in a cup of weak meeting coffee. It wasn't like she was a poster child for sobriety. But she was here, and that in itself was astonishing. Sometimes she wondered where she'd been all these years.

She emptied the top rack of glasses and loaded the few new ones from the sink. Hanging the damp dishcloth from the handle of the oven, she noticed the silly salt and pepper shakers her mother bought at the flea market, the pink pigs dressed like waiters. She picked them up, one in each hand, examining their happy faces, their black vests, the towels draped over their arms. They seemed to be rushing to fill someone's order, but gamely, rosy-cheeked.

She tried to recall a morning thirty years ago, maybe in winter, because she could picture snow falling on the Mitchells' pear tree across the driveway. Her father wore a pressed shirt, his tie thrown over his shoulder so he wouldn't spill on it, and orange juice, he always had a glass. He ate first because he had to catch the bus, taking the same chair every morning, his back to the refrigerator. Then when he was gone she and Ken and their mother sat down together and had their eggs or oatmeal. These shakers would be on the table, but she couldn't see them. There were plates, but what they looked like she had no idea, as if her brain had been scrubbed clean of the memory. Glasses, silverware, the table itself—nothing. All she could recall was her father sitting there alone, reading the business section as he ate, and then the three of them sitting down without him.

She was going to put the shakers down again—foreign now, things she might have handled in a dream—but noticed a film of grease on the stove top. She soaped and wetted a sponge and wiped between the burners, then set them back where they were supposed to go.

She did the counters and the chopping block, pensive, in slow strokes, her eyes going unfocused. While it was still dark, her father would walk down Grafton Street with his briefcase to the corner of Farragut and wait for the bus by the sign. In winter he wore galoshes over his good shoes and a black watch cap. There were three or four other fathers who waited with him, discussing money or sports, whatever it was fathers discussed. When the bus came they filed on and it rolled off, blowing diesel exhaust, the silhouettes of their heads in the lit windows.

She rinsed the sponge, filled Rufus's water dish from the teapot and refilled the teapot from the tap. Finally, she turned the lights off in order: the outside light and then the kitchen, leaving only the brow of the stove to guide her, the yellow porch overhead, the lamp above the puzzle, and lastly the brass one by the gateleg table. At the door to the stairs she paused, appreciating the dark, then went up, her father following her, cruising through the cold city, lost in his newspaper.

25

Emily woke in the vast, blank middle of the night, as if the Lerners' alarm had gone off. It hadn't, but she sat up, head cocked, listening for what it might have been. The rain had slackened, and as the room divulged itself—the bright clock, the shadow-box mirror on the dresser, the drapes, the closet door—she was certain she heard someone prowling through the downstairs. At the foot of the bed, invisible, Rufus exhaled indignantly, and the burglar evaporated.

She tipped her head, her mouth open yet holding her breath, until all she heard was a tiny whine, a piercing set of empty frequencies like a skewer through her head—an absence of sound that she understood was manufactured deep within her skull, one she knew from afternoons when she skipped lunch, precursor of a debilitating headache.

The window flashed, a lunging shadow painted on the drapes, making her clutch the covers, unconsciously reach beside her as if to wake Henry. Just then a wall of thunder banged and broke open, uncomfortably close, echoing over the hills, slowly dispersing in crunches like distant fireworks.

"God's sake," she said, and Rufus groaned in protest, but she still was not convinced she was alone.

She sat there waiting for the next footfall as the rain picked up again, a handful of acorns lobbed onto the roof. The thunder had frightened her, and now her blood seemed to pulse in several different parts of her head, like heat lightning firing the sky. She imagined someone outside, a faceless man in a slicker, the muddy prints from his boots filling with water.

Ridiculous. Rufus was old but he could still hear better than she could. It was just the thunder, and her being excited about going tomorrow.

She'd moved from her warm spot, and as she settled back in, the sheets were cold on her arms. She'd reached for Henry—wasn't that funny. Even now she expected him to protect her.

She could hear her own breathing, and stopped. In the cup of her ear pressed against the pillowcase, her heartbeat scratched at the fabric like someone approaching over a crust of snow. She shifted to get rid of it, lay with her nose pointed toward the ceiling, knowing she'd never fall asleep in this position. When she and Henry slept together, they ended up with him tucked behind her, his stubbled chin pricking her shoulder, his breath warm on her neck, an arm crooked around her ribs.

It had not been so long ago, she knew, yet it seemed she'd been alone forever, futilely trying to heat their big bed with just her own dwindling body. It was last fall, and now it was August. Not even a year. She rolled on her side, slowly, trying not to stir the chilly air under the covers. Rufus sighed, the rain abated, and then the house was still again, all but her mind, slapping like a loose shutter in the wind.

Wednesday

Wednesday

1

Lise was up with the boys and beat everyone to the shower, even Ken. It was Wednesday, past halfway. Today would be easy, the ride eating up time, and she was glad to escape the enforced intimacy of the cottage, to turn her mind to something less demanding than his family. She could see beyond Niagara Falls to Saturday, packing the car and heading back to Massachusetts, to the crammed mailbox, the answering machine blinking with calls. Rinsing the conditioner from her slick hair, she thought she ought to feel guilty about how much she was looking forward to it, but shrugged that off. The stink of the water, the crystallized mineral deposits on the stall walls, the dark bracelet of hair ringing the drain—none of it could discourage her this morning.

"Come on, let's go, up up up," she taunted, getting dressed, Ken groaning at her enthusiasm, Meg turning her face away. From their sleeping bags the girls eyed her with disdain. "Better get your buns out of bed if you want pancakes."

"What kind?" Ella asked, stretching.

"Whatever kind we have. This isn't Perkins." She high-stepped over them and pounded down the stairs for effect.

Sam was still in his pajamas, playing his Game Boy.

"Go get dressed," she said. "And wash that crud off your face, I can still see it." He started to complain but she cut him off. "Go *now*. You don't want to mess with me today."

With a twinge, she saw Emily's coffee cup next to the sink. She'd really thought she had a shot at beating her. But there were no breakfast dishes to accuse her of sleeping in, and she ransacked the cupboard for a yellow box of Bisquick.

"There you go," she said, cheering herself along, and swung around the door to the fridge.

Milk, eggs, margarine. She spun the lazy Susan and found a bowl the right size.

As she laid everything out on the counter, she noticed the flowers she'd bought at the farm stand sticking out of the trash, the stems still wet. "Nice," she said, but resisted pulling them out to see if they were really dead. It had been four days, she didn't care.

Emily walked in as she was whisking the lumpy batter and stopped dead in the middle of the floor, shocked. "What's the occasion?"

"No occasion," Lise said, "just making pancakes. Would you like some?"

"I've had a muffin, thanks."

"You wouldn't have any chocolate chips?"

"I don't believe so."

"Oh well."

And still Emily didn't move, stuck there in the middle of the floor, staring at her as if she were on fire. Lise resisted turning and leveling her with a look, instead projected herself into the car, the fallen barns and stony hillsides passing with the miles, the hours and the day wasting away. She churned the batter, her arm hard. The powdery clumps of flour were breaking up, being absorbed. She turned the lazy Susan again and found a cast-iron skillet.

"You don't need to grease it," Emily coached.

"I wouldn't," Lise said cheerily. She had her own heavy set at home, picked up piecemeal year after year at the flea market. Lise knew Emily would say the same thing to Meg—to anyone who trespassed in her kitchen. Lise switched on a burner and waited, as if her gaze would make the coil glow. She would not let Emily get to her so easily.

Behind her, Emily sighed. "Wouldn't you know, it's recycling day."

"I can do it," Lise volunteered. "You just put it out by the road."

"By the mailbox. You have to separate the glass and the plastic and put the magazines and newspapers in different bags. I'll do it. You're making breakfast."

"It's no problem," Lise insisted, suspecting Emily of stringing her along.

"What about the pop cans and beer bottles—should we put them out or will someone take them back?"

"I'll take them back."

"Maybe we should make a special place for them in the garage. Does that sound like a good idea?"

"Sure," she said, and went back to tending her pancakes. Once the screen door swung shut behind Emily, she let herself exhale.

"Where's breakfast?" Sam asked, sliding across the dirty linoleum in his socks.

"Didn't you wear that shirt yesterday?"

"We didn't play outside."

"Go put on a clean one, please."

Alone, she stared down into the skillet, smoke rising from the black metal. Bubbles opened in the soft face of the batter, releasing steam. She tested the edges with her spatula, then flipped them, turned the oven on to warm.

Outside, Emily was lugging the recycling bin up the drive.

Lise punched the screen open with the heel of her hand. "I'll do that."

"I've got it," Emily called back.

"Just incredible," she said into the skillet, shaking her head, then caught herself, stopped, taking a deep breath and standing bolt upright.

She wouldn't play that game, not today. And honestly, she wanted to feel sorry for Emily, it was just that Emily made it so hard. All last fall, Lise had to remind herself to be nice to her, and then Emily seemed to take advantage of it, tearing down her Christmas dinner in front of everyone. Lise needed to be bigger, but she wasn't like Ken, she couldn't just slough that stuff off, pretend it didn't hurt her.

She'd burned the second set. She poured another pair and watched the batter spread, resenting the power Emily had over her emotions.

"Are the pancakes ready yet?" Sam asked, wearing his gray Nomar shirt that was too small.

"Two minutes. Go tell your father."

"You don't mind taking those bottles and cans back?" Emily asked when she came in.

"We have to go to Wegmans anyway to load up on stuff for the trip home."

"You might have to go before that. They're piling up pretty fast."

"Not a problem."

"When I was a child they were only a penny. It's not such a jump considering the price of everything else."

Lise nodded, concentrating on her pancakes, and Emily made her exit. She was like a little kid, Lise thought, always having to have the last word.

There was syrup in the fridge door, but they'd need to get more soon—put it on the list. She told Justin to pour three milks for now and leave the jug out. Yes, he could have juice, but only after he finished his milk. He asked it like she might yell at him. He was a fragile kid, timid. For all Sam's problems, she was glad he was hers.

The boys were almost done when Ken came down, and she was doing the dishes when the girls finally showed. She gave them sufficient grief before telling Ella to get the ones in the oven and to be careful of the plate. Arlene returned from walking the dog and said she didn't need any, only if there were some left over.

"I made enough for everyone," Lise said.

They would get off early, even with Meg dragging her ass. Ella was worried about leaving Rufus alone all day, but Emily said he was used to it, he'd sleep. The idea appealed to Lise. She could recline her seat and sleep in the car all the way there. Ken would want to drive anyway, with the girls chattering in the back. At the falls, she'd be busy with the kids. Nap on the way back, eat dinner, read her book.

She wondered aloud what the weather was going to be like tomorrow.

"It's supposed to clear off," Arlene said. "Eighty degrees and sunny."

"Gotta get out there and hit 'em," Ken said.

"The place will be an absolute madhouse," Emily said.

"It'll be worse on Friday," Lise reasoned, "with everyone down from Buffalo."

Finally Meg had her act together, and they told the boys to at least try to pee. They had to leave by the kitchen door, something to do with the dead bolt, and then Emily had forgotten to turn on the answering machine. "In case there's an emergency," she said, though the whole family was split between the two cars.

When Emily came out again, she made straight for the 4Runner and got in back, Sarah scooching over so she'd fit. "I'm sorry," she explained to the back of Ken's head (as if Lise weren't looking directly at her), "but I cannot passenge while your sister's driving, I'm simply not strong enough. I hope you girls don't mind."

"No," Sarah and Ella said.

"Good. Now I can catch up on all the gossip."

Lise rearranged herself so she faced the front, giving Ken a sideways look which he returned, as if to say it wasn't that bad, or that, yes, he knew, but somehow he'd make it up to her. They were in the lead, and pulled out first. She felt bad for Arlene, stuck with the boys and all the garbage in Meg's car.

"How are you going?" Emily asked, as if she knew a quicker way.

"Ask the navigator," Ken said.

"I don't know," Lise preempted her.

"You should be able to go right up 90."

She shuffled through the maps in the dash—everything was New England—and then, before panic set in, remembered New York was in the door, turned inside out so they could track their progress on the way across.

"How far is it?" Ella asked, making her turn the map over noisily and scan the mileage chart.

"About an hour and a half, but that's going fifty-five."

"How fast are you going to drive?" Emily asked, as if they were in danger. "I've heard these things tip over."

Ken checked Lise to make sure she wasn't going to jump on it, then said, "We haven't rolled it yet."

"Well, be careful."

"I always am."

"I'm serious," Emily said.

"So am I," Ken said, testy.

He braked for the highway, waited for a truck to pass, then turned on. Rain dimpled the ponds on the golf course. Lise expected Emily or Ken to say something about playing tomorrow, whether the course would be in shape—as a peace offering, just to break the silence. When neither of them apologized, Lise was secretly pleased, the way she was on those rare occasions he disciplined the children. For once she didn't have to be the bitch.

2

Ever since his father mentioned it, Sam wanted to go up in the thing that looked like a space station, but Aunt Margaret didn't know anything about it, and Justin was no help. He wished Ella was with them. She'd know.

"The tall thing," Sam said. "There's a restaurant in it that goes around. The Sky Something."

"Sorry," Aunt Margaret said.

"I think I know what he's talking about," Aunt Arlene said, and looked back at him. "A big silver tower? On the Canadian side?"

"Can we eat lunch there?"

"I don't know," Aunt Margaret said, trying to ignore him like his mother did when she was driving. "I don't know what Grandma or your father have planned. You can ask your father when we get there."

"I'd like to too," Justin said.

"I hear you, but I am not making any promises to anybody about anything."

"I'd like to see the view from there," Aunt Arlene said. "I'd think it would be spectacular."

"Spectacularly crowded," Aunt Margaret said.

"I'm not sure that can be avoided."

"I guess not."

Sam gave Justin a high five.

"Hey," Aunt Margaret said, catching them in the mirror. "What did I say? No promises. I don't want to hear any grumping if we don't go there."

He wished Uncle Jeff was here. He'd let them go. Now he'd have to ask his father, who would ask his mother, which meant they probably wouldn't.

Aunt Arlene said they could see Lake Erie, but all he saw was construction, yellow bulldozers and brown gouges in hillsides, piles of white pipes. Aunt Arlene pointed out apple orchards and vineyards like they were on a field trip and had to remember everything for a test.

"There's the lake—there," Aunt Arlene pointed.

It was just a blue line behind the electric wires and only showed for a second, then it was back to nothing, just trucks and cars, their lights shining in the rain.

"Can we play our Game Boys?" Sam asked.

"You couldn't leave them at home?" Aunt Margaret said.

"Please?" Justin asked.

She made them wait like it was a tough decision, the windshield wipers moving faster than they had to, squeaking against the glass. Sam knew to be quiet until she turned them down.

"One hour total, no more. When we get there, you leave them in the car. And no sound."

"Thank you," Justin said.

"Sam? What do you say?"

"Thank you," he said, but he already had it on, and she was speaking from another world.

3

"There goes the Bills' training camp," Ken said, "the losers," but no one laughed.

"They really seem to be going downhill," his mother said, "if their game against the Steelers is any indication."

Beside him, Lise remained silent, a bomb waiting to go off, and he felt obligated to say something, if only to be polite.

"Yeah," he said, "I'm afraid they're dead meat," then immediately regretted it.

Since his father died, he was acutely aware of using certain words around his mother. On the phone, they popped up as if he were purposely trying to torture her, yet she never commented on it. He supposed the effect was like him hearing the word "cancer" or seeing terminal patients on *ER*—a numbness and then relief once it had passed and he could slip back into everyday forgetfulness, his father not dead, just a long-distance call away, probably working in the basement or lying on the couch in his den, reading one of his historical novels about the sea.

Maybe this was his way of reminding himself that he really was dead, asking his mother to verify that impossible fact. Perhaps, he thought.

"The Steelers aren't much better, I'm told," his mother said.

4

Emily didn't remember the skyline, or any of the highways that looped them around the soggy downtown, and yet somehow they must have come this way. The roads were new, and most of the buildings, blue mirrored cubes and concrete boxes blank as graph paper. It was like Pittsburgh. The mills were gone, the rail yards obsolete, replaced by economic rhetoric, neighborhoods like the Hill and Braddock gutted, only pensioners left, the city grown old. It was a mistake to have come at all, she thought.

Their first day as husband and wife, they woke up early and made love again, and then Henry had driven the entire six hours from Pittsburgh while she fiddled with the radio, both of them singing along, pinching and prodding each other, making fun of the four-corners trout-stream towns she knew too intimately, being silly. The only person she'd ever slept with besides her mother was Jocelyn, freezing winter nights in their walk-up, and the presence of Henry in bed disconcerted her. Between the lack of sleep and her giddiness, the drive seemed an endless carnival ride. They stopped for lunch in the Allegheny Forest, laying a blanket in the shade of fragrant pines, and made love again, the trees rising over Henry's shoulders like spires. She imagined the state ranger would let them go if they explained they were just married, showed him the clean marks the shaving cream left on the car. They ate, ravenous, shoving handfuls of grapes in each other's mouths, crushing them on their faces, a burlesque of some decadent Roman movie they'd seen, Ingrid Bergman in a sheet and sandals. She'd never laughed so much in one day.

Now, surrounded by her family, she thought it was not a loss. She had had that time, and it was still hers, if only in her memory. It did no good to compare what was present with what was gone.

They turned a curve down a long, sweeping hill, and the lake spread before them, whitecapped and almost black under the dark sky. Across the water, the shoreline was mobbed with houses.

"There's Canada," Kenneth informed the girls.

"It looks like here," Ella said.

"It pretty much is," Kenneth admitted.

To Emily, newly wed, it had seemed what it was, another country, as vast and mysterious as the life she would make with this man driving beside her. It was the first time she'd ever left the U.S., and she was nervous about customs. When the uniformed guard at the booth asked what their purpose in Canada was, Henry said they were on their honeymoon, and the man ducked down to give her a smile and formally welcome them as if he were an ambassador and they were his special guests.

The Peace Bridge was familiar, traffic jockeying for the right lines.

"'Nothing to declare,'" Kenneth read. "That would be us."

The irony was too much, and Emily looked out her rain-beaded window at the other cars, taillights flaring as they inched up to the booths. She could declare so many things.

Her life was no more tragic than anyone else's. All these people in their warm cars would lose the ones they loved, ultimately, or die themselves, leaving their dearest behind. Cities would fill and empty, buildings crumble under the wrecking ball. It went without saying, and only a fool or a moony teenager would see something horrible in it, like Margaret thinking Duchess dying in the chives was the end of the world (it was the end of the chives for that year, nothing more, and the next spring their green spears peeked out again).

The first time she'd crossed this border, how little she'd appreciated time, thinking she'd defeated her childhood, shed it cleanly, like Kersey, the awkward girl she'd been and the unloved town left to starve in the wilderness. And then when she returned triumphant, she found the town was the same, and the girl, her mother's house drawing memories from her like blood—spankings and bad report cards, the night she and Laurel Saunders had been arrested for drinking brandy by the football field. And ugly—it made her sick to see the downtown with its pitiful ladies' shops where her mother's friends bought their dresses. She'd been so ashamed that she never wanted to go back, but did at Henry's calm insistence, holiday after holiday as the children grew and the streets and the cramped corner stores lost their meaning, until she missed the place she'd grown up, and then her father died, and then her mother, and there was no reason to go back, only the shells of houses, the elementary school that had been turned into apartments, the movie theater whose marquee now advertised hardware, and in the cemetery two plots like twin beds separated by a chaste strip of crabgrass. She had not gone for years, and this seemed wrong. She had barely been to Henry's grave, even though it was close. She would go when she got back, she promised—and to her parents' too, a pilgrimage while there was time. The Olds could make it that far.

"What do you declare?" Ella asked beside her.

"Money," Kenneth said, "or merchandise."

"Anything valuable," Lisa added.

"Guns?"

"Guns," Kenneth echoed. "Any kind of advanced technology. Animals that might have diseases. What else?"

He was asking Emily, checking his answer with her, a habit passed on from his father.

"I think that about covers it," she said.

Plants and produce came to mind, agricultural hazards and hitch-hiking insects, but she wasn't interested, and turned back to the cars, the scudding clouds. She was glad it was raining. She couldn't imagine facing this on a sunny day.

Just the thought transported her to Henry's Chevy, the vent window tipped out all the way backwards to funnel air into the stifling box of the car. And still it was a beautiful day, and they were happy, as if the weather, like the songs on the radio, was meant for them, stemmed somehow from their love, the rest of the world a backdrop for its two most popular stars. The sun made the day sharp and promising, as if they might drive forever, only stopping to make love and eat. It had seemed that way, though they must have waited in line like this, and sat at stoplights, and fussed with the luggage. She remembered only the best of them, compensation for the months she'd spent at Henry's bedside, memories that caught her walking across the living room or washing out her teacup at the sink, leaving her useless and fretful for the rest of the day.

"Mom," Kenneth was saying from the front.

"What is it?"

"I was asking if you knew what the exchange rate is."

"I haven't the faintest. A dollar forty? That's where it usually is."

"That's not bad," Lisa said.

"Everything's expensive," Emily said, "that's the catch. And not just here, it's the whole country. If you don't do the math you can easily be fooled."

It was Ken who finally said, "I don't think we're going to be doing much shopping."

"You don't have to. See how much lunch costs. You'll be surprised."

"The kids have to eat," Lisa said, as if she'd suggested they didn't.

It reminded Emily of Margaret as a teenager, waiting for the littlest slip, as if they were locked in some kind of contest. She chose to ignore her and look out the window. The mist in the trees beyond the tollbooth made her think of Monet, one of his studies of light they had at the Frick this spring. It was noon, but it felt like three or four, the sky an uncertain color.

In the hospital, she watched evening build, the sun withdrawing from the corners of the room, then the dull walls, leaving only the window and Henry's bed in the whisky-colored glow—last light, which she associated with summer and the lake, the lingering end of their slow days, except as fall came on, that quiet time seemed to last only a moment, a colored lens passed in front of the sun, and then the room was a uniform gray, the skyscrapers downtown cold black shadows, the sidewalks busy with commuters, the thick, institutional pane cool and soothing against her forehead. Dinner appeared, steaming under its hubcap of a cover. The heater clinked. Henry slept in odd shifts, leaving and then returning to her, as if testing himself, getting ready.

"You should go home," he said once, freshly woken up, and she could not have been angrier with him.

"And what am I supposed to do there?" she demanded, as if he might have an answer, as if he could still argue.

He did not want her to see him like this, she understood that, but the alternative was worse. They were so close to nothing already—or so she'd thought, because afterward it was harder than she could have imagined. There were days when she got dressed fully intending to go to the hospital, but there was no one there. It was like going mad, she supposed. Everything she was so certain of, everything that held intense meaning for her, no longer existed. She spent hours pursuing pointless rituals, talking to herself or people invisible to others, addressing objects, then suddenly stopped and scourged herself for it, furious with her own emotions.

In the midst of this came a barrage of phone calls from people she hadn't seen in years, Henry's old coworkers and the parents of Kenneth's high school friends, even a grade school teacher of his. How quickly she wearied of their careful sympathy. She appreciated the words meant to console her, but hung up feeling wrung, and soon she took to leaving the machine on, screening her calls, leaning over the rolling tape, hoping it might be Louise suggesting they go see the new Hopper exhibit at the Scaife or just somewhere for coffee. "Emily," she'd say, "Emily, are you there?" and sometimes Emily picked up and sometimes she didn't. She'd learned to turn the volume down without feeling guilty, Louise's sweet voice replaced by the shuttling of the cassette, then a sword fight of clicking, a new number blinking like a score piling up against her. Her record was seventeen. Didn't they know? All she wanted was to be alone.

They were almost to the booth. Margaret's van was three cars behind them. Kenneth checked the mirror obsessively, afraid they'd lose her once they went through.

He slid his window open and the breeze chilled the tip of her nose. The smell of exhaust was nauseating. Trucks idled, their air brakes sighing and letting go. On the far side, cars raced back into the States.

"Where you folks coming from today?" the guard with the clipboard asked. He smiled but ducked down to check the backseat.

"Chautauqua, New York," Kenneth said, as if they lived there.

"How long you plan on staying?"

"Just for the day."

Beside her the girls were vamping for the video cameras aimed at them from all sides, and she wondered if the guard's banter was just an excuse to keep them there while people somewhere else ran checks on the car. Even back when she and Henry crossed here, there was a sense of intrigue, the possibility of unknown laws being broken. In an instant they were foreigners, beyond the reach or protection of their government. It seemed silly now—exotic Canada—but to that Kersey girl it was the first time she'd left the country, Europe the logical next step, and they'd made it there, to Paris, less than ten years after, staying in that narrow hotel by Saint-Sulpice where you had to step up into the round shower stall and the diving bell of an elevator squeaked and shuddered threateningly. They served crepes everywhere on the Left Bank, and she was forever brushing powdered sugar off her front. Their feet ached from walking all day, but each night they made love as if to honor the city, in the morning huddled naked together at the porthole window, looking out over the steaming rooftops, the clerks filing into the ornate office buildings. They reveled in it, not knowing when they'd be back.

Never, it turned out, just as they would never return to Bermuda or the Grand Canyon or Westminster Abbey. Wall Drug. Valley Forge. The Lincoln Memorial. The list seemed endless, when in reality they rarely traveled, a pair of homebodies wary of luxury. Henry inevitably saved his two weeks for Chautauqua, coming up the weekend before Memorial Day to fix things, closing the place after Labor Day. She could pay Mrs. Klingin-smith to have someone do it, she thought.

The guard had Kenneth sign the clipboard with a pen on a bead chain and waved them through, already locked in on the next car and its occupants.

"Nothing," Ella declared as they passed under the sign.

"Ha ha," Sarah said.

"It's okay now," Lisa coached, looking behind them, and Kenneth swerved to the right, cutting off a FedEx truck to pull into the gritty breakdown lane, the asphalt hatched with white stripes. Cars shot by, tall semis drawing curtains of mist.

"Is this legal?" Emily asked, searching behind them for the police.

"It'll have to be," Kenneth said in a tone she didn't appreciate.

"Do you think it's safe?"

"I've got my hazards on."

"We're only going to be a minute," Lisa dismissed her, and Emily bit her lip. In her lap she thumbed the underside of her ring, twisting it around to busy herself.

"There they are," Lisa said, and Kenneth tipped his blinker on and waited for a break. The girls ducked so he could see.

Once they were going again, no one spoke. The main highway curled off for St. Catharines and Toronto, taking half of the traffic. Lisa directed them onto a divided road with geese in the median. It followed the river—calm as a pond, the rain making circles between the willows. They wound through a parklike neighborhood, Emily wondering at the fifties split-levels and ranches, certain she'd never seen them before. They must have come in some other way. No doubt the roads had changed.

Forty-eight years, she thought, watching the river. Hadn't they diverted it at some point because of flooding, dug a new channel? She'd seen a documentary on PBS. Henry would have remembered. She wanted to ask the car at large but knew it would come to nothing, more useless facts from the old bag. Sometimes the better part of valor was shutting up.

The road and the river curved, an island riding along beside them, a wedge of puffy gulls standing on the bank, and then the view opened up, showing them a broad confluence, the two rivers joining forces and the sky behind it. Emily recognized the sudden transition from glassy swirls to purling rapids, but was it from their honeymoon or later, taking the children, and it might have been from the other side. The sensation of danger was the same, an ageless reflex to stay away. Downstream, a line of new blaze-orange buoys rocked in the water, warning boaters off with stenciled death's heads.

"We must be close," she said, and pointed for the girls.

"It's creepy," Sarah said. "It's like the water knows it's going over."

"Why is it like that?" Ella asked. "Dad?"

"I don't know," Kenneth said, then advanced a theory even he found unconvincing.

"Your father would know," Emily said.

"He would," Kenneth agreed.

"That must be Goat Island there," Lisa interrupted them.

Beyond it rose a white funnel of mist like a stilled tornado. Emily thought they should be able to hear the falls. Ahead, traffic had backed up, and Kenneth braked, checking the mirror for Margaret. Emily touched the button and the window slid down.

The wind pushed the rain against her face. Above the murmur of the car, she could hear the river, and in the distance, the pour of the falls, solid as a blast furnace. She wanted to close her eyes and listen to it grow but she was getting the upholstery wet and pressed the button and sealed herself in again.

The last mile took them forty minutes, and then they ended up being stopped short of the falls and waved into a huge new parking lot with color-coded sections.

"We're in H9 blue," Kenneth impressed on everyone.

There were only two umbrellas, so he did without, braving the rain in his Red Sox cap and yellow slicker. The boys bounded out of Margaret's van and into the path of another car. All the way across the lot, they ran ahead, larking like dogs. Emily waited for their mothers to rein them in, then when Sam slipped on the asphalt, called them back herself.

"Please," she said, "we don't need any accidents today."

A minute later, Margaret stopped Justin and took him by the wrist, while Lisa walked behind Sam like a guard.

They waited at a crosswalk, the falls still hidden, so close Emily could smell the river in the mist, the well-like, mineral scent of wet rock. The roar was all around them now, and the air was sodden. That first time, the drenching had been a welcome relief from the heat, Henry laughing at his ruined shirt, and then later, in the caves, they laughed at themselves because they were freezing. They would have laughed at anything, the day was so rich, the whole world theirs when all they needed was each other.

The light changed and they crossed with everyone. The girls were lost in some private joke; Margaret and Lisa finally had the boys under control. As they followed the other tourists down a broad plaza, Emily tried to fit Kenneth under her umbrella.

"It's not too crowded," he encouraged her.

"No, it's not too bad."

"Thank you," she added, hoping he knew she wouldn't have come by herself.

"Sure," he said, and she thought he understood. He was like his father after all.

Ahead, the plaza rose. It was built like a stage, raised and stepped so people could see the falls from anywhere. It was new, like everything else, and foreign to her. She wished she could recall the road that had gone along here, and the restaurants and parking lots, the souvenir stands with their racks of postcards—because there must have been some then.

The crowd fanned out, sidestepping puddles, and suddenly there it was across the gorge, the solid white curtain familiar as a carved monument or the face of a coin, to the right the prettier, more human-sized plume of Bridal Veil Falls.

Yes, this was it, that first fresh glimpse again, how it lived up to its promise. The view was no different than it had been when Henry drew her to him at the rail and kissed her and the crowd had clapped because they were young and in love, but what she recalled now was not that moment but the day before, in church, the low, near-funereal thrum of the organ and the old folks' coughing echoing over the pews as she waited, cloistered in the rectory with the choir robes as if she were backstage in some chorus girls' dressing room, late for the big number. All morning people had been asking her if she was nervous, and she'd lied and told them no. She was not superstitious, but since she'd put on the dress, everything was bad luck. Outside the door, her father stood solitary guard as if she were a condemned prisoner. Her waist was cinched so tight she couldn't take a full breath, her bosom pushed up to appear more impressive. Henry had proposed to her three times before she said yes, a fact she'd heard enough of at the rehearsal dinner, but now she wasn't sure why she'd given in. Jocelyn didn't like him. Plus, Jocelyn argued, Emily was so young, and he was so . . . she didn't know—average, meaning he was from Pittsburgh and had no ambition to live the high life in New York, Jocelyn's fixed idea of success. Emily knew at heart it was true. He was earnest and dull and nice, and the whole thing was a terrible mistake. She was sorry, but she would have to call it off. It would break his heart but it was the right thing to do. They couldn't spend their whole lives hating each other because of one bad decision.

Her father opened the door, stiff in his rented tux, his thin hair brilliantined as if it were still the Roaring Twenties, his dentures ill fitting. It was like a nightmare she was gliding through, down the dark hall and into the rear, where her maids of honor were processing to the music her mother had picked. Her father kept Emily off to one side so no one could see her, and then he started forward and she followed, her arm in his, drawing even with him so she could see the faces all turned to her, drinking in her dress and her ridiculous cleavage. She had a bouquet clenched in her hands, though who had given it to her was a mystery.

A flash bloomed, and she looked up, puzzled. There, far up the aisle, Henry waited, standing straight, wearing his carnation.

She wanted to stop and discuss this with him, lay out her objections reasonably, but she was walking, keeping pace with her father, trying to smile at Aunt Ingrid and Mrs. McKenna and Carol Darling as they passed, and then her father let go of her hand and she was standing in front of Henry, the candle flames wavering all around her, and before she could stop herself she threw her arms around his neck and broke into sobs, unsure what they meant but holding on to him, pressing her face against his hard chest, saying she was sorry.

"It's all right," he said. "It'll all be over soon."

Just the sound of his voice was enough to calm her. He was kind, he was good. She was being an idiot, and rubbing at her tears with the back of one hand, she pulled away from Henry and turned to face the minister, snuffling but chastened, sure now, ready to begin their life together, whatever that might be.

What God has joined, let no man put asunder. For richer, for poorer, in sickness and in health. Till death do us part. The words were terrifying, real in a way they'd never been before and would never be again.

She believed him; everything would be all right. She would be fine, she thought, as long as she was with him.

5

Lunch was interminable, the view and the motion of the room dizzying, and then during dessert Sam came over and opened his hand to show Lise a bloody tooth. She hadn't even known it was loose.

"For a long time," he said.

"Since when?"

"Since last week."

"Did you know about this?" she asked Ken.

"It's been wiggly for a while."

He took the tooth and rolled it in a napkin, shoved it in his pocket so he could play tooth fairy later, slipping a note and a new gold dollar under Sam's pillow.

"Where have I been?" she asked.

6

In the humid elevator going down, they were jammed into the corner, Sarah pressing against Ella as if their bodies had a natural attraction, a force like magnets or gravity. Ella tried not to notice how she felt, tried not to concentrate on the spongy part of Sarah touching her arm, and then Sarah moved, breaking the connection, and Ella wanted it back.

She stared straight ahead at the top of the closed doors where there should have been numbers. Everyone except her father had to wear these stupid see-through ponchos. Sam hadn't brought a sweatshirt like her mother had told them, so they had to buy him one that cost a lot, and now he was whining about his tooth and how he was hot and wanted a drink. They'd been standing in line so long they wouldn't be able to go down in the caves. Her father apologized to everyone like it was his fault— like anyone wanted to go see them in the first place.

Ella didn't care if they went on the *Maid of the Mist* or not, or if they saw Niagara Falls. Back at the cottage she and Sarah could have been alone like yesterday, drinking beer and sharing secrets, lying across the rumpled bed and watching for their parents' cars from the upstairs window, Sarah's tin of cinnamon Altoids ready. Sarah lay back on the pillows in her shorts and her sweatshirt, her long legs deeply, evenly tan. Ella wanted to run her palms along her hard shins, cup her perfect calves. In three days they were leaving—two and a half now—and she would go back to their empty neighborhood and wait for school to start. Sarah would be five hundred miles away, going to a new high school, even if she did break up with Mark. So Ella didn't care. It was all a waste of time.

The elevator jostled to a stop, making people laugh, like it would be funny if they all died, and for a second Ella thought that if the boat sank and she had to choose between people to save, she was sorry but it would be Sarah. She would pull her to the rocks and give her the breath of life, and when Sarah realized what Ella had done, they'd kiss. It was like a movie in her mind; it was that stupid. The boat would never sink. They'd go back home and after a while Sarah would forget to answer her letters. It was the same thing that happened at camp with Laurie Burgwin, except they'd just been friends.

She followed Sam, aware of Sarah behind her and of how dumb she looked in her poncho.

"Stay together," her father was saying, even though they were the last ones out and there was nowhere to go but through the door and along the concrete walk between the green railings.

The sky was bright after being inside, and the rain was coming down harder, or maybe it was just the spray, fogging her glasses, making her squint. A metal net hung above them like a cage, dotted with rocks and soggy paper garbage. Across the water, the falls pounded like an engine. The boat was already docked and letting people off. It looked smaller against the cliffs, and the possibility that it could sink suddenly seemed real.

The walk sloped sharply as they passed the tourists coming up from the dock, totally soaked, grinning and wringing their sleeves. For no reason, they annoyed her—because they weren't in love. Most of them were too old, married already, or kids who were too young. They were lucky in a way—they couldn't be hurt. They didn't spend every minute worrying, not knowing what to do, and still she wouldn't trade places with them for anything. She couldn't believe she'd really been like that, average and untouched, walking around like a zombie with no idea why she was alive. It seemed so long ago, when it had just been last week. She couldn't imagine her life then, before Sarah. It was like she was flying above them, lifted into another world where everything was connected to her, and it all meant something—her clothes, the weather, songs on the radio. Even now it didn't seem completely real.

She was lucky, she knew. She needed to be careful. All she had to do was turn to Sarah and raise a hand to her face, lay a palm on her cool cheek, and all of this would disappear. But Sarah knew—she had to know. Sometimes Ella pictured her feelings glowing around her like an aura, a bright force field, impossible to miss. She'd never had to keep a secret this big. She couldn't even lie to her mother about blowing off her homework or not eating all of her lunch.

They bunched up at the gate, waiting for the last passengers to come ashore. Sarah watched the falls, her hands resting on the top of the fence. Taking the spot beside her, Ella could see the dolphin ring Mark had given her, proof that she was fooling herself, and for a moment she was helpless before her own hopes. Her father had his little camera out, being the big photographer. Three days wasn't enough.

"You've heard of people going over the falls in a barrel," Grandma was telling Sam and Justin. "When I was a little girl, a boy no older than you somehow lost his way in a canoe and ended up going over with nothing but a paddle. The *Maid of the Mist* here fished him out. He's the only one who's ever done it and lived. Imagine having to explain *that* one to your mom and dad."

"What happened to the canoe?" Justin asked.

"Who cares?" Sam said.

"I imagine it broke up on the rocks."

"How come he wasn't killed?" Justin asked.

"Well that's the thing, isn't it? It's a mystery. People in specially designed barrels died, and this little boy with nothing but a paddle and the clothes on his back lived."

"We should ask about it at the Ripley's Museum," Aunt Margaret said. "I bet they have something on it."

"There's an idea," Grandma said.

"Oh boy," Sarah said so no one but Ella could hear, and it was enough to keep her dreaming. Lately she was amazed at how little it took to tip her one way or the other. The terrible thing was there was nothing she could do about it. It was like she was being controlled by something bigger than herself, but sometimes she liked it.

Finally they let them on, making everyone wear an orange life jacket that snapped in front. She couldn't believe how stupid she looked. You could sit inside or stand outside, and the inside filled up quick. It was hot and smelled like wet socks. There were still some seats in the middle you couldn't see anything from, and her mother and Grandma and Aunt Arlene and Aunt Margaret took them. Sam and Justin wanted to be outside, so her father went with them. Ella thought inside would be nicer, but Sarah pulled the drawstrings of her hood tight and tied a bow under her chin and led her out into the wind.

The deck was wet, and the rocking of the boat made walking hard. She kept her arms stretched out to her sides. Justin had fallen down and his jeans were wet. Her father crouched down to console him, holding his hand. She and Sarah found a spot by the bow, away from everyone, hunched together for warmth, and that made her happy. Watching the falls, she could pretend they were alone, that this was romantic.

The wind rattled her hood, and rain dripped off her chin. There was garbage in the water, Pepsi cans and gray newspapers. All along the rail hung white life preservers with MAID OF THE MIST stenciled on them, and Ella wondered how often they had to use them. She'd heard of people killing themselves that way, taking off all their clothes on Goat Island and swimming out into the river, letting the current sweep them over. She thought of what the view from the edge must be like, the water suddenly becoming air, the tiny white boat far below, the noise.

Before they cast off, a woman's voice came on the P.A. and asked them to please listen carefully to the following safety instructions. The woman recited her memorized lines without feeling, like the guys who ran the roller coasters at Nantasket Beach. Ella couldn't think of anything more boring, just turning in circles all day long, going nowhere.

And there, like a dare, was Sarah's hand on the railing, waiting for hers to cover it, and her face, turned to the constant roar, ready for Ella's lips. She could see it happening in slow motion, like an accident, like the dream she'd had. But it couldn't be an accident, it wasn't a dream. She would have to do it herself, risk it and accept whatever happened.

She thought about the kid in the canoe. There must have been a moment when he realized he'd gone too far, that he was headed over the edge and there was nothing he could do. Did he just quit then, give up, or did he paddle as fast as he could, knowing it wouldn't help? And did it make any difference?

To him, she thought, maybe. Not to the falls. Not to the water.

7

When Arlene was fourteen and headed off to Miss Porter's, her grandmother McElheny had sat her down in her grave, antimacassared parlor, the rosy-cheeked Gilbert Stuart portrait of her great-grandfather glaring down from between the gaslights above the mantel. Here, in what passed for respectable splendor, she imparted the one nugget of wisdom her travels had instilled in her: that no matter where one happened to be in the world, one should always bring a book. Arlene loved to quote this adage to her students, proud to arm them with such timeless advice, and here she'd forgotten it herself, sat surrounded by restless children and their weary parents with nothing to read but a foldout map of the falls, the encroaching border of which advertised gruesome wax museums and steak-and-egg honeymoon brunches for a dollar ninety-nine.

Why anyone would choose to celebrate their marriage here escaped her, and yet millions did. When she first heard that Henry would be taking Emily she'd been jealous, not so much of the place as the standard of happiness it was meant to represent, and which their family urged her at every turn to secure, setting her up with the grown sons of their closest friends until there were none left.

"What are you looking for?" her mother once asked her, and Arlene had honestly said, "Nothing."

She could not say there was nothing she regretted, but who her age truly could? She had had more children than any of her friends, and been loved and respected, fawned over and feared. She'd taught thousands of young people to read and think, and they had gone on to change the world and would continue to long after she was dust. She did not expect them to remember her, and often she could not recall them herself, had to refer to her scrapbook of class photos and grade sheets when she came upon a name in the paper. She was not surprised to find she'd given the newly indicted district attorney a solid fence of check marks for not following instructions. The directions one's life might take were determined early.

She was not sorry for the choices she'd made. She'd never needed a man, even the one she could admit she'd loved. Maybe she was too aware of how others judged her, how easily her self-sufficiency could be misconstrued as emptiness, her high spirits merely a cheerful exterior. She had thought, as the years passed, that society would retire the idea of the spinster, the dried-up old maid, and yet daily, roaming the grocery store with a plastic handbasket or taking lunch alone in a restaurant, she felt an unspoken pity directed towards her.

Emily had wandered off to gawk at the view, and Arlene spread out on the bench. She wanted a cigarette, but of course the cabin was no smoking, and immediately she calculated how much of the tour was left, then tacked on the elevator ride back to the surface. They'd wasted most of the day waiting. By the time they got home it would be dinnertime, and tomorrow was already Thursday.

She worried that her forgotten book was a sign of slippage. One of her real fears was her mind slowly deteriorating, having to give up her apartment and submit to one of those assisted-living places, her money draining away month by month. That possibility was years off, she figured, but once you noticed yourself going, it was supposed to happen fast. One day Emily would come to pick her up and find her sitting in her underthings, her refrigerator stinking of rotten hamburger and liquefied vegetables. Or she would swing by and find Emily the same way.

The tour guide was droning on over the speakers, regaling them with salient facts and points of interest. Barrels, gallons, kilowatts—the same drab litany Arlene had been feeding her kids since the fifties, all the glories of democracy and progress. In 1970–something, so-and-so was the first to cross from the American to the Canadian side by walking a tightrope. It took him so many minutes and in the middle he stopped to do something.

"Absolutely fascinating," Margaret said, and Arlene smiled back at her and thought of their talk in the garage, the tenuous bond between them, a bridge built of cigarettes.

She would have liked to have had a daughter (yes, even Margaret, troubled as she was), but that was not a regret, more of an idle wish, stillborn, not serious. The time for that had passed—like so much of her life—quietly.

The guide directed their attention to the starboard side of the ship, blah-blah, blah-blah-blah.

"Having fun?" Margaret asked.

"Always," she said.

8

When they got too close to the falls, Justin thought, something would go wrong with the rudder. The captain with the white mustache and the fancy hat wouldn't be able to steer, and the current would draw them in. "We'll all be killed!" he'd shout.

People would be screaming and diving off the sides, and then the water would hit them and drive the boat under, smashing it in half with his mother still inside, and Justin would be in the water and it would be cold like the other day at the lake, and someone would grab his legs and try to drag him down. He'd kick at them, except it might be Sarah, and he'd stop. There would be broken boards everywhere, but the life savers would be floating away, everyone swimming after them down the river, and then they'd start going around in a circle because the whirlpool would be sucking them under. He'd be caught in it, and he'd see Sarah on the other side, both of them spinning around. All they'd have to do was reach each other and hold hands and they'd be free.

"Come on," Sarah would say, "you can do it!" the way she rooted at his games (but he never did it then, he always struck out and his teammates hated him for it), but this time he would, and the whirlpool would stop and they'd be okay, they'd be safe. His father would see it all on TV and call them to say they could stay with him, and they'd go to his mother's funeral together, one on each side of him, and drive away in the same limousine.

His hands were cold but he didn't let go of the railing. The water was full of brown suds. He wondered if fish ever went over and got killed. When he looked up, rain landed on his face. Above them, a helicopter circled. It was funny, Justin couldn't hear it.

"So," Uncle Ken asked, "now that you've seen them both, which do you like better?"

"Canadian!" Sam said first, stealing his answer, and Justin had to change his.

9

"I have to go to the bathroom," Justin whispered, hunching and squeezing his crotch with his whole hand, as if Meg could conjure up a men's room on the spot.

"You should have told me when we were on the boat. I don't think there's one down here. Can you wait till we get up top?"

"I guess so."

"The elevator should be here any second. I'm sure there's one up by the line."

He was bouncing, rocking foot to foot. All the water wasn't helping, but she didn't dare make a joke. He was already embarrassed that he'd fallen down, according to Ken. She'd rolled her eyes to let Ken know it was typical of Justin, making the littlest thing into a big drama, but then Ken had been sensitive as a kid too, using tears on their mother to get attention.

She hoped that Justin would toughen up—and she'd told him this—otherwise he would have one tough row to hoe (the country phrase straight from her citified mother, applied to her own future too many times), but when she looked at Ken and how he'd turned out, she thought she would just have to get used to Justin being timid and picked on. There were worse things than being quiet and shy. God knew she knew that.

"Did you notice a bathroom upstairs?" she whispered to Ken. "Just's got to go."

"Sorry. He didn't go in the restaurant?"

"Apparently not."

The doors parted and they got on, Meg holding Justin back so they'd be the first off. She kept him in front of her, her hands on his shoulders, looking up as if she could see where they were going. When she glanced down to see how he was doing, he raised his face and gave her a pitiful grimace.

"We're almost there," she promised.

The elevator shook as if pushed by the wind, slowed and then paused, making them wait before the doors rolled open.

She'd forgotten what a mess it was up here, dank as a subway station. The noise disoriented her, hundreds of conversations from the switchbacked line rising and then ricocheting down from the open rafters. She hurried him through the crowd, trying not to cut people off, all the time searching the walls for a sign. She found the women's first, the featureless girl in her sixties A-line, and the men's just beyond.

"See it there?" she pointed, and he took off, nearly knocking over a toddler, the mother glaring after him.

Sarah and Ella were right behind him, taking advantage of the break. Ken and the rest of them headed for the gift shop, her mother waving to make sure she understood.

"I see you," Meg waved.

She positioned herself between the men's and women's and lit a cigarette. Around her waited young husbands in shorts and baseball caps. One of them guarded a stroller with a purse in it. The concrete floor was filthy, spotted with discarded brochures and flattened paper cups. She thought of the waitress at lunch asking her if she wanted anything to drink, and drew the smoke deep into her lungs.

It was a perfect day for drinking. Rainy, nothing to do. A day like today, she liked to turn off the lights and unplug the phone and sit on the couch under a blanket and argue along with the soap operas, feeling, after a sip or two, that she understood everyone's problems (and all of them were better off than her, that was the sad thing). One glass of scotch, one of water. Not a lot, just enough to get the job done. First a sweet clarity and then the muffling fog, her brain as saturated as the clouds outside, the TV tireless, showing her her own life, the rest of the room as utterly still as she was, only her hand slowly lifting one glass and setting it down, picking up the other, the mountain of butts growing in her favorite ashtray, all of it cleaned up by the time Sarah's bus squealed to a stop at the bottom of the drive, and then the purgatory of making dinner, getting ready to answer Jeff's questions or endure his silence, already dreaming of tomorrow when the house would be hers again, a slow and formal world with its comforting, deliberate rituals.

It was exactly that kind of destructive behavior she was trying to change. She wasn't supposed to miss it. She thought she didn't, and then she would remember it at times like this with something like nostalgia, her blurry days a painless, voluptuous cocoon.

She missed Jeff, and she hated Jeff, so maybe it was the same. She hated herself for what she'd done, the person she'd been then. She was trying to get rid of her and it wasn't working.

She couldn't do anything about the past except apologize and move on. Forward, not backward, no excuses.

The line shuffled herdlike through the maze of rails and she tapped the ash off her Marlboro and crossed her arms, holding herself close. All these people wasting their vacations. She searched the faces of the adults for a genuine smile and wasn't surprised when she couldn't find one. She couldn't blame them; it really was a miserable day.

And here Justin was, the front of his shirt stuffed down his pants, but happy to see her, glad he'd made it.

"Feel better?" she asked, jagging him. She suppressed the urge to fix his shirt.

"What are we waiting for?"

"Your sister and Ella felt the need as well."

"Where's everyone else?"

"They went to check out the gift shop."

"Are we going to have time to see the Believe It or Not museum?"

It was not quite five. "I don't think so, Spud. Sorry."

He seemed to be all right with it, but it was like him not to complain. He stood beside her watching the people sweep by, the sunburnt mothers and fathers in their makeshift rain gear. Everyone was trying, she thought. Nothing was easy.

"Hey," she said. "Did I ever tell you you're a good kid?"

"Yeah?" he said, unsure, like it might be a trick.

"Well you are."

10

His mother was watching him, so Sam looked at the license-plate key chain with his name on it a long time before he put it back. There were baskets full of superballs and rubber snakes and pink change purses, miniature decks of cards, pens with the *Maid of the Mist* sliding inside, giant pencils too big to hold the right way, and red maple leafs all over everything. When he moved to the next aisle she followed him.

They'd each gotten five dollars to buy anything they liked, except the metal telescope he wanted cost $6.99, and the unfairness of it was building in him. If he'd known, he would have brought money from home. He still had twenty dollars left over from his birthday check.

He kept his head down so she couldn't see him. Felt pennants, bags of cat's-eye marbles, water guns, Rugrats finger puppets. He saw himself throwing the soldier with his plastic parachute over the wall outside, watching him float all the way down to the water. He could buy five of them and throw them all over if they let him. It was all dumb stuff. With a telescope he could spy on Mrs. Parmenter from his window at home.

His father was talking with his mother now, giving her some money.

Go away, he wished, pretending to look at some pencil sharpeners. He touched his tongue to the hole where his tooth had been, the blood sweet as barbecue sauce. Go away, go away.

It was magic just like Ella said, because she was walking off and his father was coming down the aisle.

"How are we doing?" he asked, and Sam shrugged. "Can't find anything?"

"I don't know."

"Well pick something, because we've got to get going."

His tongue found the tender hole again. "There's one thing, but it's too expensive."

"How much is it?" his father asked, and then, "What is it?"

"A telescope," Sam said, and led him to it.

He wanted his father to pick it up and look through it, but he was looking around for his mother, over by the wall of coffee mugs.

"I could use my tooth money."

"Does the tooth fairy know you're at Chautauqua?"

"Then it would only be ninety-nine cents."

"Plus tax," his father added. "Unless . . ." He reached past the stack of boxes and touched the price on the sign. Sam didn't understand.

"It's Canadian."

His father explained how their money was different, how it wasn't worth as much.

"So how much is it?"

"I don't know. Under six dollars, I bet."

"Can I get it?"

"You'll have to leave the tooth fairy an IOU."

"I will."

"All right," his father said, and pulled a dollar from his pocket.

His mother caught up with them in line. "I thought we agreed on five dollars," she said, and Sam was afraid she'd take it away.

"I told him he could use his tooth money."

"That was nice of you."

"I know."

"You have a very nice father," his mother said, "I hope you realize that. What do you say?"

"Thank you," he said.

"Not me," she said. "Thank him."

11

Emily took a long last look from the plaza, the drizzle still coming down around them, the concrete the solid brown of mud. Pockets of water sat atop the rock wall like tidal pools. Kenneth waited for her, and the rest went on, heading for the parking lot.

She didn't blame them. It was a dreary day, and in truth she was glad to have a moment to herself. Kenneth kept a respectful distance, as if she were addressing someone invisible. The telescopes for a quarter with their overlarge chrome heads were their only company. Even the tour buses were leaving, dieseling at the curb, their interiors dimly lit, TVs glowing above the seats.

Across the gorge, the falls roared frothing over the edge, fed by days of rain. She gazed at the white column's endless fall, the product of countless centuries. Forty-eight years was not so long, was a blink in the larger scheme of things. It had passed so quickly—it seemed, standing here—that she was still trying to catch up with it, make sense of it the way you would an accident, slowing it down to understand what had happened, as if that might change how she felt.

There had been colored lights at night, the falls turned into a kind of giant screen they projected shapes onto—rockets and stars and planets—and fireworks after that.

She remembered Henry taking her for a steak dinner with a view and the waitress bringing champagne and asking to see her ring (she was just working them for a tip, had surely seen thousands of rings, thousands of young couples who thought the future would grant them happiness just because they were in love). She remembered both of them throwing a shiny penny from the wall for luck and then a gust of wind almost skimming the hat from her head, and Henry laughing, saying it nearly worked. She would remember more on the drive back, she knew, and yet the feeling of something left undone nagged at her, some expectation unfulfilled. She didn't feel closer to Henry here—if anything, she felt further away—and wondered if it wouldn't have been better to have simply stayed home, tended to the present rather than dredge up the past.

She twisted her ring around her finger, inspected the cracked skin beneath it, the age spots the color of mushrooms gone bad in the fridge, as if she were rotting. For years he'd joked that he would die first, being a man, and for years she'd said, "Don't you dare." Neither of them had been kidding. For a second she thought of pulling her ring off and throwing it over the wall—an extravagant gesture of protest meant to soothe her—but with her other hand she centered the stone on her finger. She would take it to her grave. But that was foolish too.

The rain suddenly picked up, tapping at her umbrella, and Kenneth was by her side, asking if she was ready.

"Sure," she said, but had to force herself to move.

Stepping in puddles was inescapable, and then at the road they missed the walk signal. Traffic was bad, everyone fleeing as dinnertime approached. With all the noise she could barely hear the water. When she looked back, a caul of mist hung over the falls, and she couldn't see anything. Good-bye, she thought, already gone.

They were waiting in the cars, Lisa driving this time, impatient to get going. Kenneth had to adjust his seat, careful of Sarah's legs. Emily set her wet umbrella in the way back before buckling herself in. By then they were mired in line.

"So has it changed much?" Lisa asked her, and though there was something artificially sweet in her tone, Emily answered seriously, for the girls.

"Not really."

Going home was supposed to feel shorter, according to one of her mother's aphorisms, but it was bumper to bumper from the exit all the way to customs. The guards made her think of Kenneth's girl from the convenience store, and then the Lerners. She hoped Rufus was doing all right by himself. Her stomach was rumbling. She hadn't given dinner a thought. The children would need to eat something.

The agent waved them through and they were back in America. It was rush hour in Buffalo. They crawled along, peering at the houses across Lake Erie, the invisible dotted line in the water separating the two countries. When the freeway turned inland, Emily thought it was another loss—and the same with the city itself, from a distance its sooty buildings lit like the spires of a magical land.

"Crummy old Buffalo," she said, testing herself. She was glad to have seen it again, to prove to herself she'd missed nothing, that other life she could have lived dissipating, a daydream left over from her teens. It was like cleaning out a house she'd lived in fifty years, throwing away all the broken things she'd never use again. She thought she should feel lighter instead of empty.

"Okay, everybody," Lisa said, pointing through the windshield at a sign, "Wendy's or Burger King?"

"Wendy's," Ella said.

"I don't care," Sarah said.

Emily said nothing. Fast food depressed her, the idea that there was nothing better available. So many things had changed for the worse. In that sense, forty-eight years were an eternity.

"Speak now or forever hold your peace," Lisa said. "Ken? Emily?"

"Wendy's," Kenneth acquiesced.

"Emily?" Lisa asked.

"Wendy's is fine," she said.

12

Of course it quit raining now that they were going home. Lake Erie was on her side, and Sarah could see where the clouds stopped and the miles of orange sky started, the day-glo sun almost down on the water. It was the kind of sunset her mother would say was made by pollution, but her mother was behind them, driving their car, and Grandma said maybe they would finally get some nice weather.

"Red sky at night," Uncle Ken said.

"Are you two still planning on golfing tomorrow?" Aunt Lisa asked.

Sarah kept track of everyone's plans, just to see where they'd be. She was afraid she and Ella would get stuck baby-sitting the boys.

"Can we go tubing?" Ella asked.

"Yes," Uncle Ken said. "When I get back, I will take everyone tubing who wants to, weather permitting."

So there went the whole afternoon, Sarah thought. She didn't have anything specific she wanted to do, just walk around, go over to the fish-ponds, maybe play tennis, ride bikes. She didn't expect to run into him, not really, but being stuck on the boat meant there was no chance—unless he had one. She saw him in it with his shirt off, tan, and herself beside him in her yellow bikini. Like her mother would ever let her go out with anyone here. Ever since that girl got kidnaped and they'd seen the guys in that van she was waiting for the big lecture.

"You're exactly what those people are looking for," she'd said once at home, and all Sarah could say was "Great."

Outside, lights were coming on. The sun wasn't gone yet, and everything was a weird orangey pink except the bright signs for gas stations and fast-food places. As they passed an exit, she watched the traffic on the road below, the restaurants busy with families, some of them waiting out front to be called, standing in little cliques like kids did before school.

Behind an Applebee's, a girl not much older than her in a green uniform was throwing cardboard boxes into a dumpster. She was blond and her ponytail was pulled through the back of her visor. Sarah turned to watch her, followed her dwindling shape as she went back inside, imagining the people she worked with, the jokes they made and the radio playing in the kitchen. She probably had her own car, Sarah thought, and didn't have to ask her mother for anything. She would be saving her money to escape. One day she would take a suitcase of clothes and leave a note and her real life would begin, just like that. Maybe tomorrow, maybe next week. Whenever she was ready. The only hard part would be what to say in the note, and who to address it to.

13

Arlene was glad Margaret was driving. The one bad accident she'd had was at twilight. She'd stopped at a stop sign by Frick Park and looked both ways and thought she was all right, except the parked cars right beside her had hidden an oncoming car, and when she pulled out she turned directly into its path. No one had been seriously hurt, just shaken up, and the woman hadn't had her lights on, so it was not all Arlene's fault, but she'd been careful at stop signs ever since, especially around this time of day. That must have been twenty years now.

How many thousands of miles had she driven in her life? The circumference of the earth, she liked to remind her students, was just under twenty-five thousand miles, and her Taurus already had seventy-something. She'd put a good two hundred on the Volvo before it quit, and another hundred fifty on the dog of a Peugeot she'd liked the styling of (though Henry had warned her), and there were the two Chevys before that, her mother's Olds she inherited, and the rusty Ford she'd kept going through grad school. A million miles. It seemed an improbable, even boastful figure, seeing as she didn't like to drive, but the numbers added up. Give or take, she'd driven around the world forty times, and yet she remembered most clearly her one accident, kept the memory fresh, ever vigilant.

She was tempted to see it as an analogy for her one attempt at love, a disaster that precluded all further risk, but it was not the same and there was no sense going over it again, not here.

In the back, the boys were asleep, their seats reclined like dentist's chairs. She fished for a Lucky but the pack was done.

"Can I borrow one?" she asked, holding up Margaret's box of Marlboros.

"I could use one too."

The first tug was sweet, and Arlene looked at hers, surprised.

"Aren't they nice?" Margaret said.

"Very."

They cracked their windows at the exact same time and laughed.

"You're sure I'm not your daughter?" Margaret asked. For an instant Arlene wanted to confess to a plot straight out of the Brontës, a home for wayward girls, a cloaked midwife smuggling a bundle through the woods under a bloody moon. In a way, it was true—soon enough she would be all that remained of her on earth, thoughts of moments like this floating up like her own memories of her old Peugeot or Walter's face inches above hers.

"Reasonably sure," she said.

14

He opened his eyes in the darkness and lifted his head from the musty cushion. Something thumped outside, followed by voices—them—and he stretched and rolled himself off the couch, his stiff legs protesting. He shook his head so his ears flapped, and blinked until he could see, stopped in the middle of the living room and arched his back, giving off a soft puff of gas, then padded into the kitchen, offering a warning bark. He sniffed his empty water dish and stood watching the back door as it rattled open.

The light was blinding. She was the first one in, and he went to her, his head down for her to scratch, the smell of mud rising from her shoes.

"There you are," she said. "I heard you protecting the house, yes, Mr. Ferocious. Did you miss us? I bet you did. I bet you slept all day, didn't you? What a rough life, huh? What a hard and terrible life you have."

15

"You've got a letter," Grandma said, holding the envelope up and popping her eyes wide for her mother's benefit. "Must be from an admirer."

"It's probably from Mark," her mother announced, and started telling everyone about him before Sarah could take it and get away, her own surprise and uncertainty turning to pure anger so that when she flopped down on her sleeping bag upstairs she didn't know how she felt.

He'd promised he would write her and then their last night together they'd had that fight. All July she waited for the mail jeep, watching the flag on their box from the kitchen window, then trudging up the driveway with her arms full of catalogs for her mother, the magazines that still came for her father. She had to stop herself from writing him first. All day she spoke to him in her head, said his name to the blue sky. Lying on a towel beside the Kramers' pool, she composed quick and simple letters, sometimes just one question. An ant skittered by on the concrete, skirting the dark stain of a drying footprint, then vanished into the jungle of grass. Bees crawled over the clover blossoms, working, while she lay there waiting for the day to end and tomorrow to come, another shot at the mail jeep.

She'd stopped him from unbuttoning her cutoffs and he'd called her a tease and she'd hit him and called him a fucker. He just wanted her body, to get whatever he could.

He tried to apologize but she said, "I'm going home."

She didn't, not right then (he knew she was serious, and that was all she wanted). But by her curfew they hadn't completely made up, and the next morning he was gone, leaving her to rethink her decision and remember the nights she'd come in sopping and wanting more.

The pool was just a place to waste time. She rode past his house going home, even though she had to push her bike up Stagecoach so she could coast down Carriage like it was on her way. It was one of those big, perfect homes her mother pointed out when they drove by, impressed with the flowerbeds. The driveway was empty except for the backboard, the garage doors down. One day she'd seen a newspaper, and the next day it was gone, so his parents were home. She wanted to run into them by accident and rode by on Saturday, hoping his father would be out in the yard, but it looked like it did all week, so maybe they were away. Maybe a neighbor was taking care of things. Mark hadn't said anything about them going on vacation. She wondered if his mother was inside all the time, watching her.

The days ran into each other like a looped sample, the same cereal for breakfast, Justin in his PJs playing Pokémon Stadium in the basement, their mother asking the same questions: Weren't the Kramers getting tired of her? Why didn't she ride her bike to the library? Did she want to invite Liz over?

Every day the flag was still up, still up, still up, and then it was down and she went out in her bare feet, stepping gently, flipping through the pile as she walked back up the drive, but it was all for her mother. There was no mail on Sunday, and Tuesday it came early and was all junk, and suddenly it was August and they were supposed to go to the cottage.

And so she'd given in and written him, sent him a short, carefully worded letter that said she missed him and hoped he was having a good summer. She was fine and getting tan, he wouldn't believe how dark she was. She'd bought a new swimsuit. She even joked that she was getting tired of waiting by the mailbox every day, but not anymore because they were leaving. If he wanted to write back, he could use this address. When she came to the end, she wondered how she should sign herself, and finally decided on "Love." *Love, S.,* she wrote, and licked the envelope closed and added a ladybug sticker to be safe.

If she set it on her desk she might not send it at all, and she didn't want her mother to see it, so she slipped it in her backpack along with her rolled-up towel and found her flip-flops and headed off, stopping at the box on the corner of Buckboard and sliding it in as she straddled her bike. The metal was hot, wavy lines coming off the top. Once the weighted door swung shut, she wanted it back, but it was too late, and really she was glad. If she hadn't, she'd be thinking of him the whole time she was at the cottage. At the pool, she imagined the jeep coming to pick it up, the guy unlocking the box and dumping it into a sack, then driving away, as if she had nothing to do with it. On the way home she passed the box and wondered if it was already gone.

That had been a week ago, and this was postmarked Monday from Petoskey. So he'd gotten her letter and written back immediately. She wished she could remember exactly what she'd said in hers, every word.

Saturday she would see him. It seemed months away, but it was just three days. Two and a half.

She turned the envelope over in her hands and slit the end of one flap with a nail as far as it would go, then dug a finger in and tore the hole open.

16

"Your machine's blinking," Margaret called.

"Just a second." In the kitchen, Emily finished refilling Rufus's water dish and gingerly set it down in the corner, Rufus crowding her knee. "There you go," she said, and he looked up from drinking as if to thank her.

"Okay," she said, breezing into the living room, "what's all the hollering about?"

The answering machine had been a late addition, and they'd never found a suitable place for it. She had to lean over the arm of the couch and reach under the lamp to hit the button. It was so seldom used that she was surprised to find there were two messages.

"Hello, Mrs. Maxwell," Mrs. Klinginsmith said, "this is Dorothy Klinginsmith. Friday I have a man coming to inspect the septic system, if that's all right. I'll be there to coordinate things so you won't have to do a thing, I just wanted to warn you."

"She couldn't wait till next week?" Margaret asked.

Emily just shrugged, still intent on the machine, waiting for the second message. She hoped it was Mrs. Klinginsmith canceling. The thought of anyone intruding on their last day at the cottage was dismaying.

"Hey guys," a man said, and it took Emily a second to recognize him as Jeff.

"Dad!" Justin said, turning from the TV.

"I guess you're probably out on the boat or something. I'll call back tomorrow. Nothing big, just wanted to say hey. Hope everyone's having a great time. Okay, bye-bye."

"Can we call him?" Justin asked.

"It's late," Margaret argued, though it was only nine. "You can talk to him tomorrow. Okay?"

"Okay," Justin said glumly, dragging back to his spot on the floor slump-shouldered, and Emily had to restrain herself from butting in. She couldn't imagine denying Kenneth or Margaret their father. It wasn't her right.

"'Just wanted to say hey'?" Margaret asked later, while Lisa was getting the boys down. "What the hell is that?"

"Maybe he's just checking up," Kenneth said.

"I don't think it's that odd." Emily had no reason to doubt Jeff's sincerity. All along she'd suspected Margaret of exaggerating his irresponsibility, especially toward the children, whom she was certain he loved. Emily's only criticism of him—unspoken and, she hoped, unfounded—was that he hadn't protected them from Margaret at her worst and was now abandoning them to her.

"You don't think he did that on purpose? Come on!"

"Am I missing something?" Emily asked.

"She thinks Jeff's trying—" Kenneth started.

"He's playing games," Margaret said. "Pretending he's Mr. Reasonable. Did you hear the voice he used—'Hey guys.' I mean, please. You don't want to hear what he sounds like when he talks to me."

Emily thought that what evidence she had was to the contrary. She could bring back all too easily Margaret's distorted face and the torrent of saddening profanity and vicious threats leveled at her, the late-night finger waved in her face, prodding her to retaliate. At times she had, and then had been ashamed at what could never be retracted, the measured, devastating words that lingered between them even now like wreckage.

She'd never seen Jeff get mad. Maybe that was saved for those closest to him, and was all the more horrible for it, like the few times she'd seen Henry angry. You could only know people so much.

"He wants you to think it's all my fault," Margaret went on, "and it isn't. I'm not perfect, I admit that, but I was trying to make things work, and the whole time he was sneaking around on me. So I don't want you buying any of that 'Hey guys' bullshit."

The room went silent around her, and Emily felt a responsibility to reassure her they were on her side, no question. Because that's what she was asking.

"Do you want me to unplug the phone?"

Margaret checked her face to make sure she was serious, and this seemed to placate her. "No. Now Justin *has* to talk to him. I'm sure Sarah will want to too. It's not that, it's the whole thing." She waved her hands to indicate how large the problem was, and how sick of it she was.

"I understand," Emily said, and she thought she did. She was more puzzled by her own hesitation to give Margaret her support from the beginning, as if she needed to earn it. That was how Margaret must see her— stingy, setting conditions on her love. She'd been accusing Emily of this since she was a teenager, insisting she'd been wronged, that at bottom Emily was disappointed in her. She was surprised to discover it was true.

17

Lise had been trying to be nice because of Sam's tooth, and then he couldn't find his damned Game Boy. They were all exhausted.

"It's not in the bathroom?" she asked, because Sarah was taking an endless shower and had thoughtlessly locked the door. Lise had bullied the boys into their PJs and then into their sleeping bags with instructions to brush their teeth when Sarah was done, but had gotten stuck on this one last point. "Could you have left it in the car?"

"No," Sam said, sure.

But he was always sure. Last winter she'd had to search the school's lost and found for his new ski jacket three times. He couldn't tell her how it had ended up there. Things were never his fault, they just happened to him.

"Did you take it into the restaurant with you?"

"No."

"Ella, have you seen your brother's Game Boy?"

"No," she said venomously, as if Lise had accused her of something. She was still angry at him for elbowing her in the mouth while they were horsing around before bed. Her braces had cut her lip and Lise had had to intervene to prevent further bloodshed. It seemed the hardest thing in the world for him to say he was sorry. She wouldn't put it past Ella to kidnap the game in retaliation, but unlike Sam she wouldn't lie right to her face.

The room was a shambles, clothes thrown about, towels on the floor. She was too tired to make them pick up, her patience sacrificed to the drive, the makings of a headache branching like an aneurysm behind one eye. She thought she should take some Advil, but the bottle was in her kit sitting on the back of the toilet.

"Well, if it's not in the car and you didn't leave it at the restaurant, it's got to be around here somewhere. Maybe tomorrow we can clean up in here."

Sam sighed, unhappy with her answer, but she held back. "I'll look downstairs. I don't see why you need it now because you can't play with it anyway, you've had more than your hour, but I will look for it. In the meantime, entertain yourself with this."

She took the cheap tin telescope Ken had let him buy from off the low wardrobe and handed it to him. He held it as if he didn't know what it was.

"Good night," she ordered.

He barely answered, Justin drowning him out. She retrieved her book from the cedar chest, determined not to let him get to her. On her way to the stairs she knelt down and asked Ella if she was okay and she said yes coldly.

In the shadow of the stairwell she composed herself, an actress waiting for her cue. The day had gone fast, thankfully. Her plan was to read for a little and then excuse herself, whether Ken was ready to go up or not. She could have died for a glass of wine, but it was late, and with Meg she thought she ought to be careful. She took a breath and stepped down, turning the knob and letting her weight open the door.

Arlene hunched over the puzzle, a dish of ice cream at her elbow. Meg had taken the far arm of the couch by the light, her legs tucked to one side. Lise noted Emily's absence not with relief but apprehension, as if she were lurking for her. She raked her gaze over the floor but didn't see the bright yellow case.

"Have either of you seen Sam's Game Boy?"

"No," they both said.

"Is your car open?" she asked Meg.

It was, and when she went out to check she saw the light was on in the garage. Framed by the doorway, Ken was holding up a fat golf bag while Emily wiped it down with a rag.

She snuck by and tried to slide open the door of the minivan quietly, the oiled rollers gliding along the runners. By the dome light she leaned across the old french fries and lollipop sticks bonded to the carpet, involuntarily making a face. She twisted her head to peek underneath the seats but saw nothing except greasy bags and dented cups, straws pushed through their cracked lids. She had to climb in to check the far door pocket, and then the pouches in the backs of the seats, stuffed with trashed maps and atlases.

Kneeling backward on the seat, she thought of calling the restaurant. Information would have the name. She could even picture him taking it on the *Maid of the Mist*—he was that addicted. She wished it was lost. No, because if it really was, Ken would buy him another one, and think her mean if she suggested any different (while Emily could say whatever she wanted and then hold her responsible as the last line of defense). She should have never given in in the first place. TV was bad enough.

"What in the world are you doing in there?" Emily joked, Ken at her shoulder, carrying both bags.

"I'm looking for something of Sam's."

"If it's his video game, I put it on top of the fridge. It was lying in the grass there. I figured that wasn't the best thing for it."

"Thanks," Lise said.

"You could have asked," Ken said later, in the kitchen, the two of them whispering under cover of the radio. Emily had turned it on, supposedly for the weather. "How could she have known what you were looking for?"

"I don't know," Lise said, "but I don't like being made fun of. I know you don't think so, but I'm telling you that's how it felt to me."

"I'm sorry," he said, as if he could apologize for Emily. And still he didn't see it; he was just trying to appease her. Typically, they ended up mad at each other while Emily skated away untouched.

"Forget it," she said, not forgiving him but not hard enough to really hurt him either, and took her book into the living room. Sam could wait till tomorrow for his Game Boy.

"Any news on the girl?" she asked Emily.

She held up a hand as if Lise were interrupting her concentration, except the story was something about road construction in Jamestown.

"They haven't said anything yet," Arlene answered her.

Emily put the hand up to her as well, so that when the newscaster switched to the latest in the continuing case of missing convenience-store clerk Tracy Ann Caler, they could all hear it.

State police investigators were using infrared cameras mounted on helicopters and had brought in specialized K-9 units, but so far they'd turned up no significant leads. The nineteen-year-old Mayville woman was last seen more than four days ago. Today's Jammers game that had been rained out would be played tomorrow as part of a single-admission double-header. The weather would be sunny and warm for a change.

No one spoke until Emily turned it off, and then it was Ken, saying they'd have to wake up early if they wanted to get a decent tee time, as if talking about the girl was bad luck. Lise thought it was morbid the way Emily had adopted her, not that it surprised her.

"Well," Emily announced, rising, "I think I've had about enough excitement for one day." She thanked them all for taking her to Niagara Falls, then negotiated a time she and Ken should get going.

"Be quiet leaving," Lise joked, thinking that would give her the whole morning. The afternoon she would spend on the boat with Ken—but as soon as she caught herself thinking this, she erased it, afraid of jinxing the day. Counting her chickens, as Emily would say.

They all watched Emily go, so when she stopped by the TV and asked if anyone minded if she left the bathroom light on tonight, they all responded, nodding or mumbling.

"The Lerners' alarm must have me conditioned. I keep waking up at three in the morning or some ungodly hour."

As if anyone cared, Lise thought, and the sour taste of this stayed with her once Emily had brushed her teeth and closed her door.

"Why the big sigh?" Ken asked, beside her.

"I'm just tired," she said, bypassing any real explanation, and went back to her book.

Harry was learning how to use spells and curses. The rules were confusing, and all the cute names were losing her. She found it hard to believe Ella thought this was funny, and very soon the pages revived her headache and she had to stop.

Around the room, they each sat quietly in their own circle of light, Ken bent over an old *New Yorker,* Meg reading, Arlene intent on her puzzle. In the bathroom, the toilet trickled, refilling, a jet rushing, then suddenly cut off. They had reached the peaceful end of the night, the children down, Emily safely in bed, yet instead of a feeling of release or freedom Lise felt constricted, the darkness pressing at the windows. If it were just herself and Ken it would be different, but the silence, being shared, was almost enforced. To put on the TV would be an affront. There was nowhere to go but outside, and then everyone would watch you leave and wonder where you'd gone and what you were doing.

Across the room, Arlene straightened up in her chair and clicked off her light. She rose and hauled on a padded jacket thirty years out of date, checking the pocket for her cigarettes.

"I'm going to take Rufus for his constitutional, if anyone's interested."

Lise saw it as an opportunity to excuse herself, telling Ken she was heading up. He seemed disappointed, as if to say, Stay, it's still early.

"Don't be too late," she said. "Remember you've got golf tomorrow."

If he wanted to stay up all night with Meg, that was his decision, but upstairs, reading on the pot, she marked the time on her watch.

She'd forgotten the Game Boy on the fridge. It didn't matter.

Harry Potter was boring. She wished she'd bought that Oprah book. She was becoming as cheap as he was.

She set Harry down on the fuzzy crescent rug at her feet and rubbed her hair with her hands, her scalp loose on her skull. With her palms over her ears, she could hear a great trembling like an earthquake, a herd of buffalo a mile away. Why was she so tired? She'd done nothing but sit in the car. Her back hurt from standing in line. She wiped herself and stepped out of her underwear, catching her face in the mirror.

"Oh God," she said, trying to be funny for someone.

She took three Advil, cupping a handful of sulfurous water to wash them down, the sweet coating lingering after. When she opened the medicine cabinet, her face slid off the mirror. She turned her back on it to brush her teeth.

She decided not to read. She took the side by the wall so he wouldn't have to crawl over her. The sheets were freezing, her headache that much clearer. She could hear the liquid hiss of Ella snoring. She wondered if Ken had a dollar to give Sam from the tooth fairy, because she knew he'd do it anyway, he couldn't be that ruthless. She wasn't either, Sam would discover that soon enough.

She was just frustrated, having to compete with everyone for Ken. She wasn't used to it, or was too used to it here, tired of fighting the same old ghosts. There was always a moment like this during their visits when she felt unstrung, her world provisional, at the whim of primal forces. She had to remind herself that as eternal as these positions seemed, they were temporary, that in a day or two they would go home and all of this would vanish, become nothing but a weekly phone call, or, in the case of Meg, a monthly one. Their lives would go on with minimal interruption. For whole days they would talk to no one but each other. They'd go to bed and then wake up together, fix breakfast and tend the children, just the two of them, the bills their only worry, and the disasters on NPR.

She thought she should be alarmed at how tightly she held on to that promise, because at heart it was false—their problems were larger than she wanted to admit—and yet she wasn't. The week would end, as it had to. Eventually Ken would come to bed, first turning to her, then rolling over so she could nestle against him. She just needed to be patient, to forget about her watch ticking on the cedar chest. It wouldn't be long.

18

Without the rain, Arlene realized how loud the night was, how unserene and wild. She loved the peepers over by the marina, riotous, screaming away like frightened birds, the cicadas keeping time in the trees. As Rufus neared the dock, frogs plopped into the shallows, a musical handful of stones, and there, as the trees gave way to the oily calm of the lake, the sky opened up, a bowl of stars.

Arlene stopped and tipped her chin, gawked at them like a child, openmouthed with delight. There were things in life that had a power over her, things that could not be denied—autumn, Schubert, a child who wanted to learn. They restored her faith, she supposed, the same way the Institute had refreshed her mother every summer. This was why they came to the lake, why they muddled through all the crossness and soft water, the lumpy pillows and rainy days. She wanted to run back to the cottage and drag Margaret out to see it, this proof of goodness or reward, but knew that would ruin the feeling, send it fleeing like the brief illusion it was.

On the dock, Rufus waited for her, stock-still, as if she might take off and ditch him.

"You just hold your horses," she said, and stepped onto the boards, a much different proposition than during the day.

The wind was mild and it was hard to see the water. Rufus went ahead, his nails tapping.

"Oh, now you can't wait for me," she said, but he kept going, sure of their destination.

The bench was wet. She slicked off a spot with the palm of one hand, but still it soaked cold through her trousers, making her sit up straight and clench a breath. She lit a cigarette and tucked her other hand in her armpit for warmth.

The moon threw a surprising amount of light. It lay puddled on the water, cast shadows of the pilings across the motorboat. Perhaps she'd go out with them tomorrow if there was a spare seat. When Henry first bought it, the three of them used to boom up and down the lake, taking turns at the wheel, leaping wakes and skidding through turns, waving a rooster tail of spray. He stood up to drive, peering over the windshield, bare-chested and wearing his Ray-Bans, a can of beer in one hand. They'd come in sunburnt, bleached blond, the roots of their hair throbbing from the wind. She'd wanted Walter to see her like that, the ravishing beach bunny, but of course he couldn't come up. She told Henry about him, sure he would keep their secret, even if he disapproved, and he did—both disapprove and keep it.

"I think you're kidding yourself," he'd say, or "In my experience, that's not how it works," or "Don't let Emmy hear you say that," but he stayed out of her affairs.

He would have been within his rights. Their love had been improper. She'd been Walter's teaching assistant, the two of them sneaking around campus, meeting in his dark office after the rest of the department had gone home. She could still bring back the thrilling strangeness of being stretched naked across the cool leather inlay of his desk, the patterns the flowered border left on her skin. He had a phonograph he played when they made love, and weekends when he was occupied with his wife and daughter, she haunted the record stores, trying to find a piece that described how she felt about him.

She'd brought a copy of Prokofiev's *Love for Three Oranges* that last Monday. They never listened to it. He took her to the Ramble instead, clasped his hands behind him as they walked through the ankle-deep leaves. Back in her apartment she dropped the unopened record in the garbage and smoked most of a pack before calling Henry, only then giving in to tears. All that fall he checked in on her, making her eat and holding her while she wept, and not once did he remind her of how silly she'd been.

Rufus sighed and she looked up, movement drawing her eye. What she thought was a satellite resolved itself into two dots and then three, an invisible airplane blinking across the stars, small and high up enough to be silent, tiny compared to the vast backdrop. The summer sky was fixed with the season, had been with her since she was a girl here, quietly abiding the turning of the world, the wars and great changes. She felt lifted out of herself, as if she could look down on the dithering old woman who sat on the dock, and the trees and dark cottages along the shore, felt buoyed up towards the larger question of the stars and the earth and eternity.

She could not see Henry in her mother's version of heaven, a place not much different from the Institute, with beveled hedges and Mozart lilting from the woods, the inhabitants robed and earnestly discussing philosophy like the ancient Greeks. She hoped there was a time in his life when he was happy with everything that he would return to, like those mad, breathless days she thought Walter could be hers.

She had no real idea of heaven, she thought, even less than the cottonball clouds and harps a child would have: a carless small town blessed with good weather, houses lifted from fairy tales. That didn't mean it didn't exist. She couldn't believe Henry was just gone, lost.

Her mother would scoff at her apostasy, see it as prideful and self-inflicted, one more useless thing she'd learned, but it wasn't. Her whole life had been dedicated to giving others the courage to say "I don't know" and then go further, the search for truth itself a sacred rite. It made no sense to stop now just because she found herself faced, in the end, with her mother's favorite questions.

Behind her, a car glided down Manor Drive, its headlights picking out the sides of houses, its taillights painting the leaves. A truck, chugging, probably a fisherman on his way to the marina. Her neck hurt, and the stars had lost their majesty. She was almost done with her cigarette, and it was too chilly to wait for the bell to ring.

She did not plan on going to heaven. She would simply no longer be, just as, in a minute, she would no longer be on this dock. The bell would ring anyway, as it would next week and next year, when they were no longer here. The stars and the earth would turn, the cottage fall down. It was not a mystery. Someone would take over her apartment and stalk the small rooms, pace from the kitchen to the front door the same way she did, set their plants on the fire escape to take the sun. All she would leave behind were her scrapbook, a few pieces of her mother's jewelry, a stack of fading snapshots. She would be the old woman in the video they strained to name, a difficult trivia question, their great-grandfather Maxwell's sister, the one who never married. What disturbed her most was not the idea that they would think her a lesbian (though she'd fielded that one more often than she cared to remember) but unhappy, that even in death she would have to defend her choices and, as in life, inevitably lose to the opinions of those who didn't know her.

She stubbed out her butt on the piling behind her, smearing the ember, then scratching at it with the filter.

"You ready, old man?" she said, and Rufus grumped and struggled to his feet.

She could see easily now, the water a silvered, reflective black like the waxed finish of a limousine. As they approached the bank, the frogs dove for safety. Rufus stayed obediently at her heel until they reached the grass, then loped over to the kitchen door, lobbying for a treat. In the woods, the locusts screamed, eternal as the stars. The night was full of sex and predators—life, Arlene thought. Near the stairs, Rufus wagged his back end, prancing frantically.

"All right, all right," she said. "I see you."

19

There was no remote, another rustic feature of the cottage, and when he stood up to turn on the eleven o'clock news he saw with a twinge of disbelief—followed sharply by annoyance—that they'd forgotten to take the tapes back.

"It's okay," Meg said, "I can take them back tomorrow."

"I can drive," he said, and it was true, he'd crisscrossed most of the U.S. stoned during his college years, going on road trips with his Deadhead friends just for something to do, the thrill of being out there, moving, spending the shows grooving in the parking lot, driving the whole way back because everyone else was fried. Maxwell Cassidy. It had been a while.

"I'll come with you," she said, and after they made sure the back door was open, they hopped in the 4Runner and started off, Freedy Johnston on the CD player.

Meg had never heard of him. It didn't seem like her, as if she'd changed, lost some precious skill or sense of appreciation, the years and the booze dulling her. Ken remembered how she'd introduced him to music, spinning her 45s for him with her door closed. They played a game where he had to name a song by its first notes, Meg dropping the needle, the record scratching around, then the thump of a bass, a drum beat, and she'd lift it again. "I Think We're Alone Now!" he'd shout. "Sky Pilot!"

So what was she listening to now?

"Nothing," she said. "The Stones. Old stuff. Jeff took all of his CDs, so we're a little short on tunes right now."

"I guess I know what to get you for your birthday."

"Yeah," she said, as if it didn't matter.

He babied the 4Runner up Manor Drive, obeying the fifteen-mile-an-hour limit. Their neighbors were mostly asleep or away, only a few windows still awake. The feeling of being stoned and the only ones up reminded him of high school, cruising the empty streets, the radio wired into the night. Meg had been gone by then, leaving him to deal with his parents, to take on the unfamiliar role of the favorite.

"You oughta lock that door," Freedy Johnston sang. "Somebody might get in. Didn't I teach you that?"

There was no one on the highway, only a light above the corn-field, bugs orbiting the hot bulb. He turned and the neat green rows riffled in his headlights like a deck of cards. The Snug Harbor Lounge was doing a decent business, its neon making a carnival of the parking lot. Then darkness, farms and unlit billboards, the white line stuttering under the tires, a familiar, dreamy feeling. Trees and signs floated by, invisibly suspended. The moon traced a creek through a field.

"Niagara Falls," Meg said, and it took him a second to process it.

"Slowly I turned . . ."

"Did you get some pictures of her?"

"Some."

"Will you do me a favor," she said, "and take one of me with her before the week's over?"

"Sure," he said, but waited for her explanation, let the road occupy his mind.

"She's not young."

He thought this was ridiculous but agreed. "So have you talked to her about the house?"

"When have I had time?"

"I'll have four hours with her tomorrow morning," he said, and she laughed.

"All I want is a picture, that's enough for me. Four straight hours. Man."

"So I guess I'm representing us, is that it?"

"Hey, she'll listen to you before she'll listen to me. I know Arlene's tried to talk to her."

"I don't think she can back out now. It's pretty much a done deal from what I can tell."

"They're still doing a septic inspection. How done can it be?"

He'd tried that angle because he wanted it to be done. The money just wasn't there.

"Who's going to pay the taxes on it? You know how much they are?"

"Three thousand a year," she guessed. "Ballpark."

"Do *you* have three thousand dollars?"

"*She's* got three thousand dollars. She doesn't need the money, she just doesn't want to deal with the hassle. I bet if you offered to take care of the place, she'd keep it."

"I don't want to take care of the place," he admitted.

"I'll take care of it."

"Right. I'll tell her that."

He knew it was a mistake as soon as it escaped, an unfunny joke. But he couldn't take it back, and he couldn't blame it on being stoned, though he never would have said it straight.

"Fuck you," she said, and went quiet on him.

She sat there, a statue in the dark, as they sped past Willow Run and crested the hill by the campgrounds, the shuttered Book Barn.

"Lovers cry," Freedy sang. "One last kiss by the edge, then hand in hand, two lovers fly."

The reason it was so hard to talk about money, he thought, was because it revealed how they really felt about each other. Maybe it was the same with the cottage, his willingness to let it drift away an unrealistic wish to rid himself of all the difficulties he associated with his family, the misgivings, both real and imaginary, he felt when he thought of his mother or father or Meg and his own nonsupporting role in their lives.

"I'm sorry," he said.

"Don't be. It's true. That's why you're the one who's got to offer. I don't count."

He wanted to contradict her but knew better.

"I thought you liked the cottage," she said.

"I do." He searched for a reason that wouldn't convict him, then resented her for forcing him into a corner. "It's just the money."

"She's *got* the money," Meg said, as if he didn't understand. "You think she *wants* to sell the place? She just doesn't think she can take care of it without Dad. All we have to say is we'll take it over, both of us. That's what she wants. I'm telling you. What is she going to use the money for? She can't take it with her."

"I don't know," he said slowly, as if mulling the whole thing over.

He didn't want to think of his parents' money, whatever money there was (his father's insurance on top of the stocks and bonds and mutual funds, the joint accounts and the two houses). At his most desperate he fended off the idea that it alone could save him, her death a windfall not far down the road. No, their money was theirs (was hers now), as separate and secret from him as their love life, and best left that way.

"Talk to her," Meg said. "See how she feels. What else are you going to talk about for four hours?"

"You."

"I figured that."

"She still hasn't reamed me out about the job yet."

"And I'm going to miss it."

"I'll give you the highlights."

He was glad to joke about himself, joining with her to make fun of his mother and the expectations they would never live up to. He could still make her laugh by playing the fool, her goofy little brother.

"Can I smoke in here?"

"Sure," he said, anticipating Lise's objections, "just open a window."

He cracked his as well.

Far off, at the bottom of the hill, high clusters of lights bathed the on-ramps of the Southern Tier like a crime scene. Hogan's Hut was closed for the night, only the Mobil pumps aglow, reminding him that he needed to buy gas tomorrow, and he found himself thinking of Tracy Ann Caler, somewhere out there, probably dead. He could dedicate his work to her, use it to commemorate her life, the house she grew up in, her family, her room—very Bill Owens, the mystery of the everyday. He could see how much it would require, the time and patience. That was what he wanted to do with the cottage, and he'd barely started. Tomorrow was Thursday, and half of that was golf. He'd take the Holga in his bag. There would be time on the tees and greens, driving the cart—not too much, just what Morgan ordered.

They came down past the Ashville marina and into Busti, where the speed limit changed. The gas and convenience mart there was closed, no surprise, and the Ice Cream Shack, back in its gravel lot. A van passed them coming the other way, then two cars, two more, a steady stream headed north. It wasn't until they went under the railroad overpass outside Lakewood that they saw the movie complex was letting out. On their left the Dairy Queen was still serving, the entrance and exit of the parking lot marked by lighted cones three feet high, complete with the curl on top.

"Very nice," Meg said.

"How many times a year you think those are stolen?"

"I'd take them. Hell yes."

Up a rise by the restaurant where they'd been served bloody chicken the one time they went there, and the run-down motel with the derelict trailer in the lot, and then they were into Lakewood with its orange-tinted streetlights and extra lanes, traffic in front and back of them, the sprawling strip-mall ugliness of Wal-Mart and Rite Aid replacing the spooky intimacy of night in the countryside. Blockbuster was up ahead, its trade-mark colors drawing cars in.

"You've got the tapes, right?"

"I thought you had them," she said, and when he turned to her in stoned disbelief she was holding them up. "You are so easy."

He inched up to the drop box, afraid of scraping the side, and then had to open the door to reach the slot. Above it hung Tracy Ann Caler's face. PLEASE HELP FIND ME, the flyer read, and gave all the information, and he thought unsteadily that if he were alone he would have taken it for himself, a sick keepsake. He'd have to shoot it with the Holga, a whole series.

"What do you think about some ice cream?" he asked Meg, to deflect any questions, but then at the Dairy Queen there was the same picture on the inside of the drive-thru. Five-five, 110 pounds. He had time to memorize it while the girl in the headset made change, cracking a roll of nickels on the drawer like an egg. He remembered Sam's tooth and asked if they had any of those gold dollars, but of course not.

"That's all right," he said, his all-purpose reply, and she went to get the cones. Lise once told him it sounded phony, like he was trying to come off as a nice guy, and since then he'd been self-conscious about it, often stopping it halfway out of his mouth.

He could do one of every place that had a flyer—the hardware in Mayville, the Golden Dawn—and show her world that way. Her parents, the cops, everyone who was trying to find her—that was what he was doing too. He was part of the project, incorporated organically, as Morgan would say.

"I always think I see you," Freedy sang with perfect timing. "Across the avenue."

It was hard to shift with the cone in his hand, and Meg had to hold it until they were into fourth. His buzz was fading, and he felt the day closing around him, the possibilities narrowing down, like the end of a date. For all his dread of her, he liked being with Meg. In some ways she was easier than Lise or his mother. She could take him back further than anyone, the memory of their rooms on Grafton Street a safe space to retreat to, the years ideal, nothing serious intruding on their after-school reruns of *Superman* and *Gilligan's Island,* nothing gone wrong yet. It was as false as the soft ice cream they were eating, and as comforting. Lise regularly told him to grow up, charged him with acting like a little kid. Sometimes he thought it was more than nostalgia, that he would actually be happier if he'd stopped around nine. Or no, later, a teenager, believing the lyrics from the records he taped from his friends, all of them falling for the rock'n'roll dream that if they went far enough fast enough they'd never run out of open road.

Meg had been his only role model, and he'd seen her disregard for convention as heroic. The world seemed very large then, and home very small, a place to get away from, their parents jailers. In college he'd stayed awake for days, read books that told him everything was possible, the systems that held everybody down were an illusion bound to crumble before the truth, but as he aged the world had solidified, become real. It was that excitement he missed, that freedom so closely allied with irresponsibility and nothingness. He had betrayed it or it him, or maybe it was just a stage, as he was tempted to see it now. He wondered if Meg was as baffled at how things had turned out as he was. Maybe that was just life. Their dashed hopes weren't a tragedy, just something they needed to get used to.

"Good idea," Meg said, toasting him with her cone as if she'd read his thoughts.

His was dripping over his fingers, a spot dotting his jeans. The stiff little napkins were inadequate. The CD started again—"I know I've got a bad reputation"—and Ken stabbed at the eject button with a thumb.

"No," Meg said, "I like that one."

And so they listened to it again, and the next song, and the next, riding along through the dark, limitless night.

20

She didn't want him anyway, Sarah thought. He never loved her. He only said it that time so she would take her top off, let him slide the wet straps of her suit over her shoulders, and then he squeezed her breasts too hard, like they were baseballs, and she gasped and he pulled back and apologized, stood there as if she might send him away.

She didn't understand why she took his hands and placed them on her again. To prove she was tough, not as fragile as he thought. Because she had power over him then. He would do anything to touch them, and after a while she came to resent it, pulling him up by the tip of his chin so he would kiss her. She could make him do anything.

He didn't know how to touch her, cramming his hand down her jeans, his watchband tearing out hairs, and then fumbling around and her getting wet anyway, her hips turning to find the right pressure but then him changing, losing his place. She wanted to tell him to stay still, but instead she let him explore her, thinking it was early, that she could teach him.

He was about as romantic as a roll-on deodorant. He lied to her when he told her he would write. She wrote. He never wrote, only this: *I'm sorry. I hope you're not angry.* Two pages of excuses. Fuck him.

She thought of Saturday, and of not seeing him. Her mother would ask if there was something wrong, and then there'd be this big thing. They'd fight, which would frighten Justin, and she'd go to her room and close the door. She'd cry and rage and slam her fist into her pillow as if it were Mark's face, and it wouldn't change anything. He didn't want her. He'd found someone else better, someone who would pretend he was the sexiest guy in the world.

It was his plan from the beginning. He'd used the summer to break up, the days and weeks apart building up to the news. She'd done it herself with Colin last year, but now she saw how cruel and cowardly it was. Mark should have just told her in June instead of making her wait.

She lay there, Ella whistling through her train tracks beside her.

The door opened below, throwing a shaft of light up the wall, and Sarah rolled over, nose to nose with Ella. The room went dark again until some- one clicked on a flashlight, a circle flying around like a trapped bat. She heard her mother and Uncle Ken giggling, trying to be quiet, and she wondered angrily if they were stoned. Ella slept with her mouth open; it made her look even more like a little kid, and Sarah thought she was lucky, not having to worry about guys hitting on her all the time.

The fucking prick. She could make him change his mind anytime. It wouldn't take much.

She wasn't that desperate.

They turned at the top of the stairs, the floor creaking under their feet. She closed her eyes and tried to slow her breathing, waiting for them to step over her, to leave her alone again so she could think. Like it would do her any good.

21

Sleeping was not the problem, it was what flew through her head as she lay awake: the moments after the accident rendered in a blinding flash; Jeff making love to Stacey in their bed (the bed she still slept in, though she stripped it and sprayed the mattress every week with Lysol, as if that could kill the memory); the woman in rehab who screamed herself to sleep, exhausting all of them. This was her version of that, with visions instead of hallucinations, her demons real.

She'd been pinned in the car, her knee mashed under the dash- board and hurting, blood running down her face, flecking the cuffs of her shirt, wetting the front. For some reason she was off the road, a stretch of wire fence filling the passenger window. Her car had stalled but her lights were still on, the speedometer on zero. The other car sat attached to hers, T-boned, smoking, the other driver partially eclipsed by the air bag, a woman her age, her one arm rising and falling as if she were waving to her, flagging her down for help. Her first conscious thought after the impact was ironically relieved—that she hadn't been drinking—as if the woman had caught her at just the right time. She didn't remember what happened, only that she'd been driving. It was not her fault.

She had a cigarette somewhere—knocked from her hand—and thought the cars' might catch fire like they did in the movies. She could open her door. It swung free, and the cold and snow poured in, attacking from all sides. Her arms were fine, and her one leg, but the other wouldn't budge. She thought someone should be here already, the police at least. It was a busy road, even at this time of night.

"Help!" she yelled, but the snow seemed to swallow her words. The other woman waved her hand mechanically. On the road another car sluiced by. "Help us," she said weakly. For Christ's sake, stop.

Of the moments in her life she would never forget, this one returned to her most often. It was the one she singled out as the turning point, the reason she decided to become another person, though Jeff never tired of pointing out—as she herself did, remembering—that she hadn't been drinking that night.

"I just as easily could have been," she argued, until he no longer listened to her. That was when Stacey came into the picture, walking out of their bathroom naked, noticeably younger than her, perky and carefree, a lover Jeff might have dreamed up, jumping on the bed like a trampoline, trying to touch the stucco ceiling as he laughed beneath her, while Meg lay in her private room at Winding Trails, freezing under the covers, the stitches in her knee healing. Down the dark hall, night after night, she heard the woman pleading with Jesus, screaming for him to save her.

These were the secrets she didn't tell anyone but selfishly held on to, bringing them out in the last minutes before sleep to turn them over again, trying to glean some meaning from the awkward combination of the three. The woman in the other car suffered a serious spinal injury but survived. It had been the other woman's fault, the police report determined, she'd been driving too fast for conditions. The woman down the hall she never found out about. The screaming stopped after her first week, the room empty when she passed it, awaiting its next occupant. The third woman was herself (Stacey wasn't a woman, just a symptom), and there her analysis foundered, leaving only what had occurred, vivid and irreducible, meaning she was free to revisit the events anytime, which she did.

Thursday

1

Emily stood at the sink, sipping, not a hint of a breeze filtering through the screen. Here was the day they'd been waiting for, warm, the sun already sharp on the rhododendron, threatening a breathless heat. The brightness held everything in place, the only motion the bees that patrolled the Lerners' trumpet vines. The humidity under the trees promised thundershowers, but not until dusk, a brief, steaming reprieve. It seemed a different season altogether, the last few days erased. They'd have to get out early and wear some headgear, rub on sunblock. She couldn't imagine how bad it would be in the city—roasting, an absolute sauna—and pictured Louise going out to water her roses.

She hoped her postcard would arrive tomorrow. She was beyond worrying about it now.

She unearthed a white visor in a pile of baseball caps Henry kept for the boat and found her clip-on sunglasses in a dish on the mantel. The boys were relentless, playing video games in their pajama bottoms. She didn't feel up to ruining their good time and went into the kitchen and rinsed the stray dishes from last night and wiped down the counters before taking her coffee outside, Rufus sticking close to her, worried. He stopped at Arlene's car, pointing at the door and wagging his tail as if they were going somewhere.

"My," she said, "we *are* antsy, aren't we?"

The lawn bristled with dew, the new light angling between the tree trunks, laying the black stripes of their shadows along the garage and across the Lerners' yard. Overhead, the birds were busy, all talking before the noise of the world drowned them out—chirps and whistles and trills, the lonesome two-toned hoot of a mourning dove. The lake was still, a skin of cottonwood fluff glazing the surface. Walking out onto the dock was like taking the stage, and she was pleased to see she was alone, no neighbors to wave to. She stubbed her toe on the raised lip of one section, spilling her coffee, and swore, the chain reaction almost comic. Rufus stopped when she stopped, as if he'd done something wrong, but she just held the dripping cup away from her, unhurt, more amused than embarrassed by her own carelessness.

She decided against the bench, set the cup on the dock and lowered herself to the edge, her feet dangling inches above the water. Rufus folded himself down beside her uncertainly. She wondered if he knew she'd be gone all morning, the familiar golf bag a tip-off. And after she'd left him alone the whole day yesterday.

"Is that why you're acting so goofy? Huh? You poor neglected dog."

He regarded her solemnly, then, slowly—all the time watching her, as if for permission—listed until he was flat on his side, his one eye wide open, keeping her in sight.

"You are something," she said, thumping his ribs, and heard the echo of Henry in her words.

The basement was cool in summer, and Rufus had a spot in a corner of his workshop, the concrete floor delicious. She was convinced Rufus missed him. Sometimes he would nose around the house, sniffing the ruffle of Henry's chair or the half-filled shoe rack in his closet, and then come to her looking puzzled, as if to ask where he'd gone. "I know," she'd say, but—it was so silly—she couldn't bring herself to tell him, sit down with him as you would a child and patiently explain everything. And maybe he was asking something completely different, maybe she was just projecting her loss onto him. So she said "I know" and left it at that.

She wondered if Marcia had emptied the dehumidifier like she'd asked her. A day like today it would fill up quick. Last year she'd let it go and then Emily had had problems with mold, her best gloves and scarves musty, the new fleece vest Kenneth had given her for Christmas mildewed. Things like that were maddening, so easy to prevent.

She used two hands to drink from her cup, as if it were winter. The birds hadn't shut up. A pair of swallows dueled, zipping across the water, then sailing high and stalling, falling again, veering away when they came too close to her. Their sudden cutting made her appreciate her own stillness. She wished she had the ability to absent herself, to become part of the dock and watch without intruding. She could happily sit here forever, a morning like this. The peace of the day became hers, quieted her mind, if only for a moment. At home it was impossible, any daydream leading to Henry or the children's old rooms, the past flashing like a photo album, but here she was justified, the setting—the spirit of the place—designed to let visitors forget time, open oneself to larger contemplation. The same was true of golf, she thought. She ought to get out more. She'd have to badger Louise.

Behind her, a mallard glided between the docks, dipping his green head to feed, tipping his feathered rump up, a sinking ship. He worked his bill as if tasting the grass, smacking his lips. He pushed himself along, his ridged wake glossy, swiveling his head, stiffly vigilant. Rufus was drowsing and didn't see him.

And where is Mrs. Mallard? she thought, but not heavily. She could not see Henry everywhere. There were ways of short-circuiting these things, stopping them before they started. The first was learning to recognize them.

She noticed she was kicking her feet like a child, letting them swing for no reason, a hedge against thinking. It was just the day, the gift of perfect weather. The sun was hot on her arms and knees, and she hoped Kenneth was up. She wanted to get off before the rush. There was nothing worse than waiting for other people to hit.

A breeze wrinkled the surface, bringing the boggy vegetable smell of algae. She closed her eyes and listened to the different birds, identifying them, the sun burning red through her lids, insistent, and all the time she was aware of her legs, still kicking. In the distance, a lawn mower snarled. Smart—the afternoon would be brutal.

A tremor ran through the dock, and she opened her eyes and turned to see Arlene tromping toward her, carrying something black. Beside her, Rufus lifted his head, then subsided. Emily consciously stopped her feet.

"Finally, a decent day," Arlene said, waving an arm at the sky.

She had her camera, and wanted to borrow that film they talked about. She needed new shots of the children for her refrigerator, and she wanted a good one of the cottage. Maybe Kenneth would lend his professional skills.

Emily checked her cup—almost done. "Did you look on my dresser?"

"I didn't see it."

The mantel, the kitchen table, maybe by the phone.

No.

"Can it wait a minute?"

"Sure," Arlene said, but instead of taking the hint, she sat down on the bench and started talking about going out in the boat. "Remember when it was new and we'd drive the heck out of it?" she asked, ruining any chance Emily had of losing herself.

She remembered. She knew that Arlene missed him too. She was just annoyed at having to leave the birds and join the rest of the world again. It was inevitable, and not Arlene's fault, but still she felt hurried, gave up her perch unwillingly. Rufus wasn't happy either.

She was surprised to find Kenneth stalking the yard with his camera, as if he'd forgotten their game.

"I was under the impression that we had a golf date," she said.

"The light's so good, I thought I'd get in a quick roll. It'll take ten minutes."

"We're leaving in ten minutes then."

"I'll be ready."

"I hope so. It's going to be a zoo."

Inside, the boys were killing each other with guns. Margaret and Lisa and the girls weren't up yet—no surprise. She found the yellow box on her dresser where she'd left it, in plain sight. She didn't understand why Arlene felt the need to stand on ceremony after so many years, but didn't have the time or energy to get into it with her. She washed her coffee cup and brushed her teeth and rubbed sunblock on her face and arms and legs. She had enough cash, and her credit cards, in case, and going through the musty zip pocket of her bag she discovered an unopened package of tees—two years old, at least. A bottle of water would be a good idea, but the one in the fridge was nearly empty, obviously the work of one of the boys.

"Please do not leave empty bottles in the refrigerator," she told them both, holding it up.

The blame fell between them, unacknowledged.

Outside, a car slowly rolled by the windows—the Wisemans' red Cadillac coming up the drive. She followed it through the screenporch, caught up to it before Marjorie could open her door. Herb Wiseman sat strapped into the passenger seat, emaciated, barely managing a wave, and Emily had to temper her reaction, freeze her surprised smile. The windows were closed for the air-conditioning, and Marjorie left the car running. Arlene and Kenneth came over to pay their respects.

"We're leaving," Marjorie explained, and enveloped Emily in a perfumed hug.

"We've been meaning to come see you," Emily protested, looking her over.

Arlene hugged Marjorie as well. Kenneth shook her hand with manly concern. Emily marked how unchanged she was—the neat white hair and enviable tan and even teeth, her summer uniform of faded alligator shirt, madras shorts and moccasins. She seemed fine, untouched by his illness, if anything more capable. Emily worried that that was how she'd looked, her health shocking next to Henry, vampirelike.

"I hear you sold the place."

"I did," she admitted.

"It's a shame. The old gang's breaking up. I'm so sorry about Henry."

Emily thanked her—a reflex she thought she'd lost. She wanted to ask after Herb but couldn't with him right there. He hadn't moved, and wouldn't, out of pride or infirmity she didn't know.

"I don't think I've ever seen you drive this car before," she said.

"On the highway it's fine. You'd be surprised, you get used to it."

"You're brave," Emily said.

When they'd said their good-byes (she and Arlene craning their heads through the open window to give Herb a scratchy kiss) and the Wisemans had driven off, she puzzled over her own remark, wondering what part of it was directed at herself, self-congratulatory after the fact. They were only driving to Buffalo. She could tell from Herb's mushroom color what was in store for Marjorie, the hope and panic, the preparation and the waiting. She'd have to call her when she got home, already dreading it along with the bills and her estimated tax payment, and reluctantly added it to her list.

"Are we ready?" she asked Kenneth, to get him going, and he dragged himself inside to find the sunblock.

Arlene took the rocker on the porch, her mission forgotten. The Wisemans had crushed whatever momentum they had, changed the tone of the whole morning. Emily didn't dare sit down or she would succumb too, and she couldn't afford to, not now. At home she'd have nothing but time to dwell on these things. Today she was playing golf.

She lugged her clubs to the back of Kenneth's car and figured out the latch, got a good grip and hefted the rattling bag in, surprised at how light it was. She'd always taken care of herself, and her mother had lived to be eighty-three. Again she thought of trim, prim Marjorie. They could each have another twenty years, hunched and shrinking to nothing inside their empty houses until the children worried for their safety and installed them in old-folks' homes.

Kenneth came out of the house with his bag, walking flat-footed, fussing with his zippers, taking his sweet time.

"Let's go!" she called, a tough coach. "Come on, Maxwell, let's see some hustle!"

2

Lise heard the car start and turned her face toward the open window for a minute—the curtains motionless, the chestnut dusty and sun-dappled beyond the screen—verified the familiar engine, then turned back to the page with Harry eating Christmas dinner, hundreds of plump roast turkeys followed by flaming Christmas puddings and crumpets and cakes. Filch, Professor Snape and Professor Flitwick. It was like Dickens, everyone had funny names.

Across the room, Sarah opened the bathroom door and clicked it closed behind her. Lise checked her watch on the cedar chest. It was still early. Meg was asleep, and Ella. Outside it was blinding, but inside the light was flat, the room shadowed. Emily was gone, and she was free, the whole morning hers. She slouched down, curling her back, making mountains of her knees, vowing not to get out of bed until she absolutely had to.

3

Sarah took Rufus with her—any excuse to get away from them. Aunt Arlene was busy taking pictures and didn't ask to tag along, just looked at her funny, as if it was too early for her to be up.

"It's so nice," Sarah said, "I thought I'd go over to the ponds."

It was simple lying to her, she didn't even have to try. With her mother it was tiring, keeping track.

I hope we can still talk the way we used to.

She hated the way people said they were sorry about things like it wasn't their fault, like someone else was doing them. Like Mark apologizing when he was getting what he wanted.

It was sunny and she'd barely slept, and the walk seemed farther than usual. Her stomach hurt. There was nothing in it, but she was sure she'd throw up if she tried to eat anything. The hot asphalt smell of the road reminded her of last month, riding her bike past the mailbox, the slow days she waited to hear from him, and she felt stupid and pathetic, let down again.

The hardest thing was not being able to talk to him, to scream at him all the things she'd thought of last night, to ask him why. At least with Colin she'd told him face-to-face. "I think we should break up," she said, not "I want to break up." It wasn't a request. She had reasons if he needed them, as if he might agree with her, think it was a good idea. She didn't say she was sorry. Once the words were out and she could see his face change, she thought he would hit her, but suddenly he was helpless, blinking and red-cheeked, stunned, saying he didn't understand, asking her to explain, and she knew it would be easy. She wanted it to be over and for him to go away, but otherwise she felt nothing, not even relief, just a dull impatience like a headache.

That was how Mark felt about her now, and she was just as confused as Colin had been. "What did I do wrong?" Colin had asked, and she'd tried to be nice, saying, "Nothing." Now she saw how useless that answer was, how cruel. It said, There's nothing you can do, so don't try. You don't exist. It was the same feeling she had after her father dropped her and Justin off, when he said he'd have to ask their mother if a certain day was okay—the feeling of not being wanted the way you wanted someone else. She knew it too well.

And still, she wanted to call the camp office long-distance and talk to him. She'd started a dozen letters in her head full of biting lines, selecting exactly what she could say to hurt him—that he was clumsy and dumb, a child—and then pulled back, thinking they weren't true, not completely.

The terrible thing was, she didn't even like him that much. She'd known it from the start. She never expected him to write. All July she'd been fooling herself. It was the time of year more than anything. She'd felt the same loneliness last summer at Grammy's, spent the cool, buggy evenings wishing she were home, and then when they were back in Silver Hills she couldn't stand her room, the stuffed animals and yellow walls reminding her of how long she'd been in that house, how long she still had to go.

The thought of school starting soon only made things worse. She'd wasted the whole summer. She was supposed to be excited—"Think of all the new people you'll meet," her mother gushed—but secretly she was afraid. She didn't think it would be that different from middle school, the same gray routine of the bus and the cafeteria and band practice while the weather turned, the days growing shorter, made up of phone calls and homework, but the place was huge and Liz's parents were sending her to Dearborn Academy. For the first time since kindergarten they would be split up. When she asked her mother how much it cost to go to Dearborn, her mother laughed and said, "Too much," as if she couldn't be serious. Her father said the only reason they moved to Silver Hills was for the school district. "For you kids," he said, as if it was a sacrifice and she was supposed to be grateful.

Rufus pulled her toward the shortcut, passing the empty A-frame. The grass hadn't been cut, and the ditch by the road was high with black-eyed Susans. Ahead of them, insects circled out of the woods, specks caught in the light, then swung back into the shadows. Rufus padded along, panting, a drop hanging from the tip of his tongue. She'd have to make sure he had water in his dish when they got back.

She heard the truck before she saw it, jolting and squeaking over the road to the marina. Her first reaction was to hide, to duck into the cool woods, tugging Rufus with her, but it was coming too fast and on principle she didn't want to give in. Fuck them. She saw the black shape of it flashing through the leaves and thought it was a van or a big pickup towing a boat. It was only when it crossed the intersection ahead that she saw it was a small dump truck hauling a trailer with lawn mowers on it. In the bed, leaning on the back of the cab, were two guys in baseball caps and T-shirts, and without seeing their faces, she knew one of them was him.

They hadn't seen her, and for an instant she stopped, trying to decide whether to turn around and hurry and cut them off or pretend she hadn't seen them. Rufus looked up at her and then back down.

"You're a big help," she said.

She thought of how desperate she'd been with Mark, and walked on, slowly, checking over her shoulder, and when the truck crossed Manor behind her, she kept going. She wasn't going to run after it waving her arms. She didn't even know his name. She didn't even know if it was him.

If he was cutting their lawn, she didn't want to miss it. There were only two days left—one, really, since today had already started.

She kicked a white stone from the A-frame's driveway and watched it skitter and hop along the asphalt, adjusted her course and caught up to it and kicked it again, and then again until it slid off into the weeds, and by that time she was almost to the road, her mind filling with possibilities.

The sun made her squint, the flat ponds shadowless. The crooked lines of tar used to fix the road were soft and smelled strong, intoxicating as magic markers. There were no cars coming, so she walked Rufus down the middle, past the hatchery. The same official pickup stood by the door of the building, the same hum of a pump coming from inside. Once they left the road and climbed the dirt path up the side of the dike, she took Rufus off his leash.

The closest row of ponds was dry, so she headed for the center where she knew they were stocked, and found one, the dark water busy with slowly opening circles as if it were raining—the fish feeding, kissing the surface. She chose a patch of grass to sit on, facing the road. Rufus hunched beside her, bored, his head on his paws. Up here anyone could see her, but she didn't care. Through the liquid shimmer wriggling above the fields, she could see the cars on the highway slow before they turned in and the marina road far down past the hatchery. The chances that he would come back so fast were slim, but she kept checking, pretending to be interested in the even row of pines across the road, sharp in the harsh light, the tips of which were reflected, softer, in the pond. From the murky bottom, a string of pearly bubbles ballooned to the surface—a sign of life— then stopped, all done.

Her mother would ask what Mark had said in the letter, maybe seriously, in private, or as a joke in front of everyone, and she would have to say something. She'd hidden it in her flute case, under the blue velveteen, and the idea of it there now made her want to take it into the bathroom again and reread it, tear it to bits and flush them down the toilet. She wouldn't. She'd take it home and save it in the shoe box in the bottom of her closet with the other ones, a rubber band around them—the ones she wanted to reread now, to torture and reassure herself that it had been love.

She sat, the heat like a weight on her head, the monotonous cycling of the pumps drifting to her, small and faraway, over the empty ponds. She'd barely slept, would probably not sleep tonight either. She needed to eat something. The grass was itchy, and she scratched at her shins, made a painful cross on a mosquito bite with her fingernail. A cloud of gnats buzzed Rufus, and he rubbed his face with his paws. Two fish came over, knives in the brown water, paying them no attention, then vanished with a flick, impossible to follow, lost in the mirror of the sky. The wind lisped in her ears and the water shivered like skin.

It was beautiful, she knew, but it didn't change a thing between her and Mark. It didn't change anything, who she was or how she felt. It all took place outside of her, disconnected, like the rest of the world. Her life would be the same when they went home and school started and she only saw Liz on weekends, her father whenever he felt like showing up. It would be just her and Justin and her mother, with nothing to look forward to.

Two days. She wasn't being realistic. And yet she kept hoping to see the truck, would stand if it did come rattling up the road, would turn to face it as it passed, obvious, offering herself. He would see her, that was all she wanted, no wave, no words, just the two of them seeing each other, knowing.

The sun rose higher. A man in a ranger uniform came out with what looked like a crowbar, turned a wheel in another pond and went back in, totally ignoring her. A fish flopped out of the water. Her hair burned, and the shimmer made the highway break up, the cars blobs of color that shot spears of light. With his shaggy black coat, Rufus was too hot, panting in the grass. They ought to get back. Out of habit she went to check her watch, but it was gone, lost, her belt loop empty. She knew she would use it as an excuse. And in the end it was true: it was impossible to tell how long she waited.

4

They had to pull up the wickets to let them cut the grass, so Justin and Sam went around the side of the house and practiced whacking the balls as hard as they could, knocking them off trees and through bushes, gouging up clumps of mud. They played hockey, clacking their mallets together, then quit when the ball hit Justin on the ankle. They spun each other on the swing, stumbled off like drunks. They had a buckeye fight until Sam hit Aunt Arlene's car. She was out on the dock and didn't hear it with the mowers going. It didn't make a dent, but they stopped anyway. The guys finished and drove off, and Sam and Justin put the wickets and stakes up again, trying to find the same holes.

In the shade the cut grass was wet and stuck to their sneakers. It was a lot easier to hit the ball. Their shots went straight instead of bouncing, and when you knocked the other guy's ball, it went a long way. Justin was winning, and then Sam missed a wicket on purpose so he could hit him.

"Yes!" Sam taunted him, dancing like an idiot. "Who's the man?"

Justin stood off to the side while Sam settled his orange ball next to his red one. Sam's idea was to knock him forward, toward the porch, so he would have to come all the way back to go through the middle wicket. Sam clamped his own ball underneath his sneaker, keeping his balance, lifted the mallet, then chopped down hard. He caught part of his foot, but got enough of the ball to send Justin's shooting over the low grass, headed straight for the porch. It didn't stop when it got close, it rolled right under, disappearing into the black gap, a hole in one.

Sam laughed, doing his stupid Nelson—"Ha ha!"

"Shut up. You have to get it."

"It's not my ball."

"You hit it."

"If I get it, you have to forfeit."

They both got down on their hands and knees and looked. Sam brushed away the cobwebs with his handle, and as their eyes grew used to the dark, they could see the cool mounds of dirt in back that could be hiding anything—rats or giant spiders or worse.

"There it is," Sam said.

The ball was too far in to reach with a mallet. Maybe Sarah or Ella could get it later.

"Let's play wiffle ball," Sam said, and jumped up, and Justin followed him. Losing the ball bothered him—it was his, and he thought they should tell someone—but Sam was already whipping the bat around like a light-saber.

They couldn't find the wiffle ball anywhere. They looked on the porch and in the garage, Sam even ran around back. It wasn't under the porch. Rufus sometimes chewed them up, or the wind blew them into the lake and they floated away. Maybe the mowers ran it over.

Sam picked up a buckeye and tried to hit it and missed. He tossed another one up and connected with a plastic smack, the buckeye whistling off across the yard.

"Whoa!" Justin said.

The two of them collected enough buckeyes to fill their pockets and made sure home plate faced the lake so they wouldn't hit the cars. Justin pitched first. He wasn't very good, but the buckeyes were so small it was hard to make contact, and Sam struck out twice before he even foul-tipped one. The next three pitches bounced in the grass at his feet.

"Throw strikes," Sam ordered him.

Justin did his best, lobbing the biggest buckeye he had over the heart of the plate. Sam swung hard and lined it cleanly, the buckeye coming straight at his face. Justin put his hands up, sure he was going to catch it, but somehow his hands moved or closed too soon—as if it had changed direction or slowed in midair, a trick—and he could see it had sneaked through, was still coming. He had just a split second before it hit him to remember the feeling he had leaving the croquet ball under the porch, and thought: I should have gotten it.

5

"Get right," his mother cried, waving an arm at the ball, which continued to hook for the woods, disappearing into the trees with a leafy ripping.

They both listened for the knock that would mean it had struck a limb or a trunk and might kick out, but there was nothing, just the shadows on the grass.

"Oh crap."

"It's not that far in," he said, and teed his ball high.

He hadn't played in two years, and then just the one time with the two of them, his father's last round with him, though none of them suspected at the time. While both of his parents were ardent golfers, and encouraging, his swing was the product of thirty years of softball, his short game strictly from the Putt-Putt. Sometime today he would let loose a long sky-climbing bomb of a drive or sink a thirty-footer, and his mother would say, "Imagine how good you'd be if you played regularly," but he knew he possessed no hidden skills, that the few moments he rose above his own mediocrity were flukes, gifts to be appreciated, not relied on.

He skulled his tee shot—thinking too much—and it bounded over the cart path, a weak grounder just clearing the light rough and stopping on the nap of the fairway.

"You'll have a nice lie," his mother said.

She took the passenger seat while he stabbed the shaft of his wood into his father's bag. He drove the cart no matter where their shots were, just as his father had, the scorecard clipped to the middle of the steering wheel, the Holga stuck in a cup holder. They were playing the fifth, a small par-four, 360 yards with a dogleg left, and so far she hadn't gotten into his job. He wasn't foolish enough to believe she'd let an opportunity like this slide. His strategy was to answer her questions head-on and then turn the conversation to her plans, hoping she'd respond to his honesty with her own. The only hard part, he thought, would be defending Meg, stating her case with both tact (a strength) and force (his great weakness). He was prepared to lose any argument they might have, bow out, satisfied that he'd done his best, introduced the issue, leaving the real work to Meg, whose idea it was in the first place. They'd played the same game when they were kids, nothing had changed. He was still trying to make peace between them, and he wondered how much of his personality—how much of his life—had been decided by his position in the family and the role he chose, however unwillingly. He thought it was unfair, being the youngest, but here he was doing it again, the faithful messenger risking his head.

"There's you," his mother pointed, and he swung the cart alongside his ball. The lie was slightly uphill. He took a three-wood, one of the few clubs he could hit with any consistency.

He paused before he addressed the ball and gazed down the fairway, gauging the trees for a sense of the wind. His father had taught him to concentrate on every shot, not let emotion control him. "They're all worth the same," he loved to say, and "You need to think before you hit." As a child, Ken had felt helpless before his advice, certain it didn't apply to his loopy, inside-out swing. He could think all he wanted and the ball would still rocket out of bounds or duck-hook into the scrub. He would chase after it with his bag, angry, slashing the underbrush, then dumping his clubs with a clank when he found it, gritting his teeth to slow himself so he could think again, inevitably developing a headache he would blame on the sun. His father was infuriatingly calm and self-deprecating of his own play, wry and lighthearted, as if they were having a good time. "I liked your decision to lay up there," he'd say, or "That was the smart shot."

The smart shot here wasn't a three-wood. It was too much club. If he hit it thin, he'd overshoot the dogleg and end up in the woods, the rough if he fluffed it. He'd wanted to use some muscle to make up for his drive, a tactic his father would shake his head at—teenage caveman stuff. The smart thing to do was to take maybe a five-iron and leave the ball right so he'd have an approach shot, except he was shaky with his five-iron, horrible with his four.

He walked back to the cart and pulled out a five-iron, scratching at the ridged club face with a thumbnail, as if for luck.

"I *see,*" his mother said theatrically.

"Well," he said, "we shall see."

His precise but unconscious imitation of his father shocked him, made him suspect his spirit was near. It made sense, here where they'd been together. His father's money club was his five, the one in his hand. If he was channeling him, Ken thought, now was a good time.

He took a practice swing, scuffing the grass, then settled his feet a half-step closer, checked the fairway where he wanted it to go, getting his shoulders in line (front shoulder closed, head down, follow through—all the moves his father taught him in the backyard, posing him in slow motion, one hand on the club), then lifted into his backswing and let it fly.

He barely felt the ball at all, and—a small triumph—he'd kept his head down, didn't jerk up to watch the shot.

He heard a familiar click from the cart. His mother had the Holga pointed toward him but had turned to see where he'd gone.

"Looks good," she said.

Now he could pick it out, still rising, a black dot in a white sky, dead right but clear of the trees, one of those shots that could fool him into thinking he might be able to play this game. The ball touched down, got a true hop and a long roll, stopping well past the turn, in the middle of the fairway.

"Very nice," his mother said.

"Hey," he shrugged, "it's Dad's five."

"It's your father's driver too, and I haven't seen you hit that all day."

On the way to her tee shot, she apologized for taking a picture of him. "I couldn't resist."

He said he knew the feeling. "Probably be the best shot on the roll."

"No," she said coyly, pleased they were teasing each other.

He had no problem getting along with her. It was when Lise or Meg entered the picture that they ran into trouble. It wasn't just jealousy but a female love of control, at once social and familial, the complicated opposite of the macho dream of independence, dominance through intimacy. It was politics on a dangerously heartfelt level, where the smallest disagreement could be taken as a betrayal, and out of sheer self-interest he'd developed the slippery skills of a pawn. Even alone with her, joking, he was aware of a subtle positioning, as if he were attending a queen.

"How's your work going, by the way?"

"Good," he said, a reflex, and slowed the cart. "I think it's somewhere in here."

"I thought it was a little farther."

"I'm sure you did. It's definitely in bounds though."

Passing into the shadows beneath the trees was like entering a dark house. The ground was bare back to the white stakes except for the trees' tortuous roots and some swaths of moss, a few skunk cabbage and sunstruck ferns. This reprieve was only temporary, he knew. After she hit, they'd get in the cart and she'd circle back to the topic, her criticism taking the form of puzzlement, his job incomprehensible—what it was and why he would choose to do it—as if paying the bills and saving money on supplies wasn't justification enough. Building his skills, as Morgan would say. He wasn't being realistic, she'd imply, painting him as naive, a dreamer. He had nothing tangible he could point to, not even the promise of success. His friends from high school were doctors and lawyers—an alarming number of them, as if the country were locked in the grip of illness and litigation—and their neighbors' oldest daughter, whom he remembered as a shrieking baby, was a full-fledged editor in New York.

A ball was hiding under the skunk cabbage like an Easter egg, right about where he'd figured. The simple juxtaposition was a surprise, elemental (for an instant he envisoned Tracy Ann Caler's naked foot, the trees strung with crime-scene tape). He wished there was enough light for the Holga, but there wasn't.

"Titleist 2?"

"Thank you," she said.

He stood back, watching all the time, afraid of a ricochet off a tree. She'd brought a seven-iron with her, and without hesitation she choked down on the grip and punched it under the branches and out into the fairway, nearly even with him.

"Nicely done."

"I got lucky with my lie. If it gets in those roots I have to take a drop. So tell me about this job, it's at a photo lab?"

He had to remind himself to be honest, to stand his ground. She had a way of making him a child again, the boy who needed to please her.

"It's steady," he said, "and it's in Davis Square, right by us." He said it casually, concentrated on the path as if it were a racetrack, stone-walling.

"So you're not teaching?"

"I might pick up a course in the fall if there's overflow."

"What about Merck?"

"That was just a onetime thing."

Her mouth was set, and he could see she was thinking, disappointed that she was learning this after the fact. They were almost to their balls, and she let him dangle. Over the years he'd gotten better at anticipating her objections, cataloging her tactics—not that it did him any good. It only meant he could see what was coming from farther away, giving him longer to worry. He consoled himself, thinking someone with less of a conscience would have sidestepped her long ago. Lise was right, he was the good son, the lifelong martyr.

He parked the cart halfway between them.

"I think you're away," he offered, and while she set herself he tried to remember why this was supposed to make breaking Meg's idea easier. His mother would resent having to justify herself just as much as he did. She'd do it though, painful as it was, because, like him, she thought he deserved an answer. On the phone they might evade each other, relying on silence and omission, but not here. They wouldn't change each other's minds, though it had happened in the past. It was enough that they let their desires be known.

His mother lobbed a decent-looking iron at the green. "Get up!" she said, stepping back, but it didn't, stopping on the ramp of apron between the two sand traps.

"What was that?"

"A six. I didn't hit it."

"It's safe," he said. And to prove it, dropped his seven, plop, in the right-hand trap.

"Is it salaried at least?" she said in the cart.

"Hourly."

"Good benefits?"

"No."

It's actually a pretty crappy job, he wanted to say. To be completely honest, I hate it.

"I take it Lisa's working then."

"Her job's got the benefits."

"Who looks after the children?"

"We both do," he said, though what she meant was: Who looks after them after school, when you're both at work? He preempted her, explaining that Ella had taken the baby-sitting course offered by the Red Cross.

He blasted a sand wedge on. She chipped close but ended up two-putting.

"*Hit* the ball, Emily," she said. "I know Ella's responsible, but Sam's what, ten?"

"He'll be eleven next month."

In the cart they sparred over his old choices, the neighborhood they couldn't afford, the lost jobs and useless degrees, and he was relieved to stop at the tee. She hopped out after him as if he were running away.

"And why am I just finding all this out now?"

The sixth was a par-three, a straight shot across a pond, and the foursome in front of them was still finishing up, making them wait. She had him. The conversation had gone as he expected, reached its inevitable destination, and yet he dreaded admitting he'd lied, though they both knew his reasons. While he accepted his penance, it seemed a double punishment, unnecessary.

He selected a club and rolled his eyes—his entire head, as if it tired him—appealing to their familiarity and the shallowness of chat, trying to make it into a joke.

"I didn't tell you because I didn't want you to worry."

"You knew you'd have to eventually. Maybe you thought you were buying time."

"Maybe."

"What am I supposed to say?" she said. "That I'm happy you're working at all?"

"No."

"I wish I could say I'm surprised."

She made her voice tired and dispirited, when minutes before they'd been trading punch lines, and Ken readied himself. Her concerns were the same he'd been hearing since he'd gotten married. He needed to be a responsible adult. He needed to think about the children. Even she was tired of hearing it, and she asked if he thought she ought to bother anymore. He let it pass, keeping it rhetorical. None of this was new, and none of it touched him, only the pointless repetition, the circle they turned in.

Across the pond, they were putting the pin back in, scattering to their carts.

It was still her honor, and she teed up by the right marker. He stood back, glad to relax for a minute, and when she turned to him after her practice swing, he needed to regroup.

"Now honestly," she said, "I want to know. Do you really think your photography is going to get you anywhere?"

It was such a large question, asked so casually—almost objectively, as if she had no opinion—that he balked at answering.

"Maybe I should put it another way. Does Lisa think it's going anywhere?"

She turned to the ball again as if she didn't expect an answer, her mind taken up by the game. She was being cruel, he thought. Because she knew.

6

Arlene had only handed Justin over to Margaret and was about to resume her picture taking when Ella collapsed in the viewfinder with a cry, flinging her mallet aside as if shot. At first Arlene thought it was an act staged for her benefit, but when she lowered her camera, Ella was sitting in the grass, bent over the upturned sole of her foot, rocking and distraught.

"Did a bee get you?"

"Yes." Ella gulped for breath, trying not to sob—probably afraid of looking like a baby with Sam there. "Stupid bee!" she said hatefully, outraged.

Arlene had seen the same clenched-teeth heroics from hundreds of boys and girls injured at recess, and knew to treat it seriously.

"All right, let's find the stinger. You're not allergic, are you?"

"I don't think so." She'd never been stung before, she said, defeated, as if this had ruined her perfect record.

The black nib was sticking from her skin like a whisker, easy to get at. While Sam told them how he'd been stung last summer, Arlene squeezed it between her thumbs and the barb slid out cleanly, a miniature thorn, along with a drop of clear fluid that might have been venom. "There we are. Let's get some ice on that." She helped Ella up and walked her to the porch, propping her on one side, depositing her on the chaise.

"Can I have a popsicle?" Ella asked, forlorn but recovered.

"Of course."

"Can I have one too?" Sam asked. He'd followed them in, drawn by the excitement, and still had his mallet.

Margaret came down to refill Justin's ice pack and saw them. "It's like a war zone around here," she said, and went back to tend her patient.

In a minute, Lisa appeared in a T-shirt and sweatpants to check on Ella. "I hear we had a major catastrophe."

She squatted to examine Ella's foot, then thanked Arlene for taking care of her, grabbed something from the kitchen and disappeared upstairs. Arlene couldn't imagine how warm it was up there under the eaves. She was already roasting from being in the sun.

It must have been the effect of Ella being stung, because when she looked out on the yard, it was a city of bees whizzing an inch above the grass, crawling over the clover blossoms, filling their sacs with pollen.

She stayed with Ella, leafing through Tuesday's *Post-Journal* as the children nursed their popsicles in bowls. An accident on the Southern Tier had killed a woman. There were forest fires in Idaho and a heat wave lay over the Plains. Here, in the shade of the porch, the song of a motorboat coming across the water, the news seemed more than two days removed, the world distant, and yet—she couldn't explain—more real, as if she herself was not part of any ongoing life while she was here, was even more powerless to prevent these tragedies. The paper could have been from ten years ago, or next year, and with the pleasure of settling into a hot bath she recognized the timelessness she wanted from Chautauqua. She felt her head clear, her sinuses open, and gave in to an invigorating shiver of satisfaction.

"Aunt Arlene!" Ella cried, pointing at her. "You're bleeding!"

She looked down in time to see a fat drop splash on the page she was reading, and brought a hand to her face. Her nose was gushing.

She tipped her head back and tasted it thick in the back of her throat.

"Just a nosebleed," she said, not wanting to frighten them (Walter's father had died of a cerebral hemorrhage, one minute complaining of a headache, the next exploding into his oatmeal). "I'm fine. One of you bring me a tissue, please."

Sam ran inside with his popsicle.

"Must be all the excitement," she told Ella, and had to swallow, the taste unpleasantly rich.

Sam brought back a box and Margaret, who took over, adding a constant, reassuring patter, cooing to her as if she might be afraid.

"I guess they're right," Arlene said. "These things come in threes."

The tissues soaked up the color—always shocking, so vivid. Margaret brought out the wastebasket from the downstairs bath. Arlene could feel her upper lip crusting over, growing itchy, and wanted to wash her face. She wished the children would leave. She didn't want them to see her like this, powerless (she would never let her students, for several reasons), but knew they needed to to make sure she was okay. She thought she was done at one point and lowered her head, only to provoke another flood. She finished the box of tissues and Margaret ripped open a second.

"Maybe if you lie down for a while," Margaret suggested, and for everyone's sake Arlene went inside and let herself be put to bed, setting her sunglasses on the night table, laying a towel under her neck.

"I'll look in on you," Margaret promised, and shut the door.

Arlene felt unfairly banished, as if she'd done it for the attention, her plans sabotaged. For years she'd heard her older colleagues joke about going through their second childhoods, and here she was, a girl confined to her room. She remembered how terrible it was to be sick in the summer when she was little, knowing Henry and their friends were playing Belgian fort and kick the can in the alley while she was stuck in bed. For hours she lay imprisoned, unattended, with the blinds drawn and luffing in the weak breeze, watching the light color the ceiling, thinking miserably, as she did now: But it's such a nice day.

7

"You can stay up here if you like," Meg told Justin. "I've got to go keep an eye on everyone else."

"I'll do that," Lise said from the other bed, but without force, a courtesy.

"You've got your book. I should get going anyway, it's almost eleven."

"Thanks. I'll make lunch."

As Meg suspected, Justin elected to come with her rather than stay with Lise. The knot on his forehead was red from the ice. He'd covered the bump at first, afraid of anyone else touching it, but now that Ella's foot was getting attention, he proudly displayed it for Sam, who was so impressed with his own strength that he launched into a drawn-out re-creation of the fatal blow.

"Sarah's still not back?" Meg asked.

Only Ella said no, timidly, the boys abstaining, reading something potentially threatening in her tone.

"How long's she been gone?"

"I don't know," Ella said. "I slept in."

"Justin?"

"I don't know," he echoed. "An hour maybe?"

The only person who could tell her was Arlene. An hour and a half at the least, she said, maybe two. Did Meg want her to watch the kids so she could go check?

Neither of them had to mention the girl who'd disappeared. Meg didn't like the way it hung between them, unspoken and melodramatic, absurd in its implications. If she thought like that, she'd never let Sarah out of the house.

"I'm sure she's fine," Meg said, but now she was doubtful. When Arlene declared herself cured and returned to the porch, Meg had to fight off the urge to walk over to the ponds, in part because it would be obvious to Sarah that she was checking up on her—treating her like a little kid, she'd say indignantly. And Meg remembered days like this when she was thirteen, fourteen, when she needed to be alone and the ponds were her only refuge. It might be Mark or her father, or it could be nothing, a baseless anger or the giddy freedom of just sitting in the sun. Meg had given up trying to figure out Sarah's mood swings but kept a close eye on her, worried—what a hypocrite—that she might be getting stoned. Once a month she casually searched her drawers, the wall of shoe boxes in her closet. Her greatest fear for Sarah was that she would turn out to be like her, just as her own greatest fear was of becoming her own mother. In their skirmishes, she could hear echoes of battles fought long ago. Back then her mother had laughed and promised that one day Meg would have a daughter of her own, as if putting a curse on her. At her worst times she thought it had come true, that they'd changed places, and it was with a kind of sick pride that she reminded herself that her failures were her own and far beyond her mother's.

Justin said he was okay but wanted to keep the ice pack. She examined him a last time, professionally solemn. The swelling was down. She could still please him by fussing over him.

She poured herself a bowl of the Cap'n Crunch her mother had bought for her, and noticed someone else had been into it. She thought of orange juice in one of her father's glasses—the Olds, maybe, his favorite—but Arlene had made coffee, and she left her Sue Grafton on the porch and took her breakfast out on the dock, indulging in the mix of sweetness and caffeine, the last socially acceptable buzzes, and ones she needed.

Since rehab she'd been tired for days at a time, a side effect, as if her body was exhausted by the change, sobriety a whole new time zone. It was easier here, given the rare luxury of sleeping late, but at home she was jittery early in the morning, her brain foggy. She felt dislocated, though she'd gone nowhere. She forgot to write notes so the kids could get out of school for doctor's appointments and ended up calling the office. The secretaries there must have thought she was a space case.

The sun cut through her. She hadn't had a chance to take a shower, and yesterday clung to her skin like grease. Now it melted. She was sure she smelled. The hell with it. She spooned up the Cap'n Crunch and followed a school of sailboats tilting by the bell tower, darting one way and then the other as they tacked through the racecourse. She wondered how Ken was doing with their mother, and the whole scene suddenly felt precarious, as if it could be taken away. She could argue for the children, the idea of a shared legacy, continuity, but ultimately she would have to appeal to her mother's love for the place. Not for her or for Ken or even their father, but for her idealized view of what their family had been here, her perfect world that had never existed and that Meg had never fit into and railed bitterly against, trying to open their eyes—the same thing she realized she was now defending. She felt she was admitting she'd been wrong all these years, asking—as in rehab—for another chance. She'd been bored here as a child, ungrateful as a teenager. In her twenties, Ken and her mother hounded her about coming east, and she used money or whatever new job she had as an excuse, glad to miss the week of phony togetherness. It was Jeff who engineered the reconciliation, her mother doing it for the sake of the grandchildren, supposedly, though Meg knew she counted it as a victory.

She was almost to the bottom of the bowl, only a few soggy barrels floating in the sweet slick. Maybe it was her lack of options, she thought. It wasn't the cottage that was precarious, it was her life. Somehow, maybe in getting straight, she'd lost the hard-boiled ability to shrug the big things off. That was progress. She didn't care if it made her feel desperate. She *was* desperate, and at least now she could tell what she was feeling.

She set the dish on the dock, the spoon jangling, had a sip of coffee and lit a cigarette. She'd dreaded this week, and now that it was about to end, the thought of driving back to Detroit, back to that mess of a life, depressed her. Jeff said he'd call today. The thought made her even more annoyed at Sarah, and when she'd finished her cigarette and carefully stubbed it out, she rocked herself up off the bench and headed for the cottage.

Ella was teaching the boys card tricks on the porch, Arlene sitting there content, not even reading. Justin had finally tired of the ice pack, his bump a small purple knob. Indoors it was ten degrees cooler, and gloomy, the sun highlighting a strip of rug. Meg rinsed her dishes and fit them in the machine, thinking that any second she'd hear the jangle of Rufus's tags or the creak of the screen door. She'd gotten some sun on the dock, and took an old Pirates cap from the pile.

"I'm going to walk over to the ponds," she said. "Why don't you guys ride your bikes? It's too nice a day to stay inside."

"When are we going to go tubing?" Sam demanded.

But Ella took the hint, rallying the boys. Meg rolled open the garage door for them.

"How's the foot?" she asked.

"It's okay," Ella said, almost pleased that she'd asked, and again Meg thought how much easier she was than Sarah. She was quiet and pleasant, and Meg could see why she was her mother's favorite of the grandchildren. Her mother flattered herself that the two of them were sisters under the skin, both tall and bony, when in reality Ella had received the qualities she admired from Ken, just as Ken had gotten them from her father. Her mother was more like Sarah, more like herself, guarded and intolerant, emotionally explosive, but she would never admit it, just as Meg tried to deny being jealous of Ella, despite liking her. She was, and she was baffled by her, in the same way Justin stumped her. Ella was good. Having been bad, Meg understood Sam better, his antics predictable, that free-floating creepiness his only wild card. She had no clue what Ella was thinking or how she felt, what she loved, just the bad girl's suspicion that it would be correct and dull.

They all set off, the boys weaving in front of her, Ella behind them, precise and upright, coasting through the shadows. Motorboats roared, skimming the gaps between the houses. Everyone would be out on the lake today, and the drive was quiet. The Lerners' birdbath was full of mucky water, last fall's leaves decomposing. The Wisemans were gone. The Diamonds had sold their place ten, fifteen years ago, and the new people had added dormers.

She was just distracting herself. She expected to see Sarah and Rufus slumping up the drive toward them any minute—and the flip side, straight out of *A Is for Alibi,* a clutch of police cars and ambulances clogging the marina road, a circle of men on the bank of one of the ponds. It was not far-fetched when she thought of her lost years, all the fearless, stupid things she did, the places she let men take her and the shape she'd been in. She could have been killed and disposed of so easily, no corpse for her mother to mourn, and at times, in her stoned bravado, she would have said that was fine with her.

Justin cut a turn too sharp and almost fell, and she had to stop herself from yelling at him. "Let's be careful!"

They took the shortcut. The A-frame that had been new and daring when she was a girl now seemed quaint and outdated, misplaced. It needed a ski slope and snow. Sam and Justin stood up on their pedals and raced ahead, Ella following, calling, telling them to wait for her at the corner. She looked back, and Meg waved for her to go ahead. Her fears were just that—hers. Sarah could take care of herself.

Ella led them around the corner, then reappeared a minute later, swinging wide, shrugging and holding up both hands. Sarah wasn't there.

Meg tried not to act surprised.

"Maybe she's at the tennis courts," Ella guessed.

"Lead on."

The road past the ponds was long and shadowless, wavy with heat, and Meg wished she had a bike. Cars shot by on the highway. If someone kidnaped Sarah, they'd leave Rufus. He'd be wandering around, dragging his leash. Sarah was smart enough not to get in a car, Meg thought, and then for a second she wondered if she'd planned it, run away with someone.

No, that was unfair—she was judging Sarah by her own life. At sixteen she'd taken off with her first serious boyfriend, James, saving up baby-sitting money, carefully packing a bag. His Mustang overheated on the turnpike and when the police shipped her home, her parents sent her to a Catholic boarding school in Ohio, where she received an education in being sneaky. She drank 3.2 beer and made straight Cs and her parents didn't seem to care. They'd given up on her, and maybe that lack of ambition or pride on their part was why she felt so incapable, why for so many years she treated herself as worthless. If she expected too much from Sarah, she had her reasons. Better too much than too little.

Before she reached the path, Ella came spinning out of the woods. Not there either. Ella rode beside her, waiting for instructions. Her eyes were fishlike, magnified by her glasses, and she seemed alarmed. Meg wanted to calm her, worried that she might upset Justin.

"Try at home," she said. "We're probably just going in circles."

Under the trees the path was humid and buggy, puddles in the deep ruts, a faded beer can in a rotted stump—maybe her own, from a lifetime ago. She picked it out, an act of penance to guarantee Sarah would be there. As she tramped by the empty courts, can in hand, she was confident. Sarah was smarter than she was at that age, more mature. And logically, she convinced herself, there was no other answer.

8

Downstairs, the door to the screenporch clapped shut, knocking Lise out of Hagrid's darkened hut and into the sticky sheets, her feet sweaty. A blade of sun lay across the cedar chest, chopping off the tail of her watchband. Harry's dragon was finally hatching, and she needed to get up and make lunch for everyone.

It took her two tries to sit up. The bottom sheet had pulled off again and she fixed it. Her back hurt from the slab of a mattress. She couldn't wait to get home to their trusty waterbed, but the thought of their bedroom brought with it all the things she needed to do—buying new school clothes for Sam and Ella, putting together Sam's birthday party. She didn't know where she'd find the time. Even when she wasn't working, she'd hated the way summer arbitrarily ended on Labor Day, suddenly cut off, the weather too nice to be inside. The kids knew it was a gyp, moping around the house until the bus showed up. A week and a half from now she'd be nagging Sam to do his homework, telling Ella she couldn't watch TV until hers was done.

She kicked Sam's balled socks out of her way and stepped over a mess of water shoes and flip-flops. She peed and turned on the shower and the fan, dug in the low wardrobe for her bathing suit and a pair of cutoffs. The zit she'd seen coming the other day was here, a red dot on her chin, a hard nodule she could press against the bone. The shower smelled. A fat black ant scurried behind the toothpaste and over the far edge of the vanity.

"This is *not* what I need," she said, but submitted.

She hadn't slept well, and with the reading she'd developed a headache, her brain a dense, heavy bread. At least there was hot water—sometimes there wasn't after the girls. Normally she'd linger in the shower, head bowed, the warm force of it on her neck a pleasure, cleansing, but even with her eyes closed she couldn't ignore the sulfur. It was almost noon and she'd gotten nothing done.

She heard them when she turned off the water, no words, just raised voices on the other side of the door, sudden and harsh, like notes sharply struck, blows dealt and parried—Meg and Sarah. She stilled herself like a hunter, an animal sensing danger, stood there naked and wet, listening. She couldn't hear clearly, and dug a pinkie in each ear.

"You don't care because you're selfish, that's why," Meg was saying. "You think the whole world revolves around you, but guess what, it doesn't."

"I don't think that," Sarah said.

"Then maybe I don't have to explain all this to you. Maybe you know all this already. Are you bored, is that why you're not saying anything?"

Lise couldn't hear Sarah's answer, just a murmur. She wondered where Sam and Ella were, as if she could protect them from this.

"I don't need this shit from you."

"I'm *sorry,*" Sarah cried. "I said I was sorry. What else can I do?"

"You can think of someone other than yourself for a change. And you can stop acting like I'm some kind of mental patient. I don't have to explain my life to you."

A dribble of leftover water fell from the showerhead. Her skin was chilled, and she noticed she was wringing her hands like an old woman.

"Did you want to say something?" Meg said. "If you want to say something, say it. Don't give me that look."

And then: "I didn't think so."

She heard one of them cross the floor and rumble down the stairs—Meg, making an exit—and then silence, though she knew Sarah was right outside the door.

She couldn't stay here forever. She pushed the glass door of the stall open with a loud click and stepped onto the bath mat. The towels were not quite dry and smelled of mildew. She did a thorough job of drying off, taking her time.

"You okay?" she'd ask if Sarah looked like she wanted to talk. She and Ella got into it sometimes, but not like this.

She tugged on her suit and her cutoffs, rolled on her deodorant. She brushed her hair carefully in the mirror, and then, hoping to give Sarah ample warning, rinsed her toothbrush and flicked it with her thumb be-fore squeezing on a blob of toothpaste, grimaced at the taste as she spat. And still she was not prepared to open the door, had to prime herself to grip the knob, ready to act natural, whatever that meant.

9

Emily was sure it was unfair of her, but she couldn't help thinking he played the same way he approached life—distracted and haphazard, conservative to a fault and then, when his execution failed him, taking risks that didn't pay off, hoping his luck would overcome his lack of skill, waiting for a break. As she watched him hit from the rough, something Henry said of him as a child returned to her: "He expects hard things to come easy." She'd defended him on principle, saying Kenneth was just a boy, but Henry hadn't said it lightly or out of frustration, and through the years she'd re-luctantly come to agree with his assessment.

As if to disprove her, he reared back and blasted his five-iron onto the green. She caught hers fat, cuffing up a muddy divot, leaving it short.

The heat was withering, even under the hard canopy of the cart. Her iced tea had become warm and thin. And the course was crowded now, after the turn. She hated when the starter sent people off on ten. Maybe they should have just played nine and called it a day.

She got out and dropped a pitching wedge on, hopped back in.

"Well done," he said. The breeze while they were driving was nice. He parked on the path behind the green and the two of them climbed the rise with just their putters, tufts of cottonwood fluff drifting down around them. Her ball had rolled to the fringe but he was still away. She steered clear of his line and knelt to fix her ball mark, patting it flat.

"I was talking with Meg last night," he said, reading the break. "She still wants to see if there's a way we can take over the place."

She couldn't stop herself from letting out a chuckle, a belch of a laugh. "It's a little late now, isn't it?"

"No, she's serious."

"You're not just saying this to get me upset?"

He had his putt lined up but backed away. "I think we'd both like to try. We don't have any money, but—"

"That would be a problem, wouldn't it?" It came out too much like a joke—she didn't mean to make fun of him. "I'm sorry, it's just that everything's set. Mrs. Klinginsmith's coming tomorrow to check the septic."

"Nothing's signed."

"The agreement's signed. I'm sure you've heard of breach of contract." She was annoyed that he would bring this up here, ruining her one sanctuary. She looked behind them for the foursome who had let them play through and saw them advancing, a cart on each side of the fairway. "You should hit."

He took it as a reproof, and rushed his putt, knocking it well wide of the hole, but said nothing. She got hers close, then missed a gimme trying to get out of his way. He babied his, and they walked off sullenly, counting up their strokes.

He filled in their card by the next tee. She admitted to a six.

He had a five. "On in two and then the three-putt. It's mine then," he said, stepping up as if nothing had happened.

He didn't mention it again, but the day had been altered, the whole purpose of the week thrown in doubt. She had asked them time and again—and not out of courtesy, but painfully, in the teeth of their disapproval—whether they wanted the responsibility of the cottage, and their answers had been identical and consistent. They didn't have the time or the money, and from what she'd gleaned this week, both of them were in even worse shape than she'd suspected. The only way they could take it over was if she paid the taxes and insurance for them, and in that case she might as well keep it in her name. That's what they were asking, wasn't it, what they'd wanted all along, for her to hold on to it.

Why this struck her now as reasonable rather than self-serving she couldn't say. Maybe it was the heat. She was tired and dehydrated and she wanted to quit and sit in the clubhouse with a gin and tonic. It was a complicated subject, and she did not want to discuss it with Kenneth and say something she'd regret later, so she noted it and filed it away, held off, all the time knowing she would have to come back to it.

Arlene was on their side too, the three of them united against her. It was too late. It was that simple. She'd already gone through this.

In the midst of her confusion, she parred the twelfth, getting up and down niftily. Kenneth totted up their scores and feigned astonishment.

"That's what happens when you practice," she said. "You get good."

"Here we are," he said. "Unlucky thirteen. I hope you brought a floater." He slipped a second ball from his zippered pocket.

It was an old family joke, a scene they replayed each year. Both Emily and Kenneth had been witnesses, and Herb Wiseman. It had to have been fifteen years now. Henry had been having a tough day, three-putting and then getting down on himself, driving away from the greens tight-lipped. On thirteen he was the last to hit. He put his tee shot in the water and his mulligan in the hole. Instead of throwing both arms in the air and dancing a jig, he turned to them, deadpan, not a change in his face, and said, "It figures." In sixty years of golf, it was the closest he'd come to a hole in one, and now they celebrated it by playing two balls.

On the far side of the pond a pair of geese cropped the grass, walking targets. She kept to the shade while Kenneth launched a six-iron wide right. The geese kept eating, oblivious.

"Have at it," she said, and he teed up his second.

Sixty years, she thought. So many holes, so many par-threes within reach. It was almost sad, and now, reconsidering Henry's reaction—which they all thought comic, repeated summer after summer on how many tiki-torched decks and nineteenth-hole patios—she wondered if he really saw his life that way, if he'd expected more. He would never complain, but as he matured he'd turned serious and reserved, went from dashing to stead-fast, absorbed in his work, the young man he'd been submerged, allowed to wink out only rarely. He withdrew into himself so quickly, one minute discussing some household necessity with her, the next lost behind the wall of his newspaper. Getting him to do anything with them was an ef-fort, though anyone who saw him with the grandchildren would think he was pleasant, even doting.

They'd been happy, despite the silences and disagreements, the little tiffs. The children had been hard on him, especially these last years, but whose weren't? Every family harbored some private heartache, some unfulfilled dream of lives that might have been.

She stood still as a white butterfly struggled past Kenneth's ball—a sign. Now would be the perfect time for him to sink one, proof that Henry was watching over them, looking down with his sly smile, finally content, at rest. She would circle it on the scorecard, frame it for Kenneth—maybe take a picture of them on the green, the numbered flag between them. She wondered if his little camera had a timer.

He settled his feet, addressed the ball, reached back and whacked it. The ball rose on line with the flag, and she stepped forward, hopeful, willing it in. Henry's had caught the apron, hopped on and rolled straight for the hole, disappearing as they cheered. Kenneth's seemed to be on the same trajectory, but faltered, dropped into the pond just short of the far shore, then bobbed up again as if it might skip over—"Get!" she said—and finally stopped, hung suspended, incredible, a white dot on the water.

"What in the world are you doing?" she said, because she'd tricked herself into believing.

"I told you, it's a floater."

"Those things don't carry."

"I didn't hit it," he said, scuffing the heel of his club.

He teed up a mulligan like Henry, but stuck it in the right-hand trap.

So it was up to her (as with everything else in this family, she thought). She took a five, more than long enough for her. Kenneth's ball lapped in the shallows, distracting. The whole concept was idiotic: who wanted to face their mistakes? Better to let them fall to the dark bottom and nest in the silt, their bright faces turning the color of mud. She'd heard of places that hired scuba divers, scooping basketfuls from the murk, but couldn't imagine it would be profitable here, with the short season. The ones she'd contributed over the years were probably still down there, Henry's too, his notorious first shot crowding its sepia brothers like a pickled egg. She didn't have to hit an impossible shot to join him, just a bad one. It would have to be honest though, no limp-wristing. She thought she could accomplish it in two tries.

A fly buzzed her ball, standing on it, then zipping off. She waved at it belatedly, reset herself. There was no wind to speak of, the tendrils of the honey locusts behind the green hanging plumb. She relaxed and shifted back as if it was any other swing, made contact and followed through like a pro, elbows high.

"Beauty," Kenneth said before she could find it, his floater hooking her attention for a second.

She was nearly dead-on, just a hair left. The ball arced and dropped, long enough. There was time for Kenneth to say, "That's going to be about pin-high," before it lighted and kicked cleanly off the front apron and ran up the green, slowing, breaking as it neared the hole, taking it farther left so there was no chance, but darn close. She'd have a five-footer for the bird.

"Best shot of the day," Kenneth said. "Very pretty."

"I'm still going to have to putt for it."

She searched for her tee halfheartedly and walked to the cart.

"You're not going to hit your mulligan?" he tried to ask casually, but she could see he was worried about tradition, and slippage.

In some ways—and didn't it drive Henry crazy—he was as sentimental as she was.

"No," she said. "I think I'll keep that."

"I don't blame you," he said, but on the way there, she thought that he did.

His floater had drifted away from the bank and into a stand of cattails, out of reach of even Henry's telescoping retriever, and they had no choice but to disown it. The geese stood their ground, watching as they passed.

Her putt wasn't a toughie, but she had time to mull it over. His wedge was too hard and skimmed all the way across the green and off the far lip. He had to come back and then get close, and she laid down the flag and told him to finish rather than mark his ball.

"Double bogey," he grumbled, standing aside, inspecting his ball as if it were defective.

The foursome behind them wasn't in sight. They might have time to get a picture after all. That might salvage the hole for both of them.

He'd shown her the break, so her only worry was the speed. As soon as she hit it, she knew it was going in. She followed the ball, took a step toward the hole as it fell and knocked around in the cup, the sound immensely pleasing, her sense of relief blossoming into pride and satisfaction.

She herself had never shot a hole in one either, but it was nothing to mourn. A two was fine. Just being alive was a gift.

"Good one," he said.

She looked for the foursome, but the tee was clear.

"Does your camera have a timer on it?"

"What, that thing?"

"Well I don't know."

"I can take a picture of you if you want."

His offer fell so short of her original vision that she scuttled the plan. "I'm not really interested in that. I wanted the two of us."

"I'll do one of you, and you do one of me. Come on. I can fit the negatives together so it looks like we're both there."

He was already fetching the camera, his enthusiasm taking over, irresistible. The foursome held off. She let him pose her to the left of the pin, holding her ball up and two fingers for the bird, waited while he framed it exactly, then followed his instructions as he stood to the right, one hand pulling the flag taut so she could see the numbers.

"Do two," he instructed as the foursome's carts puttered up to the tee.

She pushed the button but nothing happened.

"You have to forward the film," he said, pantomiming the action with a thumb.

By the time she found the little ridged wheel, she felt rushed and just wanted to leave. She took the shot and they hustled off, leaving the floater behind, a cheap memorial.

The woods were cooler but full of bugs. The path was dirt here, and the cart bumped over exposed roots so she had to anchor her iced tea with a hand. They only had five holes to go, and then maybe lunch in the clubhouse, a cold drink. She'd woken up this morning with the feeling she'd had all week, that this was the last time they'd be here, the last time they played the course. The feeling was still there, but Kenneth bringing up Margaret's desire to keep the cottage had masked or diluted it. Part of her wanted to think they would be back here next year, while the rest of her insisted she treasure every minute, store them up against the inevitable. It was unfair of Margaret, she thought, unfair of them all.

The rest of the way was a struggle, a forced march, longer than she thought possible. On the par-five fifteenth she took advantage of the ladies' tee (cheating, Henry would say), and still finished with an eight, the dreaded snowman. They were both in and out of the woods, in the creek, in the sand. The sun stopped rising and hung above them, baking the fairways. She could feel the heat on her cheeks, the sweatband of her visor wet. After her birdie on thirteen, she didn't par another hole, and Kenneth was worse—erratic off the tee and then hacking at his irons. It was disheartening. After she'd been so looking forward to it, it turned out to be a chore.

"Well," she said after eighteen, "I don't know about you, but I've had enough."

"It was fun," he said. "I missed it last year."

"I know," she said, the whole of last summer coming back to her— the view from Henry's room, the bad cafeteria food, the hot, darkened house. She fended it off, pulling at the fingers of her glove. "So did I."

They returned the cart and stashed their bags in the car. She changed her spikes right there in the lot, sitting on the back bumper. She'd had this tasseled pair at least ten years, yet they looked brand-new. She'd convinced Henry their old ones were getting ratty and drove him out to the Waterworks. His were still in the garage, cobwebbed. She'd have to remember to bring them home.

For what? The house was turning into a museum.

"Don't," she said, throwing a hand in front of her face, but too late, he'd already taken her picture.

"Do you do this to Lisa? I can't imagine she puts up with it."

"She's used to it," he said.

Rather than open that subject up, Emily let it drop.

"I'm starving," she said, "and you look like you could use a beer."

Inside, the air-conditioning raised goose bumps on her arms, her sweat drying, sealing over like a coat of paint. They had a window table with a view of the seventh green and a spacious yellow-and-white-striped tent being set up for some weekend function, a wedding reception maybe. They ordered, and when the drinks came, toasted themselves. Kenneth had brought the scorecard in. Since he was a boy caddying for them, it was his job to add up their scores, a duty he took seriously. He held the card flat beside his beer glass, as if to prove he was being honest.

"A hundred and three for you."

"And that's with a two on thirteen," she joked. Her gin and tonic was delicious, lifting her above her own grubby, sunstruck exhaustion, making the day seem full and golden, if only for a moment.

"Yeah, all that practice is really paying off."

He moved through his own back nine, tracing his progress with the stubby green pencil.

"Well?" she asked, knowing it wasn't close.

"A hundred and eleven."

"That's dreadful. With the way you hit there's no reason you shouldn't break a hundred. That's more than six strokes a hole."

She commandeered the scorecard to see where he'd gone wrong and noticed that he'd circled her birdie on thirteen, given the two an exclamation point. They'd have to save the card on the mantel with all the others (their names boiled down to H, K and E, the holes and days forgotten), another thing for her to take back, and again she worried that Arlene's car wasn't big enough, that she should have rented a truck.

"How did you get a nine on sixteen?" she asked.

"I was out of bounds twice."

"That'll do it."

The waitress brought her chicken Caesar and his club sandwich and they tucked in. The truck weighed on her, and as she was thinking of Saturday and leaving, a cloud covered the sun and the light in the room changed, in tune with her mood. The food was mediocre at best, and she'd drained her gin and tonic—mostly ice—its buzz solidifying into a numb denseness. A stock-car race whined above the bar, though no one was watching it. The long mirror doubled the last tier of bottles, and there was Henry's Cutty Sark, its dark green shoulders and periscope of a spout.

She thought of Margaret's drinking. She remembered Henry giving her sips of beer as a child, and once, in high school, Margaret being dropped on their frosted lawn in the middle of the night, reeking of vomit, a clot in her hair. Margaret had apologized to her, slurring, as Emily peeled off her jean jacket, her blouse already half unbuttoned, her bra gone, and again Emily felt that enervating, helpless mix of anger and sorrow only Margaret—her first—could elicit from her. Now Margaret wanted her to keep the cottage.

Across from her, Kenneth ate his messy club over his plate, dripping gobs of mayonnaise. He'd purposely not told her about his job, or about Lisa working. Why were her children's lives a secret from her? Why did she have to drag everything out of them?

"Did you know about Margaret?" she asked, making sure the waitress wasn't coming.

"What about her?"

"What about her. About her drinking." She couldn't be plainer than that.

He had to think about the answer, which meant yes.

"Not while it was happening," he said.

"So you knew."

"I knew she was having some problems, I didn't know exactly what. She's been going through a lot."

It was gallant of him, she thought, but misplaced, too late. "She didn't tell you she was going into rehab?"

"No," he said, and she believed him. It was just like Margaret to deliver whatever bad news she had when it was too late for anyone to help her. In her eyes this passed for independence.

"I think she's doing pretty well though," he said. "She's a lot better than she was last year."

Emily agreed, with her usual reservations, knowing everything with Margaret was temporary, fleeting, one crisis yielding to the next more pressing one, and all of them beyond her control. Emily could imagine the two of them trying to keep the cottage afloat after she was gone, the bounced checks and leaky ceilings.

She hadn't meant to let any of this ruin their last round together. She thought of ordering another drink to buoy her, but she was almost done with her Caesar and Kenneth still had half his beer. She had to search her mind for a topic that would make them both happy, leave them both untouched.

"So," she said, "Ella must be excited about high school," and he was glad to change the subject.

He insisted on paying. Out of politeness she argued with him, then gave in, promising to get it next time. He took a mint for her and they walked out into the lung-crushing heat. The closed car held the familiar smell of baking vinyl, and a rush of summers cut through her, coming back from the swim club with the children, the endless trip out west, Henry's old Chevy with its two-tone seats and stainless-steel buckles dangerous as cattle brands.

Kenneth got the air-conditioning going, the cool with its mechanical scent of hoses and antifreeze neutralizing the memory. Across the road, behind the spiked wrought-iron fence, stood the new condos the Institute had put in—identical town houses with buttercream vinyl siding and mint-green plastic shutters. The lawns were false, obviously sod, and she thought with distress that Arlene couldn't even afford splitting one of these monstrosities.

She couldn't see herself at the Lenhart, a sad remnant of the past. Better the We Wan Chu. Yet when they passed it, the low motel in front seemed uninviting, badly painted, lacking all charm—and still she watched it slide by, hopeful. She wasn't surprised. The reason never left her, a lesson from Henry. As meager as the present seemed, it was all she had.

10

Ella wanted to go upstairs so bad, but stopped herself. The thing to do was to wait for Sarah to come to her.

She stalled, sitting and working absently on the dumb puzzle while her mind flitted from hatred for Aunt Margaret—out reading on the porch with her mother—to worry for Sarah, to confusion over why she'd been left behind. It had nothing to do with her, it couldn't. This betrayal had to be a mistake. Sarah would explain it away, erase it with a few words, and they would be the way they were before, an unbeatable team.

Ella nearly believed this, or some of it, fitting together the pigeons at the feet of one beefeater, but when she was done with them the feeling of being deserted returned and the pieces stumped her, vague and shapeless, just color. She held one in her hand and searched the ragged edges for a match.

She couldn't think of anything she'd done. She'd tried so hard to be low-key, to resign herself to the fact that it was never going to happen, but once she'd succeeded (easy, because it was true, and safer for her;

impossible, because she couldn't give up), she began to dream of Sarah again, her thin arms and knobby wrists and long fingers, the whole cycle starting all over for no reason. It was like she wasn't listening to herself, and she felt even more helpless, a bystander, angry at her own hope.

She dropped the piece she was holding so the cardboard side showed, a blot on the picture. Beefeaters guarded the empty courtyard, the rows of blank windows. The sky above the palace was unfinished, the wood grain of the table a dull brown cloud.

Her mother came in from the porch, flopping in her swim top. "I'm taking lunch orders. We're having sandwiches."

She said it hard, like a final warning, because she knew Ella hated sandwiches. Ella didn't care. She could eat the turkey and leave the bread. No one would check.

"What about your cousin, do you know what she might like?"

And what a complete loser she was, because she did. Salami with provolone cheese and lettuce, just a little mayo, on wheat bread, cut diagonally. Macaroni salad, not the mushy potato stuff. She knew Sarah liked salt-and-vinegar potato chips better than sour-cream-and-onion ones, and that she liked the garlic dills and not the bread-and-butter slices Sam liked. And Diet 7UP, nothing with caffeine.

It was just like at school. She knew all the unimportant things, the things that didn't matter.

"Maybe you can take it up to her," her mother suggested. "I think she's in the doghouse."

"What did she do?" Ella asked, a challenge.

"Just what you're doing. So keep it up."

She was glad to have an official excuse to see her, and something to do—anything to kill the minutes so she wouldn't look totally desperate. She fixed a plate for each of them, taking care putting together the sandwiches, arranging the chips between the cut halves, and the macaroni salad, the pickles off to the side so the juice wouldn't get the bread soggy.

"That's very nice of you," her mother commented.

"It's just lunch," Ella said, getting forks for them.

"Can you handle both of those?"

The thought of her mother coming up with her made her say she could. She'd have to come back and get their drinks.

"Don't forget napkins," her mother said.

Her first test was the door to the stairs, elbowing it open. She set one plate on a step to close it behind her for privacy, then headed up slowly, keeping her hands level in front of her. How stupid would she look if she dropped them, macaroni salad all over the carpet. As she climbed, the air grew thicker, a hot, stale smell of dust and plaster and bat poop and the tar shingles of the roof. Sarah didn't even have the fan on, and Ella thought she must really be pissed off. Ella wouldn't smile, she'd just be quiet, let Sarah talk if she wanted to, or not. She would be a friend and take on whatever she was feeling—and she would know what that was, the way she and Caitlin did at home, their moods matching like sisters'.

She expected Sarah to be on her sleeping bag, reading or playing solitaire, but when she turned at the head of the stairs, Sarah was going through the red, white and blue dresser, piling the clean clothes on top of it, then shoving them back in the drawer, moving on to the next. Each time Ella saw her she was surprised by the fact of her body, struck by something new.

"What are you looking for?"

"My watch," Sarah said.

Ella set the plates on the low wardrobe and started helping, opening the shallow top drawer.

"I already looked in there," Sarah said, shutting her down.

Ella was hurt—stunned as suddenly as her bee sting—and at the same time it hurt her to see Sarah so upset. It was Aunt Margaret's fault, whatever happened. She looked behind the cedar chest and under the beds until Sarah said, "Forget it," and ordered her to stop.

"I'm sorry," Sarah said, meaning Ella was okay, it was everything else.

Ella followed her plan, waiting for Sarah to explain, but she just looked at the plates.

"Did my mother make this?"

"I did," Ella said, and was grateful—saved—when Sarah thanked her and picked it up. "You want a soda?"

"I'll get it."

"It's okay," Ella said, and went, not ready to let her go.

Her father had gotten home and was in the kitchen, opening a beer.

"How's it going, Ella-bella?"

"Good," she said (and he believed her, he understood nothing), and escaped again, closing the door behind her. She thought of locking it but was afraid they'd get in trouble.

Sarah was hungry. She'd gotten some sun—her hair was brighter, highlighted—and Ella noticed as she was eating her sandwich that she wasn't wearing Mark's dolphin ring, the ghost of it a neat white band of skin on that finger. Instead, she had on the plain silver ring Grandma and Aunt Arlene had given them, making them twins.

So it was the letter—not her.

Sarah pretended nothing had happened. Ella waited, thinking she'd have to explain, but she just ate her lunch. Mark had broken up with her and she was crushed. Ella wasn't sure how she felt about it. She thought it was wrong to be happy.

And then, about to take a bite, Sarah stopped and looked at her sandwich, held it up like she'd found something interesting. "You cut it the way I like it."

"Yeah," Ella said, pleased that she'd noticed, that a little thing like that could change her mood. "And I know you like those chips, so . . ."

Sarah laughed. "You are so gay!"

The shock of hearing it said out loud was plain on her face, Ella thought, her burning skin a dead giveaway. She knew Sarah only meant to thank her, but Ella couldn't control her reaction. She laughed, agreeing with her, nearly choking on an undigested bite.

"I know."

11

"Yah! Gah!" Emily cried, reeling back from the mailbox into the road, waving the hot letters and then dropping them, kicking them apart to scatter the ants. She slapped at her arms, and still she felt them crawling on her, turned her wrists over to check, and then felt foolish, standing there in the middle of the road, the butt of a joke.

She'd asked Kenneth to take care of this. Obviously he hadn't gotten the job done.

The sun beat down on her brow, an extra drain on her patience. She needed a shower or a dip in the water. Half the day was gone already, and she still had the unpleasant task of talking to Margaret.

She bent down and gingerly pinched up the letters—all second-class junk. The ants were panicked, zigzagging away. She stepped on as many as she could and made straight for the garage, leaving the lid open. This time she'd take care of it herself.

12

His father slowly walked over to the edge of the road and waved for Sam to stop. The way he moved, Sam thought Justin must have told on him for throwing the buckeye at Rufus. He jammed on the brakes and cut the handlebars, leaned hard and let the back end fishtail, stopping right beside him.

"Lunch is ready," his father said.

He got off his bike and bumped it over the grass, walking beside him.

"Hey," his father said, "have you seen Sarah's watch at all?"

"No," he said automatically.

He tried to remember where it was. Maybe in the pocket of the shorts he wore yesterday, somewhere on the floor upstairs. His mother would find it when she cleaned up.

"You know what it looks like. It snaps onto your belt loop."

Sam pushed out his lip in a shrug.

"Well if you see it, she's looking for it, okay?"

"Okay," Sam said.

"And please, wash those hands before you eat."

Sam leaned his bike against the buckeye tree and followed him inside. His mother was working at the sink, so he went into the downstairs bathroom, not bothering to turn on the light, and used the green squirt soap. He pushed back his upper lip with two fingers to look at the bloody hole in his gums. His dollar was upstairs somewhere too, and the change he'd stolen from the dresser.

His father didn't know, or else he'd be mad. He was just guessing.

13

The ants in the mailbox, the stove dying—everything was a crisis, Lise thought. So they wouldn't have coffee, big deal, it was easily ninety degrees out. Ken said it was probably just a fuse, he'd look at it when he was done eating, but Emily would not be calmed. The realtor was coming tomorrow (not to look at the stove, Lise wanted to say, but held back). And then, as lunch was winding down, Justin dropped his slice of watermelon on the floor of the porch, and Meg ordered Rufus and all of the kids outside. Lise could see she was having a bad day and told Ella and Sam to steer clear of her.

By default she did the dishes, not really caring. It was easy with the paper plates. In the side yard, the boys were chasing each other, spitting seeds. Behind her, Emily hovered around Ken as he searched the control panel of the stove for a fuse box.

"I wonder if it could have anything to do with the heat," Emily said.

"Possibly," Ken said.

Lise finished the glasses and started in on the knives and silverware, the empty mac-salad container Emily wanted saved for no reason. She was sweating, her suit a clammy second skin under her cutoffs. The lake looked blue and breezy and cool, though she knew the sun would be that much worse out on the water.

"There we go," Ken said behind her.

"Did you get it?" his mother asked.

He had. He held the fuse between his thumb and finger like a bullet, the glass tube burned a percolator brown in the middle. Lise was always amazed at how technically proficient he was. Perhaps that was his way of compensating, making himself useful, if not entirely involved in their lives.

Sometimes she wondered why she was with him, or why he was still with her when he found her so uninteresting. She joked with Carmela that she was jealous of his cameras, and while both of them knew that at heart she was deeply serious, they'd created a whole blue routine about what he did in the privacy of his darkroom. And she could see where it came from, there was no secret. Spending time with his family made her understand how he could see self-absorption not merely as its own reward but as a necessity, a place to hide. It was ironic—when she'd first met him, she liked him because he was quiet.

"I know Dad's got some in the garage," Emily said.

"I don't know if he'll have one this size," Ken said, and went to check, single-minded, the screen swishing and then subsiding on its piston. Lise wiped down the counters, Emily stepping out of her way, thanking her absently.

"No," Ken came back to report. "I'll have to try the hardware up in Mayville."

"Would you mind doing that now?" Emily asked, and Ken gave in.

"It'll take twenty minutes," he explained to Lise on his way to the car. "It takes that long for the kids to find their suits."

"It's almost two o'clock already."

As if to spite him, she organized the children, driving them upstairs and sorting out their suits and towels and water shoes, forcing the boys to try to go to the bathroom, then slathering their freckled shoulders and scrawny chests with sunblock while the girls did each other. She convinced Sam to wear a hat, and established that Meg and Emily and Arlene would be staying ashore.

"I think I need a break," Meg said.

Lise took the kids down to the dock, Rufus tagging along with his ball. She relieved him of it, set it sopping in her beach bag with a gentle "No," and after a while he stopped pointing at the bag and lay down in the only shade, under the bench. The kids didn't need any encouragement to go swimming. She had her book but watched them instead, boys against girls in a massive splash battle. Justin wasn't a strong swimmer, and she'd promised Meg she'd keep an eye on him, even though the water was only waist-deep.

The heat melted whatever resistance she had left, made the day seem ideal. The lake was buzzing with motorboats, thick with sails, the weekend starting early. After the crappy weather, everyone was out. It reminded her of the beach, the sudden crush of weekly renters determined to get their money's worth. That part of the summer was over, just as this part was almost gone, and she cast forward to next weekend, dragging Sam through the mall (he was a size 12 now, and she was sure he'd outgrown his winter coat). The middle school had sent home a whole list of supplies he needed. Ken had read it aloud, incredulous, as if they were being ripped off, though each of the past three years they'd received the exact same list for Ella. She'd take Sam to Staples after supper one night and fill up a plastic basket. The only thing Ken would see was the flyer. Ella had an orthodontist appointment in there somewhere to get her braces tightened; Lise would have to take off work for it, use a few hours of hard-earned comp time. She could see the blocks of the calendar filling with ink—September, October. It was their turn to have Emily and Arlene for Thanksgiving—earlier, true, but easier than Christmas.

She shrugged the thought off, shaking her head to clear it. The sky was cloudless, a thin blue bleached white at the horizon. The kids were doing handstands.

"No," she told Sam, "we're not throwing mud."

"Yes we are."

"Do you want to go on the boat?"

"Yes," he said brightly, as if the two weren't connected.

"Then smarten up."

They wanted her to come in with them, splashing and taunting her from the edge of the dock. She hid behind her book, looking back toward shore, expecting Ken to show up any minute. She'd left her watch on the mantel but it was well past time. She didn't think he'd taken a camera. Her worry was that he'd stop at the gas station or buy a paper, catch up on his missing girl. She promised herself not to ask. Beneath her, Rufus murmured in his sleep.

Finally the kids quit, bored with tormenting each other. They laid out their towels on the gray boards of the dock and shivered in the wind, the water drying to dots on their skin, then disappearing. She'd have to goop them up again.

Lying side by side, Ella and Sarah seemed years apart, Ella still bony and girlish, her proportions all wrong, where Sarah had filled in and rounded out, her body pronounced, the only baby fat left in her face. Lise hoped Ella wouldn't compare herself to her. Lise had been a late bloomer too, and knew that impatience—the fear that things would never develop or would stop partway, her body left unfinished (she was reconciled overall but would never be happy with her nose, her legs, her stingy upper lip) . She could see that Sarah would attract boys and then men, whether she wanted to or not, the same as her mother. Lise wished she could have given Ella better genes, or more, since her eyes—Lise's best feature—and the shape of her face were unmistakably Ken's. She'd survive, but how much easier the coming years would be if she had Sarah's looks.

Lise wished she could just give in to sensation, let the heat bleed away all her thoughts. Stopped, stilled like this, it was hard for her not to think of the future—to worry, really. At home she didn't have time to wallow, her pleasures and defeats fleeting, attenuated by her schedule. Here there was nothing to occupy her mind but their problems—common enough, and stultifying, since she saw no improvement ahead, let alone real solutions. They would talk in the car on the way back, a sort of enforced communication, but with the kids right there they couldn't discuss anything serious, and by the time they pulled in the drive they would be too tired, so wiped out she'd be lucky to get the laundry started.

Two jet skis racketed past, spewing rooster tails, freeing her. She'd never been on one, just as she'd never ridden a motorcycle—Meg had owned one once—and she had a secret urge to try it, though she hated the noise, and the way at the ocean people came in close to jump the breaking waves. It looked like mindless fun, just going. There were so many things she wanted to try but had somehow never gotten around to: skydiving, bungee jumping, snowboarding, windsurfing. She had to believe it was circumstances that had prevented her, not timidity. At the pool, she'd been the first in her grade to climb the high dive, and there was the time she and Tammy Artman sneaked into school on Sunday, walking the dark halls like girl detectives, every corner a thrill.

"When are we going?" Sam asked, half sitting up.

"When your father gets back."

"How long is that?"

"Not long."

"I'm thirsty."

"Then go get yourself a drink."

"Can I have a ginger ale?"

She hesitated before she said yes, made him say please.

"Can I please have one?" Justin echoed.

"Yes," she said, and then had to holler "Walk!" to stop them from killing themselves. The girls barely stirred.

None of them had a watch. She followed a large sailboat as it patiently approached and then passed beyond the bell tower. A seaplane roared over the far shore, waving its wings for the beach crowd at Midway, a maneuver she'd only seen on TV and thought was dangerous.

The bell rang once. Two-thirty? Two-forty-five?

"This is ridiculous," she said out loud, and looked over her shoulder. Nothing.

The boys came back with their cans and a bag of Doritos and sat tailor-seat on their towels, eating, Rufus nosing between them, gobbling up anything that dropped. And then, before she could stop him, Justin held up a whole chip in front of him and frisbeed it out over the water.

In two steps Rufus was off the dock, airborne. He hit with a smack, the splash carrying the chip away from him so he had to paddle after it, making the boys laugh.

"No," Lise scolded them, already up. "He can't do that. He's too old."

"Yeah," Sarah said to Justin. "Don't you ever listen?"

Lise could see him cringe as if he'd been hit.

"It's all right, we just need to get him out now."

The boys walked down the dock toward shore, whistling, as Rufus swam alongside, snorting like a seal. He hacked something up on the grass, then shook, ears flapping, and trotted out to her again, panting, his gums pulled back in a smile. There was no reason to be mad. She'd just have to watch him. She was getting everyone resettled, confiscating the Doritos in the confusion, when the 4Runner turned in.

The boys popped up.

"He still needs to look at the stove," she said, and Sam sat back down, resting his chin on his fists. "Okay," she said, "enough with the poo-poo face."

Ken waved getting out of the car. He had a paper, and something in a brown bag.

She would not go in and check on his progress. She would not pull off the cover and get the boat ready. She would not move.

He got like this, obsessed with things. It didn't absolutely have to do with his photography, or didn't necessarily spring from it. Once it was matchbooks, once it was telephone poles. Old Volkswagens, Greek restaurants, patterned Formica counters. He would come home with an idea for a series, and for weeks she would have to listen to him spout about the cultural significance of tow trucks, and then a month later he would be off on some other kick, sometimes not even developing the rolls he'd taken. The first burst of infatuation was enough for him, and enough to spur her jealousy. At home he would forget the missing girl, whatever her name was, but for now she couldn't help but feel replaced—like Meg, dumped for a younger, less complicated woman. She would win him back by default, not through any grand romantic development. At her age, it was the most she could hope for.

As if to answer her, Sarah rolled onto her back, firm and perfect, and Lise looked away, scratched at a suddenly demanding mosquito bite.

Finally he came down to the dock with the square wheelbarrow his father had assembled from a kit.

"All fixed?" she called, and he gave her a thumbs-up. His new trunks were shorter than the ones the other day, a bright white line peeking out from each leg. He let the boys help him get the cover off, then asked them to stay out of the way as he straddled the gunwale and loaded the long red gas cans like bombs. She stood aside with the girls, useless, untrustworthy.

There wasn't room for him to work, so they hauled the inner tube and its snarl of rope onto the dock.

"Life jackets, everybody," she instructed, and helped the boys adjust their straps.

"Is my mom coming?" Justin asked.

"I'll be your buddy," Ken said, "okay?"

This prompted the girls to claim each other, leaving Sam with her. As if, at this point, she could feel any more undesirable.

Ken left the empty gas can under the cover and the boys' sodas in the wheelbarrow. Emily and Arlene and Meg came down to see them off, Arlene snapping away with her camera while they paddled out, the breeze pushing them at an angle for the Lerners' dock. Lise could see the weeds reaching up through the dark water, wrapping around the blade, and imagined the girl bobbing to the surface, rotted, something out of *Deliverance*. It was a wicked wish—killing his dream girl.

He left the wheel and pushed through them to the stern, bending over the edge to lower the engine, then came back and tried the key. The motor whirred but didn't turn over. He pushed the throttle up, thumbed the choke button and tried again, getting it to sputter. They drifted sideways into the blue smoke.

"Keep paddling," he said, as if he'd never rescinded the order.

"Need a jump there, Captain Ahab?" Emily shouted from the dock.

He twisted the key and the motor revved hard and long, not catching. He took his shades off and shouldered through them again and squeezed the rubber bulb to prime the engine. He was sweating and frustrated, and Lise knew not to bother him.

"Watch the dock," Meg called.

"Use your paddle to push off," he told Lise—as if they didn't go through this every time they tried to go out—and she did, the bow coming around.

He tried again, and this time the engine caught—the boys cheering, Ella looking worried—and he eased the throttle up until it was steady, deafening. He didn't look back as he aimed them for the center of the lake. With the wind in her hair, Lise felt freed, as if they were really departing. She waved along with the kids, leaving Emily and the others behind, their figures diminishing as the wake grew and tilted and curved, finally dwindling to dots, the dock one among dozens, and then just a distant, green piece of shore, indistinguishable from any other.

"Sorry," he shouted from behind his shades.

"For what?"

"For being a jerk."

"That's okay. You can't help it," she said, an old joke, worn but still with shifty implications, in this case a peace offering, temporary and happily accepted.

The windshield was crazed, nearly opaque. She sat up to help him with traffic, swiveling to check on the kids. They skirted the no-wake buoys for the marina at Prendergast Point, cut behind a big cabin cruiser with two women in their twenties in bikinis and joined the main lanes. It was like getting on the highway. The hull thudded against the waves, Sam shouting "Unh! Unh!" to get a laugh. She held on to the bare grab bar built into the dash, letting the speed and noise pour over her, washing her clean. It had to be past three but the sun was still high. On the far shore the trees gave way and she could see a truck climbing a long hill. It was Thursday, somewhere people were working, and for the first time since they'd arrived she felt truly on vacation, emptied of all responsibility.

They curled around Long Point, and Ken cut the throttle. As they slowed, the boat settled into the water. The air thickened, the humidity clapped back in place, and they could hear birds and, behind them, the motors of other boats. In the woods, behind a chain-link fence hung with signs, the old mansion glided by, a stucco imitation of a French villa. It was part of the state park, but they'd run out of money to fix it, so it sat there derelict, windows sealed with plywood, and each year when they swam in the cove Lise wished they could take it over, the whole family eating their meals on the broad stone patio. She and Ken had been inside once, years ago, before the children. The place smelled of mold and campfires. Deep maroon wallpaper from the twenties was peeling off in sheets;

someone's sneaker sat on the mantelpiece, decoratively centered. She'd been too spooked to make love, and Ken had been disappointed, a fantasy of his thwarted.

She so wanted romance now. This should have been enough—a motorboat and a ruined villa, a moody starving artist of a husband. Mary Stewart could spin a thriller from less, with the right heroine. As a teenager Lise had wanted to be like the young, untried women on her covers, governesses and college students abroad unfailingly described as lissome or winsome. She really thought she would grow up to be one of them, plucky and windswept. What an idiot she'd been.

Ken killed the engine and climbed over the windshield and she handed him the ceramic anchor, an overgrown ashtray. He tied it off on the bow cleat and played out the line until it hit bottom, then lashed down the excess.

Sam asked why they couldn't go tubing. Lise ignored him, stepping out of her shorts.

"How come we always have to go swimming first?"

"Don't be a wiener," Ella finally answered him.

"Okay, who's going to go first?" Ken asked, unfolding the ladder.

Usually the boys could be counted on to do anything that put them in the spotlight, but Sam was grumpy and Justin wasn't biting. Ella and Sarah hung back, loath to show enthusiasm.

"Somebody," Ken said.

"I'll go," Lise said. "I'm not afraid."

There were no protests, so she climbed over the windshield and pushed herself upright on the hot bow. The boat rocked beneath her feet, making her shift her weight; she crouched and put her arms out for balance. She chose to go off the starboard side, straight at the mansion. She needed a step or two to clear the edge of the bow. She thought of the kids paralyzed from diving in quarries, telephone poles and old pilings lurking under the surface. The mansion must have had a dock. Steamboats probably stopped here to let guests off.

"Jump," Sam prodded.

"How deep is it?" she asked.

"Don't worry," Ken said, "it's like twenty feet."

She decided to play it safe and go feetfirst, then wavered.

"Come on," Sam urged.

She gathered herself up, swayed back and hurled herself toward the edge, measuring her steps. She pushed off, flying not up but straight out, and tucked her knees to her chest, wrapping her arms tight around her shins in a cannonball.

She hit the water hard, a shock to her bones. The cold closed over her, and the silence. She let her weight take her down into even chillier depths.

When she opened her eyes there was only a yellowy, shining hint of the surface above, the water green and swamplike, silted. The cold stilled her heart, isolated its beating against the faint, silvery sound of propellers passing far out in the middle of the lake, submarinelike. She could see herself on the muddy beach, limp and white-lipped, eyes open like a fish, her slicked hair a shocking contrast. He'd take pictures of her then, rolls and rolls of film, coveting her a way he never did in life.

She'd never know. Her own buoyancy pushed her, will-less, to the surface. The castle was gone, nothing but trees above her.

"How is it?" he called, and she found him, standing on the bow in his silly short-shorts.

"It's nice," she lied.

14

The whole point of her not going on the boat was so they could talk. Meg had hoped Arlene would clear off and leave them alone. While Meg invented likely errands to send her off on, she installed herself on the porch with her novel and a tall glass, half listening to the Pirates game on the Erie station.

It was too hot to walk Rufus, too hot to sit on the dock. Her mother took the rocker beside Arlene and Meg took the glider, conceding defeat, if only for the moment. As always, Ken had left her the hard job, slipped away, blameless, while she confronted her mother. Despite her train wreck of a life, their roles had stayed the same. She thought it was by default, or weakness on his part, not a show of faith in her, but she was willing, maybe even eager, to be wrong.

The three of them read in the shade while the sun glittered on the water, the noise of the boats like a racetrack, then quiet for a time. The Pirates were winning in Chicago. In the middle of a sentence she would be drawn into the game, the shouts of the crowd or the announcers joking with each other. They were still advertising Iron City beer, a staple of her teenage years, Vitamin I, and she remembered cutting school and drinking in Frick Park, walking the gravel paths far into the woods, sitting on the side of a hill and looking down the valley at the busy steel mills and the gray Monongahela. She would be with James and Gina and Sully and Ray, and Teddy, who smoked Newports. Spring or fall, it didn't matter; the days seemed promising, an adventure. For lunch they'd hit the Open Pantry, getting gross premade hoagies wrapped in plastic and cold quarts of pop, more cigarettes, a new lighter. As the afternoon wore on, they'd slow down, knowing they had to go home.

"How was school?" her mother would say over the dinner table.

"Boring," she'd say, and go up to her room and listen to music.

It didn't seem twenty-five years ago. Nothing seemed twenty-five years ago, but it was, and for a moment she saw the past like a forgotten country spread out behind her, a landscape seen from a speeding car, the backwater towns and cracked streets and shabby apartments she'd lived in still there, and the girl she'd been, as if she could recapture her (redeem her) by returning to that hillside in Frick Park and start again.

She couldn't, just as she couldn't help but fall under this spell of regret. She was especially susceptible here, now, afraid she wouldn't be able to persuade her mother to keep the place, that—as with her life and her sobriety—it was already too late.

"You're thinking," Arlene said. "That's not allowed."

It's dangerous, Meg wanted to say, but blamed the mesmerizing glare of the lake. "It's like diamonds."

"I hope the children have their sunglasses," her mother said. "Sun like this can do permanent damage to your eyes."

"If you look directly into it," Arlene tweaked her, but too quickly, as if coming to Meg's rescue.

Meg appreciated the gesture, but thought it called too much attention to her, and really, she didn't need any help. As with so many of her mother's random observations, there was a judgment attached, an implied failure on her part, even if Sarah and Justin happened to be wearing their sunglasses. At another time in her life, Meg might have seen her warning after the fact as purposeful, designed to hurt, but this summer, with larger things on her mind, she'd acquired enough distance to understand that this was simply the way her mother saw the world—as a place you had to prepare yourself against or face dire consequences. She wasn't so much malicious as thoughtless. She would have said the same thing to Lise or Ken or to Arlene. She would have said the same thing twenty-five years ago.

Maybe it was the way her mother was raised, her grandfather and grandmother White religiously strict. Yet when Meg remembered them, she recalled how the two of them watched TV after dinner, planted in matching chairs for hours, both of them smoking, sharing the same ashtray, her grandmother heaving herself up to get them each a bowl of ice cream to eat with the local news. No, it was just her mother, her tentative, judgmental nature. If you made the right choices in life, you might be rewarded, but if you made the wrong ones, you were doomed. Meg had been wrestling with that idea for forty years, hoping to disprove it. Only her pride kept her from admitting that she'd given up, that her mother had won.

She needed a cigarette, needed to get up and move around. As she expected, Arlene tagged along after her, the screen door slapping shut. They stood under the chestnut and watched the boats, their dazzling sails. She looked for an opportunity, waited until Arlene had gone on about the heat wave in the Plains and the forest fires in the west as if they shared a personal stake in them.

"They were bad last year too," she agreed, and paused, clearing the air. "Listen," she said softly, and bent closer. "You wouldn't be insulted if I needed some time to talk to Mom alone, about the house?"

"Of course not. I think it's a good idea."

"Any suggestions?"

"Tell her we like it here," Arlene said. "Tell her it's cheaper than anyplace else. I know she still wants to come up next year. The only reason she's selling the place is because of your father, I'm convinced of that. It's not hard to care for, especially with the new roof."

She gestured toward the cottage in full view of her mother, and Meg had to turn her around.

"You don't think it's the money?" she asked.

"I think she sees it as one more thing to take care of. She's taken care of a lot in the last year."

"She didn't have to do it all herself."

"That's her way," Arlene said.

Meg didn't respond to this, relying on Arlene's solemnity to cover her. The lake and the radio filled the silence. It was too large of a subject, her mother misguidedly trying to insulate her and Ken from their father's illness, if that's what she really thought she was doing. Helping him die with dignity. It was a fight for another time.

"I was thinking you might go out to the store and get something we need for dinner."

"The shish kebabs. We've got an order in at the Lighthouse. I don't know if that'll give you enough time."

"All I need is an hour. Not even."

"I'll just drive around if I have to," Arlene said, and now Meg wanted to say she was sorry, that she wasn't in the way.

"Thank you," Meg said, and laid a hand on her shoulder, and Arlene brightened, grateful—like Justin, Meg thought—to be part of things.

"Good luck," Arlene said.

Back on the porch, Arlene waited until the Pirates had batted before she announced she was going out to the Lighthouse. "Any special orders?"

"We have more than enough dessert," her mother warned. "Someone's going to end up taking one of those pies home."

"Not me," Meg said, comic relief, as if to distract her.

When Arlene had gone, her mother turned off the radio. "I think it's a habit," she said, "always having something on. I do the same thing now when I come home. Two minutes haven't passed and I've got my music going. It's like having someone else in the house."

"I know," Meg said. "With me it's the TV."

"That's worse."

"I don't watch it. It might not even be in the same room. It's just hearing another voice."

"I'm sure that's it," her mother said.

They subsided, pleased with this rare agreement, and turned to their books. Meg held off, not wanting to be too blatant. Her mother was quick to see any serious difference of opinion between the two of them as criticism, and took criticism as a personal attack, went defensive, whether that meant dismissing her concerns as foolish or lashing out at her. Her father and Ken had spoiled her, Meg thought, going along with anything just to placate her. Stoned or sober, Meg refused to, and their fights escalated from clashes over small concrete issues into tests of higher principles and finally, irrationally, into proofs of who they were and what they owed each other. She had to avoid anything that sent them down that track. She thought everything depended on how she started.

The day couldn't have been a better example of why they should keep the place. It's so nice, she might say—a misstep, since her mother would know she was leading her somewhere.

I wish it was always like this.

This is what I love about Chautauqua.

In her book, Kinsey was driving around in her little red Bug, tailing someone, breaking down the case in her head. Meg needed to think like that, analyze the situation and get ahead of it, know what buttons to push. Good luck, she thought. She'd never had that ability, not with anyone, let alone her mother. All she could do was tell her how she felt and hope she would be merciful, a tactic that worked in group but nowhere else.

She closed her book and set it on the table, an opening move her mother noted. The light through the trees was turning golden, honeyed like a beer commercial. The water near shore had gone glassy. Her mother looked up from her book to see what she was doing, and Meg was waiting for her.

"Do you think we could talk about the cottage?"

Her mother paused to see if she was serious, giving her a chance to retreat.

"Why not?" she said, and stuck a bookmark between the pages, shifted so they were facing each other. "Kenneth said you'd want to."

"Did he tell you what I was going to say?"

"The gist of it."

She waited, and Meg could see she wasn't going to make this easy. She would have to state her case plainly, cleanly, without making her feel guilty or ganged up on.

"We'd like to try to keep the place. We all would—Ken, Arlene and myself. We're all willing to do whatever we can to help."

She thought her mother would interrupt and crush her argument before she started, but she sat there, expectant, as if she needed more reasons, more information, proof they'd thought it through. This was somehow worse. "We don't have money, I know that's a problem. And I know you don't have a lot of money either."

"True enough."

"What we're proposing is that we take care of the place. We open it and close it and take care of the repairs."

"And emergencies like the pipes breaking last winter?"

"And emergencies like that. And if and when we're in a position to do it, to help with the taxes." Her mother didn't scoff at this, a good sign. She had more, but most of it was emotional, how much they loved the place, how her father would want them to keep it, and she thought that would be a mistake. "Basically that's it," she said. "We all love coming up here, we're all going to be here next year, and this way would be cheaper than having to rent a place."

"It sounds fine," her mother said. "I can't tell you how happy it would make me to have you kids take it over. But I needed to know this six months ago. Telling me now doesn't do me any good. I've already signed the papers."

"You can back out of the deal, it happens all the time."

"That may be the way you operate, but that's not how I was brought up to act."

The tone was familiar, a note from her childhood. The danger was striking back at her mother in the same vein, or attacking her moral high horse.

"I know it's late," Meg said. "I wish I was in better shape six months ago or I would have told you I'd take it over myself."

"It's not realistic. I don't mean to sound unfeeling, but you have enough on your plate right now. You said you were worried about losing the house. If you had to make a choice, I think you'd have to choose the house over this place, for the children's sake, if nothing else."

"Of course," Meg said, "but that's not—"

"Then here, this is what *I'm* proposing. With the money from this place, I give you enough to keep you where you are until the kids are done with school. It's only seven more years, that's not a long time. In the meantime, we find a nice place to rent, somewhere close. It may be more expensive, but it doesn't make sense to pay taxes when we're only up here one week out of the year now. I'm not going to come up any more than that, my life's in the city."

The offer stopped her, emptied her head.

"What about Arlene?"

And Ken, because to take the deal would mean she'd betrayed them, and the idea of being able to stay in Silver Hills was more than tempting. She'd agreed to it immediately, her problems solved. She would put away her paychecks and build her savings.

"Arlene is tougher than you think. This is going to sound awful, but Arlene's had her life, so have I. You and Kenneth are going to end up with everything sooner or later and it's entirely up to you what you do with it, no strings. I would *hope* you'd want to take care of your family first. One reason I decided to sell the place, and I don't want you repeating this, is because I want to be able to control what happens to me ten or fifteen years from now when I can't take care of myself. I don't expect you or Kenneth to take me in, I wouldn't do that to you, but it's expensive, whichever way you choose. I'd like to have some say in the decision, and the only way to do that is to have some money in the bank. So yes, I admit it, it's selfish on my part."

"I never said it was."

"What did you think I'd do with the money?"

"I didn't think about it like that." She said it without thinking, a reflex, but it wasn't true. Being broke, she'd been jealous.

"You didn't wonder?" her mother pressed.

"I did."

"I had my reasons for doing this. It wasn't easy, believe me. I *tried* to involve you all in the decision."

"I know."

"Then why didn't any of you speak up when you had the chance?"

"I don't know," Meg said, but she did. Ken wouldn't have wanted to upset their mother, and from experience Arlene knew that she wouldn't have listened. They hadn't wanted to think of it, hadn't wanted to deal 'th her, and so she had done it alone, just as she'd done everything else.

t was true as far back as Meg could remember. Her mother had been the driving force in the family. Her father was either getting ready for work or recovering from it, too tired to do anything but give in to her demands or hide from her in the basement.

"Well I wish you'd have said *something*. It's hard enough being here without everyone being on my case."

"I'm sorry," Meg said, though this seemed an overreaction on her mother's part. No one had actually challenged her.

The phone rang from inside, loud through the open window.

Shit. Him. Whatever he had to say, she didn't want to hear it.

"The machine's not on," her mother said.

"I'll get it. It's probably Jeff."

"Say hello."

"Right."

The screen was surprisingly light. Inside, in the dim, humid room, she approached the phone with scorn and a new strength, as if the promise of money gave her a power over him. It did, strangely. The sudden reality of the change was palpable, hundreds of miles away—the lawn, the front door, the garage. They could stay. The kids wouldn't hate her.

She thought of just letting the phone ring, but her mother was right outside, her mother, who had unexpectedly rescued her, guaranteed their future. Of all people.

She understood.

Ken and Arlene wouldn't.

The phone rang, insistent. She picked it up before it could ring again, then hesitated, making him wait.

"Maxwells," she said.

15

Justin had to wear a life jacket but Sam didn't because he took lessons when he was little. He could almost dive as good as Ella now. He did a better straight dive and a perfect jackknife but she could do a back flip because she took gymnastics.

"Slow down, pal," his father said as he was climbing the ladder, trying to catch up with Sarah and Ella, who were standing on the nose of the boat.

Ella stopped at the edge and turned around so only her toes were still on, then squatted and launched herself, turning in midair, her hands feeling for the water. It was the flip part he couldn't do, snapping his knees around so he'd go in clean. Plus he was afraid. Bobbing next to Justin, his mother clapped and held up both hands wide to show her fingers. "Ten!"

Show-off, he thought.

"Come on," Ella called, daring Sarah to try it.

"I can't," she said, but turned backwards, laughing.

She was wearing her yellow suit that pushed her boobs together, drops of water trickling into the dark line between them. He looked at everyone else to see where they were looking. He looked at the castle in the woods, at the jet going over. The dark line curved where it disappeared, about to make a circle.

Sarah bent her knees and dove and he put his hands out for balance. She snaked her arms above her head the way Ella did, but instead of turning in the air, she went half over and landed on her side with a smack.

"Ouch," his father said from the driver's seat.

"Are you okay?" his mother asked.

She was, and now it was his turn. They all waited for him like this was the Olympics.

"Show us what you got, champ."

"Be careful," his mother said.

He didn't have anything special, and he didn't want to try the back flip because he knew he couldn't do it, so he chose his best regular dive, took two steps and pushed off, his hands together in an arrow. The water took him in, filling his ears, then pushed him up into the sun again. He shook his head, wiped his hair out of his eyes, pinched his nose.

"Nice," his mother said, holding up nine fingers. "You bent your legs a little, otherwise it's a ten."

Sarah and Ella were at the ladder. When Sarah climbed up, a line of water ran off the bottom of her suit. On the boat she seemed taller. She twisted her hair with both hands, squeezing it out like a towel. It was easier to watch in the water, harder for other people to see you.

"I'm going to swim all the way around," Sam told his mother. She had to ask Justin if he wanted to go, but he said he was cold and wanted to get out.

"Come straight back," she said.

The girls were still on the front. He was careful going around the motor and the rainbow the gas made on the water. It felt colder over here. You could see where the fence around the castle ended. It went right down into the water so no one could swim around it. He checked to make sure his father wasn't looking, then turned away from the boat and reached into his pocket. The watch was there, solid against his fingers.

"You all right there?" his father called.

He didn't turn, kept treading water. "I'm peeing."

"Oops. Hope everything comes out all right!"

He tried to pull the watch out but it was caught in the mesh of his suit. He got it on a second try, felt the knob on the side and the plastic strap. For a second he thought it might float, a bubble of air trapped under the glass, but when he opened his hand and let go, it disappeared, tipped off the top of his foot and was gone.

Already he wanted it back, wished he'd never taken it. He was sorry—he liked the watch. He hoped it was still good. Maybe someone scuba diving would find it. It was supposed to be waterproof, and swimming around the front where Sarah was, he imagined it sitting on the bottom of the lake, faceup, ticking, still alive.

16

The phone wasn't portable, so Emily could hear Margaret talking through the window right behind her. Out of delicacy, she walked Rufus down to the dock and sat there watching the traffic, rehashing her offer, convinced it was rash. A pair of fishermen drifted by on their swivel seats and tipped their caps, and Emily waved, neighborly, a flip of her wrist. Locals, she thought, or a good imitation. She didn't say it was too late in the day to catch anything, though she could see Henry shaking his head at them.

What kind of money did Margaret need? And after taxes, wasn't what Henry had left her enough? Their safe-deposit box was crammed with bonds and stock certificates Emily had never seen or had forgotten over the years. Heinz, PPG, Allegheny Ludlum. She'd received a proxy card from Alcoa and thought the number of shares had to be a typo, but no, he'd piled it up the way he collected those aluminum-colored pencils from work. The house was infested with them. She'd find one in her hand as she added to the grocery list or halved a recipe. The paper said the price was up to sixty-something, meaning their shares were worth well over a hundred thousand. She could talk to the accountant who did their taxes and see what her choices were. She should do that anyway.

The shadow of the Lerners' oak covered the dock now, the far shore softened by the mild light. Creamy thunderheads were building to the north, blown off Ontario. Kenneth and the children would be back soon, hungry from swimming.

She tried not to imagine what Margaret and Jeff were saying to each other. When she and Henry fought, they stayed out of each other's way, a hardened silence their weapon of choice. Margaret had a mouth on her she hadn't gotten from either of them, and Emily inwardly cringed whenever she heard it, followed its explosions, knowing it was just a precursor. One night at a barbecue she'd seen Margaret, drunk, punch Jeff in the neck and mean it. She'd been holding a cigarette, and the end burst over him like fireworks. Emily had never seen her hit anyone else, but had feared for the children ever since, checking their limbs when they visited. Thank God that was done with.

When she thought she'd waited long enough, she stood and walked back to the porch. Before she could open the door, she saw Margaret by the garage, smoking, one arm across her body as if she were holding herself. Closer, Emily could see she'd been crying, her eyes puffy.

"I'm okay," she said, almost casually, as if Emily shouldn't bother herself worrying. As if this happened all the time.

Perhaps it did, Emily wouldn't know.

"Is there anything I can do?"

"Short of just killing me, no." She gave her a mocking smile, false and dismissive.

"I'm only trying to help."

"I appreciate it," Margaret said. "Right now I'd rather not get into it, if that's all right with you."

"Should I just go away and leave you alone, is that what you want?"

"Don't take everything so personally."

"I only asked because I'm worried about you." Emily felt herself rising to the fight and had to rein herself in, take a breath. "I'll leave you alone," she said, and left, calling Rufus.

She went straight into the house to her suffocating room and closed the door and sat on the bed like a scolded child, rubbing the nubbly chenille spread with her hands, thinking of what she should have said. She could say whatever she wanted and Margaret would still behave the same way. She had no influence over her, or perhaps a negative one, the two of them repelling each other like magnets, made of the same volatile stuff.

With a crunching and a hydraulic squall of protest, Arlene's car turned in the drive and floated by the window. She understood that Margaret would tolerate Arlene's intervention, that she felt if not on the same level with her aunt then at least a sympathy that joined them against her. Emily wasn't so much jealous of the bond as resentful, left out. She'd had Henry as a sounding board for so long, as emotional ballast. Now, with no one, she felt outnumbered and alone, wildly unreliable. Her offer to Margaret seemed imprudent, could easily be misconstrued as a crude stab at reconciliation.

Margaret hadn't said that she'd accept it. She might not, out of pride. That would be truly foolish, Emily thought, but not at all surprising.

Well, she'd tried.

She heard Arlene's voice and stood up and went to the dresser, ignoring the gray face that loomed in the shadow-box mirror. The tiled tray Kenneth had made at camp one summer was full of junk they'd accumulated—bent nails and brass picture hangers, dark pennies and a pair of rusty nail clippers, a black electrical adapter, a cat's-eye marble and a squash-colored one from the Chinese checkers, dusty movie stubs (ONE ADMISSION $3.50), a battery crusted with some chemical. She picked up a curled golf pass from the club, like a price tag for an appliance, the string still knotted. Why Henry had saved it she couldn't say, but it had his initials penciled in, and the date indelibly punched in the tiny, precise numbers of a time clock, five years ago next week. She couldn't remember the day, and that was a failure. Herb Wiseman probably played with them. She would keep it and throw the rest away.

She suddenly wanted to keep everything—the mirror, the dresser, the house itself. She had enough money, she could figure out a way. That would make everybody happy.

She opened the top drawer. Inside, among her underthings, was a travel alarm clock of his, fake alligator, an old windup job with radium-painted hands. When he first started working, he'd taken it around the world with him, flying BOAC to Europe to help rebuild their plants.

She closed the drawer. She had too much to do to be moping around like this. The bathrooms had to be cleaned, the closets and cupboards emptied, the fridge defrosted, the oven scrubbed. Kenneth had barely started on the garage.

What she really wanted was to take a nap, let the heat of the day lull her to sleep.

She went into the kitchen, saw on the way that Margaret and Arlene were out on the dock, Rufus with them. It was almost five, and she fancied a gin and tonic, but didn't want to start before everyone else. She poured herself a glass of water and emptied the dishwasher while the ice cracked and chimed against the side.

In the middle of the top rack she stopped to admire one of the tumblers Margaret had asked for, the cheap silk-screened design of the car on the side, the glass itself darker by the thin rim and the thick, slanted bottom. She wondered if she saw them at a flea market if she would give them a second thought. Strange what could take ahold of you. Maybe that was why so many women her age surrounded themselves with knickknacks, their shelves and mantels ranked with pleasant memories. That was what she was doing now, wasn't it, gathering keepsakes. Again, she was surprised that she'd come to that part of her life so soon, where everything was remembered, as if she'd skipped ahead, her sixties missing.

She made shrimp dip, a ritual she'd inherited from Henry's mother, the queen of cream cheese. She covered it with plastic wrap and set it in the fridge to firm. Someone hadn't put the clip back on the potato chips, and they were rubbery. She fed them to the disposal and took down a new bag, propping it on the chopping block. There was enough ice, enough of the children's drink things.

It was too hot to be inside, and she went out on the porch where she'd left her book. Margaret and Arlene were still on the bench, Arlene gesturing to the world at large with one arm, explaining something. Emily thought another mother might see it as a defeat—sitting here by herself while someone else counseled her daughter—but she understood. As much as she might wish it, it was too late to change their places in the family. All she could hope for was a softening of their roles, if not trust then a grudging respect for what they'd put each other through, if that was not too much to ask.

Rather than watch them, she read her book. She'd just fallen into it when the boat pulled in with Kenneth and the children.

Arlene came flapping off the dock and across the yard. "I need my camera!"

"You're worse than he is."

It was on the table beside Emily, and she handed it to her. At the door, Arlene looked back as if she were coming, holding it open, an invitation to join her. Ever the diplomat, she thought. Arlene knew them both too well.

"Go ahead," Emily said. "I'll be there in a minute."

17

He couldn't read the face Meg gave him as he unloaded Lise and the kids. His mother and Arlene were there, so she would be using code, but her even look—closed and matter-of-fact—didn't seem hopeful, confirmation that things had gone the way he expected. He thought she had no reason to be upset. She didn't really think their mother would change her mind this late.

Meg helped the kids lug everything back to the house while he and Lise put the boat up, and by the time they finished, she and Arlene had gone out to the Lighthouse. He didn't bother with a shower, not with the crowd. He'd just get dirty going through his father's workbench anyway. He'd have time to wash up before he had to grill the shish kebabs. It would be cooler then too.

He smuggled the Nikon outside. He was dull from the sun, his forehead tender, and a cold Iron City revived him. He set the sweating bottle on top of the little refrigerator—his now. The garage was hot and airless, a rich, secretive smell from childhood he associated with loneliness and spying. How many times had he watched Meg and her summer boyfriends making out on the dock? A mellow light slanted through the side window, intersecting lengths of scrap wood jutting from a barrel, a strange bouquet. He bracketed it, hoping one setting would catch what he'd seen. He thought of just freestyling, but nothing jumped out at him, not the campy mermaids or the geometry of the ladder hung on the far wall. He could hear Morgan warning him and shook his head to banish the voice.

He started with what he knew he wanted, his father's tackle boxes. There were two: the rounded green metal-flake one he remembered, and the new square two-tone brown plastic one his father actually used. They were not quite his yet, not until he took them down to the basement at home and set them in a respectful place. Here they were still his father's, on the workbench where they belonged. He opened the green one, stepped back and bracketed it, pleased with the symmetry of the trays, the different hooks and lures in their uniform spaces.

The brown one he wasn't as happy with. It was cheap and common, not really his father's at all but a functional substitute. The green one's latch had given way. After it had dropped most of its contents on the lawn, his father had picked this one up at Wal-Mart. In his father's eyes, it was simple: this one worked and that one didn't. Ken wondered if he could have the green one fixed. Maybe the differences between the two would create something interesting.

He was going to close the brown one when he noticed a Zippo lighter in the bottom compartment among the bright bobbers and packaged leaders. His father had supposedly quit smoking years before he bought the new box, so it was out of place, an anachronism. He palmed it, then flipped it over, hoping for an inscription (a retirement present, a door prize from some convention), but it was just brushed steel, scratched and nicked with use. The wick was charred and the flint was good, but it didn't light, the fluid long since evaporated, the cotton wadding inside dried up. As a teenager, Ken and his friends had all carried Zippos as part of their style, though they were actually useless for lighting pipes. He'd mastered the switchblade flick that popped the top, ready, any second, to light some untouchable girl's Marlboro.

There were no cigarettes to go with the lighter, and he vaguely remembered his father once using it in lieu of a knife to melt his line when a snag proved impossible to free. Rather than upset his mother, he thought he would give it to Meg as consolation.

He thought she would interrupt him as he framed the beer bottles neatly cased for return, the kindling cut from scraps of some forgotten project, but when she and Arlene returned from the Lighthouse they took the bags inside, leaving her van under the chestnut, its engine ticking.

It was Lise who finally came out and asked him if he was done yet. "Your mom's making noise about dinner."

"Is everyone out of the shower?"

They were, leaving him zero hot water. He ducked his head under the spray, clenching his muscles, and then when he got out, the humid room made him sweat. He dropped the lighter in the pocket of his shorts, a conspicuous lump.

Meg was on the lawn, helping the kids shuck the corn. She looked up as he passed, and this time he was sure she was asking him something, that she needed to talk. He got the coals going with the starter, and Lise brought out the packages of shish kebabs, Rufus loping alongside her, champing his loose lips and drooling.

"I guess Jeff called," she said.

"What about?"

"I'm just piecing things together. It sounds like they talked for a while."

"She was going to talk to Mom about the place."

"You said," she said absently, and he thought she was bored with his family's annual melodramas, that in the end she only wanted to go home.

"I'm just worried about her," he said.

"That's good of you." She gave him a kiss as a reward and discovered the Zippo. "What's this?"

He showed it to her. "I thought she might like it. I didn't think Mom would want to see it."

"No, she wouldn't."

From the porch, Meg called, "Should I put the corn in?"

"Go ahead."

Lise went in to do the salad, and again he found himself imitating his father, waiting, a long barbecue fork in one hand, a beer in the other. Rufus stayed with him, curled up on the concrete apron of the garage. Finally he got the kebabs on, the smoke floating over the garage and the dock. The kids started a game of croquet. The sun was gone from the sky, and the air over the lake was gray, a touch of mist building. The *Chautauqua Belle* chuffed by, tooting its whistle. The locusts whined.

He knew what his mother's answer had been—that was never in question. He wanted to know how Meg felt about it, and what he could do to help.

He could not pick out a single instance that he'd helped her, a particular time he lent her money or took care of her or the children. They were too far apart for that. He called her, and sometimes she called him back. After talking with her on the phone he felt powerless and ashamed, as if her problems were his fault. They weren't, just as they weren't their mother's, but the feeling would stay with him for days, dispersed only when

Lise teased it out of him. "She's an adult," she'd say, the exact opposite of his mother, who loved to mock Meg from a position of wisdom: "She thinks she's still a teenager."

For him she was both, and also his big sister in the fifth grade, the face that had peered through the bars of his crib at nap time. She had paved the way for him, often to places he feared to follow, but she'd always been on his side, his advocate in all matters, even when they sent her off to boarding school. She sent him thick letters covered with vines and flowers, melting psychedelic designs. On the phone she joked that they should run away together.

The kebab on the end was burning, flames licking through the grill. He doused it with a spritz of his beer, stirring up a cloud of ashes, and backed off. He rearranged them and ran inside for a knife, peered into a bloody cut and decided they were done enough. The burnt one would be his.

"You don't want that," his mother said in the kitchen, raising a hand to take it, and he had to protect his plate.

Meg built a steaming pyramid of corn on a pink flea-market platter and broke out a new stick of butter—"*Not* margarine," she boasted.

If she was overcompensating, he couldn't tell. Maybe he was the only one thinking of the place, tomorrow being their last day. Maybe it was Jeff.

They barely all fit on the porch. Rufus stood outside the door, peering through the screen, wriggling his nose.

"There's no room for you," his mother apologized. "You just wait."

His meat was tough. The boys had trouble cutting theirs, and then he sliced through Justin's paper plate, the juice staining its wicker holder. "Get a new one," his mother instructed, and Meg went. Ken brought the whole thing inside, trying not to drip on the carpet.

Meg peeled a paper plate from the stack and fitted it in, and he transferred the meat, his hand underneath it, in case.

"Hey," he said, "you talked to Mom."

As he asked, he was surprised to find that, after everything, he still held out some hope. She could tell him their mother had changed her mind and he wouldn't be shocked.

"I did," she said, and even though she was busy cutting Justin's meat, he could read her voice easily. He'd heard it over the phone for years. It was the flat, disinterested tone that said his mother would never change, that it was foolish to think she might.

"What did she say?"

"What did she say," she repeated, working, a signal that she didn't want to talk about it. "She said we should have said something earlier. And she's right, I understand that. She says she needs the money, which I didn't know, but that's fine. We had a good talk, actually."

He checked the doorway to make sure no one was coming, but she was done, ready to head back out.

"Look what I found," he said, to stop her, and showed her the lighter.

"Where'd you get this?"

"Dad's tackle box."

"Nice." She tried to give it back.

"Keep it. I've got no use for it."

He wanted her to be thrilled with the gift, touched the way he'd been when he discovered it. She just thumbed the lid open and flicked the wheel, testing it, then folded it closed, unimpressed.

"Arlene might like it," she said, and despite himself, he agreed. Nothing could make up for losing the place. He couldn't believe he really thought it would comfort her, a lighter that didn't even work.

They went back outside and reclaimed their chairs, laid their napkins in their laps. His meat was gristly and tasteless, dots of fat congealing on the plate. His mother was telling the story of Duchess being sprayed by the skunk who used to live behind the woodpile and the shopping cart full of tomato juice they bought to wash her, how in the middle of it Duchess got away from them and they had to chase her through the neighbors' yards. She was young then, and too fast for them. They finally found her hiding under the Loudermilks' toolshed, covered with dirt.

"Can you imagine, on a hot day? It was worse than the skunk."

She laughed at her own story, enchanted with their history. In her corner, Meg was busy eating, completely ignoring her, cool and solitary, and Ken thought that she was right. Things didn't change.

18

They didn't have to do the dishes tonight, Grandma and Aunt Arlene would take care of them so they could play miniature golf.

"Go," they said, "have fun," and everybody jammed into his mother's van and went to Molly World. Usually they only went there for bumper boats and go-carts, but the old Putt-Putt was closed. This was supposed to be a harder course.

"I'm gonna kick your butt," Sam said, sticking a finger in Justin's face.

"I'm gonna kick *your* butt," he said.

"I'm going to kick all your butts," Uncle Ken said from the front.

He would, too. Uncle Ken always won at miniature golf. He was even better than his father.

"Can we do the bumper boats?" Sam asked.

"We'll see."

"That means no."

"That means we'll see."

"Are we going to have ice cream?" Ella asked from the middle seat.

"Yes, we are going to have ice cream," Aunt Lisa said, right beside Justin. "You can't go to Molly World and not have ice cream."

It was weird sitting in the way back with Sarah's scrunchy in front of him. She was mad about something, because she didn't talk the whole way there, and Justin thought it was because their father had called and they didn't get to talk to him. Justin missed him too, but come on, they were going to Molly World. And besides, it wasn't their mother's fault. They'd see him when they got back. She promised.

They went by the house with all the goofy stuff in the yard, and the one with a goose for a mailbox. They went by the sign for the

McDonald's and the bar like a log cabin with all the motorcycles outside, by the Pizza Hut and the Blockbuster.

"Can we go to Blockbuster?" he asked his mother.

She made him say it twice because she couldn't hear, and by the second time he already knew the answer.

"We won't have time tonight."

"What about tomorrow?"

"Tomorrow we're going to Webb's for dinner."

Sam groaned.

"Can it," Uncle Ken said.

They went to Webb's every year on the last night. They had to get dressed up, and it was boring. Even the gift shop didn't have anything except gross goat-milk fudge.

The lights were on at Molly World even though it wasn't all the way dark yet. Inside the fence he could see fake palm trees and the Eiffel Tower and the Empire State Building with King Kong waving at a plane. The ice-cream stand was a giant sundae with a cherry on top.

On the roof of the booth where they got their putters was a flashing yellow light like on a tow truck. When it was lit, the guy in the Molly World shirt explained, the first person to make a hole in one won a free game.

"Why do they have to play the music so loud?" Aunt Lisa asked.

"Because it's fun," Ella said.

Justin took a green ball and Sam took a blue one. They had a sword fight until Aunt Lisa stuck an arm between them.

"Calm down," she said.

There were too many of them, so they had to split into two groups. His mother and Uncle Ken went with him and Sam while Aunt Lisa went with the girls. They had a choice of two courses.

"Let's play both," Justin said.

"We're only playing one," his mother said, "so pick the one you want."

They picked the one with King Kong; the girls wanted the Eiffel Tower.

"Okay," Aunt Lisa said, "we'll see who's faster."

"I don't know," Uncle Ken said. "You've got Miss Pokey there."

"Dad," Ella said.

"We're gonna cream you," Sam said, but then they had to wait to tee off. The people in front of them had three little kids and none of them could hold their putters right. They chased their shots around like hockey.

"Come *on*," Justin said.

"Shush," his mother said. "It's not a race."

"But—"

"But nothing."

It was just like at home. She was always yelling at him for no reason.

"And don't give me that face," she said. "You start with that, you can go sit in the car."

By now the other people were done.

"Sam, you go first," his mother said, like she was punishing Justin, but she wasn't because he didn't want to play anymore.

The hole was boring. It was straight and went up a bump like a triangle at the end. If you hit it to either side, it would send the ball down a dead end. Sam hit his too hard; it went up the bump like a ramp and jumped the back wall, bouncing past the other family and under a pine tree. He chased it down and did it over again, and this time it was too soft, and then he almost kept it on the bump but it just rolled off; he did that again, then came back the other way, bouncing it off the back, and it went in.

"How many?" Uncle Ken asked.

"Four," Sam said.

"Okay, Just," his mother said.

It wasn't a four, but he knew not to say anything, his mother would just get mad at him.

Justin put his ball on the center spot on the rubber mat and looked at the hole.

"Nice and easy," Uncle Ken said.

His mother said nothing, and he thought of Sarah in the van, if she was mad like he was now. When his father got mad he yelled so you could hear it upstairs.

He didn't want to hit it too hard. He pulled back the putter just a little and swung.

It was straight, and going for the hole. He was afraid it was too soft, that it would stop or swerve when it hit the bump, but it climbed the triangle and rolled past the hole.

"Get in!" Uncle Ken yelled as the ball knocked off the back wall. It almost stopped, then curled, made a slow turn like water swirling down the drain, and went in the hole.

"Who's the man!" Justin said, and raised his putter like Steve Yzerman when he scored.

"Wow!" his mother said. "Nice going."

"Good job, Just," Uncle Ken said.

And then Sam was in his face, pushing him, almost knocking him over. Justin thought it was part of the celebration, like when you won the Stanley Cup, but Sam was shoving him, shouting like he'd messed up. "The light's on, you idiot!"

It was.

Both of them ran, dashing past the soda machines with their putters. There was another kid there and Justin thought he'd lost, but he was just getting change. Sam called to the guy, "We got a hole in one."

"I got it," Justin said.

"What hole?"

"One—the first."

The guy looked over their heads at his mother and Uncle Ken. "Must be your lucky day. What's your name?"

Justin told him. The guy picked up a microphone and pressed it with his thumb and the rock'n'roll stopped.

"*Just*-in Carlisle," he said, making his voice crazy, like the commercials for the monster-truck show, "*you* are the lucky *hole-in-one* winner of *one*—count it, one—*free pass* to the fabulous thirty-*six* holes of *Molly* World! How does it feel, big guy?" He held the mike in Justin's face.

"Great," Justin said, and he could hear his voice come back to him over the speakers.

He wished his father was here to hear it, but that was okay.

"Next *lucky* hole-in-one *con*test in just *five* minutes," the guy said, handing Justin an orange ticket good for a free game. It was the first time he'd ever won anything.

He let Sam look at it, and they ran back to his mother and Uncle Ken.

"Let's see," his mother said. "Very nice. Do you want me to hold it for you?"

"I won't lose it."

The rest of the game he kept checking his pocket, touching it, feeling the piece of paper through the material, and then when they were eating ice cream, he took it out and set it on the table in front of him. No one else made a hole in one, not even Uncle Ken.

It was dark out when they drove home. Sarah was talking with Ella, so she wasn't mad anymore. Squished in the way back, Justin held the ticket up, reading the words by the headlights of the cars behind them. As he did, he saw the ball coming off the back wall and slowly turning, curling for the hole, and the same feeling spread through him like a shiver, perfect happiness. It was something he'd never forget.

19

Emily joined her on the dock to watch the stars come out, both of them bundled up in their jackets and caps. She sat down on the bench beside her, and Arlene saw she was drinking Henry's scotch. For a while they said nothing. A radio was playing somewhere behind them. A duck came in for a landing, skiing on its feet.

"It's very still tonight," Arlene said.

Emily murmured assent, and then silence enveloped them again, the slop of the water.

"Why am I selling the place," Emily said, "if none of you want me to?"

Arlene looked at her and then up at the stars, but there was no answer there. "I don't know."

"I feel like I'm being put in a position here, and I don't think it's fair."

Nothing's fair, Arlene wanted to say. Being alone your whole life isn't fair. Henry being dead isn't fair.

"It's your decision," she said. "It's your place."

"That's exactly what I'm talking about," Emily said. "And then everyone resents it."

"What did you expect?"

"I expected some help. Some support. I guess I should have known better with this family."

"Yes," Arlene said, "we're evil. We've been sent here to torture you."

"It seems like it sometimes."

"Uh-huh. Well, you know what, Emily? Join the club."

"Touché."

Emily sighed and set her glass down at her feet and sat back, and Arlene thought the serious part of their talk was over. It never ceased to amaze her how successful she was when she talked to people as if they were her students, how willing they were to be treated like children.

They sat side by side, not talking. A thread of music blew across the water. The stars beamed and twinkled. The bell tower rang the half hour.

20

They wanted to stay up and play cards, but her mother told them to go to bed.

"Tomorrow's going to be a long day. First thing after breakfast, that upstairs is getting picked up. I want all your dirty clothes in one pile."

It wasn't even her regular bedtime, but rather than argue with her in front of everyone, Ella climbed the stairs behind Sarah, trying to ignore the white fringe of her cutoffs, the taut hollows of her knees. Earlier in the week this would have filled her; now she bit her lips and kept her eyes on the steps. She had no chance, and it seemed cruel that Sarah was so close.

She really didn't know. At the miniature golf she'd grabbed Ella's arm and whispered, "Did you see the guy in the white?" She still hadn't said anything to her about Mark's letter.

Ella wasn't mad at her, it was just a feeling—on top of feeling like she was lying all the time, pretending to be her friend.

She wasn't even that.

Upstairs the air caught in her throat. There was nothing they could do. The fan was already on. Justin and then Sam used the bathroom while they changed into their PJs, Sarah pulling on her nightshirt before taking off her bra. Ella didn't want to see her like that anyway, it wasn't right. She turned her back and slipped on her pajama top, tossed her shorts on the floor. The room wasn't that bad.

Sarah was taking her earrings out in front of the mirror. "I can't believe I lost my watch."

"I know," Ella sympathized, thinking: Sam.

"I loved that watch."

Because it was from Mark. Sarah didn't have to say it. Ella knew it was wrong to be glad that it was gone but couldn't help herself. Lately she'd been having all these crazy thoughts.

The bathroom door was unlocked.

"Get out," Sam said, on the pot.

"At least turn the fan on." She did, half for the noise. She didn't want Sarah to hear them. "Where is it?"

"What?"

"Where is it?"

"Where's what?"

"You know."

"What do you mean?"

"Where's the watch? I know you took it."

"I did not."

"Sam, don't lie, I know you did it. I'll tell Mom."

"Go ahead."

"I will."

"I didn't do anything. Now get out, I'm trying to poop."

She couldn't tell if he was lying, he was that good at it. The watch was exactly the kind of thing he'd steal.

"Hurry up," she said. "The rest of us have to use the bathroom too."

It would show up tomorrow, she thought, just like at home. He'd stick it under the dresser or drop it behind the cedar chest, somewhere someone else would find it when they were cleaning up.

"What is he doing in there?" Sarah asked. She'd gathered her hair in a ponytail to wash her face, a strand curling by her ear, and again Ella was aware of how powerful she was, how far from her.

When Sam was done they brushed their teeth together, jostling each other at the sink, elbowing and joking. It was an act. Every touch made Ella cringe inside like she was telling a lie. She was just lucky to be with her like this. She should enjoy it now.

"Here," Sarah said, "try this," and handed her a tube of peppermint scrub.

Ella lathered her face and splashed it off, her cheeks tight and tingling. At home, alone, with her face straight on, the mirror let her pretend, but with Sarah there beside her, she had to admit the truth. She would never be beautiful, not like that. No one would ever think of her the way she thought of Sarah.

"This is my favorite," Sarah said, and squeezed a pink blob on Ella's palm. "It's called Strawberry Smooth."

Ella watched her rub it into her cheeks, then imitated her, working the excess into the backs of her hands. It felt sticky and smelled sweet, and even though she and Caitlin made fun of the girls who wore candy-flavored lip gloss and stunk up the bus, she said, "It's nice."

Her mother came up to bug them, tucking Sam and Justin in. "It's like an oven up here," she said to no one, and tried to open the window higher but it was stuck, her father had already tried a million times.

She and Sarah lay on top of their sleeping bags. Ella had to take off her glasses to read, and she knew she looked squinty and stupid.

"At ten o'clock that light goes off," her mother threatened, then finally left.

Ella wanted to talk, but Sarah was almost finished with her book. Ella had lost interest in her own, the fortune-teller warning the queen of the upcoming battle between Good and Evil. The books were all the same. In the end, something magical happened and everyone got what they wanted. They were so fake.

The boys were noisy across the room, rustling the slippery skins of their bags. Ella shushed them once, twice.

"Stop," Justin said.

"Sam," Ella warned.

"Oooo, I'm scared."

She thought she'd have to get up, and then a couple of minutes later they were both asleep, whistling. Ella looked to Sarah to show her they were alone.

Her eyes were closed, her face turned from her book, still upright on her chest. With her hair covering one eye, she looked like the princess after she drank the sleeping potion. Even asleep she was beautiful, and the urge to kiss her rose again. She could see how it would be, bending to her, their lips sticking together, the sweet strawberry smell of her skin, the soft, worn nightshirt. For a long moment Ella watched her breathing, and then, afraid Sarah might catch her, took the book from her hands—Sarah murmuring, rolling—found her bookmark and saved her place.

She got up and turned out the light and for a while she couldn't see her, but then her eyes got used to the dark, and there she was, right beside her. Ella shifted so her face was even with Sarah's.

She couldn't tell her. It would ruin everything. She'd end up with nothing. This was as close as she'd ever get.

She didn't say the words out loud, just mouthed them.

21

He didn't think he was that stoned until he tripped over a wicket and dropped one of the beers he was carrying, the bottle thudding on the lawn, rolling to a stop. The moon helped him find it—his now, a slippery time bomb. It was cool out, dew settling in the air, the dank smell of the water pronounced, and the locusts were slower, only a few of them still going. The lake held the light; the dock was outlined in silver. At the far end he could see the black shadows of Meg and Lise sitting on the bench, the gap between them he'd vacated. Above the hills on the far shore the stars were locked in their turning, fastened to an invisible pane of glass, and he sensed in their vastness and permanence the curvature of the earth, the smallness of its orbit, the swiftness of the seasons.

He was wrecked. Polluted, they used to call it.

He'd only sneaked a couple of hits from the torpedo Meg left for him in the garage, but he was sure he reeked. He stopped to open the good beer (his hands were sore from golf, and the bottle cap dug into his skin) and swished it cold through his teeth, let it fizz on his tongue. He took another swig on the dock for insurance, knowing Lise would see his indulgence as a betrayal, siding with Meg against her. Even after so many years he was leery of leaving them alone too long, afraid their conversation might stray into dangerous territory, old slights and sudden confessions.

Lise held up a hand for her beer, took it without looking.

"What I don't understand," she was saying, "is why she couldn't find a way to transfer ownership to you guys, if that's what she really wanted. She could have done that anytime after the estate was settled. This way everyone has to come to her."

"I don't think so," Meg said. "You know she can't stand any last-minute stuff. It makes her nervous."

"That's even better. It gives her an excuse to freak out."

He sat between them, a referee. Lise twisted the cap off and the beer burped, a puff of gas, nothing.

"She doesn't need an excuse," Meg said. "She's already got enough of them this summer."

"Like that thing with the ants," Lise persisted.

"That's going to happen no matter what," Ken said. "Hey, are we signed up for tennis tomorrow?"

"Change the subject," Lise said. "All we could get was eight o'clock."

"That's good. We have to get going early if we're going to get everything in."

"What else?"

"I told the boys we'd go to Panama Rocks."

"Why?" Meg asked, like it was a waste of time.

He shrugged. "They wanted to go."

He didn't have to say that he remembered the whole family going when he was a boy, that the week wouldn't be complete without a visit. It was as much a part of Chautauqua as Friday night at Webb's or the mornings he spent at the Putt-Putt honing his stroke. And Meg didn't have to counter, saying she hated the place and the sad outcast she'd been then. Tomorrow he'd offer to take them himself, and she'd relent, hurrying them through the tour, never leaving the path, a new, stingy tradition, one the kids laughed at, not knowing they were being cruel.

"Where are these meteor showers we're supposed to be seeing?" Meg asked.

"In the east," he said stiffly, swimming against the warm currents in his head. He was afraid he'd say something stupid or unintelligible and give himself away. "They say you can see them best between two and five, but there should be some singles starting about now."

The words didn't fit his mouth, came out square and ready-made, odd boxes that evaporated, leaving meaning. It must have been some new kind of hybrid.

He scanned the stars for movement, checking one section of the sky, then another. Lise took his hand as they looked up, knitting her fingers with his, and he thought he wouldn't get to talk to Meg. Everything she'd said so far had been censored for Lise's benefit, and meant to feed his curiosity, the same way his mother kept them in suspense, whether the issue was what was for dinner or what was in his father's will. Maybe everything in their family really was about attention, that infantile desire—including his pictures, his need for approval and lack of success. He couldn't write the thought off to being high.

"I see a plane," Meg said. "Does that count?"

"I've got two," Lise said, and helped them find the other one.

A few houses toward the point, someone turned on a dock light, then turned it off again, an accident.

The bell came across the water.

"Anything?"

"Nope."

"Nothing here."

Except he was watching one bright star winking, as if there were a disturbance in the lens of the atmosphere like a drop of water that drew the light to one side and then let it go, all in an instant, again and again. He thought of how far they'd traveled to be here, and how much further his mother and Arlene had come, their lives trailing behind them, dense with memories of rooms, though the ones that came to him were his own—

those college apartments in Boston, their living room window looking out on sunny Beacon Street, Lise's parents' beach place. Twenty years. The idea tired him.

Meg lit a cigarette with a Bic, her face and hands flaring, then disappearing again. "My neck hurts. I think you're supposed to do this lying down."

"I think you're right," Lise said, but none of them moved, so he didn't suggest the blanket.

Tomorrow—somehow—he would find the time to do the Putt-Putt. Maybe he'd go to the hardware for some lighter fluid. There'd been no word on Tracy Ann Caler, and there probably wouldn't be. Her flyers would fade on the telephone poles, shreds held by rusting staples.

The last of his beer was warm and he didn't want another, a signal that the night was over. Lise finished hers.

"Come on," he said, "shower!"

Lise squeezed his hand, embarrassed.

High up, planes silently drew lines between the stars. They all turned toward the bell. He thought of using it as an excuse; tomorrow was going to be long.

Meg stretched and glanced around as if checking the weather.

"Well," she said, slapping her hands down on her knees, "it doesn't look like this is going to happen."

Before he could agree, she stood and said her good nights and tottered off—so suddenly that he knew Lise would comment on it once she was gone, wonder out loud if she'd been drinking. That was wrong, he thought. She was being generous, leaving, and he was grateful. It meant that—tonight, at least—he didn't have to choose between the two of them.

22

In the middle of the night Sarah got up to pee. The fan was like a train. She sat on the toilet by the orange night-light, her elbows on her knees, her face in her hands. A breeze came through the screen, and the moon was over the big pine tree, and she thought of Mark, whether he was still awake, who he'd be with. She thought of school, and now she was glad it would be all new. People would still talk but not as much.

She wouldn't have to listen to Korn or the Deftones anymore. She wouldn't have to go to his stupid hockey games or eat dinner with his parents. She'd be free.

She was done but sat there watching the shadow of a small moth on the screen, heart-shaped and motionless among the other bugs. They crawled and bounced off the mesh, busy, while it stayed there, stuck, like it might be dead. What was it waiting for?

Friday

1

"Come on," Grandma said, "help me get rid of these," so they had eggs instead of Lucky Charms. They had to be quiet or they'd wake everyone else up. They couldn't go out on the dock without an adult. They couldn't play their Game Boys—they'd have to ask their mothers about that.

They were going to play tennis later, but the badminton net wouldn't stay up, and then Sam knocked the big wiffle ball in the lake and Aunt Arlene had to take off her flip-flops and wade in to get it.

"That can't be good for those racquets," she said. "Why don't you play a nice game of croquet?"

Justin wanted to play golf, after last night, but Grandma said the clubs in the garage were expensive and not for children. "Why don't you go ride your bikes?" she said.

Sam was better at it than Justin was, and kept pretending to crash into him, slamming his brakes on at the last minute and fishtailing sideways, leaving thick skid marks. He did it too hard once and almost knocked Justin down.

"Stop!" Justin said. "Idiot."

"Ya ya ya," Sam said, and did it again.

"Stop it!"

"Don't be such a spaz," Sam said, and pulled ahead, slowed almost to a stop, then turned around and circled behind him.

Justin did his best to ignore him. It was quiet with no one else out. Bugs flew through patches of sun on the lawns. He was glad it was the last day.

At home his PlayStation was waiting for him in the basement, and their old refrigerator full of ginger ale and Hi-C. Upstairs in the cupboards there would be Pop-Tarts and Easy Mac, and if it was nice Sarah would take him to the pool. If Michael Schulz was back from vacation they could go over to Turtle Pond and fish from the bridge. *Pokémon* was on every day now except Sunday, and next weekend his father would take them somewhere in his Camaro, maybe to a Tigers game at the new stadium, which looked really cool. He could stay up late because there was no school yet, and then he would read under the covers with his flashlight until his mother told him to turn it off.

Sam came wailing by and hit the brakes in front of him, showing off. "Race you to the marina."

"Okay," Justin said, and let him go.

Sam turned around. "Come on."

"Your bike's faster than mine."

"I'll give you a head start."

"How much?"

As they haggled, they passed the shortcut to the fishponds. It wasn't that far, just around the bend and down the long straightaway. "To the dock or just the parking lot?"

"To the dock."

He thought if he got ten seconds he might beat him.

"Okay," Sam said, "ten seconds. Starting . . . now."

It took him to one-thousand-three just to get going, tilting the whole bike right and then left with each long push until he couldn't hear Sam anymore. He ducked his head, and the road rolled under his tires, white stones stuck in the black asphalt. He tried to ride in a straight line, hunched against the wind like a racer. He should have counted to himself so Sam couldn't cheat, because in no time he was right behind him, calling, "You're meat, Carlisle!"

Justin cut the curve tight so Sam would have to go outside and beat him on the straightaway. A few more houses and they'd hit the entrance with the brown wooden sign and the log guardrails like a park, the tall grass on both sides, except there was a police car parked sideways blocking the road, and more police cars back under the trees in the middle of the lot, one of them a Winnebago with its doors open, and policemen standing around, and they both slowed and looked at each other, the race forgotten. Finally there was something to do.

2

"I know you want to," Lise said in the garage. "Why don't you just go and get it over with?"

"I don't, actually," Ken said. "They don't want me there. Besides, we already signed up."

"Seriously. We can start without you, it's not a problem."

"That's all right." As if that was the end of any discussion, he grabbed the racquets and went out to round up the boys.

Lise had seen this reasonable act before and knew what it hid, his evenness itself a symptom of obsession. Not the grand, romantic kind but its opposite, a methodical, nearly detached concentration on one thing, because the world to him was made of things, objects and moments that could be frozen and contemplated rather than lived and appreciated. He wanted nothing more than to run down to the marina and shoot a few rolls, find out what the story was—not, she thought, because he was worried about the girl, but because the idea of her being missing intrigued him, tempted him like any other project, and he needed coverage. Maybe it was cold of Lise to see it this way, but there was no other explanation. He'd never met the girl, and even he wasn't so sentimental that he could fall in love with a picture.

The idea was ridiculous, and yet she couldn't deny that she was jealous. She wasn't twenty, she didn't have a tragic story, never had. A girl from the suburbs, she'd gone to school and married, raised her children, worked. She had all the glamor of a bowl of oatmeal. Part of that was his fault, her life bent to his wishes, though he would claim the opposite was true, but ultimately her plainness came, like Meg's wildness, from within. At bottom she had a cautious heart, maybe from trying to please her parents, afraid she'd fall short of their expectations. She saw the same dutiful pleasantness (colorlessness, really) in Ella and feared her daughter would be like her, sadly adequate, part of the background, never the star.

She dug through the milk crate where they kept the balls.

"What do you think?" Meg asked, in shorts and worn sneakers, her ponytail pulled through the back of a cap. "Should we bother the girls?"

"Let them sleep."

"Do we have any new ones, or is that a stupid question?"

"Just these." Who knew how old they were. The can she held was metal, yellow and red with a mouth that would slice open your wrist if you weren't careful—long since outlawed, she assumed. They played once a year here, maybe twice, since Emily and Henry had given up tennis. There was even a can of dull white ones, still fuzzy and oily-smelling, and those had been on the way out when she was a teenager.

"Let's check them before we get up there," Meg said. "Give me a couple."

"The boys can do that."

They sent them out to the road, then called them back when they started having too much fun. She gave Rufus a dead one, and he took it under the chestnut and lay down, turning his head to gnaw on the rubber. Meg got some water and they were all set.

"The girls aren't coming?" Ken asked.

"By the time they get ready, we'll be done."

She knew the police wouldn't be finished by then, if it was what she thought it was. They'd be there all day, probably all weekend, taking pictures, searching the woods and bushes, sifting through the high grass, troopers in rubber gloves bagging cigarette butts and underwear, dusting a Coke can. And he'd be down there, he'd find a way—not long, no, he'd feign a natural curiosity, maybe leave his camera to placate her. That was almost worse, a kind of sacrifice to her.

They walked up the shadowed road between the oaks, past the Wisemans' and Nevilles', the boys swerving ahead on their bikes. Between the houses, the lake was bright and blue, fishermen trying the reeds, a few sailboats out, and she was surprised at how fast the week had gone by. It was the same at the beach—it took her a while to get into vacation mode, and then it was over. She was already thinking about the drive tomorrow, cleaning out the car. She thought she'd had enough of summer, or this summer. It was wrong of her, she knew—she'd liked Henry so much better than Emily.

"Look at that sweet Bug," Ken said, meaning the Nevilles' VW convertible, sitting in their garage.

"Did you see the Smiths' new addition?" Meg said. "It's huge."

"They're winterizing it."

It drove her crazy, the way they spoke of their neighbors, as if they actually knew them. Emily knew them socially, and Arlene, but those friendships hadn't passed to the next generation. She couldn't recall a single time in all their years together that Ken had said more to one of the Nevilles or Craigs than a hello on the road. Lise had done it herself, a casual half-wave hedging rejection, and yet she still felt an outsider, lacking that easy familiarity he and Meg shared like a secret language—Lerners and Crattys and Loudermilks.

The path wound through the cool woods, between the dappled ferns, a thin skin of moss showing the scars of shoes and bike tires, exposed bony roots scuffed to a dirty sheen. The light caught a giant spider-web, its owner weaving in the center, its long legs working like the fingers of a single hand. She could hear the boys opening the chain-link gate, then pulling it shut. She wondered if someone had found the girl and called the police, and she immediately thought of Ken, where he was this morning (in bed with her), as if he were a suspect.

He was. Whatever wasn't right with their marriage, she thought she could trace it to his evasions, what he dwelt on but didn't reveal, another reason she resented him talking so easily with Meg. At home she had to ask him questions in bed to get anything out of him, and then, cornered, he gave himself up grudgingly, their lovemaking afterward a reward he hadn't earned.

They came out into the sun and saw they had the courts to themselves—a good thing, because the near net was drooping, the cable slack. The boys had dropped their bikes on the ground and were inside, trying to hit home runs. The door protested when Ken pushed it open. Cracks an inch wide ran like fault lines through the asphalt, and because there wasn't a garbage can, around the green park bench lay a dangerous collection of rusty can tops, their pull rings sticking up.

"Nice," Meg said.

"I'll get them later," Ken said, and toed them under the bench. "How are we going to do this? We've got an extra."

"Let's just hit for a while to warm up," Lise said. "There's room."

She double-knotted her Tretorns and fitted her visor in place, sloughed her racquet cover and took Sam's side. The far side was in the sun, and Justin had to shield his eyes and then missed the ball completely, the force of his swing spinning him. Meg came to his rescue, backing him up, but Sam hit it to his backhand and he just waved at it, spaghetti-wristed. Every volley stopped with him, the balls multiplying behind him.

"You can borrow my sunglasses," Sam offered, and they met at the net, but it didn't help. To make things even, Ken joined them, putting Justin in the middle, and Lise felt sorry for him. Meg and Jeff were both athletic, so was Sarah. At best Justin was tentative. He was flat-footed and turned the racquet as he swung, so when he did hit the ball, it caught the wood and shot off in odd directions. She could see him reddening, hunching his shoulders after each whiff, dragging his racquet. She tried to guide the ball to Meg and Ken and then a soft hop to his forehand, rooting for him, while Sam sprayed all over the place, happy to chase the balls into the far court.

"Good one," Lise said when Justin returned one just wide, but he was scowling, and when he missed again and whacked his racquet on the ground, Meg took him aside, bent over, lecturing him face-to-face.

"I've got one," Ken said, and started them again.

Sam had run off and it was just the two of them ranging alley to alley. She played so seldom now that she was surprised to find she could still hit her backhand with some power. She couldn't remember the last time she really ran. She was sweating, loosening up, a lifetime of private lessons flowing back into her limbs, her footwork returning. Topspin, drop shots—it was all there. Back when Henry and Emily still played, the couples paired off and had a doubles tournament, which invariably came down to how Ken was serving, and even then she could pull out some breaks to give them a win. There was a long stretch of years they'd been unbeatable, probably still were.

Justin took a seat on the bench, and after some long volleys Sam joined him. He'd brought his Game Boy and the two hunched over it, lost.

"Unbelievable," Ken said.

"Looks like Canadian doubles," Lise said.

"You up for it?" Meg asked.

"Are you?"

"Oh, so that's how it's going to be?"

"Better get ready to do some running," Ken said.

"You better get ready to do some losing."

Lise served first, usually her forte, but had trouble getting her first serve in and ran more than she wanted to. She won her serve, then lost Ken's. When she let up at all they played her side to side, trying to wear her down. She lobbed the ball deep to get back into position, then tried to split the middle. Soon she was conceding points, looking for easy kill shots, like the high hops Meg left on her second serve. Lise knew it was mean to go to Meg's backhand so often, but then her serve deserted her and anything was fair game.

"Vicious," Ken said.

"Brutal," Meg said.

Lise smiled and waved her racquet at their compliments. She was running too hard to talk. She retreated to the one patch of shade between points, clinging to that magical advantage. She couldn't remember Ken serving so well and thought he was pressing just to torture her. She came up with a pair of aces and went up 4–3, then broke Meg again—the weak link.

All she had to do was hold service—easy. She took her time. The sun was above them and her throat was a flue. The line of sweat on her visor inched toward the tip of the bill, her hair slick on her neck. She walked back after winning another point, her eyes on the ground, and caught a fat ant crossing the baseline, looked up and saw the clouds moving behind the trees, the entire sky shaking with every step. The heat came off her face, pulsed behind her eyes. Her head felt light as a dry gourd, a bright, empty room holding only the score. Even Ken's girl stood off to the side, by Emily, the two of them spectral, bleached by the white light.

"Forty love," she said, "set point," and missed long with her first.

She looked around the fence for another ball and thought she saw someone walking through the woods. The boys were gone, maybe it was them.

To her surprise there was a ball in her pocket.

"Wide," Ken called from the other side, and she shifted over, careful not to foot-fault.

She was disappointed. She'd wanted to end it with him—because it was between the two of them, finally. Meg was just in the way, the same with Emily and the girl. Lise imagined a line of searchers sweeping past the courts while they played, wading through the ferns. If she won, they would keep going, walk on into the woods and never bother them again. If she lost, they'd stop and find her, his precious dead girl, let him take pictures of her laid out on the ground. And then Lise thought it didn't matter. It wasn't like he'd ever be fascinated with her.

He had been once, but that part of their life was gone and impossible to get back, like her game.

"Forty fifteen," she said, and let it rip.

3

They sat on the porch with the radio playing the classical station from Jamestown, the occasional powerboat or car drowning out the strings. A breeze rustled the leaves without disturbing the shadows on the lawn. By the door Rufus lay capsized, his legs stretched out, paws twitching in his sleep.

"I'll tell you what," Emily said. "If I had the money I wouldn't be looking around here. I'd try somewhere like Point Chautauqua where they're done building. You've heard about the lady from Chicago and her party barge?"

Arlene hadn't.

"Oh, you're in for a treat. The road association is all up in arms. It seems this lady from Chicago bought the Smiths' other lot, the one back by the marina road, thinking it has lake access, which it doesn't. Now she wants to park her party barge at the common dock."

"How big is it?"

"Twenty-five feet, I don't know. There's supposed to be a meeting next week. We've been getting letters on it since last fall. You can bet this kind of thing doesn't happen at Point Chautauqua."

She couldn't be serious, Arlene thought. They'd never stayed at Point Chautauqua. She didn't honestly think they could buy into some-one else's genteel tradition the way the meat people from Chicago scooped up all the old Victorians at the Institute.

"I've always liked that area," Emily confessed. "There are some beautiful period places there."

"Expensive."

"I'm sure they don't come up for sale very often. It's all families that have been there forever."

"I've never stayed on that side," Arlene said.

"You get the sunset. I think it's more of a camp-type atmosphere."

"It would be different."

"*I* think it would be nice."

Arlene thought she might be fishing for her approval. They both knew she was powerless in this, that Emily was including her as a cour-tesy, like her father mentioning the family finances over dinner, a tactical flash of a closely kept hand.

The music returned, buoyant and joyful, something in flight. Over toward Midway the makings of a race were gathering, a school of Lasers tacking back and forth, weaving like cars before the starting line. She was so used to this view. She tried to imagine what the boats looked like from that side and couldn't quite.

There was so little to hold on to that the smallest change was a loss. She would even miss the Lerners' alarm going off, the dank smell of the shallows, the mildewed rooms.

She was tempted to ask Emily flat out, offer to buy the place her-self, borrow on her life insurance.

She wouldn't, of course. Couldn't, out of some sense of dignity, an invisible line. Emily wouldn't take her seriously.

Beyond the trees an engine brayed, steady—a big speedboat, but they couldn't locate it, and then a shape cut through an opening above them, an old silver seaplane banking low over the water. They followed it haltingly through the gaps until the racket passed.

"I'm sure that's not legal," Emily said.

"It's a pretty one."

"Kenneth would know what it is."

Henry would have, but neither of them said it. They sat back and watched the water like a stage, waiting for something else of interest to appear.

Arlene thought that this time tomorrow they would be packing up to leave, and imagined Pittsburgh, the hot park, her apartment musty from being shut up, her plants wilted. In the past she would have been preparing for her classes, laying out the calendar by chapters. Now the days ahead seemed endless, space that needed to be taken up somehow. Reading, and trips to the Frick. She liked the park in the fall, kicking the leaves, the paths that wound down under the bridge. She'd tried it last year when Henry was in the hospital but gave up before she passed the tennis courts. She knew how things got ruined, and didn't want to do that to something she relied on. Instead she visited dutifully until it felt like a vigil, and by then it was. The last month he couldn't stop apologizing for putting them through this, and it was true, every day she had to steel herself so she wouldn't seem shocked by his thin arms sticking out of the gown. In the parking garage Emily cursed him for worrying about them, as if he should be thinking only of himself now, the world a distraction unworthy of his attention.

"They're going over," Emily warned, pointing, just in time for Arlene to see one of the Lasers heel dangerously before recovering.

"It must be blowing out there," she said, and again the music returned like a soundtrack, filling in the silence. Bees zigzagged through the croquet set. She didn't have much to pack, yet she wanted everything— the fireplace, the awful drapes, as if she could turn her apartment into the cottage, keep this lazy feeling year-round.

"Are you making the trek to Panama Rocks?" Emily asked.

"I'm afraid I'll have to decline."

"Discretion being the better part."

"Exactly. You?"

"Mrs. Klinginsmith's supposed to call. Are the girls up yet?"

"Not to my knowledge."

"Well they better get their act together because they're not lounging around here."

The race was a chaos of sails. They must have been rounding a buoy. There was a break in the music and Emily took up her book.

"Want anything?" Arlene asked, getting up.

"No, I'm fine."

Inside, Arlene noticed the puzzle was half done but thought she didn't have the energy to finish it, or the time. It didn't make sense—the day was maybe the nicest they'd had. The wasted effort nagged at the teacher in her. She'd never been to Buckingham Palace, unlike Emily, and she wondered when the picture was from. Forty, fifty years ago, when she should have gone, Walter taking her in stiff hotel sheets, ordering room service while she showered. It would be left unfinished, swept into the box, the completed sections bending like good lace, and she had the absurd idea of taking it home and setting up the card table she used for grading, working quietly under the hot light late into the night. She could imagine what Emily would say. She might as well take the board games while she was at it.

She hoped Goodwill would be able to use it, some underprivileged child from Jamestown fitting the spiked iron fence together. She could see it ending up in a wet dumpster, the pieces sprinkled over donated sheets and gray underwear. She'd never even liked the puzzle. It was pure selfishness, childish, like her instant rejection of the mere idea of Point Chautauqua.

Some of that was jealousy, the ancient hurt of being displaced by Emily and then the children, her birthright traded away, all because she'd chosen to make a life for herself. That was childish too, picking at old wounds, yet at times she felt justified. Not that it made a difference at this point.

She would take anything. Pride was a poor companion. She could see why women her age fell for boyish con men.

She made it into the kitchen and stopped between the fridge and the sink, stood there frozen, squinting just short of closing her eyes, concentrating. For the life of her she couldn't remember what she'd come in for. Iced tea? A peach?

The damn puzzle. Let it rot for all she cared.

What was it?

She tried retracing her steps like she did at home—she'd been sitting with Emily, came inside, saw the puzzle—and when that failed, looked around the room for clues. The dish soap stood honey-colored by the sink, the teapot sat cold on the stove. The only thing on the red-and-white-checked tablecloth was a stack of paper napkins, the fancy kind Emily liked. Outside, the cicadas were already beginning to simmer, shrill as an

electrical charge, dissipating then winding up again. At home they would
be the same, and then one day they would be gone, the season over, their
empty shells stuck to the trees.

"Oh fudge," she said. And then she remembered.

4

Ella watched her. There was nothing else she could do. She watched the
way she walked, the way she stood in the sun from the window, the way
she bent over to close her sleeping bag. She watched the way her body
filled her nightshirt and the way she gathered her hair back and kept the
barrette in her teeth. When there was no one else around Ella found herself staring, absorbing or memorizing her, marveling at how perfect she
was. It was sick.

And it was dumb. It only discouraged her more.

She rolled over so she wouldn't have to see her go into the bathroom, then tried not to imagine what she was doing from the sounds. Sarah
closed the door but she could walk in and Sarah wouldn't think anything,
so she lay there waiting, searching the ugly jungle of the carpet and feeling stupid.

The shower pounded the stall. Now Sarah was pulling her nightshirt over her head, now she was stepping in, the shock of the water raising goose bumps. Now she was getting her hair wet.

Ella rolled over again to make herself stop. Her shorts from yesterday reminded her that she was supposed to pick up her dirty clothes,
and she yawned and rolled halfway back so she was looking at the ceiling, the pillow holding her head, the rest of her pinned to the floor by
gravity and other facts. She didn't want to go to Panama Rocks or tubing
or to stupid Webb's for dinner, she just wanted to lie here until it was time
for the fireworks and then go to sleep and get up tomorrow and leave.

At home no one would know. She'd think about her when she was alone, but once school started she'd be busy. She wouldn't forget, she wouldn't be that lucky, but the feeling wouldn't be like this all the time—at least she hoped not. If it was, she didn't know what she'd do. She had her e-mail address, she could call her, but the phone was even harder than talking face-to-face.

She thought of Sarah taking her hand during the fireworks—like at the party in her dream—and then the two of them kissing in the dark and no one noticing.

The water stopped. Sarah would stand there a second to drip-dry, then open the door and start toweling off, bending to do her legs, wrapping her hair in a turban.

Ella shook her head and pushed the flap off, irritated at the trapped heat of the bag. She would be with her all day today, but with everyone else around, and tomorrow she'd be gone. The thought brought up the same flush of panic she'd felt since Niagara Falls. It was like being sick, the alarming waves of nausea that warned you right before you threw up. She pressed it down, a reflex. Tomorrow would be a relief, though she couldn't see how she would get through the weeks before school. All she could see was her room, her made bed, the day stretching out ahead of her and nowhere to go.

In the bathroom Sarah blew her nose—using toilet paper, Ella knew. She'd throw it in the toilet, not the wastebasket, they'd agreed that was nasty.

And then the door opened and there she was in her nightshirt, a wet spot clinging to one hip, and even lying down Ella was conscious of her own posture.

"It's all yours," Sarah said.

Ella obeyed, then with the door closed took off her glasses and rubbed her eyes. In the mirror she was disappointed with her hair, as if it might have saved her face.

It didn't matter anyway.

The water was still hot, and she hung her PJs from the knobs of the linen closet. As she stepped in, the fine spray touched her first and she gasped at it, and then the heavy warmth spread across her chest and ran down her stomach. The sulfur reeked. She bowed her head and felt the chill around her legs, turned up the heat and stood with the water matting her hair until everything was one solid temperature. She closed her eyes, surrendering to the feeling, and remembered a horror movie where the scalding water wouldn't turn off and the stall door wouldn't open so this girl drowned behind the glass, a fish in a tank. It was dumb but made her check that the drain at her feet was working. She bent down to reach the shampoo in the corner and her butt bumped the stall, knocking her forward so she had to catch her balance with a hand on the wall.

"Graceful," she said, echoing her mother, and squeezed a handful of shampoo.

She was just rubbing it in when the door opened, a cold gust stirring the fog above her. Her instinct was to turn away, but she stopped herself, twisted to make sure by the shape of the person that it was Sarah, and it was, stopping in front of the mirror, probably to brush her hair. Ella stood straight, facing the shower. She knew from experience that if Sarah leaned her head to the right she could see the blurry outline of her, the abstract patches of color. Compared to Sarah, she had little to offer, and again she felt the urge to turn toward the wall and hide herself.

There was no reason. Sarah wouldn't be looking.

Ella lathered her hair and ducked under the rush, closing her eyes like she normally did. She rinsed, feeling daring and paranoid, the air touching her everywhere. The water suddenly turned cooler, losing strength, and blindly she twisted the knob all the way. It helped for a second but that was it. It always happened at Chautauqua—she was the last one.

Sarah had the dryer out, and Ella thought she might finish her shower before Sarah was done brushing her hair. She would notice if Ella stalled until she was gone.

The water was cold, puckering her front. Sarah teased her hair and smoothed it with a hand, and Ella thought of stepping through the door wet, standing on the bath mat, dripping, without a towel. Sarah could turn away or make a joke, but at least she would have tried.

It sounded good when she put it that way, but that wasn't how it would turn out, and anyway, that wasn't what she wanted. That wasn't who she was.

The dryer refused to stop. Even freezing, the water smelled. Ella turned sideways, but that was just as bad. She needed to grit her teeth and finish. She bent down for the conditioner and stood straight in the spray, face front, as if nothing was wrong.

5

"How am I supposed to know what time it is when I don't have a watch?" Sarah protested.

"You still can't find it?" Aunt Margaret asked.

"No."

"I'm not surprised," his mother said. "You can't find anything up there."

"We cleaned up," Ella said. "It's not there."

"Whoa, whoa," their mother said, "try another tone," and the way Ella shut up, Sam thought she would tell on him. He felt like the time at the Stop-n-Shop when he thought the lady behind them in line saw him.

"Did you look in the car?" his father asked. "It could have fallen between the seats."

"When was the last time you saw it?" his mother asked.

They were all hot from tennis and were sitting on the porch. The argument had started because the girls hogged all the hot water, and now he was the one who was going to get in trouble.

"I had it when we went to the movies because I remember looking at it when we came out."

"What day was that?"

"That was Monday," his father said.

"Did you look in the couch?" Aunt Arlene asked.

"No."

"You're not going to find it if you don't look," Aunt Margaret said.

"I'm sure it will turn up," Grandma said. "I'll keep my eye out for it while I'm cleaning this afternoon."

"Why are you cleaning?" his mother asked, and the conversation swerved away from him, turned safe and then boring.

He and Justin went outside and knocked around the croquet balls in the sun. They were supposed to go to Panama Rocks, but what he really wanted was to go tubing. When he thought of the boat he saw it blasting across the water with him behind it, and below, way down at the cold brown bottom of the lake, the watch ticking in the weeds.

The meeting on the porch was breaking up. They weren't taking showers, they were going to go all grubby. They'd just get dirty anyway.

"We need to wear shoes," his mother announced to everyone. "No sandals or open toes. Boots are best but sneakers are okay."

All morning he'd been riding his bike in his flip-flops and thought he might get in trouble for it, but when she came out to bug him she didn't say anything. She made him put away his mallet the right way, and his ball, so no one would trip over it (but not the wickets). Aunt Margaret took Justin inside and they were alone.

"Thank you," his mother said when he was done, and stopped him with a hand on his shoulder like she might give him a hug, except she didn't bend down, just held him there so he had to look up.

Her face was serious and he realized what she was going to ask him.

He'd kill Ella, the tattletale.

"You haven't seen it, have you?"

"What?" he said, making his face blank.

It wasn't fair; they had to catch him.

"What. Your cousin's watch." She made it sound obvious, sick of him playing dumb. She seemed sure, as if the only thing he could do was confess. He could say anything and she wouldn't believe him—and without any proof. Later he'd be sad about this, but now he was angry that she was blaming him just from what Ella said. It made it easier to say no.

6

They went out by the drive, for the children, though the boys had reported it. As they cruised by the neat white houses and professionally tended lawns, the lake glinting between them, Ken felt an odd sense of loss, an opportunity missed, as if they were leaving for good and he was abandoning her. Lise had told him to go, shoot, but he knew it was just another test, and those had become more important to her, and not only because they were here. She was unsure of herself and therefore of him, and he couldn't figure out what he'd done or not done to trigger this latest fit of insecurity. Nothing had changed between them.

They had to go past it. There was only one road. From the highway he could see the cars far across the ponds, and for an instant processed the shot, already composed for him, the low line of trees and giant sky, the insignificance of Man (with the shadow of his father in there somewhere). Morgan would groan and flip the print over as if it hurt his eyes. Don't try to make statements, just feel what's there. Like most of Morgan's advice, it was too sixties, too groovy for Ken, but he'd never say that, not until he did something worthwhile.

Beside him, driving, Meg let the scene slide by without a word, as did Lise behind him. In the way back, the boys craned for a look, the girls ignoring them, bored, and he wondered if his fascination was only a poorly rationalized version of theirs, juvenile and mindless, at base sensational.

He could feel something around Tracy Ann Caler, he couldn't say what—a buzz, a current—but it was there, good or bad. What was almost more exciting was that no one else seemed to have caught on to it. He wanted to believe his attraction was real and noble, if mysterious, and took the lack of any actual connection between them and the strength of his feelings as proof of rather than evidence against that. She was as much his as she was her abductors', and he could see the slipperiness of his position. He wondered if that would change if they found her. It would have to, he thought. Otherwise it was just rubbernecking, *Life*-magazine crap.

"Everyone ready for Gravity Hill?" Meg asked the car at large.

From the back came mocking, halfhearted cheers.

"Ah, let's skip it this year," Ken deadpanned. "They're probably too old."

"I want to do it," Justin spoke up.

"What about the rest of you? Let's take a vote."

All he got was muttering, though a real vote would have been close. Lise was only here because she didn't want to be stuck in the house with his mother, and Meg only came for the kids. Sam and Justin were on his side, but that was it—boys against girls.

"How many say yes?"

"Not funny, Dad," Ella said.

"Okay," he said, "we'll go."

He used the ensuing silence to look out the window, his eyes sifting, gleaning. He'd brought the Nikon, but the light was too strong, shadows sharp on the trees, every leaf precise. The road was so familiar he could see beyond the fronts of the Snug Harbor Lounge and the rotting billboards and the cabin of the pro shop at Willow Run to the pastel asbestos houses and their sorry garages, the high weeds in the ditches gone brown. September was coming. He could feel the day getting away from him and he wanted to stop the car and walk along the berm, saving it all. He could follow the road around the lake that way, make a circle; all it would take was patience. He could shoot the seasons, show skaters standing where the ferry ran, the Rod and Gun Club's built-in grills capped with snow. Thousands of dull, unassuming photos. He would head out every morning with his lunch and a water bottle in a backpack. He wouldn't think, he'd just bang away, then sort them out later on the contact sheets. When he died they'd find hundreds of undeveloped rolls, every inch of Chautauqua documented, a kind of map.

"Our turn must be coming up," Meg asked, testing him.

"Up on the right," he said, but she was already signaling.

She knew. They used to come every year.

The land back here was rolling, dairy farms cut from the woods, rusted wire fences. The barns tempted him, but it was pointless from the car. They had to go under the interstate, and then halfway across a yellow field the road abruptly turned to oiled gravel, stones plinking beneath them.

"I don't remember it being this bad," Meg said, sounding just like his mother.

It stopped, and the asphalt was all patches, jostling them. The woods closed in on both sides. Ahead, a kid Sam's age was driving an ATV on the wrong side of the road without a helmet. Before they caught up to him he turned onto a dirt trail and was lost in his own dust. The road rose to cross some train tracks, and as Meg slowed to save her suspension, Ken could see far down the green tunnel of leaves. They could have buried her anywhere out here, just left her back in the woods somewhere. The marina seemed too public.

It shouldn't matter to him. The day was taken up. Tomorrow they were leaving, Monday he'd be at work again. If he had another week—but it was typical of him to come up with an impossible project and then not follow through. This was no different. All summer he'd gotten nothing done.

"Gravity Hill," Meg read, and slowed for the turn.

It was in the middle of nowhere, marked by a blue sign like a rest area with a boxy picture of a camera on top. There was an official pull-out. A couple of chained picnic tables sat in the grass by the roadside but there were no garbage cans, and a sign at the back of the lot advertised the fine for dumping. In the past they'd all gotten out to watch, the children running alongside the car, but now Meg just stopped at the fat white decal that served as a starting line.

"Everybody ready?" she asked.

Nothing.

"I said, is everybody ready?"

"Yes!" the boys said, and she shifted into neutral and took her hands off the wheel.

They waited. He'd actually taken pictures of this, yards of video over the years, all the different cars they'd owned. As a child, he'd watched home movies of his parents' two-tone Chevy creeping uphill, his father waving sheepishly from the window in his Ray-Bans. His mother had her turn in a mid-sixties Cutlass, her hair an embarrassment. Even he and Meg had squared off as teenagers in their beaters, a drag race in slow motion.

The effect had something to do with how the roadbed had been laid out and graded. The road appeared to dip between the two hills—or it only appeared that the second hill was a hill. You looked up and couldn't see over the hump so you were tricked into thinking you were going uphill. His father could explain it. Sam and Ella knew better than to ask.

"Are we moving at all?" Lise asked.

"It takes longer if it's windy," Meg said.

"Is it windy?"

He zipped his window down and peered over the sill like the gunwale of a ship. The road was inching beneath the running board. "We're going."

"You can barely tell," Lise said.

"Just wait."

There was a pop can on one of the picnic tables, and he imagined Tracy Ann Caler here with her family as a girl, the pictures they would have taken, pictures her parents would look at now and remember her by. He'd never known her, so how was his project supposed to be a memorial, if that's what it was?

He didn't know what it was, and he was right to worry. The feeling—whatever it was—wasn't simple. If it made him queasy, what did it do to Lise? But wasn't that even more reason to follow it? The police would still be there when they got back.

"I can feel it!" Justin said.

"Now we're going," Meg said, though the needle she pointed to pointed to zero.

He could feel it too, and shouted, "Here we go!"

It seemed impossible, looking at the hill rising in front of them, but slowly the van began to freewheel, leaving the picnic tables behind, the trees creeping by on both sides.

"Weird," Ella said.

Every sense said down but they were going up, or maybe it was the other way around. It was a trick, impossible except for the feeling in his stomach that they were falling—faster and faster, as if they couldn't stop. Meg held her hands in the air to prove she wasn't doing anything. They all clapped as they gathered speed, even the girls, all of them headed for the crest, drawn on by invisible forces.

7

The parking lot for Panama Rocks was starred with weeds. Theirs was the only car there. As a child Meg had been afraid of the place, setting nightmares here, faceless killers chasing her through the cold, mossy boulders and shadowy trees, trapping her in dead ends where she clawed her fingernails to shreds trying to climb the sheer walls. She dreaded their yearly real-life visit, the jokes that focused on Fat Man's Misery—or worse, went unspoken, all of them sorry for her. Now she was surprised at how small and harmless it was, even quaint (for a torture chamber), a half-assed roadside attraction slowly going to seed.

It looked closed except the front gate was tied back with a chain. There was an octagonal picnic pavilion in dark wood, and a long open barn, both overgrown and deserted, the eaves stitched with spiderwebs. The snack counter by the entrance was blocked off with plywood. The only person there was at the ticket window, a thin man in his sixties in a Bills cap, smoking and reading a fat Stephen King paperback. He gave them a map of the rocks, had the adults sign waivers for the children and pointed them toward the entrance.

Inside the fence a sign warned them to stay on the designated path and not climb on the rocks. There were no pets allowed, and no disposable items of any kind. RUNNING IS DANGEROUS. THERE HAVE BEEN SERIOUS ACCIDENTS.

"Oh great," Lise said. "Just what a mother wants to see."

"The liability must kill them," Ken said. "I don't see how they stay in business."

"They're not spending it on upkeep," Meg said, "that's for sure," because the warped two-by-four railing along the trail had peeled down to the bare wood, curling flakes of white paint caught in the grass. She was sure it had been there when she was a girl, but stopped herself before her memory could restore it. It seemed wrong, being nostalgic about a place she despised. There was something insidious in the way the mind worked, welcoming anything familiar, like her sex dreams of Jeff.

It shouldn't matter to her what he did now. They'd been separated in every way before except legally, and yet she saw his plan to remarry as an attack on her.

The boys ran ahead of them like dogs, and they called them back and asked them to please be careful, just as her parents had. The girls weren't interested, sauntering along behind them, Sarah picking at her split ends. When they got home the whole Mark thing would explode. Meg was grateful she would be sober for it, but knew she would receive the brunt of her unhappiness. She deserved it, maybe even desired it, as payback. She had to be strong enough to accept that, not let things get personal, a battle of wills. She needed them to have a good year, and she thought they could now that the house thing was settled. Jeff could go fuck himself. It was just the three of them now.

The railing ended and the trail curved downhill, rocky shortcuts connecting the switchbacks. Ken warned the boys not to wander. The signs identifying the different species of trees were barely legible. She read them and forgot them instantly. She saw a Butterfinger wrapper, picked it up and tucked it in her back pocket. Where the shortcuts crossed, the path was uneven, stony ruts cut by runoff. It was much cooler under the canopy, you almost needed a sweater. Years ago, this was when her stomach would fill with hot fluid, her bowels drop, knowing there was no turning back. "Oh come on," her mother would encourage her, as if this was fun.

Today she felt nothing, only a vague impatience to be home, getting ready for the beginning of school. They had to go out and buy supplies, new jeans for Justin, a good winter coat for Sarah. She could do it now without sweating every penny, all because of her mother. While she relied on that fact, she still hadn't fully digested it. She thought this must be how it felt to win the lottery—lucky and unreal, as if everything could be taken away just as suddenly.

She had to tell Ken the truth. Eventually, she thought. Over the phone.

They came to the base of the trail, a wooden square with the number 1 nailed to a stake in the ground. In the birches the rocks loomed like giant heads sunk in the hillside, their lichened faces layered and stepped, dripping groundwater. Tree roots grew like vines over the greening ledges. She waved at a tangle of gnats.

"Okay," Ken said, unfurling the map, "let's see what we have here. Castle Rock."

"Where's the castle?" Lise asked.

They tipped their heads and squinted, but none of them could see the resemblance.

"Moving on," Ken said. "Number two: the Mayflower."

"That one?" Meg pointed.

"I guess."

The boys scooted between the huge stones, Justin trying to keep up with Sam.

"Careful," she called. "It's slippery."

She could have sworn Fat Man's Misery was near the end, a kind of final test, but it was early, number 4. It couldn't have been simpler—two sheer walls that almost touched, the crevice between them Justin's size at the bottom, outlined by sunlight from the other side. There was nothing menacing about it. If she were shorter she could squeeze through easily.

"What's this one?" Lise asked, and when Ken hesitated, Meg told her.

"I could never fit through it as a kid."

"You never tried," Ken said.

"You never gave me the chance. You were too busy making fun of me, remember? Margaret's Misery."

"That's terrible," Lise said, but he didn't offer an apology, and Meg felt ridiculous dragging up the past when her own was such a mess. Especially with the secret she was conveniently keeping, waiting till it was safe to tell him.

She'd tell them about Jeff and Stacey at the last second, as if it were a surprise to her.

It had been. He'd done it just to ruin her vacation. She couldn't believe he'd be so cruel—or yes, she could. After the last year, she could believe anything.

They watched Sam and Justin squat down and shoulder through—Ken leaning against a tree to steady his camera—and then Sarah and Ella, that easy. The boys whooped and screamed behind the rocks, making their voices spooky, and she remembered Ken doing the same thing while she tagged along behind her parents, smoldering as she kicked at stones. Just thinking of her childhood made her feel childish. She wanted to climb up to the crack and see how big it was, maybe slither through just to prove she could. It wouldn't change anything, and she was self-conscious with them all there. If she were alone she would probably do it and ruin her clothes and then feel stupid.

They walked on, past Crow's Foot and Indian Fireplace and Paradise Alley, past the Golden Gate and the Tower of Babel and Counterfeiter's Den. By now it all looked the same to her.

"Who came up with these names?" Lise asked.

Ken went ahead so he could shoot from above, lying down on top of the rocks and leaning out so far that Lise yelled up, telling him to be careful.

"I swear, he's worse than the kids," she said—something her mother would say of her father, that she herself had said of Jeff.

Meg thought they had it backwards. Adults *were* worse. Kids couldn't help being self-centered—needed to be. They didn't know what would happen when they did things and how they could hurt other people. There was a difference between ignorance and stupidity.

She wanted to be honest with Ken about the house. She thought she'd have a chance to talk with him last night. And he'd understand, that was the terrible thing. He wouldn't resent her mother bailing her out or think she was a hypocrite, even if he did initially. Maybe that was why she held off telling him.

Jeff she couldn't deal with right now. She'd have to soon enough, and with all of her concentration she pushed him and Stacey out of her mind. This was her time.

They finished the lower part of the trail and she and Lise corralled the kids and drove them uphill to the bald tops of the rocks. The path ran along the edge. It was dangerous up here, the gaps and crevices tempting, and there were no fences to stop people from jumping across. She wasn't surprised there'd been accidents. Lise had to take Sam by the hand. Justin stayed clear. Here was the Ice Cave and the Covered Bridge, and the last one, the Gap, an anticlimax.

"That's all she wrote," Ken said, and folded the brochure away.

"I don't know why," Meg said. "It seemed shorter this time."

"It did?" Lise asked.

"I guess I remembered it differently."

Once the words were out of her mouth, she realized how they sounded. She only meant that the place felt strange to her, smaller, that she couldn't believe she'd ever been intimidated by it.

The snack bar was closed indefinitely, much to Justin's disgust. She remembered the wrapper in her back pocket but there was nowhere to throw it. She needed to clean the car anyway.

She got the air going and buckled up, then made sure everyone was safe. As she pulled out she gave the place a last look. The sun warmed the trees, left everything beneath them in deep shadow—a postcard. The parking lot was empty, only the flimsy railings leading to the snack bar, the old man in the ticket window reading his Stephen King. There was nothing to be afraid of. That life was behind her now—not gone, no, it was still a part of her, but it belonged to the past, and she needed to keep it there, to relinquish her grip on it, as hard as that might be, if not impossible.

She started off, driving along beside the barn and the picnic pavilion. "Say good-bye to Panama Rocks," she said.

"Good-bye!" they all hollered.

8

It was past twelve and they hadn't come back yet. Emily needed to stop reading and get something to eat, but the day was too pleasant, as was the silence she and Arlene had achieved. The radio was playing a Mozart piano concerto, a big ice-cream sundae of a piece that went with the view of the lake, the shadows on the dock. It was a perfect day for golf, and she wished she and Kenneth could go again. But then, it would be an absolute zoo today, the beginning of the weekend. Maybe it was just as well.

Henry's shoes. She should get them before they slipped her mind.

She had to remember the salt and pepper shakers, and the tumblers for Margaret. The red Fiestaware pitcher. She hadn't decided about the teakettle, and she was sure she'd find things in the drawers—old church keys and nestled sets of measuring spoons that summoned up memories. There were beer cartons in the garage she could use to pack everything, wrap the breakables in newspaper. And that was just the kitchen. She hadn't even looked at the upstairs yet.

It was easier to lose herself in the high sky, the clouds blooming heroic above the hills, very Hudson River School. Any urge to move dissolved in this vision, her inertia sharpened and sweetened by the Mozart, and then her book seemed foolish and uninteresting, a waste of time. She needed another week here without the children.

She wished Mrs. Klinginsmith would call already. She'd hoped—vainly—that the septic guy would come and do his thing while everyone was out, but no, she would be spared nothing. All the more reason to savor these peaceful minutes before the storm.

She thought she was calm, considering—too calm, possibly. Her worry all along had been that she would regret selling the place when it was too late, but that wouldn't happen, she already regretted it. She almost wanted the septic guy to find a problem—if not for Margaret.

Beside her, Arlene shifted and her cushion farted. Rufus raised his head a second, then subsided. Emily tried to remember where she'd found the cushions, and why she'd chosen the blue roses (it was probably all they had at the Jamesway). Their faded ugliness touched her, and for a moment she thought she could use them at home, a little bit of Chautauqua in the backyard. Not seriously though—there was no room in the car.

A breeze stirred the trees, sent leaves fluttering into the lake. She felt like a nap, but there was too much to do. She wasn't tired, just scattered, distracted by so many loose ends and the inevitability of leaving.

There were peaches in there that needed to be eaten, and meat from last night, and a pitcher of lemonade the children hadn't touched.

She couldn't forget Henry's plaid thermos, the one he took with him fishing—probably out in the garage. She dreaded having to burrow through that mess. It would be easier to ask Kenneth, since that was his jurisdiction.

She remembered seeing a TV movie around Christmastime about a widow who found a cigar box of old love letters while she was going through her husband's things, and in learning his secrets, discovered herself. Nothing like that had happened to her. Henry had been reliable to the end. He'd had time to go over their finances with her, the insurance and how the taxes would fall out. Later, talking with Barney Pontzer, it all proved true, rounded off to the nearest thousand.

She hadn't gone through Henry's office or pawed over his workshop yet, though occasionally she'd flick on the lights and walk through them, admiring his blotter and his circular saw (both immaculate, just as he'd left them), as if touring the house of someone famous. During his life he was steady in his enthusiasms, and they had been modest. His idea of a great treat was taking the whole family out to Poli's or Tambellini's, announcing it at breakfast so she wouldn't start dinner before he got home. The only time Henry had surprised her was by dying, and she had not suddenly become a stronger person, just alone.

From the road came the sustained squeal of brakes, a lull, then a tap on the gas, a lurch forward and the brakes again. Rufus didn't move.

"Mail's here," Arlene said without looking up from her book.

"He's early. Remind me to stop it tomorrow."

She stepped over Rufus to get to the door. The station wagon was down by the Loudermilks', the man leaning out of his window. She approached the box slowly, as if it might explode. She wasn't expecting anything, unless Louise had written her on her own. Overnight a spider had spun a web around the flag, trapping it against the side. She looked up and down the road, then jumped back as she opened the door.

Nothing, just the mail—glossy coupons, dueling flyers for the Golden Dawn and the Quality Market, and the fall issue of *The Navigator*, the high school newsletter they received for paying their taxes every year. She ducked her head, double-checking for ants, then slapped it shut. Let the new owners worry about them. They still had to schedule a termite inspection. Maybe they'd find something then.

Walking back to the house, she remembered taking care of her parents' place in Kersey before it finally sold. The realtor had suggested taking up the carpet to highlight the oak floors, and the day Emily visited (she and Henry stopping by the cemetery first), she'd found it ripped up and discarded in the backyard with the old kitchen cabinets, as if the house had been skinned. She could see what they'd do to the cottage—gut it, maybe even tear it down and build new. The lot was more important, with its frontage. The buyers came from Cleveland construction money. They'd put in a new dock, probably have a massive cabin cruiser.

"Anything interesting?" Arlene asked.

"*The Navigator,* that's it."

Emily took her seat again, then wished she hadn't. Mrs. Klinginsmith had told her the cleaning service would take care of everything, but she had to at least defrost the fridge and scrub the cabinets, do the bathrooms. It wasn't how she'd planned on spending her last afternoon here.

And she'd been so worried about the stove. She should have just left it alone. The buyers would want a new one. In a month, all these things she fretted over would disappear, leaving her mind free—for what? Was that why she was stalling now, afraid of facing those lonely hours? She felt tricked, even if she was the one who had engineered the deal.

The Mozart was over and something mawkish and overwrought was on. Tchaikovsky, she thought, making another sugary appeal to the heart, like that horrid movie. It was enough to drive her inside.

"Ready for lunch?" she asked Arlene.

"In a minute."

She'd forgotten the melon, but she could finish that at breakfast. The children would eat the cold cuts and the yogurts, the bagels and cream cheese. For some reason Lisa had bought two jars of pickles; one of them was still unopened. She actually looked forward to throwing away the ranked condiments in the door, God knew how old some of them were— the salad dressing that had separated, the chili sauce clotted like a scab around the cap. She'd have to get Kenneth to haul the garbage out to the road before he took off.

In the living room the phone rang—Mrs. Klinginsmith—and she shut the door to get it. As she suspected, Arlene hadn't budged.

"I'll get it!" Emily said.

"Thank you!"

The answering machine—she hadn't even thought of it. It was practically new. She'd have to unhook it tonight, make a diagram of the wires.

"Hello," she said.

"Emily, hey," a man said, happy to catch her. "How's it goin' up there?"

"Hi Jeff," she said, and wished she'd let it ring. "Good, good. How are *you* doing?"

9

Meg was trying to be careful with the knife, but then the tomato slipped in its own juice and she had to stop and compose herself and start over. The blade wasn't sharp enough, denting the skin instead of biting through, and she had to saw at the last slices, bending the tomato and squishing the guts to mush. The fucker. She couldn't believe he was doing this to her.

It was probably about something else entirely, something stupid. But he knew she didn't want to talk to him, he knew that. She couldn't have made it any plainer yesterday.

She laid the slices out on a paper plate with some lettuce from last night's salad and rinsed her hands. Someone else could cut an onion; she wasn't going to cry in front of everyone. There were buns if they ran out of bread. She got the mayo and ketchup and mustard and pickles from the fridge, and dug in the silverware drawer.

They'd been planning it all along, she thought, the two of them. It had to be Stacey's idea. He'd do anything for her, and screw the rest of the world. The idiot thought he was in love.

She'd promised herself not to think about it, to set it aside until they got back. At least he hadn't told her mother (so she hoped; she was overexposed as it was, at the mercy of her judgment).

It was the timing of it that hurt her more than anything, as if they'd been waiting for the divorce to be legal so she'd be out of the way—as if she'd kept them apart. And then to tell her over the phone in the middle of her vacation with her family and invite her like they were old friends.

She set out the cold cuts and cheese in their wax-paper wrappers, and the last of the mac salad. Justin came in to inspect the fridge and before he could escape she asked him to pour the milk. She'd already lined up the glasses.

"That's good," she said. "Just take yours and leave the rest."

"Can I talk to Dad when you call him?" he asked.

She was fitting the paper plates into their wicker holders, and didn't stop. She wanted to lie, to say she'd already called and left a message.

"You want me to tell him something for you?"

"I just want to talk to him."

"We'll see," she said. "I think we're going to be pretty busy this afternoon. We're going to be going home tomorrow, if you can wait one day."

He didn't seem happy with this but didn't argue.

"Can you tell everyone that lunch is ready?"

"Okay," he mumbled, barely audible, and moped off.

It was unfair, she thought. How was he supposed to understand when she didn't?

And this was just the beginning.

10

"Did you want to talk to your father?" her mother asked while Justin was on the phone.

"Not really," Sarah said, because she and Ella were in the middle of a game of rummy.

"Come on. Just to say hello."

From her tone, Sarah knew she wouldn't get out of it, so she gave in and stopped playing and stood by the couch, waiting for Justin to finish. He was telling him about Panama Rocks, making it sound more fun than it was. Then it was something about going into middle school, and the Tigers, and some car show.

"Okay," Justin said, "I love you too," and handed her the phone.

"Hi," she said.

"Hey Picklehead, how's it going?"

Terrible, she wanted to say, but he didn't really want to know about her and Mark, or how long this summer had been, and she didn't really want to tell him.

"Good," she said, and waited for him to say something else. It was easier this way.

11

It worked out perfectly. There was one last can of gas under the workbench, one of the rugged plastic ones his father had bought recently, meaning in the last ten years. He slid a case of dusty Iron City tall-necks aside to get at it—heavy and cool from being on the concrete. Setting it in the wheelbarrow, he thought he could find a use for it at home (though he already had one in the shed for the mower, and Lise would never let him take it in the car). It seemed a waste, like the tools on his father's bench he didn't need—even the old Iron City case there, the very name making him nostalgic.

They were down to less than twenty hours now, but he felt as if they were already gone. The police had abandoned the marina, whatever that meant. He could see how today would play out, and tomorrow, the battle of packing, getting the bikes on the car, and finally the long drive. At least he'd have Sunday to recover.

He left the garage door up. He had to come back for the key anyway, and a hat. He'd steal his father's favorite, an ugly blue-and-white mesh job from a local trucking company with its phone number under a flying semi. He could salvage that at least.

"When are we going to go tubing?" Sam called from the porch.

"As soon as I get the boat ready."

"Need help?" Lise asked.

"I think I'm all set. You can get the kids' towels together."

It was easier to just take the cover off by himself, reaching across the tube to pull the hood off the motor and then down the gunwales on each side, using the driver's seat to scissor over the windshield and kneel on the bow to unhook the front bungees. He didn't risk tossing it at the wheelbarrow, just balled it up and dropped it in the passenger seat. He was sweating already and ditched his shirt. They still had a third of a tank, so he muscled the new one in and shoved it into a corner, yanking a stubborn loop of the towrope out from underneath.

"All right," he said, wiping his face on his arm.

If Meg wanted to come she'd have to grab a life jacket, otherwise they were good to go. He left the wheelbarrow on the dock, thinking he should pull the motor up when they were done. He didn't know when Smith Boys were supposed to come for the boat.

"Is there room for one more?" Arlene asked inside.

She had shorts on, and her hair tucked under a yellow NAPA cap. Meg said she didn't absolutely have to go, but he could see she wanted to.

"It can take all of us, it'll just be a little cramped."

His mother passed. She was busy cleaning out the kitchen cupboards.

"I've got more than enough to do here, thanks. Maybe when you come back you can help me with some of the heavy stuff."

"We women can help too," Meg reminded her.

"Good, because I'm going to need all the help I can get."

"Are we supposed to not go?" Lise asked when they were alone in the garage.

"She's just talking to herself."

"It didn't sound like it to me."

He slapped the cobwebs off the extra life jackets, weighing the cost of the argument. All he had to do was keep quiet.

"I'm sure she's just freaking out about everything," he said. "It's better to stay out of her way."

"Okay," she said.

They were all waiting for him on the dock, lined up to one side like his crew. There were only four seats for the eight of them, three really, since he needed the driver's seat.

"All right," he said, clapping once, "how are we going to do this?"

Again they waited for him. With his father gone, the job of captain fell to him, another responsibility he didn't want. On the water he had complete authority, and they knew to respond to his orders when things went wrong, because at some point they would. Usually it had to do with the motor, whether it got caught in the weeds or flooded and refused to start or came down with vapor lock—say, when he changed tanks. The boat was almost as old as he was, and had a way of reminding him of how mechanically inept he was and then displaying this shortcoming to everyone onboard. He would get them back if he had to paddle (and that had happened), but somewhere out there he would be reduced to turning the key and thumbing the choke button and swearing through his teeth so the children wouldn't hear. The funny thing was, he could remember his father—an engineer with skilled hands—struggling with the motor the same way, but somehow he had kept his sense of humor, made it a game or a problem to be solved. When Ken tried that, he felt phony and even more incompetent.

He assigned the life jackets and cranked the boat down so it floated before sending them on in order. Arlene and Lise could squeeze up front with him. Meg would be in back, the girls could share a seat, and the boys would sit on the tube, or in it, since that might be safer. No one complained or questioned him, they just helped each other on and waited for more instructions.

"All right," he said, "we're going to paddle out past those weeds there. When we push off, Sarah, I want you to paddle backward. Meg, you're going to go forward when we pass that last piling. The rest of you sit tight."

"Aye-aye," Lise said next to him.

"Thank you," he put her off.

He knew he was being rigid, afraid of making a mistake when it didn't matter.

They came back straight, drifting for the Lerners' dock.

"Push off with the paddle," he called to Sarah. "Okay, that's great. We want to head directly into the wind so it doesn't push us into the dock."

His first urge was to go back and paddle, but he held off. When they came alongside the dock again, he said it was all right, they were getting there.

"I'm not having fun," Meg said, and Sarah and Ella changed places.

A fisherman puttered by and Ken waved.

"You folks all right?" the man asked.

"We're fine."

"Okay," he said.

They cleared the end of the Lerners' dock, and Ken sidled his way back to prime the motor, squeezing the rubber bulb to feed it gas.

"Can we stop paddling now?" Meg asked.

"Wait till I get it going. I don't want to get stuck back in there if it doesn't start."

"Well, hurry up, I'm getting tired."

"I can paddle if you're tired," Arlene volunteered.

"You are not paddling," Lise said.

He sat in his seat and looked over his shoulder like he was backing up a car. The weeds weren't as bad as last year, but he still worried about fouling the prop this far in. He lifted the throttle past halfway, as his father had taught him, pushed the button and turned the key.

The starter ratcheted but nothing caught and he killed it quick so it wouldn't flood. The second try was a carbon copy, and the third sounded dry, as if he hadn't primed it enough. He spun and bumped his way through everyone. "Keep paddling," he said, and squeezed the bulb hard so that an oily sheen formed on the water—too much. He hustled back and tried again and got blue smoke. Again and it almost turned over, the blenderlike whine of the flywheel spinning. They were on the other side of the Lerners' dock and heading for the Smiths'.

"Keep paddling."

"We are," Ella said.

This time the motor chattered and caught, turned over and slowly chugged to life, sputtering. He inched the throttle up and listened to it grind, solid.

"Okay," he said, "stop paddling," and chunked it in gear, keeping his speed down as he steered through the weeds. Once they were in open water, he throttled down and slipped it into reverse to clear the prop, then headed for Prendergast Point and the marina, the ramp there busy now, trailers backed in on both sides. He cruised through the no-wake zone, then turned it loose. The bow rose up as they gathered speed. The wind was cool and the kids shouted when they smacked down after jumping a wave. He put his father's cap on and sat up straight, peering over the windshield, swiveling his head to watch for oncoming traffic, as if he knew what he was doing.

12

Justin wasn't as scared this time jumping off. It was only when the cold water wrapped around his legs that he remembered there were fish underneath him and pulled for the surface, and when he broke through Sam was doing a cannonball right on top of him. He got a mouthful of water and coughed it out, wiping his eyes, then swam for the ladder and hung on, catching his breath.

"Are you okay?" his mother asked.

"Yeah."

"Why don't you take a break?"

"I'm all right," he said. To prove it he pushed off and followed Sam out the towrope to the tube, where Uncle Ken was sunning with his legs hanging over the edge. Sam was right beside the tube, hiding. He put a finger to his lips for Justin to be quiet.

"Don't you dare," Uncle Ken said with his eyes closed.

"Don't I dare what?"

"Don't you dare anything."

On Sam's signal they both tugged the rope.

"I'm warning you," Uncle Ken said, but didn't move.

"Come get us," Justin said.

"I will."

Sam motioned for him to help push the tube over, but when they tried, they couldn't budge him.

"You guys are pitiful," Uncle Ken said. "You've got to stop playing all those video games and get outside more."

"Help us tip him over!" Sam yelled to Sarah and Ella, lying on their towels on the nose of the boat. They didn't look up.

They hung on his ankles and dove under and grabbed at his suit and punched him in the butt—"Okay, no kicking," he told Sam—and splashed him until, with a roar, he attacked, pitching himself on top of them, except they escaped and took control of the tube so he was the shark and they had to keep from being bitten. Even his skin could cut them, so he couldn't touch them at all, and then he came up through the hole and they both dove off and raced him to the boat. They barely made it there safely, and his mother pulled the ladder up.

"Okay," Uncle Ken said, "who's ready for some serious tubing?"

It was great, it was so much fun. Ella's top almost came off once, and Justin flipped all the way over and didn't fall off. He couldn't wait to do it again. He thought he'd ask for one for Christmas for Grandpa Carlisle's boat, because on the phone his father promised that next summer they'd go to the U.P. like they usually did. That way they could do it both places.

13

Emily had just gotten off the phone with Dorothy Klinginsmith and was coming back into the kitchen when the fly whizzed by her, fat and black and slow, weaving in front of her like a drunk driver. He lighted on the screen door, so she opened it, giving him a chance to leave peacefully. He hesitated, pivoting on his feet, then cut under her arm and through the kitchen again, zipping across the white gap of the fridge and around the corner for the living room.

"Okay," she said, corrected, and pulled the door closed so no more could get in.

She was nearly done with the cupboards, their contents spread out on the counter. She'd hoped to box up the unopened stuff and donate it to a local food bank, but some of the cans were dusty or dented. One can of fruit cocktail was a store brand that had gone out of business a decade ago, the lettering on the label space-age and obsolete. She filled two boxes and found she couldn't lift them—another job for Kenneth.

She wouldn't get it all done. She still had to go through the drawers and the dishes and do the bathrooms. Mrs. Klinginsmith said she'd be over around three-thirty so Emily wouldn't have to deal with the septic guy (meaning she'd have to deal with both of them). The fridge she'd worry about later. After they came back from Webb's she'd split what was worth saving between their coolers and let it defrost overnight.

She ran a bucket of hot water, stirring up the suds with her hand. The rag she used came from someone's navy blue T-shirt. She had to climb on a chair to wipe the top shelf, disgusted at the dead moths and their droppings. By the time she finished, the water was a gray soup; she poured it down the sink, and as she was wringing out the rag, the fly returned, buzzing against the screen right in front of her—a big bristly one, and loud.

She pawed at him with her bare hand, deliberate, afraid she'd break the screen, and of course he got away, bouncing in the space between the two panes. She laid the rag over the spigot and wiped her hands with a paper towel, watching him the whole time, willing him to stay there. She leaned over the sink, the paper towel bunched in one hand, and reached for the window like a jewel thief. In one lunging motion she shut the bottom pane and swiped across the top, trying to catch up with him, but he was too quick, lifting off before she could corner him. She turned to the room, determined to follow him, but he'd disappeared in the patterned curtains and the dark wood of the cabinets.

She flipped on the living room light and crouched down with the paper towel, hunting, trying to spy him in flight, and imagined what they'd think if they suddenly walked in on her. She stalked into the back hall and stood by the door of the darkened bathroom, listening.

He was in Arlene's room, a dot on the far window, bumping the glass as if he could escape that way. As she detoured around Arlene's bed, he made a break, taking the shortcut past her, zigzagging for the door.

"You think you're smart," she said.

She crossed the hall to her room and stood blocking the doorway, checking the windows and the air over the bed. She closed her door and then Arlene's, inspected the bathroom with her hand on the light switch (not appreciating her grim expression in the mirror), then sealed it too.

The living room was the hardest because of the carpet—and the couch and the fireplace, good camouflage. She wished there were a door to the kitchen to trap him in with all the white.

She found the flyswatter hanging on the side of the fridge. It was cheap, twisted wire with a floppy yellow plastic head. She heard him and raised it straight up before looking around.

He was on the rag draped over the faucet, as if he'd tricked her. She approached slowly, keeping her arm cocked. A shadow could make him take off, a stray air current. He sensed her and tensed, set his front legs down so he was ready to go. She watched, stock-still, waiting for him to pick them up again and begin the finicky ritual of cleaning, and when he did she banged the swatter down on top of him so hard she could feel the handle bend in midair.

She thought she'd missed, that she'd seen him dart off to the left at the last second, and she fixed the handle while she peered around and reset herself, bringing it straight up again. She didn't expect to get him on her first try, but there he was in the sink, half mangled and on his back, a leg waving.

She smashed him out of reflex, leaving a raspberry splash she thought was blood on the stainless steel, and the thrill of the chase dispersed and curdled into disgust—at him, at herself—and quickly she swabbed him up with the paper towel and threw it in the garbage and ran water over the spot. There was more on the swatter, and a sectioned leg, and she cleaned it off and hung it up again, a child hiding a secret.

She moved on to the drawers, but even then it bothered her, not guilt so much as a sense of letdown or waste, her better nature betrayed.

It was foolish, she knew. It was just a fly.

14

Lise took her shower first so she could fit the laundry in before dinner, a suitable excuse to read her book in the rumbling, linty humidity. It had become a tradition of hers, a last, necessary resting place in the sequence of the week. The laundromat sat tucked in behind the Putt-Putt, across the road from the practice huts. It had a tacky charm that came from a total lack of decoration. The machines were either mustard or avocado, and the only hint that this wasn't 1973 were the cars for sale shingling the bulletin board.

The place was empty this time of day, and she took one of the resident secondhand kitchen chairs out the propped-open back door and watched people who'd visited the Institute file through the rocky lot to their cars parked somewhere off in the numbered fields. They came in clumps, most of them older, driven by the crossing guards. When the wind was right she could hear a warble of French horn and the bright piping of an oboe. She was tired from swimming, and Harry's new predicament wasn't as interesting as the light on the page, the way it angled over her shoulder, tinting the margins. She wanted to finish the book, but she found herself skimming, counting down the pages till the end. Harry had found the silver keys, everything was wonderful, blah blah blah. There was nothing real she could hang on to—it was too simple. She wanted reality, complexity, not this endless fairy tale where good was rewarded. She wanted life.

She wondered what her life would look like in a book. Now there was a depressing idea.

Meg's would make a good book, at least from the stories Ken had told her—running away, hitchhiking across country when she was eighteen, being a cocktail waitress in San Francisco.

There was nothing exciting about Lise's life. Falling in love with Ken and being his model, but that was a long time ago. The rest was just what everybody did. When she was growing up she was sure she would be special, but all kids thought that; it couldn't be true for everyone. Ken still believed he was, despite the evidence, and while she didn't like herself for doing it, she knew she held that against him. One of them had to be realistic.

Flipping a page, she thought that her life was average and nothing to be ashamed of. The world wasn't as magical as people liked to believe. That was why they read books to escape it.

She checked her washers. The darks were done, and by the time she'd switched them over, the whites were ready. She couldn't get back into Harry and tipped her head up and massaged her neck with one hand. She thought of accidentally leaving the book there so she wouldn't have to pack it—or just dumping it in the garbage can with all the purple lint and dryer sheets. She couldn't remember ever throwing a book away, it wasn't done, no matter how bad the book was. There was always the library sale.

The sky was blue and the sun was warm on her arms. Traffic passed on the road, and the old people crunched across the lot. She had another forty minutes or so, and less than fifty pages. There wouldn't be time to read tonight, with the fireworks, and with a sigh she bowed her head and started in again.

15

They had to search for it, and then it was Kenneth who finally found the pebbly cover—like a patio stepping stone—in the far corner by the road. How was Emily supposed to know? Henry took care of these things.

"Doesn't it have to be pumped out before they can inspect it?" Kenneth asked, though why he was telling her this now eluded her.

"Is that right?"

"Maybe they'll do that first."

"I haven't the foggiest," she admitted. "All I know is that the buyers asked to have it inspected. The rest is up to them."

Mrs. Klinginsmith said in the case of summer homes it was rare to find a full tank. They were only there a week while the bacteria worked year-round. They didn't have a clothes washer, so they were probably okay. How many people did they have using the shower? How often did they run the dishwasher? She carried a clipboard and wrote down their answers with a pen with her name on it. Emily asked what else the inspector could find wrong with the system that would frighten the buyers.

"I can't imagine you have one of those old steel tanks," Mrs. Klinginsmith asked, tramping over the grass in a box pattern as if searching for another opening. "They're a real nightmare to replace."

Emily looked to Kenneth, but he didn't know either.

"I'm sure it's been upgraded," Mrs. Klinginsmith said.

Emily couldn't remember anyone tearing up the yard. She wouldn't forget a project that size.

Mrs. Klinginsmith stopped and looked around at the trees, clutching her clipboard to her chest. "You don't have any maples that I can see. They're what kills a system. Their roots go through the holes in your pipes and next thing you've got a ball of them inside there. By the time you call Roto-Rooter, you're looking at two hundred dollars minimum, and that's going to happen again and again. You end up having to take the tree out. You don't want to know how much that costs."

The real trouble around here was the water table being so close, and keeping the leach field away from the lake. Frost heaves were a problem. The boxes could tilt and overload the pipes on one side, or move them so that when the ground settled, dirt would work its way into the leach field. Emily wasn't sure why that was a problem. Wasn't the leach field dirt to begin with?

No, it was stone laid around the pipes. The tank itself was concrete and watertight. When the inspector came he scratched a rough diagram on a pad for her. He was older, in a maroon Chautauqua Girls' Softball windbreaker, his hands nicked like Henry's. He drove a clunker of a van with a ladder tied to the luggage rack with twine, so she assumed they weren't going to pump the tank. He had a toolbox and a checklist to go over. He scraped open the lid and got down on his hands and knees with a flashlight to look inside, and Emily stepped back from the smell.

He dipped a steel rod in as if taking its temperature and wrote down some numbers, then left the rod leaning against the fence.

"Level looks fine," he said, and asked where their toilets were.

Kenneth led them in through the kitchen.

"Pardon the mess," Emily said.

Kneeling on the bath mat, the inspector took a brown bottle from his toolbox and squeezed an eyedropper until the water in the bowl turned bright purple.

"That'll wash right out," he assured her. He flushed the toilet and they all stood there and watched the purple swirl. "What we want to see when we go outside is this particular water coming in through the input to make sure there's no blockage. We'll do the same with the upstairs and then we'll run some plain water to flood the tank. That pushes the dye out the outlet and into the leach field. Then while we're pumping the tank we'll have time to sniff around and see if there's any breakthrough to the surface or out into the lake. We definitely want to keep it out of the lake."

"So you *are* pumping the tank," Kenneth asked.

"Got to," the inspector said. "Otherwise there's no way to check the condition of the baffles. You'd be surprised, I've found actual tanks with cracks in them."

"The buyers pay for the pumping," Mrs. Klinginsmith interrupted.

"New ones too," the inspector said. "You get a bad mix, that concrete'll fall apart. It's like laying a road when it's too cold."

She couldn't follow what he said after that, something about the chemicals in detergents and the water level getting too high. She trusted Kenneth to remember. For her purposes, it was enough to know what could go wrong.

The bowl had filled again, only a tinge of purple at the edges.

"I'm going to give it one more," the inspector said, then checked around the base before he flushed.

Emily thought of the boys missing the toilet upstairs. She was glad she'd cleaned the bathrooms.

"So the water should be purple," she asked on the way across the yard.

"The water should be purple," the inspector said. "If it's not, you've got a blockage somewhere."

He turned his flashlight on and stood aside. The water was purple.

"So far so good," Mrs. Klinginsmith said, and Emily thought of her commission, how much it was, then remembered that the two of them were rooting for the same thing.

The second test was identical, and while the inspector was running water to flood the system, the pumping truck showed up, parking in the street for the neighbors to see. They couldn't pump yet, the inspector said. They had to wait a good half hour for the dye to break through. The driver unrolled a hose like a fireman, then sat in his cab with the door open, reading the paper while the inspector walked around the side yard and down to the lake, taking measurements with a wheel on a stick. It was four-fifteen and their reservation at Webb's was for six-thirty.

"How long will it take to pump the tank?" Emily asked.

"It depends on how full it is," Mrs. Klinginsmith said. "I can't imagine it'll be more than a half hour."

But at five-thirty the truck was still chugging away. Emily needed to get dressed for dinner and left Kenneth with Mrs. Klinginsmith, and while she was changing she heard the truck shift up and leave. She brushed her hair and pushed her earrings in and hustled out to see if they'd found anything.

The inspector was just dragging the lid back on, Mrs. Klinginsmith marching across the lawn with Kenneth, swinging her clipboard at her side.

"It all checked out fine," she said, as if she'd known all along.

"Good," Emily said, and thanked the inspector. Kenneth went inside to get ready.

"I think that's it," Mrs. Klinginsmith said at her car—a Taurus like Arlene's, in a sensible dark blue. "I probably won't see you before you leave, so if you could just leave the kitchen door unlocked for the cleaners, that would be a big help. And don't worry about any furniture you're not taking, or anything. I use these guys all the time and you should see them, they'll have the place emptied out in one day."

"When is that going to be?"

"I know this," she said, and flipped the top sheet on her clipboard. "The Wednesday after Labor Day. I've already called Goodwill."

"Would it be better if I left you a key? I don't know if I like the idea of leaving the house open for that long."

Even as Emily said this, she knew she was just stalling.

"Of course, if you have an extra."

"I do," Emily said, and went inside to get it.

She could back out right now, nothing was stopping her. She could save it to announce at dinner, deliver the good news over dessert, a last-second reprieve.

The key was in a dish on the mantel, part of a heavy ring with the extra boat key and the keys for the garage and the pump house and the front door and the lock on Henry's toolchest and a dozen more—all labeled with tape in Henry's neat hand. She had to fight to get it off, but she did.

16

"Come on," Sam yelled at Arlene's back, "strike him out! Throw him the old radio ball!"

"All right," Arlene said, "no mercy. What's the count?"

"Two and two," Justin said, rocking in the batter's box. He was supposed to be Nomar Garciaparra.

"Maxwell working from the stretch," she said. "Checks the runner—he's invisible. Here's the windup, and here's the pitch."

It bounced in the grass, running the count full, and she bent over and bulged one cheek out and pretended to spit, then glared in at Justin. He glared back, dead serious.

At recess she pitched to both teams, so she knew her way around the plate, but there she was strictly business, trying to give them something to hit, every minute precious. Henry entertained, throwing behind his back and between his legs, all the while delivering a ridiculous play-by-play—"Here's Sammy 'Whammy-bammy' Maxwell, he's oh for ten today." He'd been doing this routine since Kenneth and Margaret could swing a wiffle bat, and Arlene was surprised to find she'd absorbed so much of it.

"Two out, man on first, and a full count to the squirt from De-trert. Maxwell looks like she's tiring out there. This could be her last bat-ter, depending on how long those girls take to get ready."

"No batta," Sam chanted. He was playing shallow, halfway to the lake. Justin had already struck out twice, and the single they'd given him was a tapper. She could barely bend over in her dress to field it.

"Sets and checks the runner, and here's the payoff pitch."

She wanted to lay it out in the middle of the plate to give him a chance, but the ball ran in on him. He swung in self-defense as it plunked him square in the chest.

"The whiff!" Sam said, running in to take his place.

"No," she said, "it hit him."

"He swung at it."

"I swung," Justin surrendered.

"Nope. Take your base. First and second. They're giving Max-well a warning. Watch out, it could get ugly out here."

She was trying to groove one for him when Emily stepped out of the screenporch with her white purse and a camera. "What in the world are you doing?"

"Playing wiffle ball."

"Not in those clothes you're not. I swear. Come on, I want to take all of your pictures in front of the house."

"Grandma's no fun," Arlene said.

"Yeah," Sam said.

"Grandma is so fun," Emily said. "Now stand right there and look this way. Everybody say 'Aunt Arlene is crazy.'"

"Am not," she said after the flash.

"Are too."

17

On the way they passed the Putt-Putt, and with a twinge Ken realized that he'd missed his chance to shoot it. Next year it would probably be gone, replaced by a gas station or turned into a parking lot for the Institute. He'd had all week, and he'd wasted it chasing after Tracy Ann Caler. He thought he should get Webb's too—the boys standing on the huge flukes of the anchor out front, the hokey gift shop—but he'd come unarmed. By the time they got back to the cottage the light would be gone.

He had a whole list—Hogan's Hut and the True Value and the ferry seen from the bridge. He needed another week, another three days. He could do it in one day, make that the frame, wake up at four and do nothing but drive around shooting, arrange them by time like those awful coffee-table books. One Day in the Life of Lake Chautauqua.

He could mock the obviousness of the idea and still see the potential in it, and thought that said something about him. He was unoriginal, even his best work secondhand, his worst bordering on incompetent.

Lise slowed for someone turning in, and he caught a fat marmalade cat bolting for cover under a hedge, a basketball on the lawn. The light was soft on the grass, bringing out motes and flying insects under the trees, wafting seeds—pretty clichés. He could see them on Hallmark cards or posters with inspirational slogans. Maybe that was his calling.

In back, Ella said, "Stop it!"

"Stop it," Sam mimicked.

"Mo-om!"

"Stop it, both of you," he said, too hard, for knocking him out of his thoughts, and then Ella was pissed off at him.

He just wanted to get through this dinner and see the fireworks and go to sleep, but it seemed that was too much to ask. And then he recovered, or gave up, clicked into that mode where nothing could touch him, and he sat back and watched the world fly by outside, recording it like an open lens.

He saw a grackle perched in a mulberry tree, the branch it was on waving as it ate.

He saw a balloon tied to a mailbox painted like the flag.

He saw a house that was half Tyvek with roses growing around the foundation.

He saw trolls in a rock garden.

He saw a woodpile between two trees.

He saw a bored girl selling corn.

He saw a sparrow worrying a crow.

He saw an Indian woman in a squash-colored sari rolling a stroller away from the Root Beer Stand, an antique truck parked over her shoulder.

It always happened when he didn't have a camera.

18

"I hope Rufus will be all right by himself," Emily appealed to Ken for the third time, and Lise clenched his thigh under the table.

He covered her hand and held it still. She and Emily were seated directly across from each other, a mistake Lise recognized immediately but could do nothing to remedy. The kids wanted to sit together, leaving the adults bunched at one end of the table. She had Sam on one side of her so she could keep an eye on him, and Ken on the other. She caught exchanges from both the kids' and grown-ups' conversations without being part of either, which she thought was even more tiring than making small talk.

"You leave him alone at home, don't you?" Meg said—exactly what she wanted to ask.

"That's different. I know I shouldn't worry, but he's old. I know one of these times I'm going to come back and . . . you know."

But he'd been fine when they left him all day the other day.

Emily never explained. She was off into a story about Duchess, who Lise had only seen pictures of.

"When she got sick I could tell because she just wasn't herself. Remember? She'd growl at Kenneth and he used to be so good to her. And she was just the sweetest dog before that, but that's what happens. You can understand why."

Everyone agreed, or no one objected. Lise didn't see her point, if there was one. It seemed that her conversations circled more and more around sickness and death, though as far as Lise knew she was completely healthy. Maybe that was natural, after Henry, but Lise couldn't help but find it morbid. She suspected the stories Emily told had some connection to the way he'd treated her or the way she'd treated him those last weeks, though Ken said things had gone as well as could be expected. In any case, Lise thought she was trading on their sympathy, bringing it up over and over again, lightly disguised.

"Does anyone want more calimari?" Sam asked, shakily handing Lise the plate.

"I think we're all right," she said, but he'd done it to make room for him and Justin to do the word search. She reached over her wine and combined the two plates and stacked them. She thought that their dinners should be here soon. The waitress had already faked her out once, setting up the folding stand for the table next to them.

"You do have to admit that Mr. Bush is a moron," Emily was saying, and Lise checked on Ella, looking cute in her pearls, sipping at her virgin strawberry daiquiri.

Across the room it was someone's birthday, the whole wait staff serenading a table, a flash stunning the air.

"That reminds me, Lisa," Emily said. "What do you want for your birthday?"

She *would* have to do this. "I don't know. Nothing."

"Really? Nothing?"

"I'm serious, Emily. I have everything I need." Ken patted her thigh and she stopped his hand.

"I know it's early but I want to get a jump on it. If you have any ideas, let me know."

"I will."

Great, now Emily would use it as an excuse to badger her for the next two months. She'd have to look through her catalogs and come up with something. In the lull, she smiled at Ken to let him know how much fun this was, and he smiled back.

The waitress came by to say their dinners would be right out and asked if they were ready for another round of drinks. Yes, Sam could have another Slice, but that was it for the night. Lise had finished her wine but held off like the rest of them, for Meg's sake, and anyway, she had to drive.

"That's where they get you, with that second drink," Emily said when the waitress had left. "Now this is a question for everybody. Did any of you hear any new news on what was going on down at the marina?"

Thankfully no one had. Lise thought it was probably not an appropriate subject to discuss in front of the kids. Ella and Sarah were intently pretending not to listen.

"You know what's funny," Emily said. "No one's called and followed up on what we told them."

"You mean Ken," Lise corrected her.

"You'd think with such a big operation they'd cover their bases a little better. If they're looking in a certain area, you'd expect them to ask people who live there if they've noticed anything peculiar."

"Has anyone noticed anything peculiar?" Arlene asked.

"You know what I mean. Like the Lerners' alarm going off. You'd think they'd be interested in that kind of information."

"Maybe they have enough information," Meg said. "Who knows what they were looking for. They could have been looking for a weapon. They could have someone in custody who told them where to look."

"Maybe it's not a mystery anymore," Ken said reasonably, and she could tell he was covering something. He wanted them to change the subject and leave her alone, his girl.

"You don't think she could still be alive?" Lise asked.

She couldn't resist. It was a sign of how deep her jealousy went that she picked the meanest thing she could think of, leaving him no way out.

And then Emily saved him, saying, "After a week, I wouldn't think so."

"No," Arlene agreed.

She'd forgotten how badly she was outflanked here. Now she wanted another wine, Meg or no Meg.

The meal came, a break, people craning around to see what everyone else ordered. The food here was basic, aimed at the place's clientele, who were mostly Emily and Arlene's age. Everything came with a baked potato and a tiny bowl of very green broccoli. Lise had gone with the broiled sole, thinking they couldn't ruin that, but after she helped Sam cut his ribs, she found it dried out and overdone.

"How's yours?" Ken asked, offering her a bite of lamb chop.

"No thanks. It's fine."

She checked on Ella to make sure she was eating, not just rearranging the food on her plate. Ella caught her and Lise returned the look and tipped her chin for her to take a bite. Next week it was back to making dinner for them every night, trying to come up with a menu they could all live with.

"How is everything?" the waitress asked.

"Good," Emily said, and Ken nodded with his mouth full.

Lise was tempted to send hers back. If it was just the two of them, she would have. Instead she loaded her baked potato with butter and sour cream and watched the constant traffic of aproned wait staff and older couples in their summer best passing behind Emily and Arlene. Over the stone fireplace hung an impossibly pink-bellied trout curved like a wurst. She couldn't imagine what it would be like to work at a place like this.

Sam tapped her arm. "I have to go to the bathroom."

"Go ahead."

"Where is it?" he asked. She almost told him to go ask his father, but saw her opportunity.

Justin had to go too.

"Anyone else?"

No, the girls were too cool to be seen with her.

"I can take them," Ken offered, but she was gone, blazing a trail between the tables, pausing at a crossing to let a waiter by.

She remembered where the rest rooms were, back in a dim hallway near the kitchen with the pay phones and an out-of-date cigarette machine. As she waited for them, each time the swinging doors opened she could see into the bright, busy kitchen, the pots hung above the steel counters and the smoking grill. It seemed more exciting than being out here, and she envied the chefs. The boys came back too fast and she sent them in again to wash their hands. Technically she wasn't stalling. They were right out anyway and then practically ran for the table.

They were all done except Ella, what a surprise. She'd picked her chicken apart and gutted her potato. The only thing she'd eaten was her broccoli—that and the two daiquiris.

Now that Lise was back, the girls decided they needed to go. When Ken asked, Ella said she was finished.

"She doesn't eat much, does she?" Emily said, once the two of them had left the table.

Lise knew Ken would downplay it later as honest concern, but she thought this line of criticism was directed at her.

"She eats," Ken said, "she's just particular."

"Is she like this at home?"

"She's like this everywhere," Lise said. "The doctor says she's normal for her height."

The waitress saved them, asking if people would be interested in seeing the dessert menu. They all were, the boys noisily. She cleared half the table and said she'd be right back, leaving them becalmed. As a starting point, Meg wondered what was going on at the Institute.

Friday was pops night. Arlene thought it might be Dionne Warwick.

"Walk On By," Ken said, Mr. Trivia.

"Or the other one, what's-her-name, Natalie Cole. I always get those two mixed up."

The girls returned, and the waitress, with a busboy who stared at Sarah. When he was gone they gave her grief but she took it well. She was used to the attention. Lise supposed it could be tiring, putting up with that kind of aimless desire all the time, but was more concerned about Ella, sitting right beside Sarah, invisible. These were the same lessons she'd learned at that age, the basic unfairness of the world and her place in it.

She hoped Emily noticed that Ella had ordered dessert, but didn't draw attention to it.

Somehow they'd gotten around to talking about the septic tank, all the things that could go wrong. In the course of a few hours, Ken and

Emily had become experts. A diaper was all it took to plug up the works and have everything back up into the house.

"Wouldn't that be a shitty situation," Emily punned. She seemed to think this was risqué. Lise just smiled, playing along.

She was tired. The drive tomorrow would be long, but in a way she was looking forward to it. It was their last long drive of the summer, their last time together before the school year scattered them.

The coffee came, and her crème brûlée, a raspberry on top, the same as Ella's. Lise tapped at the crust, then ate with just the tip of her spoon, savoring every bite, making it last. The sundaes the boys ordered were huge; they could have split one.

The waitress wasn't dumb. She'd figured out who was in charge and set down the leather folder with the bill next to Emily.

"Let me get that," Ken said, but Emily already had her wallet out.

"You can get it next year," she said. "How's that?"

"Are we going to be here next year?" Ken asked.

It almost sounded rehearsed to Lise, a setup.

"We're going to be somewhere here. I'm not staying in the city for the whole summer."

Lise had never expected to get off that easy. It felt like a defeat, everything settled without a word from her.

The gift shop was the next stop. The boys wanted to run ahead and meet them there, but she made them wait while Emily finished the dregs of her coffee. They all rose and pushed their chairs in. Arlene nearly forgot her purse.

There was a bowl of peppermints by the coat check. "One each," she had to warn the boys.

The way to the gift shop was through the lobby, across its nautical blue-and-green indoor-outdoor carpet. The windows of the front doors were translucent and impure, the color of beer (colonial, she supposed, as if this had once been a tavern), and a tiered rack by a fake rubber plant offered brochures for places like Panama Rocks and the Lucille Ball Museum. Inside, the aisles were bright, full of people they'd just eaten dinner with, looking over pot holders and china bells and glasses of all sizes, maple syrup and muskie refrigerator magnets and local cookbooks. The muzak coming from above was the same as in the dining room but seemed louder in such a small space, and the smell of chocolate was toxic.

The back wall was a glass display case, behind which three women in hair nets cut blocks of fudge on a marble-topped table; a crowd had gathered, clutching numbers. Sam made straight for the corner with the squirt guns and superballs, Justin right behind him. She was almost glad to have the job of watching them. Ken and Emily were over by the fudge, Meg and Arlene probably outside smoking. The girls were drawn to the jewelry, modeling bracelets for each other.

Sam ran back to her, desperate. "How much are we allowed to spend?"

"Five dollars."

"That's all we ever get to spend."

"Five dollars is a lot of money," she said—and it was. She'd never been given five dollars to spend in a gift shop. Her parents were too aware of spoiling her.

"You can't get anything for five dollars."

"I think you can find something," she said, and accompanied him to the corner to prove it.

What he wanted was a balsa-wood glider on the wall that cost $6.99. "See?" he said, and showed her the other price tags.

He was half right. Everything on the wall was over five. The cheap stuff was in the bins behind them—windup ducks and frogs, decks of cards and monstrous erasers.

In one bin were dozens of miniature bottles with shiny new pennies inside, a gift she remembered buying as a child, pinching the tiny cork out. The penny was supposed to be lucky. These cost a dollar ninety-nine.

"What's wrong with these?"

He didn't answer her, and from Justin's blank look she realized it was a dumb question.

"Look," she said, "I'm not going to argue with you. Do you want the five dollars or not?"

"Yes," Sam said, as if she were persecuting him.

"Good. Find something."

She just wanted to get out of here, the ugliness of it was that oppressive. They'd been there long enough.

Sam and Justin conferred over the bins, and then Sam came back.

"Can me and Justin go in on it together?"

"And then who gets it—you? That's not fair. We're leaving tomorrow. He'll barely get a chance to play with it."

"That's okay," Justin said.

He was such a pushover.

"We'll play with it tonight," Sam said.

"It's dark out," she reasoned, then heard herself. She knew she shouldn't give in, but she didn't want to make this a battle, not here, not now. Let Emily say what she wanted.

"Fine," she said, and comforted herself with the thought that more likely than not they'd break it tonight.

She knew that they'd be back here next year, or somewhere with his family. She didn't expect to be rewarded for her patience, not by Ken. He got along with her parents. He had no idea how she dreaded this week, the days paid out like a sentence—almost over. She had to focus on that.

At the register, Justin set a bottle with a penny in it next to the glider. She'd misread him, or maybe he'd been waiting for Sam to say it was uncool, because when she paid, the bottle went straight into his pocket. Sam grabbed the glider like it was his, and now that it was too late she wanted to take it back.

Ken and Emily were still waiting for their number to be called. No, she didn't want any fudge, but thank you. She gave Ella her five and took the boys outside.

As she pushed through the door the heavy air closed over her, warm and fresh after the chocolate air-conditioning, smelling of the lake and the asphalt of the parking lot. It was not quite night out, the sky a strange blue-green between the trees. The WEBB'S LAKESIDE RESORT sign was lighted, the white anchor surrounded by geraniums. Meg and Arlene were standing by the van, looking out over the water.

"Walk," she told the boys, already racing away from her, and she slowed. It was a relief to be by herself for a minute.

A tractor-trailer whined by on the road, its wind stirring the leaves, making gravel hop along the berm, and in the quiet that followed she saw what Meg and Arlene were looking at—the *Chautauqua Belle,* outlined in white Christmas lights, its reflection glimmering in the dark water. A band was playing on the top deck. She could hear the horns and a snare drum muffled by the distance. It was a dinner cruise, or a wedding reception, and she wished she were on it.

It reminded her of their wedding, the end of that endless day, leaving the hot, loud ballroom of the beach club to drunken applause and stepping into the cool humidity of the cape, the ocean detonating somewhere behind the dunes. The lot was calm like this, a promise of rest. Their friends had decorated their car with crepe paper and shaving cream and balloons—no, up close they were tied-off condoms—and she and Ken laughed, popping them with his cigarette, smearing the windows clear so they could drive off to the motel they'd been able to keep a secret, knowing that in a few minutes they would be completely, totally alone.

Tomorrow, she thought, and relaxed. It was easier in the dark, not as much work.

"Where's the rest of the crew?" Meg asked.

"They're coming," she said.

19

"Yes, yes," Emily said, "I know, we forgot to leave a light on for you. I'm sorry. Were you scared or were you sleeping? Sleeping would be my guess."

She took her jewelry off in front of the mirror and hung up her dress and changed into her clean jeans, sitting on the bed to roll up her cuffs. When she bent down, Rufus shoved his nose in her hair and knocked the closet door with his tail.

"All right, all right, I hear you. Can you wait till I get my tennies on?"

She chose an old windbreaker of Henry's and after a few tries—shining them into her palm—found a working flashlight on the mantel. She took Rufus out in the side yard and told him to go. He watched her as he squatted, looking worried, as if asking her for a little privacy. She paced the septic field like the inspector, bent and sniffing. Fireflies lifted from the rhododendron, locusts called from the trees. With every step she ex-

pected purple puddles in the grass, her tennies bleeding, but all she discovered was a wiffle ball.

Rufus was done, and pleased with himself. She fetched him a treat
from inside and left the flashlight by the sink, and they walked down to
the dock. She'd have to take him in before the fireworks started, turn her
radio on and close the door to her room, and still he would end up quiv-
ering under the bed. Now he stuck close to her though. He'd seen her
filling boxes in the kitchen and knew they were leaving. She wondered if
he'd had a good week, and thought so. The days would have seemed
normal to him, tagging after the children or flopped on the concrete, the
smell of the carpet. Next year would be harder.

The dock shimmied under her feet, Rufus clicking by her side.
She'd done this unthinkingly so many times, and now she wished she'd
paid more attention. Bless him, Kenneth had covered the boat like she'd
asked. The moon was low over Prendergast Point, and to the north the
Gothic arches of the bell tower shone orange. A couple of docks up, the
Nevilles had congregated, their laughter floating across the water. A whole
flotilla of boats stood off of Midway, eclipsing one another's running lights.
She sat on the bench and Rufus laid his head on her knee.

"You missed us, huh? Yes, I know you."

She scratched and he stopped panting and then began again,
harder, his wet breath warming her hand. A mosquito landed on him and
she shooed it. The kids would have to put on bug spray.

The stars were up, the lake still. It hadn't been a bad week, everything considered. She hadn't expected to see Niagara Falls. They'd managed to fit their golf in, and seeing Herb and Marjorie had been important.
She and Arlene had had a good day at the Institute. It had been a full
week, maybe that was more accurate.

She would miss the place, it was that simple. After taking everything into consideration—Henry and Arlene and the children and the
money—she would regret her decision because she enjoyed coming here
every summer. The cottage was familiar, a place she still knew while the
rest of her world had changed. She'd been wrong to think she could break
that bond so easily. And yet tomorrow she would. She would lock the
door and drive away and that would be that. Already it nagged at her like
a task left unfinished. She didn't even have to stop by Mrs. Klinginsmith's

and drop off a key. There was something dishonorable in such convenience, as if she hadn't suffered enough.

She'd felt the same way when Henry died—that night, riding back from the hospital, all her worries and terrors fulfilled and obliterated at the same time, and nothing to take their place. Kenneth and Arlene had put her to bed, but in minutes she was in the bathroom, doubled over the bowl, and the next morning she was frantic, a kind of mindless anxiety that remained with her through the funeral and into the following week, leaving her empty and bedridden. She couldn't imagine going through that again.

She wouldn't. She would go home and pick up where she'd left off, working in the backyard all morning, swimming at the club after lunch, paying the bills. They'd find a nice place for next year. They could even take a drive by and see what the new owners had done.

Rufus belched under her hand.

"Well, excuse you."

The *Chautauqua Belle* was out in the middle of the lake, lit up like the Fourth of July, and she thought she should take him inside before things got going. She stood and tottered back toward shore, the boards jiggling underfoot. Henry had built this dock. She remembered him and Herb Wiseman sinking the pilings—she had home movies of them in their plaid swim trunks. Every year at the end of the season they'd pull the sections up and stack them behind the garage. The new owners would probably rip the whole thing out and put in a new one. That was their prerogative.

The boys passed her as she crossed the lawn, each of them carrying something white—popcorn. She stole a handful for Rufus, who hunted in the grass for a kernel she'd dropped. She had to grab him by the collar. If she didn't get him inside before the first big boom, he'd run away and they'd spend all night trying to find him. Kenneth and Lisa had the boys' drinks, and here came everyone else with blankets and sweatshirts and bug spray. She kept heading for the door with Rufus, who didn't understand what he'd done wrong.

"Where are you going?" Sarah asked. "You're going to miss the fireworks."

"I'm coming," she promised over her shoulder. "Don't let them start without me."

20

They sat together like always, but there was no point. Sam and Justin were right beside them, and her mother and father, all of them crowded onto the dock. And even if they were alone, Ella wouldn't risk it. She'd had her chances this week and done nothing, and still she felt cheated.

The thump of another rocket going off came across the lake as it traced its orange path upward, disappeared between the stars and opened in a green circle, a white flash at the center giving them a second to brace for the boom and then the echo rumbling over the hills. Beside her, Sarah leaned back on her elbows and tipped her chin up like she was sunbathing, waiting to be kissed.

Another thump, and another. Ella could read the colors on Sarah's cheeks—a red one, an orange one that turned blue at the last second. She had to stop herself from watching her, but the fireworks were so not what she wanted right now, and she fought them, sharp-eyed, flattening them as they tried to jump out at her. In between she could hear clapping from the other docks. The embers fell in streaks, drifted with the wind.

"Whoa," Sarah said at a double one, purple blooming through green.

A huge orange one like a sun that stayed together till it went dark. "Oooo."

A small white one that broke into pinwheels that squirted away. "Those are the ones I like," her mother said.

A red one and a flash and Justin stuck his fingers in his ears. It was like a giant drumbeat thumping her heart, impossible to ignore. She tried not to let it surprise her again, alert for the next flash, letting the rest of them break up and fade. Her neck hurt and she twisted it and resettled. On the blanket, Sarah's hand was inches from hers.

She'd had this argument with herself so many times that she was sick of it, and out of anger more than any real hope, she turned her wrist and reached her pinkie toward Sarah, but still fell short. She left her hand there, waiting through two more rounds, aware of how close she was to touching her, tensing when a bomb went off.

It would have to be an accident, and it had to be now.

She didn't even know why she was doing this. She should be happy that she was this close to her.

"Nice," Sarah said, to a shower of twinkling silver stars.

The sky filled in again to scattered clapping, and as if this were her cue, Ella tucked her knuckles under and pushed the heel of her hand across the rough blanket so the side of hers rested against Sarah's, the contact soft and incidental. She could say it was a mistake.

Sarah picked up her hand and shifted so they weren't touching. Ella drew hers back. By the time she thought to say sorry, it was too late.

It didn't mean anything. Sarah had barely noticed. Everything was okay.

The launchers thudded and thumped and they had to track all the different rockets.

"It's not the finale," her father said. "Not yet."

"I should hope not," Grandma said.

The colors exploded on top of each other, showing the puffs of smoke beginning to move away, ghosts gliding across the water. The waves turned red and blue and green, and the trees. Sarah's face hadn't changed, open to the glow. They were sending up more, their trails like comets.

"Wow," Sarah said.

"Look at that one," Sam said.

Whistling spinners and gold plumes, a low spray of Roman candles ending with a heavy barrage. The bombs came one after another, a clump flashing white and then the impact deafening them again and again. Ella sat there inside herself and followed a plane blinking high above it all, imagining how it looked from up there, wishing she were far, far away.

21

Meg didn't know why she was crying. Not because of the glasses. Because she was exhausted. Because she was stoned and the week was over and she was feeling emotional. She recovered quickly, shooing Ken and laughing at herself even as she wiped the tears. The rest of them watched her like she was out of her mind, and she realized they weren't used to seeing her cry. It was new for her too.

"It's just sad," she explained, and looked again at the way her mother had nested the glasses in the box marked with her name—a beer carton, ironically. She thanked her for wrapping them.

"I didn't think you'd have time in the morning. I've also got you down for the cedar chest. I emptied it out but you're still going to need a hand getting it in the van."

Ken and Lise volunteered as a team. Arlene said they'd all help each other, and Meg thanked them, knowing she was the one who needed the help, the only single.

"Is that all you're taking?" her mother asked. "That's not very much. I'm still trying to get rid of that blender you like."

"Does it work?"

"It works *fine,*" she said, surprised.

She had one at home that she hardly used, and a Cuisinart, but she did like the thick glass pitcher and the old-fashioned chrome controls.

"If no one else is going to take it."

"It's all yours," Ken said.

While they went over his list, she wrapped the heavy pitcher in newspaper and thought it was typical of her mother to take advantage of her one moment of weakness, then saw she was being petty and let it go. Her mother knew she liked the blender, and Ken had gotten stuck with way more junk than she had. She noticed it was all their father's stuff—like the glasses—and that Lise didn't want anything.

It was late and they had to get up early, but her mother couldn't let them go without letting them know how much she and Arlene were taking. The TV, the nightstand and dresser, the answering machine—the list went on and on. Meg didn't see how it would all fit in the car.

Neither did Ken, upstairs. They whispered, separating the kids' books and things by the glow of the night-light. She was burnt from the fireworks, her eyes tired. There wasn't time to tell him what her mother said, and she accused herself of taking the easy way out. She'd tell him over the phone, and even then she'd just say her mother was helping her with the house, not mentioning the cottage, as if there were no connection between the two.

Maybe that was why she cried, she thought under the covers. Because she saw it as a trade in a way, and her fault.

It wasn't.

Which left Jeff getting remarried, an idea she vetoed immediately, if only because it was so humiliating.

It was everything, she thought, the whole week. But she didn't believe that either.

22

He was dreaming he was still working at Merck, and then he was taking Sam and Ella to a hockey game, except somehow he was out on the ice in his tennis shoes and had to go through these brown doors like a stage set someone had built for a skit, only there was nothing on the other side.

He had just gotten a puck with a sticker on it from someone official when his stomach woke him up, a sharp pain that he thought would stop. When it didn't he slid out of bed and made his way through the dark to the bathroom, barely sitting before everything gushed out of him, loud and hot and loose, and he sat there in his own sour stink with his ass stinging and thought with an awful feeling that he'd caught some splash-back. It was the food at Webb's, too rich, greasy lamb chops and a buttered potato, everything lubricated to go through. Maybe the lamb had been bad, because he wasn't done.

Nothing came, but he could feel it waiting to pour out, he had no control. He flushed, still sitting there, and felt the wind from the whirl-pool, cooling. The moon wrapped the room in shadows, the toothpaste levitating above the marble of the sink. His stomach dropped and bubbled like a swamp. He tried and then bent over, eyes closed, breathing through his teeth. It was cold, but if he went back to bed he'd just have to come back.

Someone was snoring, a short steady exhale—Meg. Outside, a single locust shrilled like the underlying whine of a TV, otherwise the night was quiet.

What time was it? They had to get up and drive. Maybe he was upset about leaving, maybe that was it.

He pushed again and got nothing, and then, like a mud bank giving way in the rain, everything slid down and out, plunking under him. He flushed and took a breath and squeezed until there was nothing but foam. He couldn't imagine there was more, but he didn't trust his stomach. He sat up straight and then bent over to test it, pressed his fingers into his gut like a doctor checking an appendix.

It hurt to wipe, and he folded an extra handful to make sure, then rinsed his hands in the sink.

"You okay?" Lise asked when he got in.

"Yeah," he said, "I think I ate too much."

Her body was warm, and soon she'd gone back to sleep. He was wide awake. He still didn't know what time it was, and now he didn't want to. He was fine on his back, just a little tender; it was when he rolled on his side that he felt the soggy wad shift and fill his intestines, the hot juices gnawing at him like poison. He rolled onto his back, hoping that would fix things, but in a minute he was up again. It would be like this all night.

Emily was surprised to find it was 3:36; she thought it was earlier, that she'd just dropped off. At the foot of the bed, Rufus was licking himself.

"*Rufus,*" she said in the dark, and he stopped.

He started again, lapping evenly.

"*Stop,*" she said, and he did.

Saturday

1

They were the first ones up, and Emily took her coffee out on the dock with Rufus, flushing a family of ducks. Mist rose off the water in wisps that broke in the cold air. Only the real fishermen were out. The day was cloudless, the lake a mirror; it was a shame they were leaving. Beyond that she didn't allow herself to think. She would appreciate every minute of this. She would save it.

When Arlene shook the planks, she didn't look around, and Arlene just sat down beside her, sipping, as if they'd made a pact not to speak. The bell tower rang the half hour, and they both turned toward it, then faced the lake again, two old ladies.

They were like sisters now, Emily thought, with everyone else gone. No one else was going to take care of them. She wanted to thank Arlene for understanding, except she wasn't sure she understood, or could, and she didn't want to risk this fragile agreement between them. And so they sat, quiet as the time of day, while the rest of the world woke up around them.

2

"Do you have all of your stuff together?" his mother asked.
"Yes," Sam said.
"All of it?"
MAGNETON GREW TO LEVEL 40!, his screen blinked. He showed Justin.

"Sam?"

"Yes."

"Where's your suit from yesterday—hanging on the back line? Go get it. Bring in everything that's on the line—please. Justin, you go help him."

"Just," Aunt Margaret warned. "I don't want to hear any sighing."

They both saved and shoved their Game Boys in their pockets and stepped around the open suitcases.

Downstairs, Grandma was cleaning the refrigerator and had the blue Koolers lined up on the counter. They stopped to see who was getting what. Sam didn't see any sandwiches and hoped they'd stop at the barbeque place halfway. There was an ice-cream stand right next door.

"Are you two looking for something to do?" Grandma asked.

"No," they said, and went to get the suits and towels.

Outside, his father and Aunt Arlene were folding down the back-seat of the van. Like usual, the girls had disappeared so they didn't have to do any work.

"Why do we have to have so many towels?" Justin asked.

The ones on the ends were too high to reach, and they pulled at them until the clothespins let go and fell in the grass. They filled their arms so full Grandma had to open the back door for them.

"Thank you both very much," his mother said, and they headed for the stairs, thinking they'd sneak away, but his mother stopped him. "I just need you for a second. Justin, you can go ahead."

At first Sam thought she wanted him to sit on a suitcase or something, but Aunt Margaret had come over beside his mother, the two of them standing there serious. He knew what it was when she told him to sit down.

3

Lise's anger made her pack faster, bagging Ella's shampoo and cramming it in their toiletry kit, tossing the dregs of her conditioner. And she'd been looking forward to this all week.

"I wish I knew why," she told Meg. "That's what bothers me."

"There may not be a reason."

"There has to be a reason. And then he'll lie about it, you saw him. It drives me crazy. I don't know what to do about it. I don't know if talking with someone would help or not."

"Not if he's like that," Meg said.

"I know. I'm sorry. How much was it? Because he's going to pay for it, I don't know how, but he will."

"I'd have to ask Sarah."

"Please do. And let her know it has nothing to do with her. He's always liked her."

"That might even be a part of it."

"It could be," she agreed.

She gathered their toothbrushes and threw away Ken's razor. She checked the medicine cabinet and the shower stall again, searching it up and down. The bathroom was done. She'd already gone through the dresser drawers and checked under the beds. There was nothing on the clothes tree or the low wardrobe, and the handmade ashtray was staying. If there was anything else of theirs it was downstairs.

Ken came up, sweating.

"Got the cedar chest in, barely. How are we doing up here?"

"This one's ready," Lise said. "We were just having a talk with Sam about Sarah's watch."

"What did he say?" Ken seemed hopeful, as if it had all been taken care of, the problem magically solved.

"What do you think he said? I'll tell you what, it's going to be a long ride home."

Justin was already in the van with Tigger, buried under Sarah's sleeping bag laid out flat across the backseat. Aunt Arlene reached in through the window and kissed him. Aunt Margaret was still talking with Grandma, the keys in her hand. The front doors were open and Sarah's backpack sat in her seat. Ella waited until Sarah was done hugging her father, and then she turned and opened her arms and she was holding Ella the way she'd dreamed of, her hair smelling sweet. Ella had to be careful.

"I'm going to miss you," Sarah said.

It surprised Ella so much that she could only say, "I'm going to miss you too."

"Write me," Sarah said, "okay?"

Ella promised to, and held her hand a second before letting go. Sarah got in and shut the door. She'd saved Ella for last. She couldn't roll her window down until Aunt Margaret started the car, and then she waved, saying good-bye as they backed out. Ella walked beside her to the edge of the road.

"See you, Just," she called, but he was already playing his Game Boy.

"We'll see you at Christmas," Aunt Arlene called.

"Drive safe," her father called.

The van started forward and Aunt Margaret honked for them.

"Good-bye, we love you!"

When they were little, Ella and Sam used to chase after Aunt Margaret's station wagon on their bikes, Sarah and Justin in the way back, facing them. Now everyone stood on the lawn watching them go, shadows flowing over the van as it rolled by the other driveways. Ella kept her eye on Sarah's arm, still waving, like she might have a last, secret message for her. The van reached the patch of sunlight by the Nevilles', and all they could see was the back of it, moving away.

"There they go," Grandma said, and then the road was empty, just the trees and the other houses, and they all walked back to the porch.

"Okay," her father said, "time to saddle up. Now's a good time to go to the bathroom if you haven't been already."

She used it as an excuse to go upstairs and get away from everyone. She was going to be with them in the car all day. She almost didn't care. Climbing the stairs, she felt tired, like she might fall asleep.

The fan was off and the air was hot. The beds had been stripped so there were just the silvery blue mattresses and the pink blankets folded at their feet. Squares of sun from the far window showed the dust floating above the carpet. The box of toys was gone. The only thing left that reminded her of Sarah was the dresser they shared. She ran her hand over the top, but it was just paint and wood. She walked to the spot where they slept every night and sat down, pushing her fingers through the loose strands of the rug, then smoothing it flat again. She thought of Sarah in the van, moving away from her, and looked at the ring Grandma had given them that made them twins. She turned it on her finger, wishing it was magic, that she could send her thoughts through it and that wherever Sarah was she could feel what she was feeling, all she had to do was touch her ring.

It was different, the way they would miss each other. To Sarah, she was just her cousin.

She slid the ring off so her hand was bare and squeezed the thin band in her fingertips. She turned it so it was an O and looked through the circle at her bony knee, more proof that she was fooling herself.

"Ella," her father yelled up the stairs. "C'mon, hon, we're leaving."

She didn't want to go, but she didn't want him to come up either, and she slipped her ring back on and stood. She took a last look at everything—the slanted ceilings and the window at the end, the beds, the dresser, the rug. She'd thought it would be easier if she could stay here instead of going home, but now she saw that it didn't matter. It would be bad anywhere.

"Ella!"

"Hang on!" she said. "I'm coming."

"I forgot my seethreepio," Justin said.

"Your what?" Meg said, turning down the radio and leaning back to hear him better.

"My C-3PO I got at the flea market."

"Well, bud, we can't go back for it now. Sorry. Maybe Sam will remember it for you."

"He'll remember it," Sarah said.

"Stop, that's not nice."

"It's true."

"It is not, and you need to be more forgiving. We're not all perfect like you."

"What?" Justin asked, puzzled.

"Nothing," Meg said, and Sarah looked away, disgusted. "I'll call Uncle Ken tonight and see if they have it, okay?"

It was—it would have to be—and Meg turned the radio up again, watching the cars in front of her change lanes and brake for the exit ahead, a line stopped on the ramp, all of them signaling right.

"Must be something going on at the Institute," she said, but they weren't interested.

She moved to the left and slipped past and there was open sailing. She checked her speedometer, a steady seventy. The road was new through here and she had to make sure she didn't go too fast. The median was full of wooded islands the cops liked to hide in.

17 was the easy part of the drive—once they hit 90 it would be wall-to-wall trucks. Here she could let her mind roll out over the dairy farms or follow a hawk, her hands unconsciously keeping the van between the lines. She needed the time to think. The week hadn't been the nightmare she'd expected. She'd actually been able to talk with her mother—it shocked her even now how understanding she'd been. Ken she knew

would be supportive of her, and Arlene, but she couldn't remember ever spending so much time with Lise, and thought they'd grown closer. It was strange how she felt, away from them, as if she were realizing only now what they meant to her—like her life, she was tempted to say, but didn't trust the feeling. They were her family, that was enough.

"Look," she said, and turned the radio down, because they were passing a sign that said they were now on INTERSTATE 86/OLD 17.

"*Old* 17," she said, but they didn't get it. "They just built this. Remember all the graders last year, and the big trucks?"

"Oh yeah," Justin said.

"That was two years ago," Sarah said. "Last year it was like this."

"Is that right?"

"Last year there was that Winnebago with the flat tire."

"How do you remember that?"

They were so bored they were talking to each other, and Meg thought she'd better take advantage of it. She turned off the radio.

"Okay," she said, "who wants to play a game?"

6

Arlene was right, the puzzle would be left undone, and then when she'd cleaned it up and stacked it on the shelf, there was the problem of the card table. How many hands of bridge and Michigan rummy and penny poker had passed over its mouse-brown skin, how many drinks spilled over its edges?

"There's no room," Emily said. "Besides, I think we've gotten our money's worth out of that one."

Rufus had been banished for being underfoot, and the house was quiet as they moved from room to room, unplugging everything. The radio was coming, and the answering machine, the two of them bound with their own cords and waiting on the ottoman. Some of the windows were stuck from the humidity. Arlene found a mallet in the garage and wrapped its head in a dish towel, tapped the frames so she wouldn't crack the glass. Upstairs she latched the trapdoor for the fan so the squirrels couldn't get in. She remembered Henry painting the dresser for the children. The daybed was from their guest room at home; as a girl she'd been warned repeatedly for bouncing on it like a trampoline. She couldn't believe they were leaving so much. She wanted to take the toilet paper and the wastebaskets, the frosted ceiling fixtures.

"What about the water?" she asked downstairs.

"I think they want us to leave that on."

Right, the cleaning people. She hadn't thought. "What else is there?"

"That's pretty much it. All we have to do is take the food out and lock up."

"Is the garage locked?"

"I'm getting to it."

"What about the fireplace, did Kenneth close it up?"

"It's all taken care of," Emily said. "Why don't you take the cooler out to the car if you're done in here?"

But she wasn't done. She had to do another lap of the downstairs, and grabbed a box of tissues and a cherry-wood nut dish from the mantel. There had to be room for that.

"Enough," Emily said, and herded her out the kitchen door and locked it behind them.

Rufus was waiting, whisking his tail as if they might forget him.

"Don't worry," Emily said. "You can ride on the roof."

While she closed the garage and the pump house, Arlene walked across the lawn to the water's edge. Out in the middle it was a busy Saturday, powerboats hot-rodding back and forth, but here in the shade it was calm, a gentle sloshing. The rocks at the bottom were the color of tea, and then the smooth, gray mud, a few grassy weeds reaching for the surface. She sat on the bank and slipped off her shoes, rolled up her cuffs and stepped in, wading straight into the shallows with her arms out like a child, and like the girl whose family came here every year before the war, she promised the lake that she'd be back.

7

All morning they drove into the sun. There was nothing from Jamestown all the way to Corning, and Ken was glad they had gas. The scenery was relentlessly forgettable, and he felt vaguely disloyal, as if he were escaping for good, freeing himself from the tangle of jealousies and hurt feelings. He accused himself of getting what he wanted, of getting away too cleanly. At home, in their own bed at last, he would thank Lise for putting up with them, a further, necessary betrayal.

PLOW REPAIRS, a sign on a fence advertised, ALL KINDS. The road curved and dipped with the hills, past cows lounging under weed trees and trailers with plywood mudrooms and used tires on the roof—second-hand Walker Evans. Lise borrowed a pillow from Ella and fell asleep. Every so often she'd wake up, her face creased, and ask if he was doing all right.

"I'm fine," he said. "You rest."

She missed the exit for Steamburg and Onoville, and the sign welcoming them to the Seneca Nation. The Allegany Reservoir was higher than when they'd crossed it coming the other way, the mudflats and stranded logs covered. It seemed longer than a week ago. Tracy Ann Caler had only been missing six days. He could check on her through the Internet to see if there was any news.

He wasn't sure if the pictures would be any good, or if Morgan would be disappointed. He'd shot all forty rolls, a lot considering the weather. He'd tried the Holga, even if he didn't believe in it, and he'd gotten solid coverage of the garage with the Nikon.

He hadn't taken Sam fishing, and he regretted that. Maybe they'd go for a weekend when they got home. His father's tackle was in the back with his clubs.

In the mirror, Ella was scrunched sideways against the cooler, out with her mouth open. Sam had been playing his Game Boy nonstop since they left. Finally he turned it off and curled up with his sleeping bag. Ken set the cruise control to seventy-five, ten miles above the limit but not fast enough to attract attention. He had Bill Evans simmering on the CD player and the air-conditioning on low, and as they ate up the miles he felt pleasantly in between the two worlds of vacation and home, satisfied that he was done with one and equally happy that he didn't have to start the other, not yet. He felt light, and lucky, inside this cushion of time, as if he'd gotten away with something. And he had—they had. Once again, they'd survived.

8

The city was still there, unchanged, the towers of downtown rising like a wall on the far shore. Emily couldn't see how the new stadium was doing, but the Pirates were playing at Three Rivers, the ferries docked on the near side. Emily had had a coffee with her McDonald's, and the water called to her bladder. She distracted herself with the Bayer clock and the Incline, finding the two red cars on the hillside just as they passed each other, one climbing, one falling. She couldn't remember the last time she'd been on it—with Henry, an anniversary dinner at Le Mont or the Tin Angel, but exactly when she had no clue, maybe the eighties.

They took the parkway, riding low beside the Mon and then cutting up through Oakland, past the hospitals and the library, the streets empty in the heat.

"What's the weather supposed to be like this week?" she asked.

"Couldn't tell you," Arlene said. "How's Rufus doing?"

He'd lost his seat because they had so much junk. He was curled on his towel next to the TV set, his head tucked to his tail as if he were freezing.

"He's fine."

She thought she was getting low on his food and hoped there was a new bag in the laundry room. It didn't matter. She'd have to go to the store anyway.

"Are you sure you're going to be all right with that dresser?" she asked.

"*I'm* not carrying it. That's what they pay him for. I'm sure he's got a dolly."

She didn't sound convincing, but Emily let it go. She'd offered, that was all she could do.

From here she could count the stoplights. In the week she'd been gone the neighborhood hadn't changed. It hadn't rained—the lawns were still burnt, the roses blown. Every porch, every sycamore was familiar, and she noticed her anticipation growing, as if there were someone waiting for her.

They turned up Grafton and she saw the house was fine. Rufus knew, raising his head and panting.

"Here we are," she said. "Home again, home again, jiggety-jig."

Her house key was in her purse. She had it out before Arlene parked.

"Thank you for driving."

"Thank you for the furniture."

She was surprised by how hot it was—she'd been spoiled by Chautauqua, she thought. Her first steps were creaky from sitting for so long. Rufus had to christen the lawn, and she could feel the coffee. She opened up while Arlene popped the back hatch.

It was dark inside, a veiled twilight leaking through the curtains, and the air was stale and thick. The dehumidifier was probably full. She didn't have time to check. She set her purse on the front hall table, closed the bathroom door and sat before flipping the switches. The bulb flashed white and died with a fizzle; the fan whirred.

"Welcome home," Emily said.

She'd have to stand on a chair to unscrew the fixture. She didn't even know if she had the right size bulb. It would have to wait. She needed to get her things in and start the laundry.

Of course Arlene needed to pee too.

"The light *would* have to give out now," Emily apologized.

She brought her bags in one at a time, trying not to overdo it. Her golf clubs she walked to the garage—locked, the Olds safe in the window, a cobweb strung from the antenna. The toys she had Arlene leave by the basement stairs. She'd have to wash the box of kitchen stuff, meaning she had to put away the load she'd run before she left, and there was the food in the cooler to deal with. Rufus had begun to pester her, so she put him out in the backyard. He stood on the porch, looking through the sliding door at her.

Arlene was at the car, wiping the carpet in back with his towel.

"Did he have an accident?" Emily asked.

"It's just drool."

There was nothing else of hers. She asked again if Arlene would be all right with the dresser and the TV. It was no problem, Arlene said. Her super liked her. They said good-bye in the street, pecking each other's cheeks.

"Give me a call on Monday," Emily said. "I'm going to need tomorrow to get things in order."

She waved Arlene away and went inside. Rufus wagged at the back door, and she relented.

"But you have to stay out of my way," she said.

She went around throwing open the curtains and windows, trying to get a breeze going. Upstairs it was worse, and there was Henry's dresser, large as ever, and the picture Kenneth had taken of him reading the paper. She'd had a vacation from him as well.

"Back to reality."

She started with the laundry, tossing in a load of darks and draping her slack bags over the newel post. Next she emptied the cooler and wiped it out with a paper towel. There were three messages on her machine, but they could wait. Kenneth and Margaret wouldn't be home yet anyway. She'd have to call Louise.

The dehumidifier, she'd forgotten it. She took the cooler down to the moldy basement and brought back the heavy plastic catch bucket and splashed the musty water into the sink. On her way down again she took the box of toys and the orange extension cord nobody wanted and set them on Henry's bench. She'd find a place for them later. As she passed the fridge at the bottom of the stairs, she thought she should get rid of those old bottles, but not now. There was too much to do.